STUDIO
SEX

Also by Liza Marklund

The Bomber

STUDIO

a novel

SEX

An
Annika
Bengtzon
Thriller

LIZA
MARKLUND

Translated by Kajsa von Hofsten

ATRIA BOOKS
New York London Toronto Sydney Singapore

ATRIA BOOKS
1230 Avenue of the Americas
New York, NY 10020

Library of Congress Control Number: 2002104623

ISBN: 0-7434-1786-0

First Atria Books hardcover printing August 2002

10 9 8 7 6 5 4 3 2 1

ATRIA BOOKS is a trademark of Simon & Schuster, Inc.

For information regarding special discounts for bulk purchases, please contact Simon & Schuster Special Sales at 1-800-456-6798 or business@simonandschuster.com

Printed in the U.S.A.

AUTHOR'S NOTE

Sweden is an odd little country close to the north pole. There are fewer than nine million of my fellow Swedes. We experience one of the world's highest standards of living, we live longer than people any-where else, and we enjoy the greatest gender equality of any country in the world. Nonetheless, our suicide rate is high, we're way up near the top in the taxpaying league table, and men still beat their women to death regularly.

This is the place where my novels are set. It's a society full of con-tradictions. It is strange and very ordinary at one and the same time. Since 1932, Sweden has been run almost continually by the Social Democratic Worker's Party. (The liberals and conservatives have ruled in short terms for a total of nine years over this period.) This has, not surprisingly, created some arrogance among the people in power. The Social Democrats started bending the rules early, and then making up their own.

One of the rule-bendings resulted in the illegal espionage organiza-tion called the IB. Party spies worked both inside and outside Sweden for decades. Tens of thousands of Swedes were registered and defined as "security risks," which meant they might lose their jobs and their elective offices. The crimes these "security risks" were alleged to have perpetrated included parking their car too close to the wrong political meeting.

The truth about the IB organization was revealed in May 1973 by two young reporters, Jan Guillou and Peter Bratt, who wrote for the small, alterantive magazine *FiB.* Both journalists were sentenced to a year in prison for the article, making them two of very few political prisoners in modern Swedish history. (Everything turned out fine for the journalists. Today, Peter Bratt is an investigative reporter at the biggest and most prestigious Swedish morning paper, *Dagens Nyheter.* Jan Guillou is the chairman of the Swedish Publishers Club, and also a best-selling author. Together we own one of Sweden's biggest publishing houses, Pirat. Ha ha!)

Everything describing the IB affair in this novel is true, up until the conclusion. But since Sweden is an arms-exporting country, who knows? Sweden is militarily neutral. Squeezed beween the NATO member nations Denmark and Norway on one side and Finland and the former Soviet Union on the other, this seemed like the smart thing to do for a long time. Not having any allies during the cold war forced us to maintain a strong national military defense. It also made us build an advanced weapons and arms production infrastructure, and the Swedish parliament has agreed to a limited and controlled export of this matériel.

In 1986, the Indian government closed a deal with the Swedish company Bofors, worth 8.4 billion Swedish kronor. The Social Democratic government was deeply involved in the agreement. Prime Minister Olof Palme talked the whole deal through in several meetings with Indian prime ministers Indira Gandhi and, later, Rajiv Gandhi.

It became clear that Bofors got the order after 300 million kronor of bribes. The scandal dominated the Indian election campain in 1989 and actually caused Rajiv Gandhi to lose his office. (There have been several deaths in the aftermath of this deal, which might be quite coincidental. Olof Palme was shot dead in Stockholm on February 28, 1986. The man in charge of controlling the Swedish export of war matériel, Carl Algernon, was killed in a strange accident in the Stockholm subway January 15, 1987. A Swedish journalist who investigated the Bofors affairs, Cats Falck, was found dead in her car on the bottom of the ocean, and Rajiv Gandhi was murdered in 1991.)

The role of the Swedish government in this affair is still not clear. The Social Democrats have promised, again and again, to publicly "wash their dirty laundry" in this matter.

We're still waiting.

Our society is well regulated. We don't mind that Big Brother is watching. Every citizen is given a personal number at birth. This number follows you everywhere: bank accounts, taxes, phone bills, car registration, stocks, employment records, and so on. Everybody's number is published (with few exceptions, which I will explore in my novel *The Paradise Trust*) and can be located through the tax office. Using this number, you can find out a man's income, his wealth, his previous wife's maiden name, and his kids' grades in math. Everything is on the official record about us Swedes, but also about the people in power. Every piece of paper lodged with our authorities is public, as well as all the bills and receipts turned in by our officials. Anyone can check every expense by our politicians, union leaders, and other authorities.

Still, they cheat. In the 1990s, an endless line of powerful people were caught going to gambling clubs, brothels, porno theaters, and on exotic vacations at taxpayers' expense. In July 1994, I found a limousine bill that proved that Bjorn Rosengren, the leader of a huge union cartel, had lied about a visit to a porn club during the 1991 election. Rosengren had to resign, and the cartel made it no secret that they thought this was my fault.

These events inspired me to write the novel *Studio Sex*. Oddly enough, the members of this very union selected me Author of the Year for this book. And everything worked out for Bjorn Rosengren as well. His pals in the party made him governer of Norrbotten, my home region. Today he's the minister of industry in the Social Democratic government.

All of these affairs have, of course, been brought to the attention of the Swedish people by the media. The Swedes read more newspapers than those of almost any other nationality, probably because all nongovernmental broadcasting was forbidden until the late 1980s. Until then, we had two state-run TV channels and three state-run radio stations. Broadcast news programs have always been strict, official, and uncontroversial. Investigative journalism and groundbreaking news have usually been found in the tabloids.

The Swedish evening papers blend the serious and the popular in a way I haven't seen anywhere else: investigative work sits next to celebrity scandals. The papers have a true love-hate relationship with their readers. Swedes love to discuss and question the tabloids and cuss at them too. Lately, a debate has centered on a mentally disturbed drug addict who was convicted of the murder of Prime Minister Olof Palme in 1986. Later, he was acquitted by the appeals court and is, therefore, a free man. In the last ten years, the man has received 1 million Swedish kronor from the tabloids and the new commercial TV stations, mainly for giving interviews. This is still not acceptable practice in Sweden and has been strongly condemned by sections of the public. The murder of Olof Palme remains unsolved to this day.

I wish you exciting and thoughtful reading.

Liza Marklund
Avarua, Rarotonga
New Year's Day, 2002

A FEW WORDS
BEFORE YOU BEGIN TO READ

The events in this book take place nearly eight years before those of my previous novel, *The Bomber.*

Chronologically, *Studio Sex* is the first in the series about the crime reporter Annika Bengtzon. When we meet her here, she has just started work as a young freelancer at the tabloid *Kvällspressen.*

Have a good read!

Liza Marklund
Hälleforsnäs, July 1999

STUDIO
SEX

When she saw the salmon-pink panties hanging from a bush, her first reaction was one of outrage. Didn't young people respect anything these days? Not even the dead were allowed to rest in peace.

She was lost in thought about the decline of society while her dog grubbed around in the undergrowth along the iron fence. It was when she followed the animal past the small trees along the south side of the cemetery that she saw the leg. Her indignation grew even stronger—the impudence! Oh, yes, she saw them walking the streets at night, scantily dressed and talking loudly, openly inviting the men. The heat was no excuse.

The dog took a shit in the high grass next to the fence. She turned away, pretending not to see. No people were around this early in the morning, so she needn't bother with the plastic bag.

"Come on, Jasper," she called to the dog, pulling him toward the exercise enclosure on the eastern side of the park. "Come on, boy, my little darling . . ."

She glanced behind her as she walked away from the fence. She couldn't see the leg now; it was hidden by the dense foliage.

It was going to get hot again today; she could feel it already. Her brow was beaded with sweat even though the sun was barely up. She panted her way up the hill. The dog was pulling at the leash, his tongue lolling so that it was almost touching the grass.

How on earth could you lie down to sleep in a cemetery, the resting place of the dead? Was this what feminism meant, to be allowed to behave badly and disrespectfully?

She was still upset. The steep hill just made her even more irritable.

I should get rid of the dog, she thought, and was immediately seized by guilt. To compensate for her wickedness, she bent down to unleash the dog and take it in her arms. The dog wriggled free and shot after a squirrel. The woman sighed. Her thoughtfulness obviously wasn't appreciated.

Sighing again, she dropped onto a park bench while Jasper attempted to chase down the squirrel. The dog was soon exhausted and parked himself underneath the fir tree where the little rodent was hiding. She stayed on the bench until she saw that the dog was done. As she got up, she noticed that her dress was clinging to her back. The thought of the dark stains along her spine made her feel self-conscious.

"Jasper darling, little doggy . . ."

She held out a plastic bag full of treats, and the short-legged bullterrier came running straight at her. With his tongue dangling out of his mouth, he looked as if he were laughing.

"Oh, you want this, don't you, my friend . . ."

She gave the dog the bag's contents and put him back on the leash. It was time to go home. Jasper had had his treat. Now it was her turn—coffee and a bun.

But the dog didn't want to go home. He'd spotted the squirrel again, and fortified by the treats, he was ready for another chase. He protested loudly and fiercely, pulling at the leash.

"I don't want to stay out any longer," she moaned. "Come on now!"

They took a roundabout way to avoid the steep, grassy hills that faced her apartment building. She could manage uphill, but going down was hard on her knees.

She was right above the northeast corner of the cemetery when she saw the body. It lay embedded in the lush, overgrown vegetation, licentiously stretched out behind a partly collapsed gravestone. A fragment of a Star of David was next to her head. Only then did the woman begin to feel scared. The body was naked, much too still and white. The dog broke loose and rushed up to the fence, the leash dancing like an angry snake behind him.

"Jasper!"

He managed to squeeze in between two bars and continued over to the dead woman.

"Jasper, come here!"

She yelled as loudly as she dared; she didn't want to wake the people living around the park. Many slept with open windows in the heat; the inner-city stone buildings didn't cool down during the short summer nights. She rummaged frantically in the plastic bag, but she'd run out of things to give him.

The bullterrier stopped next to the body and looked at her attentively. Then he started sniffing, at first searching, then eagerly. When he got to her genitals, the woman couldn't check herself.

"*Jasper!* Come here this minute!"

The dog looked up but gave no sign of obeying. Instead, he moved to the woman's head and started sniffing at the hands resting next to her face. To her horror, the dog started chewing at the fingers. She felt sick and grabbed the black iron bars. Carefully, she moved to the left, leaned down, and peered in among the gravestones. From a distance of six feet, she was staring into the woman's eyes. They were light-colored and clouded, dull and cold. She had a strange sensation of all sound around her disappearing. She was left with a buzzing tone in her ears.

I've got to get the dog away from here, she thought. I can't let anyone know what Jasper did.

She went down on her knees and reached her hand in as far as she could through the fence. Her splayed fingers were pointing straight at the dead eyes. Her fat upper arms threatened to get stuck between the bars as she reached for the hook of the leash. The dog howled when she pulled at the leather strap. He didn't want to let go of his prey; the hand was firmly wedged in his jaws. She jerked the animal toward her as hard as she could.

"You stupid, stinking dog!"

He hit the fence with a thud, giving a yelp. With trembling hands she forced the animal out through the iron bars. She was holding him as she never had before, both hands in a firm grip around the belly. She hurried down to the street, slipping on the grass on her way, painfully pulling a muscle in her groin.

Only when she had locked the door behind her in her own apartment and saw the scraps of flesh in the dog's mouth did she throw up.

PART ONE

JULY

SEVENTEEN YEARS, FOUR MONTHS, AND SIXTEEN DAYS

I thought love was only for others, for those who are visible and who count. My mistake is singing inside me, great shouts of joy. It's me he wants.

The euphoria, the first touch, his fringe falling into his eyes when he looked at me; nervous, not at all arrogant. Crystal clear: the wind, the light, the feeling of absolute perfection, the sidewalk, the hot wall of the house.

I got the one I wanted.

He's the center of attention. The other girls smile and flirt, but I'm not jealous. I trust him. I know he's mine. I see him from the other end of the room, blond hair that gleams, the movement as he smooths it back, a strong hand, my hand. My chest contracts under a band of happiness; I'm breathless, tears are in my eyes. The light clings to him, making him strong and whole.

He says he can't manage without me.

His vulnerability lies just beneath his smooth skin. I lie on his arm and he draws his finger along my face.

Never leave me,
he says;
I can't live without you.

And I promise.

"There's a dead girl in Kronoberg Park."

This one had the breathless voice of a heavy drug user. Amphetamines perhaps. Annika Bengtzon took her eyes away from the screen and fumbled for a pen amid the mess on her desk.

"How do you know?" she asked, too much skepticism in her voice.

"Because I'm fucking standing next to it!"

The voice rose to falsetto and Annika held the phone away from her ear.

"Okay. How dead?" she said, realizing she sounded ridiculous.

"Shit! Stone dead! How fucking dead can you be?"

Annika looked around the newsroom uncertainly. Over at the news desk, Spike, the news editor, was talking on the phone. Anne Snapphane was fanning herself with a pad at the desk across from Annika, and Pelle Oscarsson was standing at the picture desk, clicking away at his Mac.

"Yeah, right," she said, and found a pen in an empty coffee mug. She started taking notes on the back of an old wire report from the news agency TT.

"In Kronoberg Park, you say. Whereabouts?"

"Behind a gravestone."

"A gravestone?"

The man started crying. Annika waited a few seconds in silence. She didn't know what to say next. The tip-off phone's official name was The Hot Line, but in-house it was never called anything other than Creepy Calls. The majority of the callers were either jokers or nutcases. This one was definitely a candidate for the latter.

"Hello . . . ?" Annika said warily.

The man blew his nose. He took a couple of deep breaths and told Annika his story. Anne Snapphane was watching from the other side of the desk.

"Where do you find the energy to keep answering that phone?" Anne asked as Annika hung up. Annika didn't respond, but just continued scribbling her notes.

"I've got to get another ice cream or I'll die. Do you want anything from the café?" Anne Snapphane asked as she got to her feet.

"I've got to check something first," Annika said, lifting the receiver and dialing the direct number to the emergency switchboard. It was true. Four minutes earlier, they had received a call about a body being found next to Kronobergsgatan.

Annika got up and walked over to the news desk with the wire in her hand. Spike was still on the phone, his feet on his desk. Annika stationed herself right in front of him, demanding his attention. The news editor gave her an annoyed look.

"Suspected murder, young woman," Annika said, and waved the printout in front of him.

Spike hung up abruptly and put his feet on the floor.

"Did you get it from TT?" he asked, and clicked on his computer.

"No, Creepy Calls."

"Confirmed?"

"It was reported to the emergency services center."

Spike turned to look round the newsroom. "Okay. Who's here?"

Annika braced herself. "It's my tip-off."

"Berit!" Spike said, standing up. "This summer's murder!"

Berit Hamrin, one of the older reporters at the paper, picked up her handbag and came over to the desk.

"Where's Carl Wennergren? Is he in today?"

"No, he's off. He's sailing the Round Gotland Race," Annika said. "It's my tip-off, it came in to me."

"Pelle, photo!" Spike yelled in the direction of the picture desk.

The picture editor gave him the thumbs-up, then called out, "Bertil Strand."

"Okay," the news editor said, and turned to Annika. "What have we got?"

Annika looked at her messy notes, suddenly noticing how nervous she was. "A dead girl behind a gravestone at the Jewish Cemetery in Kronoberg Park on Kungsholmen."

"Doesn't mean it's a goddamn murder, does it?"

"She's naked and she's been strangled."

Spike gave Annika a scrutinizing look. "And you want to do it?"

Annika swallowed and nodded.

The news editor sat down again and pulled out a notepad. "Okay. You can go with Berit and Bertil. Make sure you get some good pictures, the rest of the information we can get later, but you've got to get the pics straightaway."

The photographer put the backpack with his equipment over his shoulder as he walked past the news desk. "Where is it?" he said, directing the question at Spike.

"Kronoberg Jail," Spike said, and picked up the phone.

"The park," Annika said, and looked for her bag. "Kronoberg Park. The Jewish Cemetery."

"Just make sure it isn't a domestic incident," Spike said, and dialed a London number.

Berit and Bertil Strand were already on their way to the elevator to go down to the garage, but Annika stopped in her tracks.

"What do you mean?" she said.

"Exactly what I said: we don't meddle in family matters." The news editor turned his back on her.

Annika felt anger surge through her body and reach her brain like an electric shock. "It doesn't make the girl any less dead."

Spike began talking on the phone and Annika saw it meant the end of their discussion. She looked up, and Berit and Bertil Strand had already disappeared into the elevator. She hurried over to her desk, pulled out her bag, which had disappeared under the desk, and ran after her colleagues. The elevator was gone, so she took the stairs. Damn, damn—why the hell did she always have to take up arms? She might have lost her first big assignment just so she could take the news editor to task.

"Moron," she said out loud to herself.

She caught up with the reporter and the photographer at the entrance to the garage.

"We'll work side by side and keep an open mind until we have to split up and work different parts of the story," Berit said, writing on a pad while walking. "I'm Berit Hamrin, by the way. I don't think we've said hello."

The older woman smiled at Annika. They shook hands while getting into Bertil Strand's Saab, Annika in the back, Berit in front.

"Don't slam the door so hard," Bertil Strand said with disapproval, glancing over his shoulder at Annika. "It can damage the paintwork."

Jesus Christ, Annika thought to herself. "Oops, sorry," she said to Strand.

The photographers had the use of the newspaper's vehicles more or less as company cars. Most of the photographers took their car-care responsibilities extremely seriously. Maybe this was because all photographers, to a man, were men. She had been at *Kvällspressen* only seven weeks but was already acutely aware of the sanctity of the photographers' cars. On several occasions, she had had to postpone scheduled interviews because the photographers had been busy getting their cars washed. At the same time it showed what importance was attached to her pieces at the newspaper.

"We're better off approaching the park from the other side and avoiding Fridhemsplan," Berit said as the car picked up speed at the junction of Rålambsvägen and Gjörwellsgatan. Bertil Strand put his foot down and drove through right as the light turned red, down Gjörwellsgatan and on toward Norr Mälarstrand.

"Could you run through the information you got from the tipster again?" Berit said, leaning her back on the car door so that she could look at Annika in the backseat.

Annika fished out the crumpled piece of paper. "Right—there's a dead woman behind a gravestone in Kronoberg Park. She's naked and has probably been strangled."

"Who called?"

"A speed freak. His pal was taking a leak by the fence and spotted her between the bars."

"Why did they think she had been strangled?"

Annika turned the paper round and read something she had scribbled in a corner of the paper. "There was no blood, her eyes were wide open, and she had injuries to her neck."

"That doesn't have to mean that she was strangled, or even murdered," Berit said, and turned to face the front again.

Annika didn't reply. She turned to look out through the tinted windows of the Saab, seeing the sun worshipers of Rålambshov Park slide past. The glittering waters of Riddarfjärd Bay lay before her. She had to squint, despite the UV coating on the windshield. Two windsurfers were heading for Långholmen Island, but slowly. The air barely moved in the heat.

"What a great summer we're having," Bertil Strand said as he turned into Polhemsgatan. "You wouldn't have thought it, after the amount of rain we had in the spring."

"Yeah, I've been lucky," Berit said. "I've just had my four weeks' holiday. Sun every single day. You can park just behind the fire station."

The Saab sped down the last few blocks along Bergsgatan. Before Bertil Strand slowed down, Berit had undone her seat belt; she jumped out of the car before he had even started parking. Annika hurried after her, gasping in the heat that hit her outside the car.

Strand parked the car while Berit and Annika set off alongside a redbrick, fifties building. The narrow asphalt path skirting the park was bordered by high paving stones.

"There's a flight of steps farther on," Berit said, already out of breath.

Six steps later they were in the park proper. They ran along a path leading up to a well-equipped kids' playground.

On the right were several barrackslike buildings. Annika read the sign Playground as she ran past. There was a sandbox, benches, picnic tables, a jungle gym, several slides, swings, and other things that children could play with and climb on. Three or four mothers with children were in the playground; it looked as if they were packing up to leave. At the far end two police officers in uniform were talking to a fifth mother.

"I think the cemetery is farther down toward Sankt Göransgatan," Berit said.

"You know your way around here," Annika said. "Do you live in the neighborhood?"

"No. It's not the first murder in this park."

Annika saw that the police officers were each holding a roll of official blue-and-white tape. They were evacuating the playground to cordon it off from the public.

"We're just in time," she mumbled to herself.

They veered to the right, following a path that took them to the top of a hill.

"Down to the left," Berit said.

Annika ran ahead. She crossed two paths, and there it was. She saw a row of Stars of David standing out against the deep green foliage.

"I see it!" she yelled over her shoulder, noting out of the corner of her eye that Bertil Strand was catching up with Berit.

The fence was black, made of beautifully rendered wrought iron. Each bar was crowned with a stylized Star of David. She was running on top of her shadow and realized she was approaching the cemetery from the south.

She stopped on the crest of the hill; she had a good view from here. The police hadn't cordoned off this part of the park yet, which they had on the north and west sides.

"Hurry up!" she yelled to Berit and Bertil Strand.

The fence surrounded a small cemetery with dilapidated graves and granite headstones. Annika quickly estimated there were around thirty of them. Nature had virtually taken over; the place looked overgrown and neglected. The enclosure was no more than thirty by forty yards, the fence at the far end no more than five feet high. The entrance was on the west side, facing Kronobergsgatan and Fridhemsplan. She saw a team from their main tabloid rival stop at the cordon. A group of men in plain clothes were inside the cemetery, on the east side. That's where the woman's body lay.

Annika shuddered. She couldn't afford to screw this up, her first proper tip-off.

Just as Berit and Bertil Strand came up behind her, she saw a man open the gates down on Kronobergsgatan. He was carrying a gray tarpaulin. Annika gasped. They hadn't covered her up yet!

"Quick!" she called over her shoulder. "We might be able to get some pictures from up here."

A police officer appeared on the hill in front of them. He was unrolling the blue-and-white tape. Annika rushed up to the fence, hearing Bertil Strand jogging heavily behind her. The photographer used the last few yards to wriggle out of the backpack and fish out a Canon and a telephoto lens. The man with the gray tarpaulin was only three yards away when Bertil fired off a sequence of pictures in among the bushes. He moved a yard to the side and fired off another. The officer with the tape yelled something; the men inside the cemetery were made aware of their presence.

"It's in the bag," Bertil Strand said. "We've got enough."

"Hey, you, goddammit!" the officer with the tape called out. "We're cordoning off this area!"

A man in a flowery Hawaiian shirt and Bermuda shorts came toward them from inside the cemetery.

"That's enough now, guys," he said.

Annika looked around, not knowing what to do. Bertil Strand was already on his way to the footpath leading down to Sankt Göransgatan. Both the man in front of her and the police officer behind her looked mad. She realized she would have to start to leave soon, or they would make her. Instinctively, she moved sideways to where Strand had taken his first shots.

She peered in between the black iron bars, and there she was, the dead woman. Her eyes were staring into Annika's from a distance of ten feet. They were clouded and gray. Her head was thrown back, the upper arms stretched out above her head; one of her hands seemed to have injuries to it. Her mouth was wide open in a mute cry; the lips were a brownish black. She had a big bruise on the left breast and the lower part of her stomach had a greenish hue.

Annika took in the entire picture, crystal clear, in a moment. The coarseness of the gray stone in the background; the sultry summer vegetation; the shadow play of the foliage; the humidity and the heat; the revolting stench.

Then the tarpaulin made the whole scene gray. They weren't covering the body with it, but the fence.

"Time to move on," the officer with the tape said, placing a hand on her shoulder.

What a cliché, Annika found herself thinking as she turned around. Her mouth was dry. She noticed that all sounds were coming from a long way off. She moved, as if floating, toward the path where Berit and Bertil Strand were waiting behind the cordon, the photographer with a bored look of disapproval, Berit almost smiling.

The policeman followed her, his shoulder against her back. Annika thought it must be hot in uniform on a day like this.

"Did you manage to get a look?" Berit asked.

Annika nodded and Berit wrote something in her pad.

"Did you ask the detective in the Hawaiian shirt anything?"

Annika shook her head and ducked under the cordon, kindly assisted by the policeman.

"Pity. Did he say anything?"

" 'That's enough now, guys,' " Annika quoted him.

Berit smiled. "What about you, are you okay?"

Annika nodded. "Sure, I'm fine. And she could very well have been strangled; her eyes were almost popping out of their sockets. She must have tried to scream before she died—her mouth was wide open."

"So maybe someone heard her. We could try the neighbors later. Was she Swedish?"

Annika needed to sit down for a moment. "I forgot to ask . . ."

Berit smiled again. "Blond, dark, young, old?"

"Twenty, at most. Long blond hair. Big breasts. Silicone implants, probably, or saline."

Berit gave her an inquiring look.

Annika dropped down on the grass, legs crossed. "They were pointing straight up even though she was flat on her back. She had a scar in her armpit."

Annika felt her blood pressure drop and leaned her head against her knees and did some deep breathing.

"Not a pretty sight, eh?" Berit said.

"I'm okay."

After a minute or so, Annika felt better. The sounds came back to her in full force, hitting her brain with the earsplitting noise of a car factory: the roaring traffic on Drottningholmsvägen; two sirens blasting out of time; loud voices, their pitch rising and falling; clattering cameras; a child crying.

Bertil Strand had joined the small media posse that was forming down by the entrance to the cemetery; he was chatting to the Rival's photographer.

"What happens next? Who does what?" Annika asked.

Berit sat down next to Annika, looked at her notes, and began outlining their work.

"We've got to assume it's a murder, right? So we'll have a story on the actual event. This has happened: a young woman has been found murdered. When, where, and how? We need to know who found her and talk to him—have you got the guy's name?"

"A speed freak; his pal gave a care-of address for the tip-off money."

"Try and get hold of him. The emergency switchboard will have all the information on the call-out," Berit continued, ticking off her notes.

"I've got that already."

"Great. Then we need to get hold of a cop who will talk. Their press officer never says anything off the record. Did the Hawaii detective tell you his name?"

"Nope."

"Shame. Find out. I've never seen him before—he could be one of the new guys at Krim. Then we need to find out when she died and why. Have they got any suspects? What's next in the investigation? All the police aspects of the story."

"Okay," Annika said, taking notes.

"Christ, it's hot! It never gets this hot in Stockholm," Berit said, wiping the sweat from her forehead.

"I wouldn't know. I only moved here seven weeks ago."

Berit took out a Kleenex from her bag and wiped around her hairline. "Okay—we have the victim. Who was she? Who identified her? She'll have a family somewhere, no doubt brokenhearted. We should consider contacting them one way or another. We need pictures of the girl while she was alive. Was she over eighteen, would you say?"

Annika gave it some thought and remembered the plastic breasts. "Yes, probably."

"Then there'll be pictures of her from high school, wearing her white graduation cap. Talk to her friends. Find out if she had a boyfriend."

Annika took notes.

"Then there's the reaction of the neighbors," Berit went on. "This is practically downtown Stockholm, over three hundred thousand women live here. This type of crime will affect people's sense of security, their eating-out habits and whatnot. City life in general. That's two separate stories. You do the neighbors and I'll do the rest."

Annika nodded without looking up.

"There's one more angle," Berit said, dropping her pad into her lap. "Twelve or thirteen years ago, a very similar murder was committed less than a hundred yards away."

Annika looked up in surprise.

"If my memory serves me right, a young woman was sexually assaulted and murdered on some steps somewhere on the north side of the park," Berit mused. "The murderer was never caught."

"Jesus! Do you think there's a chance it could be the same guy?"

Berit shrugged. "I wouldn't think so, but we'll have to mention it. I'm sure lots of people remember it. The woman was raped and strangled."

Annika swallowed. "What an appalling job this is."

"It sure is. But it'll get a bit easier if you can get hold of that guy before he leaves."

Berit was pointing toward Sankt Göransgatan, where the man in the Hawaiian shirt was leaving the cemetery. He was walking toward a car that was parked around the corner in Kronobergsgatan. Annika leaped to her feet, grabbed her bag, and rushed down toward the street. She saw the reporter from the Rival attempting to talk to the cop, but he just waved him away.

At that moment, Annika stumbled on a ridge in the asphalt and nearly fell over. She staggered down the steep hill toward Kronobergsgatan with huge, uncontrolled steps. Unable to stop herself, she crashed into the back of the Hawaiian shirt. The cop fell straight over the hood of his car.

"What the hell!" he yelled. He turned around and grabbed Annika around the upper arms.

"I'm sorry," she whimpered. "I didn't mean to. I nearly fell."

"What the hell's the matter with you? Are you crazy or something?" He was shocked and startled.

"I'm so sorry," Annika said. As well as the humiliation, her left ankle suddenly hurt like hell.

The officer regained his composure and let go of her. He scrutinized her for a few seconds.

"You should watch your goddamn step," he said, then got into his burgundy Volvo station wagon and drove off, tires screeching.

"Shit," Annika whispered to herself. She squinted into the sun, trying to distinguish the fleet number of the car. She thought she saw 1813 written on the side. To be on the safe side, she also looked at the registration number and tried to memorize it.

Annika turned around and realized that the little group of media people by the cemetery entrance were all staring at her. She blushed from her hairline down to her neck. She quickly bent over and collected the things that had fallen out of her bag when she'd collided with the cop: her notepad, a packet of chewing gum, a near empty bottle of Pepsi, and three sanitary napkins in green plastic covers. Her pen was still in the bag, so she hauled it out and quickly jotted down the registration and fleet numbers of the car.

The reporters and photographers stopped staring at her and resumed chatting among themselves. Annika noted that Bertil Strand was organizing an ice cream run.

She threw her bag across her shoulder and slowly approached her colleagues, who didn't seem to be paying her any attention now. Apart from the reporter from the rival tabloid, a middle-aged man who had his picture byline next to his stories, she didn't recognize a single one of them. There was a young woman with a tape recorder marked Radio Stockholm; two photographers from two different picture agencies; the Rival's photographer; and three other reporters that she couldn't place at all. No TV teams were present—the public television local news only did a five-minute broadcast a day during the summer, and the local commercial stations only did agency stories. The morning broadsheets would probably get pics from the agencies and supplement with TT copy. The public radio news show *Eko* hadn't sent anyone, nor would they, she knew that. One of Annika's former colleagues at the local paper where she normally worked had been employed there as a casual one summer. Contemptuously, she had explained to Annika, "We leave murders and that kind of thing to the tabloids. We're not scavengers."

Already, back then, Annika had realized that this statement said more about her colleague than about *Eko*, but sometimes she wondered. Why shouldn't public radio find the curtailed life of a young woman worth covering? She couldn't understand it.

The rest of the people lining the cordons were curious passersby.

She slowly moved past and away from the group. The police—both the Krim, the criminal investigation department, and the forensic people—were busy inside the fence. No ambulance was in sight. She looked at her watch: seventeen minutes past one. Twenty-five minutes since she had received the tip-off on Creepy Calls. She wasn't sure what she was supposed to do next. It didn't seem like a good idea to talk to the police now; they'd only get annoyed at her. She realized that they didn't know much yet, not who the woman was, how she'd died, or who'd done it.

She moved toward Drottningholmsvägen. There was a wedge of shade next to the houses on the west side of Kronobergsgatan; she went over and leaned against the wall. It was rough and hot. It was only fractionally cooler here and the air still burned her throat. She was thirsty beyond belief and pulled out the Pepsi bottle from her bag. The screw top had leaked and the bottle was tacky, making her fingers stick to the label. Damn this heat!

She drank the warm, sugary liquid and then hid the bottle in a doorway among some bags with newspapers left out for recycling.

The reporters over by the police line had moved to the opposite side of the street. They had to be waiting for Bertil Strand. For some reason, the situation made her sick. Ten yards away, the flies were buzzing around a dead body while the media people were looking forward to their ice cream.

Her gaze wandered over the park. Its steep, grassy hills were dotted with clumps of large trees. From her place in the shade she could distinguish lime, beech, elm, and birch. Some of the trees were huge;

others were newly planted. The trees growing among the graves were mainly gigantic lime.

I've got to have something more to drink, she thought.

She sat down on the sidewalk and leaned her head against the wall. Something had to happen soon. She couldn't stay here much longer.

She looked at the media scrum; it was beginning to thin out. The girl from Radio Stockholm was gone and Bertil Strand had returned with the ice cream. Berit Hamrin was nowhere in sight; Annika wondered where she'd disappeared to.

I'll wait for another five minutes, she thought. Then I'll go and buy something to drink before I start talking to the neighbors.

She attempted to conjure up a map of Stockholm in her head, placing herself on it. This was the heart of Stockholm, the stony city within the old tollgates. She looked at the fire station to the south. It lay on Hantverkargatan, her own street. She lived only about half a mile away from here, on Kungsholms Square, at the back of the block of a building scheduled for renovation. Still, she'd never been here. Underneath her lay Fridhemsplan's subway station; if she concentrated, she could just about feel the trains' vibrations spreading through the concrete and asphalt. Straight in front she could see a ventilation shaft for the tunnels, a urinal, and a park bench. Maybe the guy who phoned in the tip sat there speeding in the hot sun with the pal who later went to take a piss. Why didn't he use the urinal? Annika asked herself. She thought about it for a while and eventually went over to take a look. When she opened the door, she knew why. The stench inside was absolutely unbearable. She recoiled and quickly shut the door.

A woman with a stroller came walking from the playground toward Annika. The child in the stroller was holding a bottle containing a red liquid. Puzzled, the mother looked at the cordon along the sidewalk.

"What happened?" she asked Annika.

Annika straightened up and hoisted her bag higher up on her shoulder. "The police have cordoned off the area."

"I can see that. Why?"

Annika hesitated. She glanced over to the other reporters and saw that they were watching her. She quickly moved a few steps closer to the woman.

"There's a dead woman in there," she said quietly, and pointed at the cemetery. The woman turned pale.

"No kidding?"

"Do you live around here?"

"Yes, just around the corner. We went down to Rålambshov Park, but the place was so crowded you couldn't sit down, so we came here instead. Is she in there now?"

The woman craned her neck and tried to see in between the lime trees. Annika nodded.

"Jesus, that's so creepy!" the woman exclaimed, and looked at Annika with big eyes.

"Do you often come this way?"

"Sure, every day. My son, Skruttis, goes to playgroup in the park."

The woman couldn't tear her eyes away from the cemetery. Annika watched her for a few moments.

"Did you hear anything out of the ordinary last night or this morning? Any cries in the park or stuff like that?"

The woman pushed out her lower lip, gave it some thought, and then shook her head. "This neighborhood is always quite noisy. During the first few years I used to wake up every time the fire brigade turned out, but not anymore. Then there's the drunks down on Sankt Eriksgatan. Not the winos that live in the hostel—they're knocked out long before nighttime—but the regular drinkers going home. They can keep you awake all night. But the worst is the ventilation system at McDonald's. It's on all night and it's driving me insane. How did she die?"

"No one knows yet," Annika said. "So there were no screams, no one crying for help or anything?"

"Oh, sure there were. There's always a lot of bawling around here on Friday nights. Here you go, honey . . ."

The child had dropped its bottle and was whining; the mother picked it up and put it back in his hands. She nodded toward Bertil Strand and the others. "Are they the hyenas?"

"Yep. The guy with the ice cream cone's my photographer. And I'm Annika Bengtzon from *Kvällspressen.*"

She held out her hand and the two women shook hands. Despite her contemptuous remark, the woman seemed impressed.

"I'm Daniella Hermansson. Pleased to meet you. Are you going to write about this?"

"Yes, or somebody else at the paper will. Do you mind if I take some notes?"

"No, go ahead."

"Can I quote you?"

"I spell it with two *l*'s and two *s*'s—just like it sounds."

"So you say it's always noisy around here?"

Daniella Hermansson stood on tiptoe and tried to peek at Annika's notepad. "Oh, yeah, extremely noisy, especially on the weekend."

"So if someone were to cry for help, no one would react?"

Daniella Hermansson pushed out her lower lip again and shook her head. "It would depend a bit on what time it was. By four, half past five, it calms down. Then it's just the ventilation system making a noise. I sleep with the window open all the year round—it's good for the skin. But I didn't hear anything."

"Do your windows face the front or the back?"

"Both. We're in the corner apartment on the third floor there. The bedroom faces the back, though."

"And you walk past here every day, you say?"

"Yes, I'm still on maternity leave, and all the mothers in my parenting group meet in the playground every morning. But, darling . . ."

The child had finished the red liquid and was howling like a siren. His mother bent down and with practiced movements put her middle finger down the back of the child's diaper, then pulled the finger out and smelled it.

"Whoops. It's time for us to go home. A new diaper and a little snooze, eh, Skruttis?"

Skruttis fell silent as he found a ribbon from his hat to chew on.

"Could we take your picture?" Annika quickly asked.

Daniella Hermansson's eyes grew wide. "My picture? You're kidding?" She laughed and pulled her hand through her hair.

Annika looked her straight in the eye. "The woman lying in that cemetery has probably been murdered. We feel it's important to give an accurate description of the neighborhood. I live down on Kungsholms Square myself."

Daniella Hermansson's eyes nearly popped out of her head. "Murdered? Jesus Christ! Here, on our block?"

"No one knows exactly where she died, only that her body was discovered here."

"But this is such a good neighborhood," Daniella Hermansson said, and bent down to pick up her son. The boy lost his ribbon and began howling again. Annika held on to her bag and started walking over to Bertil Strand. "Wait here," she said to Daniella over her shoulder.

The photographer was busy licking the inside of the ice cream wrapper when Annika reached him.

"Can you come with me for a moment?" she said quietly.

Bertil Strand slowly scrunched up the wrapper in a ball and pointed to the man next to him. "Annika, this is Arne Påhlson, reporter at the Rival. Have you met?"

Annika cast down her eyes, held out her hand, and mumbled her name. Arne Påhlson's hand was moist and warm.

"Have you finished your ice cream?" Annika asked tartly.

Bertil Strand's suntan got one shade darker. He didn't like being rebuked by someone who wasn't even on the staff of the paper. Instead of replying, he just bent down and picked up his backpack. "Where are we going?"

Annika turned around and walked back to Daniella. Annika glanced up at the cemetery; the plainclothes police were still there talking to each other. The child was still bawling, but his mother wasn't paying him any attention. She was busy painting her lips with a lipstick from a little light green box with a mirror on the inside of the lid.

"So how does it feel to find out that a dead woman's lying outside your bedroom window?" Annika asked with her pen poised on the pad.

"Awful," Daniella said. "I mean, all the nights my girlfriends and I have returned home after a night out. It could have been any one of us."

"Will you be more careful now?"

"Definitely," Daniella said without hesitation. "I'll never walk through that park at night again. Sweetheart, what's the matter now?"

Daniella bent down to pick up her boy again. Annika took notes and felt the hair on her neck stand on end. This was quite good, actually. It might even make a headline if she cut it a bit.

"Thanks a million," she said quickly. "Can you look at Bertil?

What's your boy's name? How old is he? How old are you? And how would you like us to refer to you? . . . 'On maternity leave.' Okay. Maybe you shouldn't look quite so happy . . ."

Daniella Hermansson's practiced movie-star smile, the one she probably adopted for all holiday and Xmas snaps, faded. Instead, she looked confused and lost. Bertil Strand was snapping away, circling the woman and her child with short, cautious dance steps.

"Can I call you later if anything comes up? What's your phone number? And the code for the door from the street? You know, just in case."

Daniella Hermansson put the child in the stroller and walked off alongside the police cordon. To her annoyance, Annika saw Arne Påhlson from the Rival stop the woman as she walked past. Luckily, the child was by now howling so badly that the woman wouldn't wait for a second interview. Annika breathed again.

"Don't try to teach me my job," Strand said to Annika.

"Fine. But tell me, what would have happened if they'd taken the body away while you were busy buying ice cream for the competition?"

Bertil Strand gave her a contemptuous look. "In the field we're not competitors. Out here we're colleagues."

"I think you're wrong. We lose out if we hunt as a pack. We ought to keep more to ourselves, all of us."

"No one would gain anything by that."

"Well, I think it would help our credibility with our readers."

Bertil Strand swung the cameras onto his shoulder. "Well, thanks for telling me. I've only been at the paper for fifteen years."

Shit! Annika thought as the photographer walked back to his "colleagues." Why can't I ever keep my big mouth shut?

She suddenly felt dizzy and weak. I've got to get something to drink, and fast, she thought. To her great relief, she saw Berit walking toward her from the direction of Hantverkargatan.

"Where have you been?" Annika called out, moving in her direction.

"I went back to the car to make some calls. I ordered up the cuttings on the other murder and had a chat with a few police contacts."

In vain, Berit was trying to cool herself by waving her hand in front of her face. "Anything happen?"

"I talked to a neighbor. That's all."

"Have you had anything to drink? You look a bit pale."

Annika wiped the sweat from her brow. Suddenly she felt close to tears. "I really stuck my foot in it with Bertil Strand just now," she said in a subdued voice. "I said that we shouldn't mingle with our competitors at a crime scene."

"I agree with you. Bertil Strand doesn't, I know that. He can be a bit difficult to work with sometimes, but he's a good photographer. Why don't you go and get something to drink? I'll hold the fort."

Annika gratefully left Kronobergsgatan and walked down along Drottningholmsvägen. She was in line to buy a bottle of mineral water in the kiosk on Fridhemsplan when she saw the ambulance turn left on Sankt Göransgatan and head for the park.

"Shit!" she cried out, and ran straight out into the traffic, forcing a taxi to slam on the brakes. She crossed Sankt Eriksgatan and headed back to the park. She thought she was going to faint before she reached it.

The ambulance had stopped at the top of Sankt Göransgatan; a man and a woman got out.

"Why are you so out of breath?" Berit asked.

"The car! The body!" Annika panted, bending over with her hands on her knees, gasping for air.

Berit sighed. "The ambulance will be here for a while. The body isn't going to disappear. Don't worry—we won't miss anything."

Annika dropped her bag onto the sidewalk and straightened up. "I'm sorry."

Berit smiled. "Go and sit down in the shade. I'll go and buy you something to drink."

Annika slunk away and sat down. She felt like an idiot. "I didn't know," she mumbled. "I don't know how this works."

She sat down on the sidewalk and leaned against the wall again. The ground burned her through her thin skirt.

The man and the woman from the ambulance were waiting inside the cordon, just inside the entrance to the cemetery. Three men remained inside the iron fence. Annika guessed that two of them were forensic people and the third one a photographer. They moved with great care, bending over, picking things up, straightening up. She was too far away to see exactly what they were doing.

A few minutes later Berit returned with a big, ice-cold Coke. Annika unscrewed the top and drank so quickly that the bubbles rose the back way and came out of her nose. She coughed and spluttered, spilling Coke on her skirt.

Berit sat down next to her and took out a bottle of her own from her bag.

"What are they doing in there?" Annika asked.

"Securing evidence. They use as few people as possible and move around as little as they can. Usually there's only two crime scene technicians and maybe an investigator from Krim."

"Could that have been the guy in the Hawaiian shirt?"

"Maybe," Berit said. "If you look closely, you'll see that one of the technicians is holding his hand close to his mouth. He's using a Dictaphone, recording everything he sees at the scene. It could be an exact description of the position of the body, the way the clothes are creased. Things like that."

"She wasn't wearing any clothes."

"Maybe the clothes were scattered around, they record that kind of thing too. When they've finished, the body will be moved to the forensic medical unit in Solna."

"For autopsy?"

Berit nodded. "The technicians will stay behind and comb the whole park. They'll go over it inch by inch to secure any traces of blood, saliva, hairs, fibers, semen, footprints, tire imprints, fingerprints—anything you can think of."

Annika watched the men inside the fence in silence. They were leaning over the body; she could see their heads bob up and down against the background of the gray tarpaulin. "Why did they cover the fence instead of the body?"

"They don't cover up the body at the scene of a crime unless it's going to rain or snow. It's all about evidence; they're trying to disturb the area as little as possible. The screen is only to shut the place off from people's view. It makes sense."

Then, suddenly, the technicians and the photographer all stood up.

"It's time," Berit said.

All the journalists got up simultaneously. Everybody went up to the cordon as if at a given signal. The photographers all loaded the cameras that hung around their necks. A few new journalists had joined the group; Annika counted five photographers and six reporters. One of them, a young guy, had a laptop marked TT, the news agency, and a woman was holding a notepad with the logo of the broadsheet *Sydsvenskan* on it.

The man and the woman from the ambulance opened the back doors and pulled out a collapsible gurney. Calmly and methodically, they unfolded it, pushing the various clasps into place. Annika felt the hair on her arms stand on end. A puff of fizz from the Coke rose into her mouth and made her burp. They'll roll out the body any moment now. She was ashamed of her morbid excitement.

"Could you move to the side?" the woman with the gurney said.

Annika looked down at the gurney rolling past. It shook as the wheels crunched over the uneven asphalt. On top of it lay a neatly folded bluish gray plastic sheet. The shroud, Annika thought, a cold thrill traveling up her spine.

The man and the woman ducked under the cordon. The orange sign saying No Entry swung after them.

The ambulance drivers reached the body. The men and the woman stood in a group discussing something. Annika felt the sun burn on the back of her arms.

"Why is it taking so long?" she asked Berit in a stage whisper.

Berit didn't reply. Annika took up the Coke bottle and drank some.

"Isn't it horrible?" the woman from *Sydsvenskan* said.

"Oh, yeah, it is," Annika said.

The ambulance people unfolded the plastic sheet and spread it over the gurney, its bluish gray, shiny surface flapping among the leaves. They lifted the young woman onto the gurney and wrapped her in the sheet. Annika suddenly felt tears come into her eyes. She saw the woman's mute scream, her clouded eyes, the bruised breasts.

I mustn't start crying now, she thought, and stared hard at the worn gravestones. She tried to distinguish names or dates, but the inscriptions were in Hebrew. The delicate characters had almost been erased over time by the elements. All at once, everything went very quiet. Even the traffic down on Drottningholmsvägen stopped for a moment. The sunlight that filtered through the enormous crown of the lime trees was dancing across the granite.

The cemetery was here before the city surrounding it. And the trees were here, smaller and frailer, when the dead were buried. But their leaves would have performed the same shadow play on the stone when these graves had just been dug.

The gates were opening and the photographers got down to work. One of them pushed past Annika, jabbing an elbow so hard in her midriff that she lost her breath for a moment. Taken by surprise, she stumbled backward and lost sight of the gurney. She quickly moved farther away.

Which direction is her head pointing? Annika found herself wondering. They wouldn't roll her away feet first.

The photographers accompanied the gurney alongside the cordon. All the camera motors were rattling out of time; the odd flash went off. Bertil Strand was jumping up and down behind his colleagues, alternately snapping away above their heads and in between them. Annika held on to the back door of the ambulance; the paintwork burned her fingers. The driver stopped five inches away from her, operating the various mechanisms of the car. Annika noticed that he was perspiring. She looked down at the plastic-covered body.

I wonder if the sun has kept her warm, she thought.

I wonder who she was.

I wonder if she knew she was going to die.

I wonder if she had time to be scared.

All at once, tears were rolling down Annika's face. She let go of the door, turned around, and took a few steps away. The ground was moving, she felt as if she was going to throw up.

"It's the smell. And the heat," Berit said, suddenly at her side. She put her arm around Annika's shoulders and pulled her away from the ambulance.

Annika wiped away the tears.

"Let's go back to the paper," Berit said.

Patricia woke up with a strange feeling of suffocation. There was no air in the room, she couldn't breathe. She slowly became aware of her body on the mattress, naked and glistening. She lifted her left arm and the sweat trickled down her ribs and into her navel.

Jesus Christ, she thought, I've got to have air! Water!

For a moment she contemplated calling out to Josefin, but something made her change her mind. The apartment was completely quiet, so either Jossie was asleep or she'd gone out. Patricia groaned and rolled over, wondering what time it could be. Josefin's black curtains shut out the daylight and made the room swim in a musty gloom. There was a smell of sweat and dust.

"It's a bad omen," Patricia had said when Josefin had come home with the thick, black material. "You can't have black curtains. The windows will be wearing mourning—you'd stop the flow of positive energy."

Josefin was annoyed. "Then don't have them!" she'd exclaimed. "Nobody's forcing you. But I want my room dark. How the heck are we going to be able to work nights if we don't get to sleep during the day? I bet you didn't think of that!"

Jossie got her way, of course. She usually did.

Patricia sat up on the mattress with a sigh. The sheet underneath her was screwed up in a damp knot in the middle of the bed. Angrily, she tried to straighten it out.

It's Jossie's turn to do the shopping, she thought, so I don't suppose there's anything in the fridge.

She got out of bed and went to the bathroom. She borrowed Josefin's bathrobe and returned to her own room to open the curtains. The light hit her like nails in the eyes and she quickly closed them again. Instead she opened one of the windows wide, wedging in a flowerpot so it wouldn't slam shut. The air outside was even hotter than inside, but at least it didn't smell.

She slowly walked out to the kitchen, filled a big beer glass with tap water, and drank it greedily. The kitchen clock showed five to two. Patricia was pleased with herself. She hadn't slept through the whole day, even though she'd worked until five this morning.

She placed the glass on the kitchen counter, between an empty pizza box and three mugs with dried-out tea bags in them. Jossie was terrible at cleaning. Patricia sighed and cleared things away, throwing out the trash, doing the dishes, and wiping counters without thinking.

She was just about to step in the shower when the phone rang.

"Is Jossie there?"

It was Joachim. Patricia straightened up and made an effort to seem alert.

"I just got up, so I don't know, actually. Maybe she's sleeping."

"Be a darling and wake her up, will you?" Succinct but friendly.

"En seguida, Joachim. Hang on a moment . . ."

She tiptoed to the end of the hallway to Josefin's room and knocked softly on the doorpost. There was no reply, so she opened the door slightly and peeked in. The bed was exactly as unmade as it had been the day before when Patricia had left for work. She hurried back to the phone.

"No, I'm sorry, I think she's gone out."

"Where to? Who is she seeing?"

Patricia gave a nervous laughter. "Nobody—or you, maybe? I don't know. It's her turn to do the shopping . . ."

"But she slept at home?"

Patricia tried to sound indignant. "Of course she did! Where else?"

"That's exactly it, Titsie. Do you have any suggestions?"

He hung up just as the anger started to surface in Patricia's mind. She hated it when he called her that. He did it to humiliate her. He didn't like her. He felt she stood between him and Josefin.

Patricia slowly walked back to Josefin's bedroom and took another peek inside. The bed really did look exactly as it had the night before, the cover on the floor to the left of the bed and Josefin's red swimsuit on the pillow.

Jossie had never come home last night.

The realization made Patricia feel ill at ease.

The air in the main entrance of the newspaper hit them like a cold, wet towel. The damp glistened on the marble floor and made the bronze bust of the newspaper shine. Annika shuddered and felt her teeth give a rattle.

Tore Brand, the porter, sat sulking in the glassed-in reception booth in the far left-hand corner. "You're all right!" he shouted as the small group passed him on their way to the elevators. "You can go outside and defrost now and then. This place is so damn cold that I've had to bring the car heater in so I don't get frostbite!"

Annika tried to smile but didn't quite manage. Tore Brand hadn't been allowed to take this year's holiday until August, something he considered to be little less than harassment.

"I'm going to the bathroom," Annika said to the others. "You go on upstairs."

She rounded Tore Brand's little cubicle and could smell that he'd smoked a cigarette on the sly again. After a moment's hesitation she chose the disabled washroom before the ladies'. She didn't want to be jostling in front of the sinks with a bunch of sweaty women.

Tore Brand's plaintive voice followed her into the washroom. She locked the door by turning the door handle upward and looked at herself in the mirror. She looked awful. Her face was blotchy and her eyes red. She opened the cold-water tap and, holding up her hair, bent forward and let the cold water run over her neck. The enamel of the sink was icy cold against her forehead. A rivulet of water trickled down her spine.

Why do I do this to myself? she thought. Why am I not lying on the grass by Pine Lake, reading *Vogue*?

She pushed the red button on the hand dryer, held out the neckband, and tried to dry her armpits. Without much success.

Anne Snapphane's desk was empty when Annika got back to the newsroom. Two mugs with dried-up coffee were on the desk, but the Coke was gone. Annika figured Anne had been sent out on a job.

Berit was talking to Spike over by the news desk. Annika flopped onto her chair and let the bag fall to the floor. She felt dizzy.

"So, how was it?" Spike called out.

Annika hastily dug out her pad and walked over to the desk.

"Young, naked, plastic tits," she said. "Lots of makeup. She'd been crying. No decomposition, so she can't have been there for very long. As far as I could see, her clothes weren't anywhere nearby." She looked up from her pad.

Spike gave her a nod of approval. "Well, I'll be damned. . . . Any terrified neighbors?"

"A twenty-nine-year-old mother, Daniella, with a small child. She'll never cross the park at night again. 'It could have been me,' she said."

Spike took notes, nodding appreciatively. "Do they know who she is?"

Annika pressed her lips together and shook her head. "Not that we know."

"Let's hope they release her name during the evening. You didn't see anything that indicated where she lived?"

"Her address tattooed on the forehead, you mean? Sorry . . ."

Annika made a smile that Spike did not return.

"Okay, Berit, you do the police hunt for the killer, who the girl was—check with her family. Annika, you do the scared mother and check the cuttings on the old murder."

"We'll probably be working together a bit," Berit said. "Annika has information from the crime scene that I don't have."

"Do whatever you like," he said. "I want a report on how far you've got before I go to the handover at six."

He swiveled round in his chair, lifted the receiver, and dialed a number.

Berit closed her pad and walked over to her desk. "I've got the cuttings," she said over her shoulder. "We could go through them together."

Annika borrowed a chair from the next desk. Berit took out a heap of yellowed sheets from an envelope marked "Eva Murder." The killing had obviously taken place before the newspaper was computerized.

"Anything that's more than ten years old you'll find only in the paper archive," Berit said.

Annika picked up a folded sheet, the paper feeling stiff and brittle. She ran her eyes over the page. The typeface of the headline seemed straggly and old-fashioned. A four-column black-and-white photo showed the north side of the park.

"I was right," Berit said. "She was climbing the steps and somewhere halfway up she met someone going down. She didn't get any farther. The murder was never solved."

They sat down on opposite sides of Berit's desk and became absorbed in the old stories. Berit had written several of them. The murder of young Eva really was similar to today's.

A warm summer night twelve years ago, Eva had been climbing the steep hill that was a continuation of Inedalsgatan. She was found next to the seventeenth step, half-naked and strangled.

For a few days the stories were both numerous and long, with big pictures high up on the page. There were reports of the murder investigation and summaries of the autopsy report; interviews with neighbors and friends; and a piece with the headline "Leave Us in Peace." Eva's parents were pleading with someone for something, holding each other and gazing earnestly into the camera. There were public rallies against violence—violence against women and violence on the streets. A memorial service was held in the Kungsholm Church, and a mountain of flowers collected at the murder scene.

Strange that I can't remember any of this, Annika thought. I was old enough to understand things like that.

As time went by the stories became shorter. The pictures shrank and ended up farther down on the page. Three and a half years after the murder, a short item reported the police bringing someone in for questioning but subsequently releasing him. After that it went quiet.

Now Eva was newsworthy again, twelve years after her death. The comparison was inevitable.

"So what do we do with this?" Annika wondered.

"Just a short summary," Berit replied. "There's not much else we can do. I'll type out what we've got—you do your mother and I'll do Eva. By the time we've done that, Krim ought to be on the case and then we can start making some calls."

"Are we in a hurry?" Annika asked.

Berit smiled. "Not really. Deadline isn't until four forty-five A.M. But it would be good if we finished a bit before, and this is a good start."

"What'll happen to our stories in the paper?"

Berit shrugged. "Maybe they won't get printed at all. You never know. It depends on what's going on in the world and on how much paper we've got."

Annika nodded. The number of pages in the paper often determined whether a story would be printed. It was the same at *Katrine-holms-Kuriren*, the provincial paper were she normally worked. In the middle of the summer, the management would economize on paper, partly because ad revenue went down in July, partly because nothing much happened. The number of pages always went up or down by four, as there were four pages to a printing plate.

"I have a feeling this may get quite high priority," Berit said. "First the news event of the murder itself, the police hunt, and then a spread on the girl, who she was. After that they'll have the recap of the Eva murder, your frightened mother, and last, possibly, a piece on 'Stockholm, City of Fear.' That's my guess."

Annika leafed through the cuttings. "How long have you worked here, Berit?"

Berit sighed and gave a faint smile. "It'll be twenty-five years soon. I was about your age when I came here."

"Have you been on the crime desk all this time?"

"Christ, no! I started out with animals and cooking. Then, in the early eighties, I was a political reporter. It was the thing to have women in such positions at the time. Then I had a stint on the foreign desk, and now I'm here."

"Where have you liked it the best?"

"I enjoy writing the most—doing the research and finding my way through something. I like it a lot at the crime desk. I can do my own thing, pretty much. I often dig out my own stuff. Pass me those cuttings, will you? Thanks."

Annika stood up and walked over to her desk. Anne Snapphane hadn't returned. The place seemed empty and quiet when she was gone.

Annika's Mac had gone into some kind of power-saving state; the loud sound when it restarted made her jump. She quickly wrote what Daniella Hermansson had said to her: intro, body text, and a caption. Then she filed her copy into the list of stories held on the newsroom server. That's it! Great!

She was just off to get some coffee when her phone rang. It was Anne Snapphane.

"I'm at Visby Airport!" she shouted. "Was it a murder in the park?"

"You bet," Annika said. "Naked and strangled. What are you doing on Gotland?"

"Forest fire. The whole island's going up."

"The whole island? Or just nearly all of it?"

"Details. I'll be away until tomorrow, maybe longer. Can you feed the cats?"

"Haven't you got rid of them yet?" Annika said tartly.

Anne ignored her. "Can you change the cat litter as well?"

"Sure . . ."

They hung up.

Why can I never say no? Annika thought, and sighed. She went to the cafeteria and bought coffee and a can of mineral water. With the coffee in one hand and the water in the other, she restlessly paced the newsroom. The air-conditioning didn't quite make it all the way up here, so the air wasn't much cooler than outside. Spike was on the phone, of course, two big patches of sweat in his armpits. Bertil Strand stood over by the picture desk talking to Pelle Oscarsson, the picture editor. She went up to them.

"Are those the photos from Kronoberg Park?"

Oscarsson double-clicked on an icon on his big screen. The deep green of the park filled the entire surface. The harsh sunlight put flecks all over the scene. Granite gravestones floated between the wrought-iron bars. A woman's whole leg could be discerned at the center of the picture.

"It's good. Disturbing," Annika said spontaneously.

"Wait until you see this one," Picture Pelle said, and clicked again.

Annika recoiled as the clouded eyes of the woman met her own.

"These are the first few pics," Bertil Strand said. "Lucky I moved, wasn't it?"

Annika swallowed. "Daniella Hermansson?"

Picture Pelle clicked a third time. A tense Daniella with the boy in her arms looking up toward the park with frightened eyes.

"Great," Annika said.

" 'It could have been me,' " Picture Pelle said.

"How did you know that's what she said?" Annika said in surprise.

"That's what they always say," Pelle said smugly.

Annika walked on.

The doors at the editorial end of the office were all shut. She had not seen the editor in chief today. Come to think of it, she had barely seen him all week. The subeditors hadn't arrived yet. The men responsible for the layout of the paper usually turned up after seven in the evening, sunburned and drowsy after a long afternoon in the Rålamb-shov Park. They would start the night by guzzling two pints of black coffee each, rant about all the mistakes in yesterday's paper, and then set to work. They would try out headlines, cut copy, and clatter away at their Macs until the paper went to print at six in the morning. Annika was a little scared of them. They were loud and brash, but their skill and professionalism were great. Many of them lived for the newspaper; they worked for four nights and had four off, year in, year out. The schedule rolled on over Christmas, Easter, and Midsummer Day, four off, four on. Annika didn't know how they could stand it.

She walked over to the empty sports desk. The Eurosports Channel was showing on a TV in a corner. She stopped in front of the large win-dows at the far end and stood gazing at the multistory garage opposite. The concrete looked as if it were steaming in the heat. If she put her face right up to the windowpane and looked to the left, she could just make out the Russian embassy. She leaned her forehead against the glass and marveled at how cool it was. Her sweat left a sticky patch on the pane and she tried to wipe it off with her hand. She drank the last of the min-eral water. It tasted metallic. She slowly walked back across the news-room floor, an intense feeling of happiness gradually spreading inside her.

She was here. She'd been accepted. She was one of them.

It's going to work, she thought.

It was after three and time to call the police.

"We don't know enough yet," came the terse answer from a lieutenant at the duty desk of the criminal investigation department, Krim. "Call the press officer."

The police press officer had nothing to say.

The police communications center confirmed that they had dis-patched patrol cars to Kronoberg Park, but she already knew that. The emergency services control room reconfirmed that they had received a police call from a private person at 12:48 P.M. There was no telephone subscription at the care-of address the tipster had given.

Annika let out a sigh. She pulled out her pad and leafed through it. Her eyes landed on the fleet number of the Hawaiian detective's car. She gave it a moment's thought, then phoned the police communications center again. The car belonged to Krim at the Norrmalm precinct. She called there.

"That car's out on loan," the officer on duty informed her after checking a list.

"To whom?" Annika wondered, her pulse quickening.

"Krim, the criminal investigation department—they haven't got their own cars. There's been a death on Kungsholmen today, you see."

"Yes, I've heard about that. Do you know anything about it?"

"Not my turf. Kungsholmen's in the Södermalm District. My guess is it's already with Krim."

"The guy who borrowed the car has short blond hair and was wearing a Hawaiian shirt. Do you know who that is?"

"That must be Q."

"Q?" Annika echoed.

"That's what he's called. He's a captain in the Krim. There's another call coming in . . ."

Annika thanked the officer and ended the call. She phoned the switchboard again.

"I'd like to speak to Q in the Krim."

"Who?" the operator said, puzzled.

"A captain called Q who works in the Krim."

She heard the operator groan. It was probably as hot there as it was at the paper.

"One moment, please . . ."

The signals went through. Annika was just about to hang up when someone answered in a gruff voice.

"Is this the Krim?" she inquired.

Another groan. "Yes, this is the Krim. What's this about?"

"I'm looking for Q."

"Speaking."

Bingo!

"I wanted to apologize. My name is Annika Bengtzon. I ran into you today in Kronoberg Park."

The man sighed. She heard a scraping noise in the background, as if he was sitting down on a chair.

"Which paper are you with?"

"*Kvällspressen*. I'm covering over the summer. I'm not quite sure how you go about these things, how you communicate with the media. Back home in Katrineholm, I always call Johansson at Krim at three o'clock, he usually knows everything."

"Here in Stockholm you call the press officer."

"But you're in charge of the investigation?" Annika chanced it.

"So far, yes."

Yes!

"No prosecutor?" Annika quickly asked.

"There's no need for that at this stage."

"So you don't have a suspect."

The man didn't confirm it, then said, "You're smarter than you look. What are you getting at?"

"Who was she?"

He groaned again. "Listen, I told you to speak to the—"

"He says he doesn't know anything."

"Then you'll have to content yourself with that for now." He was getting annoyed.

"I'm sorry. I wasn't trying to put pressure on you."

"Yes, you were. Now, I've got a lot—"

"She had silicone breasts," Annika said. "She wore heavy makeup and had been crying. What does that suggest?"

The man stayed silent. Annika held her breath.

"How do you know all that?" he asked. Annika could tell that he was surprised.

"Well, she hadn't been lying there for very long. The mascara was smeared, she had lipstick on her cheek. She must be at the forensic medical unit in Solna now, right? When will you tell me what you know?"

"What makes you think she had silicone breasts?"

"Ordinary breasts sort of float out to the side when you're lying down. Plastic tits point straight up. It's not that common on young girls. Was she a prostitute?"

"No, absolutely not," the police captain said, and Annika could hear him bite his tongue.

"So you do know who she was! When will you publish the name?"

"We're not one hundred percent sure yet. She hasn't been formally identified."

"But she will be soon? And what was wrong with her hand?"

"Sorry, I haven't got time now. Bye!"

Q, the police captain in charge of the investigation, hung up. Not until the tone was in her ear did Annika realize she still didn't know what his name was.

The minister shifted to fourth gear and sped into the Karlberg Tunnel. It was stifling hot inside the car, so he leaned forward and groped for the air-conditioning. The cooling system clicked on and turned to a hushed murmur. He let out a sigh. The road felt endless.

At least it'll cool down toward evening, he thought. He turned onto the North Circular and got in the lane for the tunnel leading to the E4. The different sounds of the vehicle echoed inside the car, becoming amplified and bouncing between the windows: the tires thundering against the asphalt road; the wheezing of the air-conditioning; a whining from a seal that wasn't airtight. He switched on the radio to drown out the sounds. The blaring music on the P3 station filled the car. He looked at the digital clock on the dashboard: 17:53. *Studio 69*, the news and current affairs program, would be starting soon.

A thought crossed his mind: I wonder if I'm going to be on.

His next thought: Of course not. Why would I be? They haven't interviewed me.

He moved over to the fast lane and overtook two French camper vans. The Haga North bus terminal flickered past, and he realized he was driving much too fast. That would be a pretty story, getting caught speeding, he reflected as he changed lanes. The vans filled his rearview mirror and hooted at his sudden braking.

It was six o'clock, and he turned up the volume to listen to the *Eko* news. The U.S. president was concerned about the Middle East peace process. He had invited the parties for talks in Washington the next week. It wasn't clear whether the Palestinian representatives would accept the invitation. The minister listened attentively; this could have repercussions for his own work.

Then came a report from Gotland where a big forest fire was raging. Large areas of the eastern part of the island were threatened. The reporter interviewed a worried farmer. The minister noticed that his concentration was divided. He had passed the turnoff to Sollentuna—he hadn't noticed driving past Järva Krog.

Eko left Gotland and returned to the studio reporter. Air-traffic controllers were threatening industrial action; negotiations were going on
and the deadline for the union representatives' response to the employer's latest offer was 7 P.M. A young woman had been found dead in
Kronoberg Park in central Stockholm. The minister pricked up his ears
and turned up the volume. There wasn't much information, but signs
indicated the woman had been murdered.

Eko continued with a short piece on the former Social Democratic
Party secretary who had written an op-ed article on the old IB affair in
one of the broadsheets. There had been a scandal involving a clandes-
tine intelligence outfit, the Information Bureau, in the service of the rul-
ing Social Democratic Party. The minister got annoyed. Stupid old man!
He should keep his mouth shut—they were in the middle of the election
campaign.

"We did it for the sake of democracy," he heard the old party secretary say floridly over the radio. "We were all that stood between Sweden and the Marxist-Leninists."

The weather report followed. The high-pressure system would stay
over Scandinavia for the coming five days. By now the water table was
below normal in the whole country, and the risk of forest fires was high.
The ban on the lighting of fires remained. The minister sighed.

The studio reporter concluded the news bulletin just as the minister
drove past the Rotebro Interchange and a hypermarket flashed by to the
right. The minister waited for the howling electric-guitar signature tune
of the current affairs program *Studio 69*, but to his surprise it didn't
come on. Instead they announced yet another program with hysterically
shouting youths for hosts. Shit, it was Saturday. *Studio 69* was only on
Monday to Friday. Annoyed, he switched off the radio. The moment he
did, his cell phone rang. Judging by the signal, it was somewhere deep
inside a bag on the backseat. He cursed out loud and threw his right arm
back. Swerving within his lane, he pulled the suitcase onto the floor and
fished out the small overnight bag. A late-model, silver Mercedes
beeped at him angrily as it drove past.

"Capitalist swine," the minister muttered.

He turned the overnight bag upside down on the backseat and
fished out the cell phone.

"Yes?"

"It's Karina. Hi." His press secretary. "Where are you?"

"What do you want?" he countered brusquely.

Svenska Dagbladet wants to know whether the new crisis in the Middle East peace talks will threaten the consignment of JAS fighter aircraft to Israel."

"That's a trick question. We haven't signed any contract for JAS deliveries to Israel."

"That's not the question," the press secretary said. "The question was whether the negotiations are threatened."

"The government won't comment on potential negotiations with potential buyers of Swedish munitions or Swedish fighter aircraft. Lengthy negotiations with prospective buyers take place all the time and relatively seldom lead to any big purchases. In this case, there is no threat to any consignment, as there won't be any—at least not to my knowledge."

The press secretary took down his words in silence.

"Okay," she then said. "Have I got this right? 'The answer is no. No consignments are threatened, as no contract has been signed.' "

The minister passed his hand over his tired brow. "No, no, Karina. That's not at all what I said. I didn't answer no. It's an unanswerable question. Since there are no planned consignments, they can't be threatened. Answering no to the question would mean that the consignments will be made."

Karina breathed quietly down the phone. "Maybe you should talk to the reporter yourself."

Goddamn it, he had to fire this woman. She was brain-dead. "No, Karina. It's your job to formulate this in the appropriate manner so that my intention is conveyed with an accurate quotation. What do you think you're being paid forty thousand kronor a month to do?"

He switched off before she had time to reply. To be on the safe side, he turned off the phone and threw it into the bag.

The silence was oppressive. Slowly, the sounds of the vehicle increased inside the car: the whining of the seal, the asphalt, the wheezing of the fan. Exasperated, he tore open his top two shirt buttons and turned on the radio again. He couldn't stand the prank phone calls on P3 so he pressed a station at random and got Radio Rix. Some old hit rolled out of the speakers; one he recognized from his youth. He had some kind of memory related to this tune but couldn't place it. Some girl, probably. He resisted an impulse to switch the radio off—anything was better than the racket the car was making.

It was going to be a long night.

The subediting crowd tumbled in just before seven, noisy as ever. Their chief, Jansson, parked himself opposite Spike at the desk. Annika and Berit had just returned from the canteen—known as the Seven Rats—both having eaten beef stew.

The food sat heavily with Annika and gave her a stomachache. The boisterous subs weren't helping. She wasn't getting anywhere with her calls. She couldn't get hold of the tipster. The police press officer was kind and had the patience of a saint, but he didn't know anything. She'd spoken to him three times during the afternoon. He didn't know who the woman was, when or how she had died, or when he would find out. It all made Annika nervous and probably contributed to the stomachache.

She had to find out something about the woman for the front page, or her name wouldn't be getting on it either.

"Take it easy," Berit advised her. "We'll get there. And tomorrow is another day. If we don't get hold of the name, no one else will either."

Of course, TV2's *Rapport* at 7:30 P.M. led with the Middle East crisis and the U.S. president's appeal to resume the peace talks. The story lasted forever and was interspersed with questions to the Washington correspondent via satellite. Lengthy narratives in officialese were spread over agency footage from the *intifada*.

Next came the Gotland forest fire, with exactly the same news assessment *Eko* had made. The aerial footage was undeniably stunning. First, they interviewed the director of the emergency-and-rescue services, a chief fire officer from Visby. Then they showed an impromptu press conference, and Annika smiled when she spotted Anne Snapphane jostling at the front with her tape recorder in the air. Last, they interviewed a worried farmer; Annika thought she recognized his voice from *Eko*.

After the fire, there wasn't much in the way of news. There was a labored piece on the election campaign's making a false start. Annika thought they could have run this about six months ago. The Social Democratic prime minister, hand in hand with his new wife, was walking across the square in his Södermanland hometown. Annika smiled when she saw the sign of her old workplace in the background. The prime minister gave a brief comment to the former party secretary's article about the IB affair.

"It's not an issue we want to drag with us into the twenty-first century," he said wearily. "We're going to get to the bottom of this matter. If the need arises, we shall order a review."

Then they'd dug out a feature they must have had on file. The public service network, Sveriges Television, had sent their masterly Russia correspondent to the Caucasus to report on the long and bloody conflict in one of the old Soviet republics there. This is the advantage of the silly season, Annika thought. They show things on the news programs that you'd never get to see normally.

The aging president of the republic was interviewed. He surprised the reporter by answering the questions in Swedish.

"I was posted in the Soviet embassy in Stockholm from 1970 to 1973," he said with a strong accent.

"Amazing," Annika said.

The president was deeply concerned. Russia was supplying the rebels with arms and ammunition, whereas he suffered under the international weapons embargo imposed on his country by a UN decree. He had been the target of repeated assassination attempts, and on top of all this he had a heart condition.

"My country is suffering," he said in Swedish, and stared straight into the camera. "Children are dying. This is wrong."

Christ, what a world, Annika thought, and went to get a mug of coffee. When she returned, the news program had moved on to the smaller domestic news items: a car crash in Enköping; a young woman found dead in Kronoberg Park in Stockholm; the strike among air-traffic controllers that had been averted after the union had accepted the final offer of the arbitrator. The bulletins were read in rapid succession, accompanied by nondescript archive footage. Some cameraman had apparently dragged himself over to Kungsholmen as a few seconds of blue-and-white police tape and park foliage appeared on the screen. That was all there was.

Annika gave a sigh. This wasn't going to be easy.

• • •

Patricia was cold. She hugged herself and pulled her feet up on the seat. A combination of exhaust fumes and pollen was being whisked around by the air-conditioning. She sneezed.

"Have you got a cold?" the guy in the front passenger seat asked. He was kind of cute but he was wearing a hideous shirt. No style. She liked older guys, though; they were less eager.

"No," she replied morosely. "I have allergies."

"We'll be there in a minute."

The woman driving the car was a real bitch. She was one of those women cops who had to be twice as tough as the guys to get respect. She'd said a stiff hello to Patricia and after that had ignored her.

She's looking down on me, Patricia thought. She thinks she's better than me.

The bitch had driven along Karlbergsvägen and was crossing Norra Stationsgatan. Only buses and taxis were allowed to do this, but she didn't seem to care. They drove under the West Circular and entered the Karolinska Institute grounds the back way. They rolled past redbrick buildings from different periods; it was a town within the town. There wasn't a soul around—it was Saturday night, after all. The rust-colored palace of the Tomteboda School towered on the hill above them to the left. She turned right and parked in a small parking lot. The guy in the loud shirt got out and opened the door for Patricia.

"You can't open it from the inside," he said.

She couldn't move. She sat with her feet drawn up on the seat, her knees under her chin. Her teeth were rattling.

This isn't happening, she thought. It's just a bunch of bad omens. Think positive thoughts. Think positive thoughts . . .

The air was so dense that it didn't penetrate her lungs. It stopped somewhere at the back of her throat, thickening, choking her.

"I can't do it. What if it's not her?"

"We'll soon know that," the guy said. "But I understand if it's hard for you. Come on, I'll help you out of the car. Do you want something to drink?"

She shook her head but accepted the hand he was holding out to her. She climbed out onto the asphalt on shaky legs. The bitch had started down a small path, the gravel crunching under her feet.

"I feel sick," Patricia said.

"Here, have some chewing gum," the guy said.

Without replying, she stretched out her hand and took a Stimorol.

"It's down here," he said.

They walked past a sign with a red arrow saying 95:7 Dep. Forensic Med. Morgue.

She chewed the gum hard. They were walking among the trees: limes and maples. A gentle wind whispered in the leaves; perhaps the heat would finally let up.

She first saw the wide canopy roof over the entrance. It protruded from the bunkerlike building like an oversize peaked cap. The building material was the universal red brick, and the front door was of gray-black iron, heavy and shut.

STOCKHOLM MORGUE she read in capital gold lettering underneath the roof, and at the bottom, Entrance for relatives. Identification. Removal to mortuary.

The entry phone was made of chipped plastic. The guy pushed a button and a low voice answered. Patricia turned her back to the entrance and looked back at the parking lot. She had a vague sensation of the ground rocking, like the slow swell on a vast ocean. The sun had disappeared behind the Tomteboda School, and barely any daylight was left under the roof. Straight ahead was the College of Health Sciences: dull red brick, sixties. The air got heavier and heavier; the chewing gum grew in her mouth. A bird was singing somewhere inside the bushes; the sound reached her as if through a filter. She could hear her own jaws grinding.

"Welcome."

The guy put his hand on her arm so she had to turn around. The door had been opened. Another guy stood in the doorway, smiling cautiously at her. "This way, please. Step right inside."

"I've got to get rid of my gum," she said.

"You can use the bathroom," he said.

The bitch and the shirt guy let her go first. It was a small room. It reminded her of a dentist's waiting room: gray couch to the left; a low birchwood table; four chrome chairs with blue-striped seats; abstract painting on the wall—three fields in gray, brown, and blue; a mirror to the right; cloakroom straight ahead; bathroom. She walked toward it with an unpleasant feeling that she did not reach all the way down to the floor.

Are you here, Josefin?

Can you feel my spirit?

Once inside the bathroom, she locked the door and threw the chewing gum in the bin. The wire basket was empty, and the gum stuck to the edge of the plastic bin liner. She tried to flick it farther down but it stuck to her finger. There were no paper cups, so she drank water straight from the tap. It's a morgue. The place is likely to be clean, she thought.

She breathed deeply through her nose a few times and went outside. They were waiting for her by another door, between the mirror and the exit.

"This isn't going to be easy," the guy said. "This girl hasn't been washed since she was found. She's also in the same position."

Patricia swallowed. "How did she die?"

"She was strangled. She was discovered in Kronoberg Park on Kungsholmen today at lunchtime."

Patricia held her hand over her mouth; her eyes grew wide and filled with tears. "We usually take a shortcut through the park on our way home from work," she whispered.

"We don't know for sure that it is your friend," the guy said. "I want you to take your time and have a good look at her. It's not that bad."

"Is she all . . . bloody?"

"Oh, no, not at all, she looks fine. The body has begun to dry out, that's why the face may look a bit sunken. Her skin and her lips are discolored, but it's not too bad. She's not horrible to look at." The guy spoke in a quiet, calm voice. He took her by the hand. "Are you ready?"

Patricia nodded. The bitch opened the door. A cool puff of wind blew from the room inside. She breathed in its moisture, expecting the stench of corpses and death. But, no, the air was fresh and clean. She took a wary step onto the shiny gray-brown stone floor. The concrete walls were white, plastered, uneven. Two electric radiators were mounted on the far wall. She raised her eyes—a cupola was suspended from the ceiling. Twelve burning lamps spread a dim light in the room. It reminded her of a chapel. Two tall, wooden candlesticks. They weren't lit but Patricia could still smell wax. Between the candlesticks was the gurney.

"I can't do it."

"You don't have to," the guy said. "We can ask her parents to do it, or her boyfriend. But that'll take longer and give the murderer an even bigger lead over us. Whoever did this shouldn't be walking around."

She swallowed. A big, blue textile screen hung behind the gurney, covering the entire back door. She stared at the blue, trying to discern a pattern.

"I'll do it."

The guy, who was still holding her hand, slowly pulled her closer to the gurney. The body was lying underneath a sheet, the hands above the head.

"Anja will remove the sheet from her face now. I'll be standing right next to you all the time."

Anja was the bitch.

Patricia saw the movement in the corner of her eye, the removal of white fabric; she felt the slight draft.

He's right, she thought. She looks fine. She's dead but she doesn't look disgusting. She looks surprised, she thought, as if she hadn't quite understood what had happened.

"Jossie," Patricia whispered.

"Is it your friend?" the guy asked.

She nodded. The tears welled up; she did nothing to stop them. She reached out her hand to stroke Josefin's hair but stopped in midair.

"Jossie, what have they done to you?"

"Are you absolutely sure?"

She closed her eyes and nodded. "Oh, my God."

She put her hand over her mouth and shut her eyes tighter.

"Can you confirm that this is your roommate, Josefin Liljeberg, with one hundred percent certainty?"

She nodded and turned around, away from Jossie, away from death, away from the floating blue behind the gurney.

"I want to go," she said in a stifled voice. "Get me out of here."

The man put his arm across her shoulders and pulled her close to him, stroking her hair. She was crying uncontrollably, soaking his ugly Hawaiian shirt.

"We'd like to do a thorough search of your apartment tonight," he said. "It would be good if you could be there."

She wiped her nose with the back of her hand and shook her head. "I've got to work. With Jossie gone, I'll have to do a lot more. They're probably missing me already."

He gave her a searching look. "Are you sure you can handle that?" She nodded.

"Okay," he said. "Let's go."

The press release dropped out of the fax machine at 21:12. Since the Stockholm police press department always sent their dispatches to the newsroom secretary, Eva-Britt Qvist, who didn't work weekends, no one saw it. Not until the news agency TT filed a brief item at 21:45 did Berit notice the information.

"Press conference at police headquarters at ten!" she called out to Annika on her way to the photo room.

Annika threw a pad and pen into her bag and walked toward the exit. Expectation was churning in her stomach—now she'd find out. She was nervous; she had never been to a press conference at the Stockholm police headquarters.

"We've got to move the fax machine from Eva-Britt's desk," Berit said in the elevator.

They squeezed into Bertil Strand's Saab, just as they had last time, with Annika in the back again, in the same place. She shut the door softly this time. When the driver sped toward Västerbroplan, she noticed that she hadn't shut the door properly. She quickly locked the door, grabbed the door handle, and hoped Bertil wouldn't notice.

"Where are we going?" Strand asked.

"The entrance on Kungsholmsgatan," Berit answered.

"What do you think they'll say?" Annika wondered.

"They've probably identified her and informed the members of the family," Berit said.

"Yes, but why hold a press conference for that?"

"They haven't got any clues," Berit said. "They need maximum media exposure. They want to alert the detectives among the public while the body is fresh. We're the alarm clock."

Annika swallowed. She changed hands on the door handle and

looked out the window. The evening looked dusky and gray through the tinted glass. The neon signs on Fridhemsplan blinked palely in the evening light.

"I should be sitting in a café with a glass of red wine," Bertil Strand said.

Neither of the women responded.

They drove past the park; Annika saw the police cordons sway lightly in the breeze. The photographer skirted the lush vegetation to arrive at the entrance at the top of Kungsholmsgatan.

"It's ironic," Berit said. "The biggest collection of cops in Scandinavia is sitting about two hundred yards from the murder scene."

The brown metal complex of the national police headquarters appeared on Annika's right side. She looked up toward the park through the back window. The green hill was in the shade and filled the whole window. She suddenly felt queasy, squeezed in between the metal house and the dark green of the park. She rummaged through her bag and found a roll of hard mints. She quickly put two in her mouth.

"We'll just make it," Berit said.

Bertil parked a little too close to the street corner and Annika hurried out of the car. Her wrist was stiff from holding the door all the way there.

"You look a bit pale," Berit said. "Are you okay?"

"I'm fine." Annika hung her bag over her shoulder and walked off in the direction of the entrance, chewing frenetically on the mints. A security guard from Falck Security was stationed at the gate. They showed their press cards and walked into a cramped office where most of the floor space was taken up by a photocopier. Annika looked around the room with curiosity. There were long corridors both on her right and her left.

"This is the identification and fingerprint section," Berit whispered.

"Straight on," the security guard ordered them.

It said National Criminal Investigation Department in reversed, blue lettering on the glass door ahead of them. Berit pushed it open. They entered another corridor with beige metal walls. Some ten yards ahead and to the right was the press conference room.

Bertil Strand gave a sigh. "This must be the worst place in Sweden for taking pictures. You can't even throw a flash off the ceiling. It's dark brown."

"Is that why their press officer always has red eyes?" Annika gave a faint smile.

The photographer grunted.

It was quite a large room with orange, wall-to-wall carpeting, beige-brown chairs, and blue and brown textile works of art on the walls. A small gathering of reporters had assembled at the front. Arne Påhlson and another reporter from the rival tabloid were there; they were chatting with the police press officer. Q was not there. To her surprise, Annika saw that *Eko* was represented, as was the highbrow broadsheet housed in the same building as *Kvällspressen.*

"Murder gains importance when there's a press conference, you see," Berit whispered.

The room was stifling hot, and Annika soon started sweating all over her body. As no TV stations were there to take the spaces, they sat at the front. Normally, TV cameras and all the equipment occupied the first few rows. The people from the Rival sat down next to them. Bertil Strand loaded his cameras.

The press officer cleared his throat. "Welcome," he said, and stepped onto the small podium at the front. He rounded a lectern and sat down heavily behind a conference table. He fiddled with some papers and tapped the microphone in front of him. "Well, we've asked you to come here tonight to tell you about the dead woman who was found in central Stockholm today at lunchtime." He put his papers to the side.

Sitting next to each other, Annika and Berit both took notes. Bertil Strand was walking around somewhere to the left, looking for camera angles.

"A lot of people have been phoning us during the day for information about the case, which is why we've chosen to call this press conference. First, I'll give you the facts of the case and then I'll be happy to answer your questions. Is that all right?"

The reporters nodded.

The press officer picked up the papers again. "The emergency services center received a call about a dead body at twelve forty-eight P.M. The caller was a member of the public."

The "junkie" Annika wrote on her pad.

The press officer went quiet for a moment, bracing himself.

"The victim is a young woman, Hanna Josefin Liljeberg, nineteen years of age and resident in Stockholm. The members of her family have been informed."

Annika felt a burning sensation in her stomach. The clouded eyes had been given a name. She furtively looked around at her colleagues to see how they reacted. No one batted an eyelid.

"The cause of death was strangulation. Time of death has not been definitely established but is thought to be sometime between three and seven this morning." The press officer hesitated before continuing, "The postmortem points to the young woman having been sexually assaulted."

An image flashed inside Annika's head—breast, eyes, screams.

The press officer looked up from his papers. "We need the help of the public to catch whoever did this," he said wearily. "We haven't got much to go on."

Annika glanced at Berit; she had been right.

"We're working with the theory that the place of discovery is the place of murder; we have forensic evidence to indicate this. The last person to see Josefin alive, apart from her killer, was her roommate. They parted at the restaurant where they both work just before five A.M. This means that we can narrow down the time of her death by another two hours."

A few camera flashes went off. Annika assumed they were Bertil Strand's.

The press officer recapitulated, "Hanna Josefin Liljeberg was murdered in Kronoberg Park in Stockholm between five and seven A.M. The injuries to her body indicate that she was raped."

His gaze had traveled over the reporters attending the press conference and finally landed on Annika. She swallowed.

"We ask anyone, I repeat, *anyone,* who was in the vicinity of Kronoberg Park, Parkgatan, Hantverkargatan, or Sankt Göransgatan between five and seven this morning to contact us. The police will gratefully accept all information that could be of interest. Several phone lines are open for the public to call in to, with a choice of speaking to a telephone operator or an answering machine. An incident may seem insignificant to an outsider, but it may fit into a larger pattern. That is why we're asking anyone who saw anything out of the ordinary at the time to contact us."

He fell silent. The dust in the air was still. Annika's throat burned from the dryness.

The reporter from the highbrow broadsheet cleared his throat. "Have you got any suspects?"

Annika looked at him with surprise. Didn't he understand what the guy had just said?

"No," the press officer answered good-naturedly. "That's why it's so important for us to get information from the public."

The reporter took notes.

"What's the forensic evidence that indicates the place of discovery and murder is the same?" Arne Påhlson asked.

"We can't go into that at this moment in time."

There were several more lame questions from the reporters but the press officer had nothing to add. At the end, the reporter from *Eko* asked if he could ask a few questions off the record. That marked the end of the press conference. It had only lasted for about twenty minutes. Bertil Strand was leaning against the wall at the back of the room.

"Shall we wait for *Eko* to finish and talk to him afterward?" Annika said.

"I think we should split up," Berit said. "One of us stays and talks to the press officer, the other starts looking for pictures of the girl."

Annika nodded; it sounded sensible.

"I could go to the National Police Board duty desk and check the passport register," Berit said, "and you could stay and talk to Gösta."

"Gösta?"

"That's his name. Will you stay here, Bertil? I'll grab a cab later."

After *Eko* it was Arne Påhlson's turn. The other Rival reporter had disappeared, and Annika could bet her shirt on Berit's bumping into him at the passport register.

Arne Påhlson took his time, as long as the entire press conference had taken. By a quarter to eleven, everybody had given up except Annika and Bertil Strand. The press officer was tired when Annika finally sat down with him in a corner of the now empty hall.

"Do you find this difficult?" Annika asked him.

Gösta looked at her in surprise. "What do you mean?"

"You have to see so much shit."

"It isn't that bad. Do you have any questions?"

Annika leafed through her pad. "I saw the girl in the park," she said calmly, as if in passing. "She wasn't wearing any clothes, and I couldn't see any clothes nearby. Either she must have climbed naked into the cemetery or her clothes were somewhere around. Did you find them?" She caught the press officer's eye.

He blinked in surprise. "No, just her panties. But you can't write that!"

"Why not?"

"Because of the investigation," the man said quickly.

"Come on. Why not?"

The man thought about it for a moment. "Well, I suppose we could disclose that. It doesn't make any difference."

"Where did you find the panties? What do they look like? How do you know they were hers?"

"They were hanging from a bush next to her. Pink polyester. We've had them identified."

"Right. The identification was quick. How did you do it?"

The press officer sighed. "She was identified by her roommate, like I said."

"Man or woman?"

"A young woman, just like Josefin."

"Had Josefin been reported missing?"

The press officer nodded. "Yes, by her roommate."

"When?"

"She didn't come home last night, and when she didn't show up at work, the friend called the police, around half past six."

"So the girls lived and worked together?"

"It appears so."

Annika took notes and considered the information. "What about the rest of the clothes?"

"We haven't found them. They're not within a radius of five blocks from the murder scene. Unfortunately, the trash cans in the area were emptied this morning, but we've got people searching the dump right now."

"What had she been wearing?"

The press officer put his hand inside his right uniform pocket and pulled out a small notebook. "Short black dress, white trainers, and a blue jeans jacket. Probably an imitation-leather shoulder bag."

"You don't happen to have a photo of her, do you? Her high school graduation photo, wearing the white cap, maybe?" Annika said.

The press officer pulled his hand through his hair. "People need to know what she looked like."

Annika nodded.

"Wearing the white cap? I'll see what I can do. Anything else?"

She chewed her lip. "There was something else about the body. One of the hands. Like it had been mangled or chewed up."

Again, the press officer looked taken aback. "Then you know more than I do."

Annika dropped her pad on her lap. "What was she like?" she said in a low voice.

Gösta sighed. "We don't know. All we know is that she's dead."

"What kind of life was she living? Which restaurant did she work at? Did she have a boyfriend?"

The press officer put his notebook back in his pocket and got up. "I'll see what I can do about that photo."

Berit was hard at work at her desk when Annika and Bertil Strand returned to the newsroom.

"She was pretty cute." Berit pointed toward Picture Pelle's desk.

Annika walked straight over to the picture desk to have a look at the small black-and-white picture from the passport register. Hanna Josefin Liljeberg was laughing at the camera. She had the bright gaze and radiant smile that you only see on a teenager who is full of self-confidence.

"Nineteen years old," Annika said, her chest feeling constricted.

"We'd better get a proper photo," Pelle Oscarsson said. "If we blow this up more than one column, it'll get grainy and gray."

"I think we'll find one," Annika said, sending a quiet prayer to Gösta while she walked over to Berit.

"Do you know the PubReg?" Berit asked her.

Annika shook her head.

"Then let's go over to Eva-Britt's desk," Berit said.

A computer with a modem was on the newsroom secretary's desk. Berit switched it on and logged on to the network. Via the Info Market, a collection of databases, she got into the Public Register, the government department for citizen information.

"You can find information about every resident in Sweden here," she explained. "Their home address, previous addresses, maiden name, national identification number, place of birth, all that kind of stuff."

"That's incredible," Annika said. "I hadn't the faintest idea."

"The PubReg is a really good tool. Sit down and check some friends out someday when you have the time."

Berit pressed the F8 key, name inquiry, to perform a national search on "Liljeberg, Hanna Josefin." They got two hits, an eighty-five-year-old woman in Malmö and a nineteen-year-old girl in Dalagatan in Stockholm.

"That's her," Berit said, and typed a *v* in front of the latter and hit the return key.

The information appeared on the screen; "Liljeberg, Hanna Josefin, born in Täby, unmarried. The latest change to her entry in the population registry was less than two months old."

"Let's check her previous address," Berit said, and pressed F7, historical data.

The computer paused a few seconds, as if it were thinking, and then another address appeared on the screen.

" 'Runslingan in Täby Kyrkby,' " Berit read. "That's a nice neighborhood. Upper-middle class. Row houses."

"Where does it say that?" Annika said, scanning the screen.

Berit smiled. "Some data is located on this hard disk." She tapped her forehead. "I live in Täby. This must be her parents' home."

The reporter ordered a printout and tapped a new command. They read the result. Liljeberg Hed, Siv Barbro, Runslingan in Täby Kyrkby, born forty-seven years ago, married.

"Josefin's mother," Annika said. "How did you find her?"

"Through a search on women with the same surname and post code." Berit ordered a printout and did the same search on men. The PubReg yielded two hits, Hans Gunnar, fifty-one, and Carl Niklas, nineteen, both resident in Runslingan.

"Look at the boy's date of birth," Berit said.

"Josefin had a twin brother."

Berit ordered one last printout and then logged off. She switched off the computer and went over to the printer.

"You take these," she said, handing the printouts to Annika. "Try to get hold of someone who knew her."

Annika went back to her desk. The subs were engrossed in their work. Jansson was shouting into the phone. The glow from the computer screens made the news desk look like a floating blue island in the newsroom's sea. The image made her aware of the dark outside. Night was falling. She didn't have much time.

Just as she sat down, the Creepy Calls phone rang. She grabbed the phone in a reflex action. The caller was wondering whether it was true that the early-twentieth-century Swedish writer Selma Lagerlöf had been a lesbian.

"Call the Gay and Lesbian Switchboard," Annika replied, and rang off.

She pulled out the pile of Stockholm telephone directories, heaved a sigh, and looked at the covers. In her hometown, Katrineholm, there was one single book for the whole of the province of Södermanland; here there were four for one single area code. She looked up "Liljeberg, Hans," in Runslingan in Täby Kyrkby. *Vicar* was his title. She took down the telephone number and stared at it for a long time.

No, she thought in the end. There had to be other ways of getting the facts she needed.

She took out the business and services directory and looked in the section for local-government information. There were two high schools in Täby: Tibble and Åva. She called the switchboard numbers; both forwarded the calls to a municipal switchboard. She gave it a few seconds thought and then tried dialing the direct numbers. Instead of 00 at the end, she dialed 01, then 02 and 03. She got lucky with 05, where a voice-mail message informed her that the deputy principal, Martin Larsson-Berg, was on holiday until 7 August. She found him in the phone book with the title BA. He lived in Viggbyholm and was both at home and awake.

"I'm sorry to call you this late on a Saturday night," Annika said after introducing herself, "but it's about a serious matter."

"Is it my wife?" Martin Larsson-Berg anxiously asked.

"Your wife?"

"She's out sailing this weekend."

"It's not about your wife. A girl who might have been one of your students was found dead today in Stockholm," Annika said, closing her eyes.

"Oh, I see," the man said with relief in his voice. "I thought something had happened to my wife. Which student?"

"A girl called Josefin Liljeberg, from Täby Kyrkby."

"Which program was she in?"

"I'm not even sure she went to Tibble School, but it seems most probable. You don't remember her? Nineteen, pretty, with long blond hair, big breasts . . ."

Now the deputy principal was with her. "Oh, yes, Josefin Liljeberg. Yes, she graduated from the media program in the spring, that's right."

Annika breathed out and opened her eyes. "Do you remember her?"

"Dead, you say? That's horrible. What happened?"

"The Jewish Cemetery in Kronoberg Park. She was murdered."

"But that's awful! Do they know who did it?"

"Not yet. Would you like to say something about her, a few words about what she was like, maybe express your feelings about it?"

Martin Larsson-Berg sighed. "Yeah, well . . . What do you say? She was like most girls that age, giggly and vain. They're all the same. They tend to melt into one, kind of."

So much for the teaching profession, thought Annika. The deputy principal thought about his reply.

"She wanted to be a journalist, on television. Not very bright, to be honest. And she was murdered, you say. How?"

"She was strangled. Did she graduate, then?"

"Yes, she got a pass in all subjects."

Annika looked at the computer printouts in front of her. "Her father's a clergyman. Did that affect her at all?"

"Is he? I didn't know that . . ."

"And she had a twin brother, Carl Niklas. Did he also go to Tibble School?"

"Niklas . . . yes, I think he graduated from the natural science program. He had quite a good head on him. He wanted to continue his studies in the U.S."

Annika took notes. "Anything else you remember?"

Jansson appeared at her side, a pleading look on his face. She waved him aside.

"Sorry, no. There are so many students."

"Did she have many friends?"

"Yes, well, I think so. She wasn't especially popular, but she had her friends. She wasn't bullied, or anything."

"You don't happen to have a class register handy?" she asked.

"For Josefin's class?" The deputy principal grunted a bit. "Yes, I have the school register. Do you want me to send it to you?"

"Have you got a fax?"

He did. Annika gave him the crime-desk fax number and he promised to fax Josefin's class photo straightaway.

As she hung up and stood up to go over to Eva-Britt Qvist's desk, the Creepy Calls phone jangled again. She hesitated for a moment but stopped short and picked it up.

"I know who shot Olof Palme," someone slurred at the other end.

"Do you really? Who was it then?"

"What's the reward?"

"We pay maximum five thousand kronor for a tip-off that goes to print."

"Only five grand? That's bullshit! I want to talk to one of the editors."

Annika heard the man gulp and swallow something.

"I am an editor. We pay five thousand, it doesn't matter who you talk to."

"It's not enough. I want more."

"Call the police. Then you'll get fifty million," Annika said, and hung up.

What if the drunk was right, she mused on her way to the fax machine. What if he really did know? What if the Rival had Palme's murderer on tomorrow's front page? She'd be remembered forever as the one who rejected the tip, like the record executives who turned down the Beatles.

The fax was lousy—Josefin and her classmates were just black specks on a gray-striped background. But underneath the photo were the names of all the students, twenty-nine young people who must all have known Josefin. On her way back to her desk, she underlined those with unusual surnames, those she had a chance of finding in the phone book. These kids probably didn't have their own phones, so she'd have to look for the parents.

"Delivery for you," the porter Peter Brand said. He was Tore's son and worked the night shift during July.

Surprised, Annika looked up and received a stiff, white envelope. "Do Not Bend," she read on the outside. She quickly tore it open and emptied the contents onto the desk.

There were three photos of Josefin. The top one was a relaxed studio shot. Wearing her white cap, she was smiling radiantly straight into the camera. Annika felt the hairs on her arms stand on end. This picture was so sharp that they could run it over ten columns if they wanted to. The other two were decent amateur photos, one of the young woman holding a cat and the other of her sitting in an armchair.

At the bottom was a note from Gösta, the police press officer.

"I've promised the parents that the pictures will be distributed to all media outlets who want them," he'd written. "Please have them couriered over to the Rival when you've used them."

Annika hurried over to Jansson and put the pictures in front of him. "She was a clergyman's daughter dreaming about becoming a journalist."

Jansson picked up the pictures and studied them closely. "Fantastic."

"We're supposed to send them over to the Rival as soon as we've finished with them."

"Of course. We'll have them couriered over as soon as they've printed their last edition tomorrow. Well done!"

Annika returned to her desk. She sat down and stared at the phone. There wasn't much to think about. It was half past two, and if she was going to get hold of any of Josefin's friends, she had to get started right away.

She started with two non-Swedish surnames but got no reply. Then she tried a Silfverbiörck and got hold of a young woman. Annika's pulse quickened and she covered her eyes with one hand.

"I'm sorry to call in the middle of the night," Annika began slowly in a low voice. "My name is Annika Bengtzon and I'm calling from the newspaper *Kvällspressen*. I'm calling because one of your classmates, Josefin Liljeberg, has . . ." Her voice cracked and she cleared her throat.

"Yes, I've heard," the girl—Charlotta, according to the class register—sobbed. "It's awful. We're all so shocked. We have to support each other."

Annika opened her eyes, grabbed a pen, and started taking notes. This was a lot simpler than she'd imagined.

"It's our biggest fear," Charlotta said. "It's what young women like us are most afraid of. Now it's happened to a friend, one of us. We all have to respond to it." She had stopped sobbing and sounded quite alert.

Annika took notes. "Is it something you and your friends have discussed?"

"Yes, sure. Though no one really thought it would happen to one of us. You never do."

"Did you know Josefin well?"

Charlotta gave a sob, a dry, deep sigh. "She was my best friend." Annika suspected she was telling a lie.

"What was Josefin like?"

Charlotta had a ready answer: "Always kind and cheerful. Helpful, fair, good grades. She liked partying. Yes, I suppose you can say that . . ."

Annika waited in silence for a moment.

"Will you need my picture?"

Annika looked at her watch. She figured it out: to Täby and back, developing the film—it would be too tight. "Not tonight. The paper's going to press soon. Can I call you again tomorrow?"

"Of course, or you can try my pager."

Annika took the number. She leaned her forehead on her hand and had a think. Josefin still felt vague and distant to her. She couldn't establish a clear picture of the dead woman.

"What did Josefin want to do with her life?"

"What do you mean, 'do'? Have a family, get a job, you know . . ."

"Where did she work?"

"Work?"

"Yes, which restaurant?"

"Oh, I don't know that."

"She'd moved in to Stockholm, to Dalagatan. Did you visit her there?"

"Dalagatan? No . . ."

"Do you know why she moved?"

"She wanted to get into town, I guess."

"Did she have a boyfriend?"

Charlotta was silent. Annika understood. This girl didn't know Josefin well at all.

"Thanks for letting me disturb you in the middle of the night," Annika said.

Now there was only one more call to make. She looked up Liljeberg in the phone book again, but there was no Josefin on Dalagatan. She'd recently moved there and hadn't been listed yet, Annika thought, and called directory assistance.

"No, we have no Liljeberg on Dalagatan sixty-four," the operator informed her.

"It could be a very new number."

"I can see all subscriptions that were ordered up until yesterday."

"Could she be ex-directory?"

"No," the operator said. "That information would have showed up on my screen. Could the number be in somebody else's name?"

Annika aimlessly leafed through the printouts. She came across Josefin's mother, *Liljeberg Hed, Siv Barbro*. "Hed. Check if there's a Hed on Dalagatan sixty-four."

The operator typed it in. "Yes, there's a Barbro Hed. Could that be the one?"

"Yep."

She dialed the number without hesitation. A man answered on the fourth ring.

"Is this Josefin's house?"

"Who are you?"

"My name's Annika Bengtzon and I'm calling from—"

"Damn it, I'm running into you everywhere." Now Annika recognized the voice. "Q!" she exclaimed. "What are you doing there?"

"What do you think? And how the hell did you get hold of this number? Even we haven't got it!"

"It was *really* hard, you know. I called directory assistance. What have you got?"

"I really don't have time right now." The man hung up.

Annika smiled. At least she had the right number. And she could add the fact that the police had been at Josefin's apartment during the night.

"I've got to know what you've got," Jansson said, and sat down on her desk.

"This is how it'll be," she said, and made a quick outline on a pad. Jansson nodded approvingly and jogged back to his desk.

She wrote the article about who Josefin was—the ambitious clergyman's daughter who dreamed of becoming a journalist. She wrote another piece on her death, mentioning her eyes and the death scream, her gnawed hand and the grief of her friend. She left the silicone breasts out. She wrote about the police hunt, the missing clothes, her last hours, the agitated tipster who had phoned the paper, about Daniella Hermansson's unease and the appeal of the press officer: "This maniac has to be stopped."

"This is pretty good," Jansson said. "Elegantly written, factual, and to the point. You've got some potential!"

Annika immediately had to walk away. She was bad at handling criticism, even worse at dealing with praise. She treasured the magic, the dance of the letters, that which gave her words wings. If she accepted the praise, the shimmering bubbles might burst.

"Let's have a cup of cocoa before you go home," Berit said.

The minister passed Bergnäs Bridge. He met a vintage American convertible halfway across, some aging rockers draped over the sides of the car. Other than that, he didn't see a single living soul.

He breathed out when he turned into the side streets behind the green bunker of the social security office. The noises and the whining had accompanied him for over 150 miles. It would soon be over.

After parking next to the rental firm office, he just sat in the car, enjoying the silence. He still had a little ringing in his left ear. He was exhausted. Still he had no choice. He groaned and climbed out of the car

with stiff limbs. He quickly glanced about him and then urinated behind the car.

The bags were heavier than he'd imagined. I won't make it, he
thought. He walked toward Storgatan, past the Citizen's Advice Bureau, then entered the old residential district of Östermalm. He got a
glimpse of his own house behind the birch trees, the old windows glittering in the early dawn. The kids' bikes lay next to the porch. The bedroom window was ajar, and he smiled when he saw the curtain flutter in
the breeze.

"Christer . . . ?" His wife looked over at him drowsily when he crept
into the bedroom. He hurried over to the bed and sat down next to her,
stroked her hair, and kissed her on the mouth.

"You go on sleeping, darling," he whispered.

"What's the time?"

"Quarter past four."

"How was the drive?"

"Fine. Go back to sleep now."

"How was your trip?"

He hesitated. "I bought some Azerbaijani brandy. We've never tried
that, have we?"

She didn't reply but pulled him close, reached over, and undid his
fly.

The sun was up and hung like an overripe orange just above the horizon, shining straight in her face. It was already hot, at half past five in
the morning. Annika was dizzy with fatigue. She had to get home. Gjörwellsgatan was deserted, and she walked in the middle of the street on
her way to the bus stop. Once there, she dropped onto the bench, her
legs completely numb.

She had seen the outline of the front page on Jansson's screen before she'd left, dominated by the graduation photo of Josefin and the
banner headline "Cemetery Sex Murder." She had written the short
front-page item with Jansson. Her stories were on pages six, seven,
eight, nine, and twelve. She had filled more columns tonight than in all
her first seven weeks at the paper.

It worked, she thought. I did it. It worked.

She leaned her head against the Plexiglas of the bus shelter and closed her eyes. She took deep breaths and focused on the sounds of traffic. They were few and far away. She almost fell asleep but was woken up by a bird chirping loudly inside the embassy compound.

After some time, she realized that she didn't know when the bus would come. Stiffly, she got to her feet and went to look at the timetable. The first 56 bus on this Sunday morning wouldn't be running until 7:13, almost two hours away. She groaned out loud. There was nothing for it but to start walking.

She got up speed after a couple of minutes. It felt good. Her legs were soon moving by themselves and set the air around her in motion. She walked down the extension of Västerbron and in the direction of Fridhemsplan. She reached Drottningholmsvägen and saw the dense green looming at the far end of the street. Kronoberg Park looked eerily dark. She knew she had to go there.

The cordons had been removed. There was plastic tape only on the fence itself. She walked up to the iron gate and traced the metal arch of the padlock with her fingers. The sun reached the crowns of the lime trees, making the leaves glow.

She would have come here around this time, Annika thought. She saw the same sun make the same pattern in the foliage. It's all so fragile. It can happen so fast.

Her hand running along the circles and arches of the wrought-iron fence, Annika walked around the cemetery and reached the east side. She recognized the bushes and the toppled gravestone, but aside from this, nothing betrayed this as the place where Josefin died.

She held on to the fence with both hands and stared into the undergrowth. She slowly slid down to the ground. Her legs gave way and she softly sat down on the grass. Without her realizing, she had started to cry. The tears ran down her cheeks and fell onto her crumpled skirt. She leaned her forehead against the bars and softly cried.

"How did you know her?"

Annika started up. Arms flailing, she slipped on the grass and landed hard on her tailbone.

"I'm sorry, I didn't mean to startle you."

The face of the young woman who had spoken was red and swollen from crying. She spoke with a faint but distinct accent.

Annika stared at her. "I . . . didn't. I never met her. But I saw her when she was lying here. She was dead."

"Where?" the young woman said, taking a step forward.

Annika pointed. The woman walked up and looked at the spot in silence for a minute. Then she sat down on the grass next to Annika, turning her back to the cemetery and leaning against the fence.

"I saw her too," she said, fiddling with the hem of her blouse.

Annika rummaged through her bag for something to blow her nose on.

"I saw her at the morgue. It was her. All in one piece. She looked fine, really."

Annika swallowed and stared at the young woman again. Jesus! This must be Josefin's roommate, the girl who had identified her! They had to have been close friends.

She thought about the following day's front page and was hit by a sudden and unexpected feeling of shame. It made her start crying again.

The woman next to her started sobbing too. "She was so kind. She never hurt anybody."

"I didn't know her." Annika blew her nose on a page from her big notepad. "I work for a newspaper. I've written about Josefin."

The woman looked at Annika. "Jossie wanted to be a journalist. She wanted to write about abused children."

"She could have worked at *Kvällspressen.*"

"What did you write?"

Annika took a breath, hesitating for a moment. All the satisfaction about her pieces she had felt earlier was gone. She only wanted to sink through the grass and disappear.

"That she was assaulted and murdered in the cemetery," she said quickly.

The woman nodded and looked away. "I warned her about this."

Annika, who was squeezing the notepaper into a small ball, stopped in midmovement. "What do you mean?"

The woman wiped her cheeks with the back of her hands. "Joachim wasn't good for her. He beat her up all the time. She could never do anything right. She was always covered in bruises, which could be a problem at work. 'You've got to leave him,' I told her, but she couldn't."

Annika listened wide-eyed. "Good God! Have you told the police about this?"

The woman nodded and pulled out a tissue from the pocket of her jean jacket and blew her nose. "I've got bad allergies. You don't have any Seldanes, do you?"

Annika shook her head.

"I've got to go home," the woman said, and stood up. "I'm working tonight again. I need to get some sleep."

Annika also got to her feet and brushed some grass from her skirt. "Do you really think it could have been her boyfriend?"

"He used to tell Jossie he'd kill her one day." The woman started walking down toward Parkgatan.

Annika stared in at the graves with a new feeling in her stomach. The boyfriend! Perhaps the murder would be cleared up soon.

"Hey! What's your name?" she called through the park.

The woman stopped and called back. "Patricia."

Then she turned around and disappeared down toward Fleming-gatan.

Not until she stood outside the street door of her apartment block did Annika remember that she had promised to feed Anne Snapphane's cats. She sighed and quickly turned the matter over in her mind. The cats would probably survive. The question was whether she would if she didn't get to sleep soon. On the other hand, it was only a few hundred yards, and she had promised. She poked about in her bag and found Anne's keys at the bottom, an old chewing gum wrapper stuck to them.

I'm just too nice, she thought.

She took the steps from Pipersgatan up to Kungsklippan; her legs were trembling before she reached the top. Her tailbone was aching after her fall in the park.

Anne Snapphane's little apartment was on the sixth floor and had a balcony with a fabulous view. The cats started meowing as soon as she put the key in the lock. When she opened the door, two little noses appeared around it.

"Hello, little kittens, are you waiting for me?"

She shoved the kittens inside with her foot and closed the door behind her. She sat down on the floor, and both the animals immediately jumped up in her arms, nuzzling her chin.

"What's this? Do you want to have a kiss?" Annika laughed.

She petted the kittens for a minute, then got up and walked over to the kitchenette. The cats' three bowls sat on a leftover piece of linoleum next to the stove. The milk had gone bad. The food and the water bowls were both empty.

"Here you go, little kittens."

She threw out the milk, washed the bowl, and poured fresh milk from the fridge. The kittens were rubbing against her legs, purring expectantly.

"Hey, take it easy."

They were so eager they nearly turned the bowl over before she'd had time to put it down. While the cats were guzzling the milk, she filled the third bowl with water and looked for the cat food. She found three tins of Whiskas in a cupboard. It made her smile. Whiskas was the name of her own cat in Hälleforsnäs. He was staying with Grandma in her cottage in Lyckebo over the summer.

"Why am I getting so sentimental?" she said out loud.

She opened a tin, wincing at the smell, and emptied it in the third bowl. She had a look in the litter tray in the bathroom; it would have to do until tomorrow.

"Bye-bye, little cats."

The kittens took no notice of her.

She quickly left the apartment and walked back down to Kungsholms Square. The day was starting. All the birds were in full voice now. She felt a bit shaky and was swaying slightly; her judgment of distance was poor.

You couldn't go on like this forever, she thought.

The air in her apartment was still stuffy from the day before. It was on the top floor at the back of the block, but it had neither its own bathroom nor hot water. But she had three rooms and a large kitchen. Annika had thought herself incredibly lucky when she got it.

"Nobody wants to live that primitively," the woman at the housing department had said to Annika when she had stated on the form that she could live without elevator, hot water, bathroom, or even electricity if necessary.

Annika had persevered.

"Here you are. Nobody wants this," the woman said, and gave her a computer printout with the address, 32 Hantverkargatan, fourth floor across the yard.

Annika took it without even seeing it. She had thanked her lucky stars every single day since then, but she knew her joy would be short-lived. She had agreed to one week's notice of eviction as soon as the owner of the block secured a loan for a complete renovation of the building.

She dropped her bag on the floor in the hallway and went into her bedroom. She had left the window open yesterday morning, but it had banged shut during the day. She opened it again and walked toward the living room to open a window in the hopes of stirring up a draft.

"Where have you been?"

Annika jumped in the air and screamed out loud.

The voice was quiet and came from the shadows over by her bed. "Jesus, have you completely lost your nerves?"

It was Sven, her boyfriend.

"When did you get here?" she said, her heart jumping against the inside of her chest.

"Last night. I wanted to take you to the movies. Where have you been?"

"At work," she said, and went into the living room.

He got up from the bed and followed her. "No, you haven't. I called an hour ago and they said you'd left already."

"I went to feed Anne's cats." She opened the living-room window.

"That's your excuse?"

She'd been there for about a minute and already they were arguing. Annika sometimes wondered what she still saw in Sven.

SEVENTEEN YEARS, SIX MONTHS, AND TWENTY-ONE DAYS

There is a dimension where the boundaries between human bodies are erased. We live with each other, in each other, spiritually and physically. Days become moments; I drown in his eyes. Our bodies dissolve and enter another time. Love is gold and crystals. We can travel anywhere in the universe, together, two and yet one.

A soul mate is someone who has a lock that fits our keys and keys that fit our locks. With this person, we feel safe in our own paradise. I read that somewhere, and it's true for us.

I long for him every moment we're not together. I didn't know that love was so compelling, so complete, so all-consuming. I can't eat or sleep. Only when I'm with him, I'm whole, a true human being. He is the sine qua non of my life and meaning. I know that I'm the same to him. We have been granted the biggest gift.

Never leave me,
he says;
I can't live without you.

And I promise him.

Patricia put her hand on Josefin's door handle. She hesitated. The bedroom was Josefin's domain. Patricia didn't have access and Jossie had been very clear about it:

"You can stay here, but the bedroom is mine."

The handle was a bit loose. Patricia had been meaning to tighten it, but they didn't have a Phillips screwdriver. Carefully, she pushed down on the handle. The door creaked. She was met by a musty smell; the air in the room was hot and stagnant. Jossie was supposed to clean her own room, which meant it never got done. The police search during the night had stirred up two months' worth of dust.

The room was bathed in sharp sunlight. The police had opened the curtains, and Patricia realized she had never seen the room like that before. The daylight exposed the dirt and the grimy wallpaper. Patricia felt ashamed when she thought of the police officers. They must have thought Jossie and Patricia were total slobs.

She slowly walked over to the bed and sat down. It was really only a mattress from IKEA that they had put on the floor. She sat about a foot off the ground.

Patricia was tired. She had slept badly in the heat—waking up, sweating, crying. She slowly lay down on the bed. When she had come home this morning, a dull and gloomy loneliness had met her at the door. The police were gone and only the traces of the search remained behind. They really had turned the entire apartment upside down but hadn't taken much with them.

She nearly dropped off among the pillows; she felt the familiar twitch. She instantly sat up. She must not sleep in Jossie's room.

A pile of magazines was next to the bed. Patricia bent down and leafed through the top one. *Woman's Weekly*, Jossie's favorite. She didn't like it much; there was too much about makeup, weight loss, and sex. Patricia always felt stupid and ugly after reading it, as if she weren't quite good enough. She knew that this was the whole idea of the magazine. On the face of it, they were helping young girls feel better about themselves but were in fact just making them feel inadequate.

She picked up the next magazine in the pile. It was smaller and Patricia had never come across it before. The paper was of poor quality and so was the print. It opened at the center spread. Patricia realized she was looking at two men with their penises inside a woman, one in her anus, the other in her vagina. You could just make out the woman's face in the background. She was screaming as if she were suffering. The image hit Patricia in the groin like an electric shock. She recoiled, disgusted, partly by the picture and partly by her own reaction to it. She threw the magazine on the floor as if it burned her fingers. Josefin didn't look at stuff like that. Patricia knew it was Joachim's.

She lay back down, staring at the ceiling and trying to repress her shameful excitement. It slowly faded. Was she never going to get used to it?

Her gaze traveled around the room. The door to the walk-in closet was open, Josefin's clothes hanging untidily on their hangers. Patricia knew this was the work of the police officers. Jossie was particular about her clothes.

I wonder what will become of them now? she thought. Maybe I could have some of them.

She got up and walked over to the closet. She ran her hand over the garments. They were expensive; Joachim had bought most of them. Patricia wouldn't be able to wear the dresses—they'd be too loose across the chest. But the skirts, and perhaps some of the suits . . .

The jingling of keys in the front door made her start. She quickly closed the closet and flew across the wooden floor in her bare feet. She had just closed the door to Josefin's room when Joachim stepped inside the hall.

"What are you doing?" He was sweating at the hairline and had dark patches on his shirt.

Patricia looked at the man, pulse racing in her veins and mouth completely dry. She tried to smile. "Nothing," she said nervously.

"Stay the fuck out of Josefin's bedroom. We've told you enough times." He slammed the front door shut.

"The cops. The fucking cops have made a mess everywhere, in here too."

He swallowed the bait. "Fucking cops." Patricia sensed a catch in his voice. "Did they take anything?"

He walked toward Patricia, who stood in front of Jossie's bedroom. "I don't know. Not from me, anyway."

He threw the bedroom door open and walked over to the bed, lifting the cover. "The sheet. They've taken the bedclothes."

Watchful, Patricia remained in the doorway. He walked round the room, seemingly checking to see everything was accounted for. He sat down heavily on the bed with his back to the door, leaning his head in his hands. Patricia breathed in the dust, too scared to move. She looked at his broad shoulders and strong arms. The light from the window made his hair glow. He really was good-looking. Josefin had been the happiest girl in the world when they became a couple. Patricia remembered her tears of joy and accounts of how wonderful he was. As if she were delirious.

Joachim turned round and looked at her. "Who do you think did it?" he said quietly.

Patricia's face was expressionless. "Some madman," she said calmly and firmly. "Some drunk on his way home. She was in the wrong place at the wrong time."

He turned away again. "Could it have been one of the customers?" he asked without looking up.

Patricia carefully weighed her answer. "One of the big shots from last night, you mean? I don't know. What do you think?"

"It would be the end of the club."

She looked down at her hands, twiddling with the hem of the T-shirt. "I miss her already."

Joachim stood and came up to her, putting his hand on her shoulder and stroking her arm.

"Patricia," he said guardedly. "I understand how sad you must be. I'm just as sad myself."

It made her skin crawl and she had to brace herself not to recoil from his touch.

"I hope the police catch him," she said.

Joachim pulled her close, a sob shaking his big body. "Shit, shit," he said in a stifled voice. "She's dead."

He began to cry. Patricia gingerly put her arms on his back, rocking him slightly.

"My Jossie, my angel!"

He cried, sobbing and blubbering. She closed her eyes and forced herself to stay where she was.

"Poor Joachim," she whispered. "Poor you . . ."

He let go of her and went to the bathroom. She could hear him blowing his nose and urinating. Embarrassed, she waited in the hall, listening to the stream of piss and then the flushing water.

"Did the police talk to you?" he asked when he came out.

She swallowed. "A bit, yesterday. They want to talk to me again today."

He studied her closely. "That's good. The scumbag has to be locked up. What are you going to tell them?"

She turned away and walked out into the kitchen and poured a glass of water.

"Depends on what they ask me. I don't really know anything," she said, and drank from the glass.

He followed her and stopped in the doorway, leaning against the door frame. "They're going to ask you what Jossie was like and stuff. How she was . . ."

Patricia placed the glass on the counter with a bang and looked Joachim in the eye. "I'll never say anything that would be bad for Jossie," she said assertively.

He looked happy with that. "Come with me," he said, placing his arm around her shoulders. He pulled her along through the hallway, into Josefin's bedroom and over to her closet.

"Have a look at these," he said, rifling through Jossie's expensive suits with his free hand. "Do you want any of these? This one, maybe?"

He took out a bright pink, silk-and-wool, fitted suit with large gold buttons that Josefin had adored. She thought she looked like Princess Diana in it.

Patricia felt tears well up in her eyes. She swallowed. "Joachim, I couldn't . . ."

"Go on, take it. It's yours."

She started crying. He let go of her and held up the suit in front of her.

"Your tits are a bit small, but maybe we could see to that." He smiled at her.

Patricia stopped crying, looked down, and let him put the hanger in her hand. "Thanks," she whispered.

"You could wear it to the funeral."

She heard him go out into the kitchen and get something from the fridge. Then he left the apartment.

Patricia remained standing in Josefin's overheated bedroom, frozen to the spot. She chased away a thought she had about being safe there. Patricia had nowhere else to go.

The Rival had talked to the father. He didn't say anything interesting, only that he couldn't believe that she was gone. But they had got a quote . . .

"You never know which way the wind's going to blow," Berit said. "If they're unlucky, they'll have a big discussion about media ethics on their hands."

"For approaching the family?" Annika asked, and skimmed through the story.

Berit nodded and took a sip from a can of mineral water. "You've got to be extremely careful when you do that. Some people want to talk, but many don't. You mustn't ever trick anyone into talking to you. Did you call her parents?"

Annika folded up the paper and shook her head. "I couldn't bring myself to do it. It didn't seem right."

"That's not a very good guiding principle," Berit said seriously. "Just because it's unpleasant for you, it doesn't necessarily mean that it will be for them. Sometimes the family feels better if they know what the papers will be writing about them."

"So you think the media should call the family when a child has died?" Annika knew she sounded confrontational.

Berit drank some more water and thought for a moment. "Well, each case is different. The only thing you'll know for sure is that people react in different ways. There is no universal right or wrong way of doing things. You have to be careful and sensitive so you don't hurt anyone."

"Well, I'm glad I didn't call." Annika got up to get some coffee.

By the time she returned, Berit had gone back to her own desk.

I wonder if I've offended her, Annika thought to herself. She saw Berit sitting hunched over a paper at the other end of the newsroom landscape. She quickly picked up the phone and dialed Berit's extension.

"Are you mad at me?" she asked, meeting Berit's gaze across the floor.

Annika saw her laughter and heard it in the earpiece. "Not a bit! You have to find out for yourself what's right for you."

The Creepy Calls phone rang and Annika switched receivers.

"How much for a really hot tip?" an excited male voice asked.

Annika groaned inwardly and reeled off the information.

"Okay," the man said. "Wait for this—you got a pen?"

"Yeah. Get to the point."

"I know a TV celebrity who dresses up in women's clothes and visits sex clubs." The man sounded as if he were ready to burst, and he named one of Sweden's most popular and admired TV presenters.

It made Annika crazy. "Bull. Do you think *Kvällspressen*'s going to print that garbage?"

The caller was taken by surprise. "But it's a big story."

"Jesus, people can do whatever they like. And what makes you think it's true?"

"I have it from a reliable source," the man said proudly.

"Sure. Thanks for calling." Annika hung up.

She saw that their tabloid rival had roughly the same copy and photos in their murder coverage as *Kvällspressen*. But Annika thought they hadn't done as good a job. For example, they didn't have the portrait of Josefin in her graduation cap. And their pictures from the murder scene were weaker and the articles more prosaic; the neighbors they had interviewed were more boring, and their update on the old Eva murder was less thorough. They had no teacher or friend, where *Kvällspressen* had short interviews both with the friend Charlotta and the deputy principal Martin Larsson-Berg.

"Well done," Spike said from somewhere above her head. She looked up and met the gaze of her superior.

"Thank you," she said.

He sat down on the edge of her desk. "What are we doing today?"

A peculiar warmth spread inside her. She was one of them now. He had come up to her and asked what she was doing.

"I thought I'd go and talk to her roommate, the girl who identified the body."

"Do you think she'll talk to you?"

"It's not impossible. I've been trying to get in touch with her."

She knew instinctively that she shouldn't tell him about meeting Patricia in the park. If she did, Spike would get steamed up about her not coming right back to write a story on it.

"Okay," the news editor said. "Who's doing the police investigation?"

"Berit and I are doing it together."

"Okay. What else? Do you think the father and mother will do a weepie?"

Annika fidgeted. "I'm not sure now's the right time to disturb them."

"He talked to the Rival. What did he say when you called?"

Annika's cheeks turned red. "He . . . I . . . didn't want to intrude so shortly after . . ."

Spike got up and left without a word. Annika wanted to explain how wrong it had felt, that you couldn't behave like that. But she didn't make the rules. The stout back of Spike drifted away and she saw him plunk his heavy body down in the swivel chair by his desk. Despite the distance, Annika could make out its heavy creaking.

She quickly grabbed a pad and a pen and a tape recorder, stuffed everything in her bag, and went over to the picture desk. No photographers were in the office and consequently no cars were available. She ordered a cab.

"To Vasastan, Dalagatan."

She wanted to know what life the dead woman had led.

He woke with a start from the light touch of his wife's hand on his shoulder.

"Christer," she whispered. "It's the prime minister."

He sat up, feeling slightly disoriented. The bed swayed and his body ached with weariness.

He got up and walked over toward his study. "I'll take it in here."

The prime minister sounded steady and clear on the phone. He'd probably been awake for several hours.

"Well, Christer, did you get back home all right?"

The minister for foreign trade slumped down on the chair by his desk, pulling his hand through his hair. "Yes, but the drive up was tedious. How are you?"

"I'm just fine. I'm at Harpsund with the family. So how did it go?"

Christer Lundgren cleared his throat. "As expected. They're not exactly ballerinas at the negotiating table."

"Well, the arena isn't exactly an opera stage either. How do we proceed?"

The minister for foreign trade quickly sorted through the thoughts in his muddled brain. When he started speaking, his words were tolerably structured and clear. He had had time to think it over on the drive up to Luleå.

After the call he stayed at his desk, his head hanging over the writing pad. It showed a world map from before the fall of the Iron Curtain. He looked among the republics' anonymous yellow patches without cities or borders.

His wife opened the door slightly. "Do you want some coffee?"

He turned around and smiled at her. "I'd love some," he said, his smile widening, "but first I want you."

She took his hand and led him back into the bedroom.

The doorbell made Patricia jump. The police weren't coming for several hours yet. Her mouth turned dry. What if it was Jossie's parents?

She tiptoed out in the hall and peeked through the peephole. She recognized the woman from the park this morning. She opened the door without hesitation.

"Hi. How did you find me?"

The journalist smiled. She looked tired. "Computers. There are registers for everything these days. Can I come in?"

"It's a bit of a mess. The police were here and turned everything upside down."

"I promise not to start clearing up."

Patricia gave it another moment's thought. "Okay." She held the door wide open to the woman. "What did you say your name was?"

"Annika. Annika Bengtzon."

They shook hands.

The journalist stepped inside the dark hall and took her shoes off. "Phew, it's hot."

"I know," Patricia said. "I hardly slept at all last night."

"Because of Josefin?"

Patricia nodded.

"Nice suit." Annika nodded in her direction.

Patricia turned red and passed her hand over the shiny pink fabric. "It was Josefin's. I've been given it."

"You look like Princess Diana in it."

"I don't . . . ! I'm too dark. I'll take it off. Just wait here."

Patricia disappeared into her room, which was the living room, and put the suit back on the hanger. She looked around for a hook to hang it on and, when she didn't find one, hung it on a door. She quickly put on a pair of jeans and a camisole.

The journalist was in the kitchen when Patricia came out of her room.

"The cops should clear up after themselves. Would you like some tea?"

"I'd love some," Annika said, and sank down onto a chair.

Patricia lit the gas stove, poured water into an aluminum saucepan, and started putting things back in the cupboards.

"Jossie's stars were lined up against her. Things weren't looking too rosy right now. Her sun sign had been dominated by Saturn for almost a year; she's been having a tough time." Patricia broke off and blinked away the tears.

"Do you believe in that stuff?" Annika thought it was bullshit.

"I don't believe, I *know*," Patricia said. "We've got English Breakfast or Earl Grey."

Annika chose the Breakfast tea.

"I brought the paper." She put the first edition of *Kvällspressen* on the table.

Patricia didn't touch it. "You can't use anything I tell you."

"Okay."

"You can't say that you've been here."

"Fine."

Patricia watched the journalist in silence. Annika looked young, not much older than herself. She dipped the tea bag in the mug a few times, twirled the string round the tea bag on the spoon, and squeezed out a few more drops of strong tea.

"So what are you doing here?"

"I want to understand," Annika said calmly. "I want to know who Josefin was, how she lived, her thoughts and feelings. You know all that. When I know, I can put the right questions to a lot of other people, without saying a word of what you tell me. You're protected by law when you speak to me. No person in authority is allowed even to ask who I've spoken to."

Patricia gave it some thought while she drank her tea.

"What do you want to know?"

"I think you probably know that best. What was she like?"

Patricia sighed. "She could be really childish sometimes. I could get really mad at her. She'd forget that we'd arranged to meet in town. There I'd stand waiting, looking like a fool. And then she wouldn't even be sorry. 'Oh, I forgot' was all she'd say."

Patricia fell silent, then added, "I miss her, though."

"Where did she work?"

She had taken out a pen and pad. Patricia noticed and straightened her back. "You won't write about this, will you?"

Annika smiled. "My memory can be as bad as Josefin's. I'm just taking notes for my own sake."

Patricia relaxed. "A club called Studio 69. It's in Hantverkargatan."

"Is it?" Annika said in surprise. "That's where I live. Where on Hantverkargatan?"

"On the hill. Not that there's a big neon sign, or anything. It's pretty discreet, all you see is a small board in the shop window."

Annika gave it some thought. "But isn't that the name of the radio show, *Studio 69*?" she said hesitantly.

Patricia giggled.

"Yes. But Joachim, the guy who owns the club, realized that the radio station hadn't registered it. He thought it was funny to use the same name. And it's a really good name—you know what it's about. The whole thing might end up in court."

"Joachim. Is that Josefin's boyfriend?"

Patricia's face turned serious. "The stuff that I told you in the park, you mustn't ever tell anyone about it."

"But you did tell the police, didn't you?"

Patricia's eyes grew wide. "That's true," she said, as if she had forgotten. "I did."

"Don't worry about having told them. It's very important that the police get to know about stuff like that."

"But Joachim's really upset. He came here this morning and he was crying."

Annika looked down at her notes and decided to drop the subject for the time being.

"So what did Jossie do at the club?"

"She waited on tables and danced."

"Danced?"

"Onstage. Not naked, that's not allowed. Everything's strictly legal, Joachim's particular about that. She wore a G-string."

Patricia saw that the journalist was mildly taken aback.

"So she was . . . a stripper?"

"I suppose you could say that."

"And you, are you also a . . . dancer?"

Patricia gave a laugh. "No. Joachim thinks my boobs are too small. I work at the bar, and then I'm trying to learn to be a croupier at the roulette table. I'm not doing very well, though. I can't count that fast."

Her laughter died out and became a sob. Annika waited silently while Patricia collected herself.

"Were you friends at school, you and Josefin?"

Patricia blew her nose on a piece of paper towel and shook her head. "No, not at all. We met at the Sports Club on Sankt Eriksgatan. We used to go to the same aerobics class and our lockers were next to each other. It was Josefin who started talking to me—she could talk to anyone. She'd just met Joachim and she was so in love. She could talk about him for hours, how good-looking he was, how much money he had . . ." Her voice trailed off as the memories came back.

"How did they meet?" Annika asked after a while.

Patricia shrugged. "Joachim is from Täby, like her. I got to know Jossie the Christmas before last, a year and a half ago. Joachim had just opened the club and it was an immediate success. Jossie started working weekends and helped me get a job behind the bar. I've got a diploma in food presentation."

The phone in the hall rang and Patricia jumped up to get it.

"Sure, that's fine," she said into the receiver. "In half an hour."

When she returned to the kitchen, Annika had put her mug on the counter.

"The police will be here in a while," Patricia said.

"I won't disturb you any longer," Annika said. "Thanks for seeing me."

Annika walked out into the hall and put her sandals back on.

"How long will you stay on in the apartment?"

Patricia chewed on her lip. "I don't know. The apartment is Josefin's. Her mom bought it so that Jossie wouldn't have to commute all the way to Täby Kyrkby when she's admitted to the College of Media and Communication."

"Would they have taken her? Were her grades good enough?"

Patricia looked hard at Annika. "Jossie's really smart. She's got top grades. Swedish is her best subject, she writes really, really well. You think she's stupid just because she's a stripper?"

Patricia could see, in spite of the dim lighting, that the journalist's face had turned red.

"I spoke to the deputy principal of her old school. He didn't think she had very good grades." Annika was trying to cover herself.

"He probably just thinks blondes are dumb."

"Did she have a lot of friends?"

"At school, you mean? Hardly any. Jossie spent most of her time doing homework."

They shook hands and Annika opened the door. She stopped short in the doorway.

"How come you moved in here?"

Patricia lowered her gaze. "Jossie wanted me to."

"Why?"

"She was afraid."

"Of what?"

"I can't tell you."

But Patricia saw in the journalist's eyes that she knew.

Annika stepped outside in the heat of Dalagatan and screwed up her eyes against the sun. It was a relief to come out of the dark and dingy apartment. Black curtains—that was a bit macabre. She didn't like Josefin's house. She didn't like what she'd found out. Why the hell would she choose to be a stripper?

If she had chosen.

The subway station was just around the corner, so she took it the two stops over to Fridhemsplan. She went out the Sankt Eriksgatan exit and walked past the gym where Josefin and Patricia had met, then took a right up to the murder scene. Two small bunches of flowers were by the entrance. Annika had a suspicion they'd soon be accompanied by many more. She stood for a while next to the fence. It was just as hot as the day before and she soon got thirsty. Just when she had made up her mind to leave, she saw two young women, one blond, one dark, slowly walking toward the park from Drottningholmsvägen. Annika decided to stay. They were dressed in the same miniskirts and high heels; both were chewing gum and had a Pepsi in their hand.

"A girl died in there yesterday," the blond woman said, and pointed in among the graves as they walked past Annika.

"No kidding?" the dark one said, eyes open wide.

The first one nodded in a bossy way and waved her hand around. "She lay in there, completely cut open. She'd been raped after she was killed."

"That's awful."

They stopped a few yards away, engrossed in the dark shadows among the stones. After a minute or so, they were both crying.

"We've got to leave a message," the blond woman said.

They dug out a piece of paper from one bag, a pen from another. The blonde leaned on the other's back to write the note. Then they dried their tears and walked off toward the subway.

When they'd disappeared around the corner, Annika walked over and read the note:

"We miss you."

At that moment she saw a team from the Rival step out of a car parked by the playground on Kronobergsgatan. She turned around and quickly walked down Sankt Göransgatan; she most definitely did not want to stand around chatting to Arne Påhlson.

On her way down to the 56 bus stop, she walked past Daniella Hermansson's street door, the cheery mother who always slept with her window open. She fished out her pad—yes, she had the entry code jotted down next to Daniella's address. Without deliberating any further, she punched in the code and entered the building.

The current of air that hit her was so cold that she shivered. She stopped to hear the street door close behind her. The entrance was decorated with murals with park motifs.

Daniella lived on the third floor. Annika took the elevator. She rang the doorbell but nobody answered. She looked at her watch: ten past three. Daniella was most likely in the park with her kid.

She sighed. The day hadn't been particularly productive so far. Especially in terms of material she could write about. She looked around the hallway. There were a lot of doors, so the apartments had to be small. On the mailboxes were the names of the tenants in plastic lettering that had turned yellow. Annika walked up and studied the one nearest to her. Svensson, she read. She might as well get some reactions from other neighbors now that she was here.

Annika rang the Svenssons' bell, and through the narrow crack that opened came the stench of acrid BO. Annika took a step back. A shape-less woman in a mauve and turquoise polyester dress peered out through the opening: myopic eyes, gray tangle of greasy hair. She was holding a fat little mutt of indeterminable breed.

"Excuse me for disturbing you. I'm from the newspaper *Kvälls-pressen.*"

"We haven't done anything." The woman gave Annika a frightened look.

"No, of course not," Annika said politely. "I'm just knocking on the doors of this house to hear how people in the neighborhood are reacting to a crime being committed nearby."

The woman pulled the door closed a bit. "I don't know anything."

Annika started regretting disturbing the woman; maybe it wasn't such a good idea. "Perhaps you haven't heard that a young woman was murdered in the park," she said calmly. "I thought the police might have been here and—"

"They were here yesterday."

"So then they would have asked—"

"It wasn't Jasper!" the woman cried out unexpectedly, making An-nika take an involuntary step back. "There was nothing I could do to stop him! And I don't believe the minister had anything at all to do with it!"

The woman slammed the door on Annika. Jesus, what had hap-pened?

A door at the other end of the hallway opened a crack. "What's go-ing on?" an old man's irritated voice sounded.

Annika picked up her pad and took the stairs down. Well out on the street, she started walking to the right without looking at the park.

"Thanks for feeding the cats."

Anne Snapphane was back and was sitting on her chair with her feet on the desk.

"How was Gotland?" Annika asked, dropping her bag on the floor.

"Scorching. Like having a fire next to a pizza oven. But they've got it under control now. But what the hell's happened to you?"

"What?" Annika said, not understanding.

"You've got a great big cut above your eye!"

Annika's hand flew up to her left eyebrow. "Oh, that. I hit my head on the bathroom cabinet this morning. Guess where I've been."

"At the murder victim's house?"

Annika smiled broadly and sat down.

"Well, I never," Anne said.

"Have you had lunch?"

They went to the cafeteria.

"So tell me about it," Anne Snapphane said with curiosity, loading a big forkful of pasta shells into her mouth.

Annika reflected. "Her roommate's an immigrant, or first-generation Swedish. From South America, is my guess. A bit odd, believes in astrology, but I like her."

"And what was Josefin like?"

Annika put down her fork. "I don't know. I can't figure her out. Patricia says she was really smart, the deputy principal that she was a stupid blonde, and her classmate Charlotta didn't seem to know the first thing about her. She wanted to be a journalist and help children, and at the same time she worked as a stripper."

"Stripper?"

"Her boyfriend runs some kind of strip joint. Studio 69, it's called."

"But that's that radio show. Boring old P3 trying to be intellectual. I hate it."

Annika nodded. "Yep. Joachim, the boyfriend, apparently thought it was hilarious. *Studio 69* must be the most pretentious radio show around."

"If his aim was to bait those hotshots at the radio station, it points to a certain degree of intelligence."

Annika smiled and stuffed her mouth full.

"Tell me more. What was the apartment like?"

Annika chewed and thought about the question. "Spartan. Like it wasn't really furnished, you know, mattresses straight on the floor. As if they hadn't moved in for real."

"How the hell did she get an apartment on Dalagatan?"

"Mommy Barbro bought it. The phone's in her name too."

Anne Snapphane leaned back in her chair. "Why did she die?"

Annika shrugged. "Don't know."

"What are the cops saying?"

"I haven't talked to them yet."

They both bought a bottle of mineral water to take back to the newsroom. Spike was on the phone; no one else was in the office.

"What are you doing today?" Annika wondered.

"New forest fires have flared up all over the realm. I'll be putting them all out single-handedly."

Annika laughed.

She switched on her computer and loaded a floppy disk. She swiftly entered the notes from her conversation with Patricia, saved the file to the floppy, and deleted it from the hard disk. She put the floppy in her bottom desk drawer.

Annika's phone rang. She knew from the signal that it was an internal call.

"You've got a visitor," Tore Brand informed her.

"Who is it?"

Brand disappeared from the phone; she could hear him hollering in the background, "Hey! Stop! You can't just walk in there—"

Steps returning to the phone.

"Listen, he went right upstairs. But I think it's all right. It's a guy."

Annika felt the irritation growing inside her. Tore Brand was there to prevent exactly this sort of thing from happening. Stupid old man.

"Did he say what he wanted?"

"He wanted to discuss something in today's paper. We're supposed to be accessible to the readers," Tore Brand said, as if it were meant literally.

At that instant, Annika spotted the man out of the corner of her eye. He was moving toward her, his eyes glaring. Annika hung up the phone and watched the man stalk through the newsroom and up to her desk.

"Are you Annika Bengtzon?" he said tensely.

Annika nodded.

The man geared himself up and slammed a copy of the day's *Kvälls-pressen* onto Annika's desk. "Why didn't you call?" His voice cracked in a spasm that came somewhere from his stomach.

Annika stared at the man—she didn't have a clue who he was.

"Why didn't you tell us what you were going to write? Her mother didn't know that this is how she died. Or that someone had been chewing on her. Jesus Christ!"

The man turned round and sat down on her desk, then hid his face in his hands and started crying. Annika picked up the paper he'd slammed down in front of her. It was open on the story on what Josefin looked like when she was found: her mute scream and bruised breasts, and the picture with the naked leg in the dense summer vegetation. Annika closed her eyes and rubbed her forehead.

This was Josefin's father, of course. Good God, what have I done? Annika felt shame wash over her like a giant tidal wave, coming at her in hot flushes. The floor started rolling. Christ Almighty, what had she done?

"I'm sorry. I didn't think you'd want to be disturbed—"

"Disturbed?" the man shouted out loud. "Do you think we could get more disturbed than this? Did you think we wouldn't see the garbage you wrote? Were you hoping we'd die too and never find out about it? Were you?"

Annika was on the verge of tears. The man was red in the face and was practically foaming at the mouth. Spike had turned around and was looking in her direction. Picture Pelle had showed up and was staring at the scene.

"I'm very sorry," she said.

Suddenly, out of nowhere, Berit materialized. Without a word, she put an arm around the man's shoulder and led him away toward the cafeteria. He went with her without arguing, shaking with tears.

Annika grabbed her bag and hurried to the back exit. She was breathing raggedly and had to make a huge effort to walk normally.

"Where are you going, Bengtzon?" Spike hollered after her.

"Out!" she yelled back in a far too shrill voice.

She ran down the steps and threw her body at the back door. Two floors down, in the stairwell outside the archive, she sat down.

I'm a contemptible human being, she thought. This is never going to work.

She just sat on the stairs for a while and then left the building via the entrance next to the printing works.

She walked slowly down to the water by Marieberg Park. The noise of kids swimming traveled over the surface from Smedsudds Beach. She sat down on a bench. This is what it's like to live, she mused. You hear the sounds, feel the wind and the heat. You fail and you're ashamed of it. That's what it's all about—to live and learn.

I'll never hesitate again to make a call or make contact. I'll always stand up for what I write. I'll never be ashamed of my work or my words. She made promises to herself.

She slowly made her way along the water's edge over to the beach. There she took the path skirting Fyrverkarbacken and leading back to the newspaper offices.

"You have to tell me when you leave the building," Tore Brand grumbled at the reception desk when she passed.

She didn't have the energy to answer but just took the elevator up, praying that the father would be gone. He was, along with everybody else. Spike and Jansson were doing the handover, the subeditors weren't in yet, and Berit was out someplace.

Annika sat down heavily at her desk. She hadn't produced anything useful today. All that remained was to call the police.

The press officer said that the investigation was in progress.

There was no reply at the Krim duty desk.

The police control room hadn't been involved in the murder case during the day.

She hesitated but then decided to call the captain in charge of the investigation all the same.

When she dialed the number for the Krim duty desk, he answered the phone. Her pulse quickened.

"Hello, this is Annika Bengtzon at—"

"I know, I know." Quiet groan.

"Are you always at work?"

"Same with you, it seems like." His tone was cold and curt.

"I've got a few quick questions—"

"I can't talk to every reporter in town. If I'm on the phone, I can't be doing my job." Angry, annoyed.

"You don't have to talk to everybody, only to me."

"You'd like that, wouldn't you?" Tired.

Annika reflected in silence for a few seconds. "This is taking a long time. It'd be quicker if you just answered my questions."

"The quickest thing would be for me to hang up."

"So why don't you?"

He breathed silently down the line, as if asking himself the same question. "What do you want?"

"What have you been doing today?"

"Routine interviews."

"Patricia? Joachim? The other people at the club? Maybe even a few of the customers? The parents? Her twin brother? People living near the park? The fat lady with the dog? And who's Jasper? And who's the minister?"

There was a pause. She'd got him. "You've done your homework."

"Just the normal research."

"We've found her clothes."

Annika felt the hair on her arms stand on end. This was news. He was giving her an exclusive.

"Where?"

"At the incinerating plant in Högdalen."

"At the dump?"

"No, they were in a compactor together with a whole lot of other garbage. They must have been thrown in a trash can somewhere on Kungsholmen. They're emptied into open wagons every day and the contents are compacted along with everything that's picked up from the street. So you can imagine."

"Will you be able to use the clothes as evidence?"

"So far the techs have found parts of a TV, fibers from couch upholstery, what look like bits of banana, and feces from a diaper among the clothes." He sighed.

"So it's useless?"

"So far, yes."

"Were the clothes torn?"

"Torn to pieces—by the compactor."

"So all fingerprints, hairs, tears, and other stuff that could have told you something is ruined."

"You've got it."

"Can I write that?"

"Do you think it's of any interest?"

"The murderer must have dumped the clothes in the trash can. Someone might have seen him."

"Where? How many people throw rubbish in a bin on Kungshol-men every day? Take a guess!"

"Like . . . everybody?"

"Correct! And it doesn't even have to have been the murderer who put them in the bin. The clothes could have been found by some concerned citizen who thought they were littering the footpath or something."

She waited in silence. "At least it shows that the police are doing something," she said after a while.

He laughed. "Which must be a good thing."

"Perhaps I don't need to state exactly how ruined the clothes are. The murderer doesn't need to know."

He grunted but didn't respond.

"What about the interviews?"

"I can't say anything about them. They're progressing." The chill was back.

"What about the people I mentioned earlier?"

"They're just a start."

"What about the autopsy? Did it produce anything?"

"It will be performed during office hours, that is, tomorrow."

"What kind of place is Studio 69?"

"Go find out for yourself."

"Do you know which minister the woman was talking about?"

"I'm glad there's something left for you to find out. I can't talk any longer now. Bye."

Annika contemplated the information she'd been given. The clothes thing was new, they could work that. Pity the police didn't rate the find highly, but at least they knew now that the murderer didn't keep the clothes.

Spike, Jansson, and Picture Pelle had returned from the handover. They were chatting over at the news desk.

"I've got an exclusive, at least for the time being."

The men looked at her, all with the same surprised and slightly annoyed look on their faces.

"They've found her clothes."

The men straightened up and reached for their pens.

"No shit. Can we get a photo of them?" the picture editor asked.

"No, but of the place where they were found. The incineration plant in Högdalen."

"They get any leads?"

Annika weighed her answer. "Not really, but the police don't want to say that."

The men nodded.

"It's looking good," Jansson said. "Together with what we've got already, this is some good stuff. Look at it."

He held out a sketch pad to Annika.

"I think we'll lead off with your story, 'New Police Lead'; photo of Josefin; photo of the dump. Soon we'll have to get a picture byline for you, Bengtzon!"

The men all laughed, kindly laughs. Annika cast down her eyes and blushed.

"Then there's the dad," Jansson went on. "Berit got a fantastic interview with him."

Annika was dumbfounded. "She did?"

"She sure did. He came up here shouting and going on about getting screwed, and Berit took care of him. Said he wanted to tell his story. She's gone out to the parents with the copy. They wanted to see the story first."

"Incredible," Annika mumbled.

"Then we need something from the murder scene. Any flowers there yet?"

"There weren't many this afternoon."

"Can you go and check out if there's any more now? Maybe talk to some mourners, someone leaving a message or lighting a candle."

Annika sighed and nodded. "What about her classmates?"

"Berit couldn't find any, apart from your Charlotta. We've got a photo of her in her room. Some of them are sure to be returning home tonight—it's the end of the industrial holidays today. But leave that for the time being, this will do for today. We've got the forest fires and the situation in the Middle East as well. It's getting pretty bad . . ."

The subeditors clattered in, raring to go to work. Annika returned to her desk, wrote her copy about the new police lead, and packed her bag to go down to the murder scene again.

Bertil Strand wasn't in, so she switched on the TV that was suspended from the ceiling above the desk. Josefin wasn't even mentioned on the local news.

Rapport spent half of their thirty-minute broadcast on the Middle East. Seven Israelis and fifteen Palestinians had been killed during the day. Three of them were small children. Annika shuddered.

After that the spokesperson for the Green Party demanded a commission be set up to look into the systematic registration of leftists in the seventies and into the IB affair.

Toward the end they showed part two of the Russia correspondent's report on the Caucasus conflict. The day before he had interviewed the Swedish-speaking president, today the reporter was with his guerrilla opponent.

"We're fighting for freedom," the leader said, one Kalashnikov in each hand. "The president is a hypocrite and a traitor."

There were women and children at the opposition headquarters. The little ones were laughing, running around barefoot, covered in dust. The women pulled their kerchiefs over their heads and disappeared into the black doorways of the houses. The guerrilla leader opened a door to a cellar and the TV reporter followed him underground. In the camera's light you could see row upon row of Russian arms: crates of mines, handguns, automatic weapons, hand grenades, antitank-grenade launchers, and on and on.

Annika was depressed. She was tired and hungry. What did it matter what she wrote about one dead Swedish girl when people around the world did nothing but destroy each other?

She went to the cafeteria and bought a bag of raspberry candies. She ate the entire contents of the bag on the way back to her desk and felt sick.

"How's it going, Annika?" It was Berit.

"So-so. I can't help thinking about all the misery in the world. It brings me down. Did you do okay with the parents?"

"Oh, yes. They had a few minor objections to what I'd written, but on the whole we agreed. We've got a picture of them sitting on the bed in Josefin's room. It looked untouched."

Berit walked over to the news desk to tell the editors. At the same moment Bertil Strand walked in.

"Have you got time for a quick trip to the murder scene?" Annika said, reaching for her bag.

"I just parked the car in the garage. Couldn't you have said something earlier?"

Patricia lay on her mattress, behind the drawn black curtains, sweating in the dark. Her legs ached and she felt sick with tiredness. She wasn't capable of spying on Joachim. They just couldn't ask that of her; the mere thought of it gave her goose bumps.

She closed her eyes and tried to shut out the sounds of the city. Night was falling out there; people were on their way to bars and restaurants. She focused inward and tried to find the truth inside, listening to her breathing and sinking into a form of self-hypnosis.

She conjured up Josefin's voice in the gloom, deep from within herself. At first the voice was lighthearted and happy, rising and falling, and Patricia smiled. Jossie was humming and singing in a high, clear voice. When the screams came, Patricia was prepared. She listened patiently to the blows and thuds, to Joachim's roaring. She hid in the shadows until he went silent and had left. She waited for the desperate tears from Jossie's room. The guilt was gone; she couldn't have stopped it. She wasn't alarmed; she wasn't scared. He couldn't do it anymore. Not to Jossie.

She took a deep breath and forced herself to the surface. The real world returned, sultry and hot.

I have to consult the cards, she thought.

She slowly got up; her blood pressure didn't keep up with her and she wobbled slightly. She took a balsawood box from a bag in the corner. She opened the box and stroked the black velvet lining. This was where she kept her cards.

She sat down on the floor in the lotus position and reverentially shuffled the tarot cards three times. Then she cut the deck three times. She repeated the procedure twice, just as the energies demanded. After the last cut she didn't collect the deck but chose one of the piles with her left hand and then shuffled these cards once more.

Finally, she put down the cards in a Celtic cross on the parquet floor, ten cards representing the quality of the moment from different angles. The Celtic cross was the most comprehensive spread to use when dealing with a significant change, which is what she felt she was facing now.

She deferred studying and analyzing the cards until the cross was complete. She then contemplated her situation. Her first card was Three of Swords, which stood for Saturn in Libra. She nodded—that was obvious, really. Three of Swords signified mourning and tension in three-way relationships. It urged her to make clear and unequivocal decisions.

The card crossing the card in the first position, standing in the way of her taking a stand, was the fifteenth of the Major Arcana, of course. The Devil, the male sex. It couldn't be more explicit.

The third and fourth cards represented her conscious and unconscious thoughts regarding the situation. Nothing strange there—Nine of Swords and Ten of Wands. Cruelty and oppression.

But the seventh and eighth cards made a big impression on her. The seventh card represented her self and was the eighteenth of the Major Arcana—the Moon. Not good. It meant she was facing a final and difficult test associated with the female sex.

The eighth card puzzled her. It represented external forces that would influence her situation. The Magician symbolized a ruthless communicator, an ingenious wordsmith, constantly moving on the edge of truth. She already had a hunch who this could be.

The tenth card, the outcome, made her feel calm. Six of Wands. Jupiter in Leo. Clarity. Breakthrough. Victory.

Now she knew she would make it.

SEVENTEEN YEARS, NINE MONTHS, AND THREE DAYS

Our happiness is so great. He holds me, always. His commitment is enormous; sometimes it's hard for me to live up to it. He gets very disappointed if I don't tell him everything. I must do better. Our travels through time and space are limitless. I love him so.

I have tried to explain that the fault does not lie with him. It's me; I'm the one who can't give him the appreciation he deserves.

He has bought clothes for me that I have hardly ever worn, symbols of love and trust. My ingratitude is based on egotism and immaturity; his disappointment is deep and hard. There is no excuse; universal togetherness brings responsibility.

I cry when I realize the scope of my imperfection. He forgives me. Then we make love.

Never leave me,
he says;
I can't live without you.

And I promise.

When Annika got to work, Spike was waiting impatiently by her desk, even though she didn't officially start for another hour and a half.

"Berit got a hot tip on another story," the news editor said. "You and Carl Wennergren will cover the murder today."

Annika dropped her bag on the floor and wiped the sweat from her forehead. "It's just getting hotter and hotter," she sighed.

"Carl's on his way up from Nynäshamn. Did you hear that he won the Round Gotland Race?"

Annika sat down and switched on her computer. "No, I didn't. That's nice for him."

Spike sat down on her desk and leafed through the rival tabloid. "We won today. They've got neither the parents nor the retrieved clothes. You did really well yesterday, you and Berit."

Annika lowered her head. "How are we going to develop the story today?"

"It won't be on the first page today. Sales always go down on the third day. Besides, it would have to be something pretty damn big to beat Berit's story. Why don't you try squeezing some kind of theory out of the cops? They should have one by now. Do you know if they have one they're working on?"

Annika hesitated as Joachim popped up in her mind, remembering Spike's dislike of "domestic quarrels."

"Perhaps," was all she said.

"If the police don't get a breakthrough, the story will soon be running on empty," Spike went on. "We'll have to keep an eye on the murder scene. Today would be the day for crying friends and stuff like that."

"Some graphics and a map detailing her last hours?"

Spike's face lit up. "You're right, we haven't done that. Get the data for it and talk to the illustrators."

Annika took notes. "Anything else new?"

"Well, our new deputy editor is coming in today. Anders Schyman. We'll have to see how it works out . . ."

Annika had heard the office talk about the new deputy editor, a presenter from a television current affairs program. She had never met him, only seen him on TV. He was big and blond and she thought he seemed boorish and unsympathetic.

"What do you think of him?" Annika asked circumspectly.

"It'll be a mess. What makes a goddamn TV celebrity think he can come here and teach us our jobs?"

Thereby he had voiced the collective opinion of the entire newsroom. Annika dropped the subject.

"Could Anne Snapphane help me on the murder case, or is she doing something else?"

Spike stood up. "Little Miss Snapphane has developed a new brain tumor and is undergoing some magnetic resonance imaging. Hey, there you are, Carl! Congratulations, pal!"

Carl Wennergren strolled into the newsroom with what must have been the sailing cup in his arms. Spike went up to him with long strides and slapped him on the back. Annika sat at her desk, numb. A brain tumor! Was he serious? Her hands trembled as she lifted the phone and dialed the number. Anne Snapphane answered on the first ring.

"How are you?" Annika said, a big lump in her throat.

"I'm really scared. I feel dizzy and weak, you know. When I close my eyes, I see flashes."

"Spike told me. Jesus, why haven't you told me about this?"

"What?"

"That you had a brain tumor!"

Anne Snapphane sounded slightly confused. "But I've never had a brain tumor. I've had all kinds of examinations, but they've never found anything."

Annika was at a loss. "But Spike said . . . So you don't have cancer of the brain?"

"Listen. You could say that I have a tendency to believe that I have various ailments. I know this, but all the same, a few times a year I will think I'm dying. Last winter I actually managed to pester the hospital into doing an MRI on me. Spike thinks it's hilarious."

Annika leaned back in her chair. She's a serious hypochondriac, she thought.

"Anyway, I've got another doctor's appointment at three-thirty this afternoon. You never know . . ."

"What are you going to do on your days off?"

"If they don't admit me to the hospital, I'm going up to Piteå with the cats. I've got tickets for the night train."

"Okay," Annika said. "I'll see you when we're back on."

They finished the call and Annika became absorbed in thoughts about her own impending vacation. This was the last of a five-day shift and she would be off for four days. She'd go home to Hälleforsnäs, see Sven and say hello to Whiskas. She sighed. She'd have to make her mind up soon. Either she'd stay and try to make a go of it here in Stockholm or she'd have to give her landlord notice and move back home.

She looked out over the newsroom. It was Monday and the place was swarming with people. She felt awkward and insecure. She didn't know the names of half the people. The warm feeling of belonging that she had felt during the weekend was gone. It was somehow linked to the quiet, the darkness outside, the empty corridors, and the low drone of the air-conditioning. During the day, the workplace was completely different, invaded by light and noise and loud people. She had no control; she had no status.

"Things have happened around here while I've been away," Carl Wennergren said, and settled on Annika's desk chummily.

Annika pointedly pulled out a computer printout from under the man's backside. "It's a tragic story."

Carl Wennergren put the cup down on top of the printout. "It's a challenge trophy," he said, handling his sailing cup. "Nice, isn't it?"

"Very."

"The owner of the boat gets the cup. The others just got a lousy diploma. The IOR class—the biggest boats—that's my kind of thing."

"I prefer to borrow Grandma's old rowing boat and row around Ho Lake. It can be pretty out there." Annika clicked to open a telegram on her screen.

Carl Wennergren looked at her in silence for a moment.

She didn't look up when he got up and walked off but made an effort to shut out him and the rest of the newsroom. She reached for the Rival. They didn't have much on the murder. She noted that they'd made something of a slip of paper at the murder scene with the words "We miss you." Annika shook her head and turned over the pages. A piece on relationships and holidays caught her attention. The divorce rate rose dramatically during the fall, she read, as the expectations that had kept marriages alive during the winter dropped with the leaves. She thought of herself and her own relationship and sighed.

"Why the long face? Do you want to grab a cup of coffee?"

Berit smiled cheerfully at her and Annika responded with a lopsided grin.

"I heard you got a tip," Annika said, fishing out her wallet from her bag.

"Yes, I did. Are you familiar with the IB affair?"

Annika quickly counted her money and saw that she'd have to go to the ATM today. "So-so. Sometime in the seventies Jan Guillou and Peter Bratt exposed how the government had set up an illegal register of people's political affiliations."

They were walking toward the cafeteria.

"Right," Berit said. "The Social Democrats panicked. They put the reporters in prison and acted pretty irrationally all along the line. Among other things, they destroyed their own archives, both for foreign and domestic affairs."

They took their coffee and sat down at a table by the window, not so much for the view as for the outlet of the air-conditioning overhead.

"So no one will ever find out what they were really up to at the In-formation Bureau?" Annika said.

"Exactly," Berit replied. "No one could find out much because the archives were lost. The Social Democrats have felt safe. Until now."

Annika stopped munching on her chocolate doughnut. "What do you mean?"

Berit lowered her voice. "I got a call yesterday, in the middle of the night. The foreign archive has been found."

"For real?"

"Yes and no. They've suddenly 'found' copies of the archive at the Defense Staff Headquarters, with no references to original sources or documents, but still."

"That doesn't mean the originals still exist." Annika blew on her coffee.

"True, but it increases the chances. Until last night there hasn't been even a scrap left of the archives. Not a single document, no recordings, nothing. These are copies of large chunks of the archive, so of course it's very valuable."

"Have you seen it?"

"Yes, I went over there first thing this morning."

"What a scoop. And right in the middle of the election campaign."

"You'll never guess where they found it."

"In the men's room?" Annika ventured.

"In the mail."

The minister pulled the swing as far back as he could.

"Are you ready?" he yelled.

"Yes," his daughter squeaked.

"Ready?" He was really hollering now.

"Yees!" the child shrieked.

With the sound of the child screeching in his ears, he rushed for-ward with the swing, pushing it ahead of him and letting it go high up in the air.

"Iiiii!" the child shrieked.

"Me too, Daddy! Me too! Run under me, run under me!"

He smiled at his son and wiped his forehead. "Okay, cowboy, but this is the last time."

He rounded the tree, tickled his daughter's tummy on the way, grabbed the boy's swing, and did his "Are you ready?" routine. Then he ran under the swing but did the whole thing a bit gentler than with his daughter. His son was of a slighter build and was more timid, despite their being twins.

"Do me again, Daddy!" his daughter yelled.

"No, that's it now. When the swing stops, you can come and sit with me over on the garden bench."

"But, Daddy . . ."

He walked over to his wife, who was sitting under a parasol. The garden furniture, made of ecofriendly blue pine, was from IKEA. Sometimes he just felt so unbelievably predictable.

"When do you have to go back?"

He kissed his wife's hair and sank down next to her on the bench. "I don't know," he sighed. "I'm hoping I can have the rest of the week off."

The phone rang inside the house.

"No, you sit there. I'll get it."

She got up and ran with a light step to the veranda where the cordless phone lay. Her skirt flapped around her calves and her hair danced around her tanned shoulders. His heart warmed. She answered the phone and was talking to someone. She looked over at him with surprise on her face.

"Of course," she said, loud enough for him to hear it. "He'll take it in his study."

She put the phone down and came over to him.

"Christer, it's for you. It's the police."

Annika couldn't get hold of Q. He was conducting an interview. She tried all the other numbers. The control room had nothing new, at the Krim duty desk she got an angry brush-off, and the press officer was busy. No one answered at Patricia's. She found the number for Studio 69 in the phone book, dialed it, and got an answering machine. A young woman's voice, trying hard to sound sexy, informed her of the business hours: 1 P.M. to 5 A.M. You could meet gorgeous girls, buy them champagne, watch the floor show or a private show, watch or buy erotic movies. All guests were welcome to the most intimate club in Stockholm.

Annika felt nauseated. She called the number once more and recorded the message. Then she tried the press officer again and this time she was lucky.

"A chief of investigation has been appointed," he told her.

Annika's heart quickened. "Who?"

"Chief District Prosecutor Kjell Lindström."

"How come?" she asked, even though she'd already guessed the answer.

The press officer stalled. "Yes, the investigation has gained some ground, and the Krim detectives thought it was time for the prosecutors to get involved."

"So there's a suspect."

The press officer cleared his throat. "Like I said, the investigation has gained some ground and—"

"Is it Joachim, the boyfriend?"

The press officer heaved a sigh. "I can't confirm that. We can't divulge any such information at this point in time."

"But that is the case?" Annika persisted.

"We've conducted quite a few interviews and there are signs pointing in that direction, yes. But I must ask you not to publish anything about it yet. It would be detrimental to the investigation."

A sense of triumph rose within her. Yes! It was him! The bastard.

"So what *can* I write? Surely I could say that the police have a clear lead and a suspect, that you've interviewed lots of people. . . . Did she ever report him?"

"Who?"

"Josefin. Did she ever file a report against Joachim for intimidation or assault?"

"No, not that we've been able to track down."

"What makes you think it's him?"

"I can't go into that."

"So it's something someone has said in an interview? Was it Patricia?"

The press officer hesitated. "Now look, please respect what I've said to you. I can't give you any details. We haven't come that far. So far, no one has been charged with the crime. The police continue to have an open mind in their hunt for Josefin's killer."

Annika realized she wouldn't get any further. She thanked him, hung up, and called Chief District Prosecutor Kjell Lindström. He was in court all day. She sighed. She might as well go down to the Seven Rats and get something to eat.

"Message for you," the porter said in a surly tone, and gave Annika a note when she walked past the reception on her way up.

Martin Larsson-Berg had called, the deputy principal at Josefin's old school. The number wasn't for his house but looked like an extension number.

"I'm glad you called back," he said energetically when she got hold of him. "We've opened up the youth club here in Täby a week early."

"Really. Why's that?"

"The youngsters need an outlet for their grief over Josefin's death. We've got a crisis management team here to take care of all these unhappy people. A counselor, a psychologist, a priest, youth workers, teachers . . . Our school is making preparations for dealing with the difficult questions."

Annika hesitated. "Did Josefin really have that many friends?"

Martin Larsson-Berg's tone was extremely serious when he answered, "A crime of this nature can shake a whole generation. Here at our school we feel we need to be there for the students and support them in their trauma. You mustn't turn your back on a collective pain of this magnitude."

"And you want us to write about this?"

"We feel it's important to act as role models for people in similar situations. Show them that you can move on. This calls for commitment and resources, and we have both here."

"Could you hold for a moment?" She got up and walked over to Spike.

As usual, the news editor was on the phone.

"Do we want to look at the grieving in Täby? Where she came from," Annika asked without waiting for him to finish his call.

"What's that?" Spike put the phone against his stomach.

"The deputy principal of her school has opened a crisis management center at the youth club. He's very pleased with himself. Do we want to visit them?"

"Go," Spike said, and returned to his phone conversation.

Annika returned to her desk. "So where can we find you?"

She was assigned a freelance photographer by the name of Petters-son. He had an old VW Golf that stalled at every other junction.

I'll never complain about Bertil Strand again, she thought.

The youth club, housed in a complex of seventies-style buildings, com-prised a kitchen, a poolroom, and some couches. The boys naturally took up most of the space. The girls were squeezed into a corner, and several of them were crying. Annika and the photographer did a quick tour before Martin Larsson-Berg received them.

"It's important to take the youngsters' feelings seriously," he said with an air of concern. "We will be open around the clock for the rest of the week."

Annika took notes, an unpleasant feeling spreading through her. It was loud in there and the young people were upset and acting out their feelings; they were yelling at each other and were generally jittery. Two guys tried to tear the T-shirt off one of the girls in the poolroom and didn't stop until the counselor intervened.

"Lotta likes the boys," Larsson-Berg said apologetically.

Annika stared at him in disbelief. "It looked like they were trying to strip her shirt off."

"They're having a hard time right now. They didn't sleep much last night. Here's Lisbeth, our counselor."

Annika and Pettersson introduced themselves.

"I feel it's very important to really listen to these young people," the counselor said.

"Can you really do that in this environment?" Annika asked tenta-tively.

"The children need to share their pain with someone. They help each other overcome the grief. We welcome all of Josefin's friends."

"Including people from out of town?" Annika wondered.

"Everybody is welcome," Larsson-Berg said emphatically. "We can help everybody who needs it."

"Do you do house calls?" Annika asked.

The counselor smiled an uneasy smile. "How do you mean?"

"Well, Josefin's best friend, Patricia—have you been in contact with her?"

"Has she been here?" the counselor asked, a puzzled look on her face.

Annika looked around the room. Four girls sat next to a crackling stereo, sobbing and playing Eric Clapton's "Tears in Heaven" at high volume. Three others were writing something to Josefin with a lit candle and the graduation photo from *Kvällspressen* on the table in front of them. Six boys were playing cards. She couldn't imagine Patricia setting foot here of her own free will.

"I doubt it."

"But she's very welcome. Everybody's welcome," the counselor declared.

"And you're going to stay open all night?"

"Our support is unwavering. I broke off my holiday to be here for them."

The counselor smiled. Something shiny and unearthly was in her eyes. Annika stopped writing. This didn't feel right. The woman wasn't there for Josefin's or her friend's sake, but for her own.

"Maybe I could have a word with some of her friends?" Annika suggested.

"Whose?" the counselor asked.

"Josefin's."

"Oh, yes, of course. Anyone in particular?"

Annika gave it a moment's thought. "Charlotta? They were in the same class."

"Oh, yes, Charlotta. I believe she's organizing a mourning procession to the murder scene. There's a lot to arrange, hiring a coach and stuff like that. This way."

They went into an office behind the poolroom. A young woman with a short bob and a healthy tan was discussing something over the phone. She glared at them for disturbing her, but her face lit up when Annika mouthed, *"Kvällspressen."* She promptly finished the call.

"Charlotta, Josefin's best friend," the counselor said by way of introduction, flashing an appropriately mournful smile.

Annika mumbled her name and lowered her gaze. "We've spoken."

Charlotta gave a nod of assent. "Yes. I'm still in shock," she said dryly. "It's been such a blow."

The counselor gave her a sympathetic hug.

"But together we're strong," Charlotta resumed. "We have to rouse public opinion against senseless violence. Josefin will not have died in vain, we'll see to that."

There was passion and dedication in her voice. She would be the perfect guest on a talk show, Annika thought.

"In what way?" Annika asked quietly.

Charlotta shot the counselor a hesitant glance. "Well, we have to be united. And protest. Show that we won't give way. That feels most important right now—to support each other in our grief. Share our feelings and help each other through the difficulties." Charlotta gave a wan smile.

"And now you're organizing a mourning procession?" Annika remarked.

"Yes, so far over a hundred people have signed up. We'll fill at least two coaches." Charlotta rounded the desk and picked up some lists of names that she showed to Annika.

"Naturally, we'll pay for all expenses," the counselor interjected.

Pettersson, the photographer, appeared in the doorway. "Can I take a picture of you two?"

The two women, one young, one older, lined up next to each other with straight backs.

"Could you try to look a bit sadder?" the photographer asked.

Annika groaned inwardly, shut her eyes, and turned her back. To the great satisfaction of the photographer, the women hugged each other and quivered their lips for him.

"We won't take up any more of your time now," Annika said, and moved toward the exit.

"There are several more weeping kids out there," Pettersson said.

Annika wavered. "Okay," she said reluctantly. "We'll ask them if they want to be in a picture."

They did. The girls cried their eyes out, the candles sparkled, and the grainy photocopy of Josefin's graduation photo floated behind them. Pettersson took pictures of the girls' poems and drawings, and while he was snapping away, the sound level rose to even higher levels. The youths were pumped up by the presence of the two journalists, their excitement growing fast.

"Hey, we want to be in a picture!" two guys with pool cues in their hands shouted out.

"I think it's time to leave," Annika whispered.

"Why?" Pettersson asked in surprise.

"Let's go," Annika hissed. "Now."

She walked off to find Martin Larsson-Berg while the photographer began to pack up his equipment. They thanked the deputy principal and left the building.

"What's the goddamn hurry?" Pettersson asked Annika testily on the way to the car. He was walking ten feet behind Annika, his camera bag bouncing against his hip.

Annika replied without turning round to look at him, "That was a freak show. It could get out of hand real fast."

She climbed in the car and turned on the radio.

They didn't speak on the way back to town.

Annika had just got back to her desk when she saw the man come walking from the far end of the newsroom. He was big and blond and the light from beyond the sports desk fell on him. She followed him curiously with her gaze. The man stopped every three feet, shaking hands and saying hello. Not until he reached the news desk did she see that the editor in chief was walking next to him, his slight figure almost invisible.

"Could I have your attention, please," the editor in chief said in his nasal voice over at the news desk. Spike was on the phone, feet on the desk, and didn't even look up. Picture Pelle gave the man a quick glance and continued working at his screen. Some of the other staff stopped what they were doing and watched the men with skepticism. Nobody had asked to have a TV celebrity for editor.

"Could you listen, please?" asked the editor in chief.

The faces of the staff were impassive. Suddenly the big blond took a step toward Spike's desk. Athletically, he climbed up on the long desk and walked along it, dodging the telephones and coffee mugs. He came to a stop right in front of Spike, whose eyes traveled up his body. "I'll call you back," Spike said, and put the phone down. Picture Pelle let go of his Mac and came over. The sound level dropped to a quiet murmur as the staff slowly gathered in the center of the newsroom.

"I'm Anders Schyman," the man said. "At present I'm in charge of the current affairs desk at Swedish Television. Starting on Wednesday, August first, I'll be your new deputy editor."

He paused; a palpable silence filled the big room. His voice had the intensity and bass that characterized the voice-overs you'd hear on TV documentaries. Fascinated, Annika stared at him.

The man took a step and looked out over another part of the news-room. "I don't know your job. You know it. I can't teach you what to do. You know that better than anyone."

New silence; Annika could hear the sounds of the evening, the air-conditioning, and the traffic in the street below.

Annika felt he was looking straight at her. "What I will do is smooth the ground for you. I won't be driving the engine. I will break the ground and plan the tracks. I can't lay them myself, we have to do that together. But you are the engine drivers, the stokers, and the con-ductors. You'll be the ones talking to the passengers and you'll be sig-naling to us so the train arrives on time. I'll be coordinating departures and make sure that we go to the right places and that there are tracks all the way. I'm no engineer. I want to become one in time, when you have taught me all the things I don't know. But today I'm only one thing: a media man."

He turned round and looked at the sports desk; Annika could only see his broad back. His voice carried almost as well.

"I feel a deep sense of duty as a journalist. Ordinary people are my employers. I have fought corruption and the abuse of power all my working life. That's the core of journalism. Truth is my guiding princi-ple, not influence or power."

He turned so that Annika saw his profile.

"Big words, I know. But I'm not being pretentious, only ambitious. I didn't take this job for the salary and the title. I've come here today for one single reason, and that is to work with you."

You could have heard a pin drop. Spike's phone rang and he quickly took it off the hook.

"Together we can make this newspaper the biggest in Scandinavia. All the qualities required are already in place, meaning you, the staff.

The journalists. You are the brain and heart of the paper. In time we'll make everybody's heart beat as one, and the roar that will issue forth will tear down walls. You'll see that I'm right."

Without saying anything more, he stepped over the edge of the desk and jumped down to the floor. The murmur returned.

"Amazing," said Carl Wennergren, who had suddenly appeared by Annika's side.

"Yes, really," she replied, still moved by the man's presence.

"I haven't heard such pretentious nonsense spoken since my dad's speech at my graduation. Did you get anywhere?"

Annika turned around and returned to her desk. "The police have a suspect."

"How do you know that?" Carl said skeptically from behind her.

Annika sat down and looked him straight in the eye. "It's quite simple, really. It's her boyfriend. That's almost always the case, you know."

"Has he been arrested?"

"Nope, he hasn't even been cautioned."

"Then we can't publish anything," Carl said.

"It depends how you formulate the words. What have you been doing?"

"I've copied out my diary from the race. The guys at the sports desk want it. Do you want to read it?"

Annika gave a lopsided grin. "Not just now, thanks all the same."

Carl sat down on her desk again. "It's turned out to be quite a break for you, this murder."

Annika threw away some old TT wires. "That's not exactly how I see it."

"First page two days in a row—no other freelancer has managed that this summer."

"Except you, of course," Annika pointed out in a silken voice.

"Well, yes, that's true, but then I had a head start. I did my work experience here."

And your father's on the board of the paper, Annika thought, but didn't say.

Carl got up. "I'll go down to the murder scene and catch a few mourners," he said over his shoulder.

Annika nodded and turned to face the computer. She created a new document, setting a dramatic tone: "The police have made a break-through in the hunt for Josefin Liljeberg's killer—"

That's as far as she got before the Creepy Calls phone rang. She swore and picked it up.

"Enough is enough," a woman's voice wheezed.

"I agree."

"We won't bow to patriarchy any longer."

"Fine by me."

"We're out for revenge."

"Sounds like fun," Annika said, unable to keep the mocking tone out of her voice.

The voice got irritated. "Just listen to me. We're the Ninja Barbies. We've declared war on oppression and violence against women. We won't take it anymore. The woman in the park was the final straw. Women shouldn't have to be afraid to go outside. Men will know the fear of violence—you just wait and see. We're starting with the police force, Establishment hypocrites."

Annika was listening now. This sounded like a genuine nutcase. "So why are you calling us?"

"We want our message to be communicated in the media. We want maximum publicity. We're offering *Kvällspressen* the opportunity to be present at our first raid."

What if she was serious? Annika looked around the newsroom, try-ing to catch someone's eye and wave him or her over. "How . . . What do you mean?" she said hesitantly.

"Tomorrow. Do you want to be in on it?"

Annika frantically looked around the room. Nobody paid her any attention. "Are you serious?" she asked feebly.

"These are our terms. We want full control over copy, headlines, and pictures. Guaranteed absolute anonymity. And we want fifty thou-sand kronor in advance. Cash."

Annika breathed silently down the phone for a few seconds. "That's impossible. Out of the question."

"Are you sure about that?"

"I've never been more sure in my life."

"Then we'll call the Rival," the woman retorted.

"Go ahead, be my guest. You'll get the same answer from them. Sure as hell."

There was a click and the line went dead. Annika put the phone down, shut her eyes, and hid her face in her hands. Christ, what the hell should she do now? Call the police? Tell Spike? Pretend nothing had happened? She had a feeling she'd be taken to task whatever she did.

"And this is where the night reporters sit," she heard the editor in chief say. She looked up and saw the senior editors of the paper over at the picture desk, and they were walking in her direction. They were, apart from the editor in chief, the new deputy editor, Anders Schyman; the sports editor; the features editor; the picture editor; the arts editor; and one of the lead writers. They were all men, and all of them, apart from Anders Schyman, were dressed in the same navy jackets, jeans, and shiny shoes.

The group of men stopped next to her desk.

"The night reporters go on at noon and work until eleven P.M.," the editor in chief said with his back turned to Annika. "They work on a roster and many of them are freelance. We see the night shift as a bit of a learning experience."

Schyman broke off from the group and came up to her. "I'm Anders Schyman." He held out his hand.

Annika looked up at him. "So I've gathered." She smiled and took his hand. "I'm Annika Bengtzon."

He returned her smile as they shook hands. "You've been covering the Josefin Liljeberg murder."

Her cheeks turned red. "You're on the ball."

"Are you on the permanent staff?"

Annika shook her head. "No—I'm just covering for the summer. My contract ends in a few weeks' time."

"We'll get a chance to talk more later," Schyman said, and returned to the group. All the eyes that had been fixed on Annika lifted and flew away over the newsroom.

She made her decision when the group left.

She was no squealer. She wasn't going to call the police and tell them about the Ninja Barbies; neither would she tell Spike. So many lunatics called the paper every day, she couldn't go running to the news editor with all of them.

She returned to her story on the police breakthrough and managed
to sound well informed without quoting Patricia. She wrote about the
suspect without betraying the police press officer as her source and
hinted the boyfriend was the wrongdoer without actually saying it ex-
plicitly. She kept the story about the Täby grief counseling concise and
terse.

She went to the cafeteria, bought a Coke, and listened to the headlines on *Studio 69*, the current affairs program. They were talking
about the role of the media during the election campaign. She
switched off and instead started working on Josefin's last hours, entering addresses and times on a grid. The only thing she left out was the
name of the club where Josefin had worked—she just called it the
Club. When she had finished, she walked over to the illustrators, who
would enter the data on a map or an aerial photograph of Kungsholmen.

When she was done, it was nearly seven o'clock. She felt hot and
weak and had no energy for more research. Instead she made herself
comfortable and scrutinized the morning broadsheets. At half past
seven, she turned up the volume on the TV and watched *Rapport*. They
had nothing on either Josefin or the IB affair. The only item of interest
came from the Russia correspondent, who rounded off his series on the
Caucasus with an expert in Moscow who gave his view of the situation.

"The president needs weapons," the expert announced. "The country has completely run out of ammunition, shells, antiaircraft defenses,
rifles, machine guns, everything. This is the main problem facing the
president. As the U.N. has imposed a weapons embargo on the nation,
he is finding it extremely difficult to get hold of anything. The only alternative is the black market, and he can't afford that."

"How come the guerrillas are so well equipped?" the correspondent asked.

The expert gave an embarrassed smile. "The guerrillas really are
quite weak—they're badly trained and have poor leadership. But they
have unlimited access to Russian weapons. Russia has important in-
terests in the Caucasus region and is subsidizing the guerrilla war-
fare."

Annika remembered the Swedish-speaking old man, the president, whose people suffered constant attacks from the guerrillas. World leaders were such cowards sometimes! Why didn't they stop Russia from supporting this civil war?

By the time *Rapport* had finished, the calm had returned to the newsroom. Spike had gone home and Jansson had taken his place in the chief's chair. Annika scanned through the latest TT telegrams, read the copy on the server, and checked the headlines on the nine-o'clock TV news *Aktuellt*. Then she went over to Jansson.

"Nice map," the night editor said. "And good copy on the suspect boyfriend. No big surprise there."

"Is there anything else for me to do here?"

Jansson's phone rang. "I think you should go home now You've been here all weekend."

Annika hesitated. "Are you sure?"

Jansson didn't reply. Annika walked over to her desk and collected her stuff. She cleared up the desk as she would be gone for four days and some other reporter would be using it.

She bumped into Berit on the way out.

"Do you want to go for a beer at the pizza place on the corner?" her colleague asked.

Annika was surprised but tried not to show it. "Sure, I'd love to. I haven't had dinner."

They took the stairs down. The evening was as sultry as the day had been hot. The air above the multistory garage was still quivering.

"I've never seen the likes of this summer," Berit said.

The women walked slowly toward Rålambsvägen and the seedy pizzeria that miraculously survived year after year.

"Do you have any family in town?" Berit asked as they waited for the traffic light to change at the crossing.

"My boyfriend lives in Hälleforsnäs. What about you?"

"A husband in Täby, a son who's away at university, and a daughter who's an au pair in Los Angeles. Are you going to try to stay on at the paper this fall?"

Annika gave a nervous laugh. "Well, I'd like to stay, and I'm giving it my best shot."

"Good, that's the most important thing."

"It's pretty tough going. I think they use the freelancers pretty ruthlessly. They take in a whole bunch of people and let them fight it out over the jobs, instead of filling the positions that are actually available."

"True. But it also gives a lot of people a chance."

The pizzeria was all but empty. They chose a table toward the back of the restaurant. Annika ordered a pizza and they both had a beer.

"I read your piece on the IB affair on the server," Annika said. "Here's to more big scoops!"

They clinked their glasses and sipped from them.

"This IB story seems never-ending," Berit said as she put down the misty glass on the plastic tablecloth. "As long as the Social Democrats go on telling lies and dodging the issue there will be a story in it."

"But maybe you need to see their side of it. It was the middle of the cold war."

"Actually, no. The first forms for the registration of people's political affiliations were sent out from party headquarters on September twenty-first, 1945. The covering letter was written by Mr. Sven Andersson himself, party secretary and defense secretary to be."

Annika blinked in surprise. "That early?" she said skeptically. "Are you sure?"

Berit smiled. "I have a copy of the letter in my filing cabinet."

They watched the other patrons in the restaurant in silence for a while, a few local loafers and five giggly youngsters who were probably below legal drinking age.

"But seriously," Annika said, "why would they want to keep a register of Communists if the cold war hadn't even started yet?"

"Power. The Communists were strong, especially in Norrbotten, Stockholm, and Gothenburg. The Social Democrats were afraid of losing their hold over the trade unions."

"Why?" Annika asked, feeling stupid.

"The Social Democrats were determined to hold block membership in the party for all workers. Section One of the Metalworkers' Union fell into Communist hands as early as 1943. When they canceled the collective affiliation to the Social Democrats, the party lost thirty thousand kronor in membership fees per year. That was a huge sum of money to the party in those days."

Annika's pizza arrived. It was small and the base was tough.

"I don't get it," Annika said after a few mouthfuls. "How could the registration help the Social Democrats maintain power over the unions?"

"Can I have small piece? Thanks. . . . Well, there were certain representatives who rigged the elections of nominees to the party conference. All Social Democrats were ordered to vote for certain candidates just to cut out the Communists."

Annika chewed, looking at her colleague with skepticism in her eyes. "Come on. My dad was shop steward at the works in Hälleforsnäs. Are you saying that people like him obstructed democratic local proceedings to toe the line defined by the party in Stockholm?"

Berit nodded. "Not everybody did it, but far too many. It didn't matter who was the most competent or who had the trust of the union members."

"And the Social Democratic headquarters had lists of all the names?"

"Not from the outset. At the end of the fifties the information was held on a local level. At its peak there were over ten thousand representatives, or 'political spies,' if you like, in Swedish workplaces."

Annika cut a slice from her pizza and ate it with her fingers. She chewed in silence, mulling over Berit's words.

"No disrespect, but aren't you making too much out of this?"

Berit crossed her arms and leaned back in her chair. "Sure, there's people who think that. More and more people have no interest in even recent history. We're talking about the fifties—that's the Stone Age for today's generation."

Annika ignored that one. She pushed her plate to one side and wiped her mouth and hands on the napkin. "What happened next?"

"IB. It was established in 1957."

"The Information Bureau, right?"

"Or 'Inform Birger,'" after the head of the IB domestic bureau, Birger Elmér. The foreign intelligence outfit was called the T Office for a while, after its boss, Thede Palm."

Annika shook her head. "Jesus. How do you keep track of everything?"

Berit smiled and relaxed a bit. "I subscribed to *Folket i Bild Kulturfront* when they published the piece by Jan Guillou and Peter Bratt that started unraveling this major scandal. It was in 1973, the famous issue nine. I've written quite a lot about IB and SAPO since then. Nothing revolutionary, but I've kept an ear to the ground."

The waiter came and removed the remains of Annika's pizza: the crusts and some particularly leathery processed pigs' snouts.

"My father talked a bit about IB," Annika said. "He thought it was all ridiculously exaggerated. It has to do with the safety of the nation, he said, and the Social Democrats should really be commended for making the country safe."

Berit put down her glass with a bang. "The Social Democrats set up registers of people's political opinions for the good of the party. They broke their own laws and lied about it. They're still lying, by the way. I spoke to the Speaker of the Parliament today. He flatly denies having known Birger Elmér or having had anything to do with IB."

"Maybe he's telling the truth,"

Berit gave Annika a pitying smile. "Trust me. IB is the Achilles' heel of the Social Democratic Party. Their great big, gigantic mistake that also happened to keep them in power for over forty years. They'll do anything to keep their secrets. Through SAPO they mapped out the entire Swedish population. They persecuted people for their political opinions, had them frozen out at their workplaces and even fired. They will go on lying as long as no one produces the hard evidence, and that's when they start to equivocate."

"So what was SAPO? A Social Democratic security police?"

"No, SAPO stands for the Social Democratic Organization for Workplace Representatives. It was completely kosher on the surface—the SAPO reps were the party mouthpieces in the workplace."

"So why all the secrecy?"

"SAPO were the ants on the floor in the IB organization. Everything they reported ended up with Elmér and the government. SAPO is the crux of the matter, the proof that IB and the Social Democrats are one and the same."

Annika looked over toward the window and the summer night outside. Three dusty artificial green plants obstructed her view. Behind them was the grimy window that laid a gray film against the busy street outside.

"So what was in this foreign archive?" she asked.

documents would be worse than the systematic registration of political affiliations. The Social Democrats didn't just lie to the nation; they were horse-trading under the table with the superpowers. This wasn't completely without risk. The Soviet Union knew what was going on in Sweden, the spy Wennerström had seen to that. It was accounted for in the Russians' war preparations. Sweden was probably a primary target if war broke out, precisely because of this double game."

Annika looked wide-eyed at Berit. "Jesus Christ. Do you really think it was that bad?"

Berit drank the last of her beer. "If the activities of IB were to be thoroughly investigated, down to the last vile detail, it would be devastating for the Social Democrats. They would lose all credibility. Completely. The key is in the archives. The Social Democrats would find it difficult to form a government for a long time if they came to the surface."

The young people left the restaurant and spilled out loudly onto the street. They left an abstract pattern of peanuts and spilled beer on their table. Annika and Berit followed them with their gaze through the window, saw them cross the busy road and walk to the bus stop, where the 62 bus rolled in and the youngsters climbed on it.

A thought suddenly occurred to Annika. Should she tell Berit about the Ninja Barbies?

Berit looked at her watch. "Time to go. My last train will leave soon."

Annika hesitated and Berit waved to the waiter.

Never mind, Annika thought. No one's ever going to find out.

"I'm off tomorrow," she said. "I'm really looking forward to it."

Berit gave a sigh and smiled. "I'll have to give this IB stuff everything I've got for a couple of days. Though I'm enjoying it, really."

Annika returned her smile. "Yes, I can see that. Are you a Communist yourself?"

Berit laughed. "And you're spying for SAPO, I guess!"

Annika joined in the laughter.

They paid the check and stepped outside. Slowly the evening had changed color and texture and become night.

"The names of agents, journalists, seamen, aid workers. People who traveled a lot. They would hand in reports with the aim of predicting impending crises. They had agents in Vietnam whose information was passed straight to the Americans and to a great extent also to the Brits. Strictly speaking they were regular intelligence reports, outlining things like the Vietnamese infrastructure, how the people lived, how they responded to the war, how bad the devastation was."

"But Sweden's a neutral state," Annika said with surprise.

"Yeah, sure," Berit said tartly. "Birger Elmér used to have lunch with the American ambassador and their Secret Service chief in Sweden. And Elmér and the Prime Minister Olof Palme met quite often. 'I'll handle the politics, you keep the Americans happy,' Palme told him. 'I've got to walk in the demonstrations, meanwhile you take care of the Americans.' "

"And a copy of their archive has suddenly shown up."

"I'm convinced that the originals still exist," Berit said. "The only question is where."

"What about the domestic archive?"

"It was entirely illegal and contained detailed personal data about people who were considered the enemies of the Social Democrats. Somewhere in the region of twenty thousand names. Everyone on that register was to be imprisoned if war broke out. They might have found it difficult to get a job and they were excluded from all union work. You didn't have to be a Communist to end up like that. It was enough to read the wrong papers, to have the wrong friends. Be in the wrong place at the wrong time."

They sat in silence for a while.

Annika cleared her throat. "Still, these things happened forty years ago. In those days people were sterilized by force and DDT was sprayed everywhere. What makes these papers so important today?"

Berit pondered the question. "They are most likely full of unpleasant details about bugging, break-ins, and stuff like that. But the really sensitive material is gone: the whole picture."

"What do you mean?"

Berit closed her eyes. "In practice it means that high-ranking Social Democrats were American spies. Today, the proof of repeated deviations from Sweden's official neutrality that may be hidden among these

SEVENTEEN YEARS, ELEVEN MONTHS, AND EIGHT DAYS

*T*ime is rent apart, leaving deep marks. Reality tears love to pieces with its pettiness and tedium. We are both equally desperate in our ambition to find the Truth. He's right; we have to share the responsibility. I lack consideration; my focus is blurred; I don't concentrate fully. I take too long to reach orgasm. We have to come closer, commit completely, without interference. I know he is right. With the right kind of love in your mind there are no obstacles.

I know where the problem lies: I have to learn to harness my desire. It comes between our experiences, our journeys into the cosmos. Love will carry you anywhere but you have to have absolute dedication.

His love for me is beyond words. All the wonderful details, his concern for every aspect of me: his choice of books for me, of clothes, music, food, and drink. We share the same pulse and breath. I have to rid myself of my egotistic tendencies.

Never leave me,
he says;
I can't live without you.

And I promise, again and again.

The draft woke her up. She stayed in bed, eyes closed. The sharp light from the open window penetrated her eyelids. It was morning. Not so late that she would feel depressed about having slept through the whole day, but enough for her to feel rested.

Annika pulled on her dressing gown and walked out into the stairwell. The cracked mosaic floor sent a welcome chill through her body. The toilet was a half-floor down; she shared it with the other tenants on the top floor.

The curtains flapped like big sails in the breeze when she came back into the apartment. She had bought thirty yards of light-colored voile and draped it over the old curtain rails—with striking effect. The walls all through the apartment were painted white. The previous tenant had rolled on a coat of primer and then given up. The matte walls reflected and absorbed the light at one and the same time, making the rooms seem transparent.

She walked slowly through the living room and into the kitchen. The floor space was clear as she had hardly any furniture. The floorboards shimmered in gray and the ceiling floated like a white sky high above her. She boiled some water on the gas stove, put three spoonfuls of coffee in a glass Bodum *cafetière*, poured the water, and pushed down the filter after a couple of minutes. The fridge was empty; she'd have a sandwich on the train.

A torn morning paper lay on the floor inside her front door. The mail drop was too narrow for it. She picked it up and sat down on the kitchen floor with her back to the cupboard.

The usual: the Middle East, the election campaign, the record heat. Not a line about Josefin. She was history already, a figure in the statistics. There was another op-ed article on the IB affair. This time she read it. A professor in Gothenburg demanded the formation of a truth commission. Right on! Annika thought.

She didn't bother going down to the basement to have a shower but washed her face and armpits in the kitchen sink. The water didn't get icy cold now, so she didn't need to heat any.

The first editions of the evening papers were just out, and she bought both from the newsdealer on Scheelegatan. *Kvällspressen* led with the IB story. Annika smiled. Berit was the best. Her own pieces were in a good place, pages eight, nine, ten, and center spread. She read her own text about the police theory. It was quite good, she thought. The police had a lead that pointed to a person close to Josefin, she'd written. It appeared that Josefin had felt under threat and had been scared. There were signs that she'd been physically abused before. Annika smiled again. Without writing a word about Joachim, the police theory was there. Then came the stage-managed orgy of grief in Täby. She was glad she'd kept it concise and to the point. The photo was okay. It showed a few girls next to some candles, not crying. She felt good about it. The Rival had nothing special, apart from the sequel to the piece "Life After the Holidays." She would read that on the train.

A hot wind was rising. She bought an ice cream on Bergsgatan and walked down Kaplansbacken to Centralen, the railway station. She was in luck, the Intercity train to Malmö was leaving in five minutes. She sat down in the buffet car and was first in line to buy a sandwich when it opened. She bought her ticket from the conductor.

Only she and three Arab men got off the train in Flen. The bus for Hälleforsnäs left in fifteen minutes and she sat down on a bench opposite the municipal offices and studied a sculpture called Vertical Tendency. It really was terrible. She ate a bag of jelly cars on the bus and got off outside the co-op.

"Congratulations!" Ulla, one of her mother's workmates, shouted. The woman stood over by a flowerbed in her green work coat, smoking a cigarette.

"For what?" Annika smiled at her.

"Front page and everything. We're proud of you," Ulla yelled.

Annika laughed and made a deprecating gesture with her hand. She walked past the church and toward her house. The place looked deserted and dead, the red rows of forties houses steaming in the heat.

I hope Sven isn't here, she thought.

The apartment was empty and all the plants were dead. A horrendous stench came from a forgotten garbage bag in the kitchen. She threw it in the garbage chute and opened all windows wide. She left the dead plants to their fate. She couldn't be bothered just now.

When she went home, her mother was genuinely happy to see her. She gave her an awkward hug, her hands cold and clammy.

"Have you had dinner? I've got elk casserole cooking."

Her mother's latest boyfriend was a hunter.

They sat down at the kitchen table, her mother lighting a cigarette. The window was ajar and Annika could hear some kids fighting over a bicycle in the street. She looked out toward the works and the dreary gray tin roofs that stretched out as far as the eye could see.

"Now tell me, how did you do it?" Her mother smiled expectantly.

"How do you mean?" Annika said, returning the smile.

"All that success, of course! Everybody's seen it. They come up to me at the checkout and congratulate me. Great articles. You've been on the front page and everything!"

Annika bowed her head. "It wasn't that difficult. I got a good tip-off. How's things here?"

Her mother's face lit up. "Oh, I have to show you!" She got to her feet. The cigarette smoke eddied in the air as she moved over to the counter. Annika followed it with her gaze as her mother returned to the table. She spread a bunch of photocopies in front of Annika.

"I like this one," she said, rapping her knuckle on the tabletop. She sat down and took a deep drag on the cigarette.

Sighing lightly, Annika looked at her mother's papers. They were prospectuses from various real estate agents in Eskilstuna. On the one that her mother had indicated with her knuckle she read, *Exclusive split-level house w/high standard, sunken bathtub in a tiled bathroom, L-shaped living room, den w/fireplace.*

"Why do they abbreviate *with?*" Annika wondered.

"What?"

"They've abbreviated about the shortest word of the sentence. It doesn't make sense."

Annoyed, her mother waved aside the smoke between them. "What do you think?"

Annika hesitated. "It seems a bit on the expensive side."

"Expensive?" Her mother snatched the Xerox copy from the table. " 'Marbled hallway floor, tiled kitchen floor, and a basement bar'—it's perfect!"

Annika heaved another silent sigh. "Sure, I was just wondering if you can afford it. One point three million is quite a lot of money."

"Look at the others."

Annika leafed through the sheets. They were all monstrosities on the outskirts of Eskilstuna, situated in districts with names like Skiftinge, Stenkvista, Grundby, Skogstorp. All with more than six rooms and a big garden.

"You don't like gardening," Annika remarked.

"Leif is a nature person." Her mother put out the half-smoked cigarette. "We're thinking of buying something together."

Annika pretended not to hear. "How's Birgitta?" she asked instead.

"She's okay. She gets on really well with Leif. I think you would like him too, if you met him." A tone of accusation and injury was in her mother' voice.

"Will she get to keep her job at *Right Price?*"

"Don't change the subject." Her mother straightened up. "Why don't you want to meet Leif?"

Annika got up and walked over to the fridge, opened it, and had a look inside. The shelves were clean but almost empty.

"I don't mind meeting him if it makes you happy. But I've been so busy this summer, as you can imagine."

Her mother disregarded the tone in her voice and also got up. "Don't rummage about in the fridge. We'll be eating soon. You can set the table."

Annika took a small pot of low-fat yogurt and closed the fridge door.

"I don't have time to stay for dinner. I'm going out to Lyckebo."

Her mother's mouth became a thin white line. "It'll be ready in a few minutes. You could wait."

"I'll see you again soon." Annika hung her bag over her shoulder and hurried out of the apartment. Her bicycle stood where she had left it. The back tire was flat. She pumped it up, fastened the bag to the rack, and pedaled away toward Granhed. She cycled past the works and glanced at it out of the corner of her eye. The works—beating heart of the small community. Forty thousand square meters of deserted industrial park. Sometimes she hated it for all it had done to her during her youth. Twelve hundred people had worked here when she was born. By the time she left school, that number was down to a few hundred. Her father had had to go when they cut it to one hundred and twenty. Now there were eight workers. She cycled past the parking lot. She counted three cars and five bicycles.

Her father couldn't deal with being unemployed. The lousy job had been his life. He never got a new one, and Annika had a feeling she knew why. Bitterness is hard to hide and unpleasant to hire.

She cycled past the entrance gate to the canoe club and automatically speeded up. That's where they'd found him, half an hour too late. His body temperature was too low. He survived for another twenty-four hours at the hospital in Eskilstuna, but the alcohol did its part. In her darkest moments she felt it was just as well. And if she thought about it, which she rarely did, she suspected she had never allowed herself to mourn him properly.

A thought entered her mind. He's the one I take after. Immediately she brushed the thought aside.

After the turning to Pine Lake, the road became narrower and full of holes. It weaved through the trees. She didn't like the late-summer color of the trees. The dense vegetation was so sated with chlorophyll that it was no longer breathing and was exactly the same shade all over. She found it monotonous.

Forest paths crisscrossed the road from the right and left. Locked barriers blocked off all the roads on the left-hand side; this was the perimeter of the Harpsund compound.

The road climbed and she breathed heavily as she stood up and pedaled. The sweat ran down from her armpits; she'd need a dip in the lake after this.

The turning to Lyckebo appeared as unexpectedly as it always did. Almost every time she nearly missed the side road in the sharp bend and skidded slightly as she braked. She unhooked her bag, leaned the bicycle against the barrier, ducked under it, and waded through the tall grass.

"Whiskas!" she called out. "Little kitty!"

A few seconds later she heard a distant meowing. The ginger cat emerged from the grass, the sun glittering on its whiskers.

"Whiskas, sweetheart!"

She threw the bag in the grass and let the cat jump up into her arms. Laughing, she lay down among the ants and rolled around with the cat, tickling its stomach and stroking its soft back.

"But you've got a tick, you little rascal. Hang on, let me pull it out."

She took a firm hold of the insect that had bored into the cat's fur and pulled. She got it out in one piece. She smiled. She still had the knack.

"Is Grandma home?"

The old woman sat in the shade under the old oak tree. Her eyes were closed and she had her hands clasped over her stomach. Annika picked up her bag and walked over with the cat bouncing around her legs, rubbing against her knees and meowing; he wanted more cuddling.

"Are you asleep?" Her voice was no more than a whisper.

The old woman opened her eyes and smiled. "Not at all. I'm listening to nature."

Annika gave her grandmother a long hug.

"You're thinner every time I see you. Are you eating properly?"

"Sure." Annika smiled. "Now look what I've got for you." She let go of the woman and rummaged around in her bag. "Look at this," she said brightly. "For you!"

She held out a box of handmade chocolates from a small factory on Gärdet in Stockholm.

Her grandmother clapped her hands together. "How sweet of you! I'm touched."

Grandmother opened the box and they had one piece each. It was a little too rich for Annika, who didn't like chocolate that much.

"So how are you?"

Annika looked down. "It's hard going. I'm really hoping they let me stay on at the paper. I don't know what I'll do if they don't."

The old woman looked at her, a long warm gaze. "You'll make it, Annika," she said in the end. "You don't need that job. You'll see it will all work out."

"I'm not so sure."

"Come here."

Grandmother reached out and pulled Annika down onto her lap. Gingerly, Annika sat down and placed her forehead against the woman's neck.

"You know what I think you should do?" Grandmother said in a serious tone. She held her grandchild and slowly rocked her from side to side. The wind rose and the leaves on the aspen tree next to them rustled. Annika saw Ho Lake glitter between the trees.

"You know I'm always here for you," Grandmother said. "I'll be here whatever happens. You can always come to me."

"I don't want to drag you into it," Annika whispered.

"Silly girl." Grandmother smiled. "You mustn't talk like that. I've got nothing to do these days. Helping you is the least I can do."

Annika kissed the woman's cheek. "Are there any chanterelles yet?"

Grandmother chuckled. "All that rain in the spring and now all this heat—the whole forest is golden yellow. Take two bags with you!"

Annika leaped to her feet.

"I'll just go for a quick swim first!"

She tore off her skirt and top on the way down to the jetty. The water was lukewarm and the bottom muddier than ever. She swam over to the cliffs, pulled herself up, and lay breathing deeply for a while. The wind tore at her wet hair, and when she looked up, the clouds were flying past at a good speed several thousand feet up. She slid into the water again and slowly floated back on her back. Dense forest surrounded the lake, and not a living soul was to be seen apart from Whiskas, waiting for her on the jetty. You could get lost in these woods. She had once as a child. A search party from the local orienteering club had found her in a forest clearing, frozen blue.

She started sweating as soon as she got up on land. She pulled on her clothes without drying herself.

"I'll borrow your rubber boots," she called to her grandmother, who had picked up her knitting.

She tucked one plastic bag in her waistband and carried one in her hand. Whiskas followed in her footsteps as she strode into the woods.

Her grandmother was right—the chanterelles grew in clusters alongside the path, as big as the palm of your hand. She found some cèpes as well, parasol mushrooms, and hoards of little pale hedgehog mushrooms. All the time, Whiskas was dancing around her feet, chasing ants and butterflies, jumping after mosquitoes and birds. Annika crossed the road and walked past Johannislund and Björkbacken. There she took a right and walked in the direction of Lillsjötorp to say hello to Old Gustav. His beautiful little house stood in the sun, a wall of huge fir trees behind it. The silence was absolute and she didn't hear the sound of the ax from over by the woodshed. That probably meant that the old man had gone out into the forest, probably for the same reason she had.

The door was locked. She continued up toward White Hill, where she climbed a hunting tower and sat down for a rest. The forest clearing stretched out below her. She'd hear an echo if she called out. She closed her eyes and listened to the wind. It was loud and hot, almost hypnotic. She sat like this for a long while, until a sound startled her. She carefully looked out over the edge.

A stout man came cycling from the direction of Skenäs. He was breathing heavily and wobbling somewhat. A dried pine twig was stuck in his back wheel. The man stopped right underneath the tower, pulled out the twig, mumbled something, and continued on his way.

Annika blinked in astonishment. It was the prime minister of Sweden.

Christer Lundgren stepped inside his overnight apartment with a feeling of unreality. He had a sense of impending catastrophe. Hot winds were blowing in his face. The electrically charged air made him realize the inevitable: the storm was blowing his way. He was going to get drenched.

The heat in the small apartment was indescribable. It had been exposed to the scorching sun all day. He was annoyed. Why weren't there any blinds?

He dropped his bag on the floor in the hallway and opened the balcony door wide. The ventilation system in the backyard was roaring.

Damn that hamburger chain, he thought.

He went into the small kitchen and poured himself a big glass of water. The drains smelled of old yogurt and apple peel. He flushed away what he could.

His meeting with the party secretary and the undersecretary of state had been dreadful. He had no illusions about his position. It was crystal clear.

He took the glass of water with him and with a heavy sigh sat down on the bed with the phone on his lap. He took a few deep breaths before he dialed his home number.

"I'll be staying here for a while," he said to his wife after the initial small talk.

His wife paused. "For the weekend?" she eventually asked.

"You know I don't want to."

"You promised the kids."

He closed his eyes and held his forehead in his hand. "I miss you so much I feel sick."

She became worried. "What's wrong? What happened?"

"You wouldn't believe me if I told you. It's one big nightmare."

"Jesus, Christer! Tell me what's happened!"

He swallowed and braced himself. "Listen to me—take the kids and go to Karungi. I'll follow as soon as I can."

"I won't go without you."

His voice acquired a hard edge. "You must. I'm telling you all hell's about to break loose. You're going to be besieged if you stay there. It would be best if you could leave tonight."

"But Stina isn't expecting us until Saturday!"

"Call her and ask if you can't come earlier. Stina's always willing to help."

His wife waited in silence. "It's the police," she then said quietly. "The thing with the police calling."

He heard the twins laughing in the background.

"Yes," he said. "Partly. But that's not all."

Annika returned home just in time for the quarter-to-five *Eko*.

"Guess who I saw in the forest? The prime minister!"

As she tipped the contents of the two plastic bags on the table, the opening chimes of the news pealed from the transistor radio.

"He's got it into his head he should lose some weight," her grandmother said. "He often cycles past here."

They sat down opposite each other at the kitchen table and cleaned the mushrooms while the radio voices droned on. Nothing was happening.

"So, you still keep in contact with people at Harpsund?"

Grandmother smiled. She had been the housekeeper at the prime minister's summer residence for thirty-seven years. The local news came on and she turned up the volume.

Annika cut the chanterelles in pieces and placed them in the bowl next to her. Then she let her hands drop and eyes rest. The wall clock ticked and the minutes went by. For Annika, her grandmother's kitchen was the very home of peace and warmth. The iron range with its white plaster hood, the linoleum flooring, the plastic tablecloth, and the wild meadow flowers in the windows. This was where she'd learned to live without hot running water.

"Will you stay the night?" her grandmother asked.

Just then the signature tune to *Studio 69* rang out. The old woman reached out to turn the volume down but Annika stopped her.

"Let's hear what they're up to today."

The music faded and the deep bass of the program presenter sounded:

"The police have questioned a man on suspicion of the sex murder of a young woman in Kronoberg Park in Stockholm. The man is said to be Minister for Foreign Trade Christer Lundgren. More about this in today's current affairs program with debate and analysis, live from Studio 69."

The signature tune resumed, and Annika put her hands across her mouth. Good God, could it be true?

"What's wrong? You've gone all pale," her grandmother said.

The music faded out and the presenter was back: "Tuesday, July thirty-first. Welcome to *Studio 69* from the Radio House in Stockholm." He continued in a somber voice, "Social Democracy in Sweden is facing one of its biggest ever scandals. The minister has been interviewed twice, yesterday over the phone and today at Krim, the criminal investigation department on Kungsholmen. We'll go direct to the police headquarters in Stockholm."

Some rustling static was heard.

"I'm standing here with the police press officer," a male reporter with an authoritative voice said. "What has happened here today?"

Annika turned up the volume. The voice of the press officer filled the kitchen.

"It's true that the police are following certain leads in the hunt for Josefin Liljeberg's murderer. However, I can't give you any details. Nobody has been arrested even if our interviews are pointing in one particular direction."

The reporter wasn't listening. "A minister suspected of having committed this kind of crime in the middle of an election campaign— what's your comment on that?"

The press officer hesitated. "Well, I can neither confirm nor deny anything at the moment. No one has as yet been—"

"But the minister was here today for an interview?"

"Minister for Foreign Trade Christer Lundgren is one of several persons that have been interviewed in the line of the ongoing investigation, that's correct," the press officer answered mechanically.

"So you will confirm that the interviews have taken place?" the reporter said in a triumphant tone.

"I can confirm that we have carried out around three hundred interviews in the investigation so far." The press officer sounded as if he was beginning to sweat a bit.

"What did the minister have to say in his defense?"

The press officer was becoming annoyed. His pager started bleeping. "As everyone must understand, I can't comment on what has been said in any interviews during an ongoing police investigation."

The control room cut in and the program presenter reappeared. "We're back in Studio 69 at Radio House in Stockholm. Now, this will naturally give the Social Democrats a run for their money during the election campaign, even if the minister isn't guilty of the crime. The mere fact that a cabinet minister should figure in this kind of context is devastating for the party image. We will be discussing this in today's edition of *Studio 69*."

A jingle played, and when the presenter returned, he had a guest in the studio, a poor excuse for a media professor. Annika knew him by reputation. He had got the post through having worked as the politically appointed editor in chief of the labor movement newspaper that also ran Sweden's biggest printing house for pornographic material.

"Well," said the professor, "this is of course a downright disaster for Social Democracy. The mere suspicion of this kind of abuse of power puts the party in a very difficult situation. Very difficult, indeed."

"Though we don't know if the minister is guilty, and we won't judge anyone beforehand here," the program presenter pointed out. "But what would happen were he to be arrested?"

Annika got up, her head spinning. So a government minister was involved. The fat woman had been right.

The professor and the studio reporter droned on, occasionally with the involvement of two reporters out on location.

"Does this have anything to do with your job?" Grandmother asked.

Annika gave a wan smile. "You can say that again. I've written quite a lot about this murder. She was only nineteen, Grandma. Her name was Josefin."

The studio reporter sounded serious and confident. "We have not been able to get hold of the minister for foreign trade for a comment. He has been in a meeting with the prime minister and the party secretary all afternoon. Our reporter is outside the Cabinet Office."

Annika opened her eyes wide. "They're wrong!" she exclaimed.

Her grandmother gave her a quizzical look.

"The prime minister—he hasn't been in any meetings. I've got to go back to Stockholm. You have the mushrooms."

"Do you have to?"

Annika hesitated. "No, but I want to."

"Take care of yourself," the old woman said.

They hugged quickly and Annika stepped out into the hot evening sun. Whiskas scampered along the path with her.

"No, go back. You can't come with me. You have to stay with Grandma."

Annika stopped and cuddled the cat for a moment before she pushed him back in the opposite direction.

"Stay there. That's it, go back to Grandma."

The cat ran past her on the path, toward the barrier. Annika sighed, called the cat to her, scooped him up in her arms, and returned with him to the house.

"I think you'll have to shut the front door until I'm gone," Annika said, and her grandmother chuckled.

The wind had picked up and was sweeping down the road, helping Annika along. She pedaled equally hard up and down the hills and was out of breath when she parked the bicycle outside the house on Tattar-backen.

"I heard you were back."

Sven slammed the car door and came walking toward her from the parking lot. Annika locked her bicycle and gave him a pale smile.

"It's only a quick visit."

Sven took her in his arms. "I've missed you," he whispered.

Annika hugged him and he kissed her hard. She withdrew.

"What's wrong?" He let go of her.

"I've got to go back to Stockholm."

The gravel crunched under her feet as she walked over to the street door. She heard him following behind.

"But you just got here. Don't you get any time off at all?"

She pulled the door open. The stairwell smelled of garbage.

"Yes, I'm off right now. But things have happened in the murder case I'm covering."

"And are you the only reporter they have?"

She leaned against the wall, shut her eyes, and thought about it. "I *want* to go. This is my chance."

He stood in front of her. He placed one hand on each side of her head, a thoughtful look in his eyes. "To get away from here? Is that it?"

She looked him in the eyes. "To get somewhere. I've already written everything there is to write about at *Katrineholms-Kuriren*: forestry supplements, auctions, municipal meetings, composting reports . . . I want to move on." She ducked under his arm.

He grabbed her by the shoulder. "I'll drive you."

"That's okay. I'll take the train."

The club was empty. Daytime business was slow in this heat. The men could ogle tits for free on the beach. Patricia took a quick look in the register—only three thousand. Five customers all afternoon and evening. Pitiful. She pushed the register closed. Oh, well, they'd make good during the night. The heat got the tourists' blood boiling.

She went into the bare dressing room next to the office and hung up her bag and jeans jacket, pulled off her top and shorts, and put on the sequined bra. Her panties were dirty and she had to remember to wash them before she left tomorrow morning. She quickly put on a thick layer of makeup. She didn't really like wearing it. Her shoes were wearing down; the heel was almost gone on one of them. She did up the straps, took a deep breath, and tripped back to the entrance.

The roulette table was gray from cigarette ash on the guests' side; she noticed yet another cigarette burn on the green baize. She removed the ashtray—smoking shouldn't be allowed at the table. She picked up the brush from the shelf on the croupier side and brushed off the ash, up over the edge and down on the floor.

"So the cleaning lady is keeping herself busy."

Joachim was standing in the doorway to the office, leaning against the doorpost.

Patricia stiffened. "It was filthy."

"You shouldn't have to think about that." Joachim smiled at her. "You should only be beautiful and sexy."

He straightened up and approached her slowly, still smiling and with his hand stretched out. Patricia swallowed. He stroked her shoulder and down her arm. She pulled back. His smile died.

"What are you afraid of?" The look in his eyes was totally different now, cold and penetrating.

Patricia looked down at her glittering breasts. "Nothing at all. What makes you think I am?" Her voice wasn't steady.

Abruptly, he let go of her. "You shouldn't believe what you read in the newspapers," he spat.

Patricia looked up with innocent eyes. "Which one of them?"

His gaze rested heavily on her; she made an effort to return it.

"They'll catch him soon," he said.

She blinked. "Who?"

"The minister—they said it on the radio. Those bigwigs that were here that night, he was one of them. He's been interrogated all day. They say the prime minister's mad as hell."

Her eyes narrowed. "How do you know?"

He turned around and walked toward the bar. "They said so on the radio. *Studio 69.*"

He stopped short, looked at her over his shoulder, and smiled again. "Now isn't that just too fitting?"

PART TWO

AUGUST

EIGHTEEN YEARS, ONE MONTH, AND THREE DAYS

Love is often described in such dull and impassive terms, a monochrome rosy red. But to love another human being can involve all the colors on the palette, vary in strength and intensity, become black or green or a horrible yellow.

This has been hard for me to realize. I've been stuck at the light crystal colors, unable to absorb the stronger colors.

I know he does it to help me, still it shakes me to the core.

His theory is that I've experienced something in my childhood that stops me from letting go sexually. I've tried and tried to think of what it could be, but have come up with nothing.

We experiment to help me move on, united in our love. I sit on top of him, feeling him deep inside of me as he hits me hard in the face with the palm of his hand. I stop short, my eyes full of tears. I ask him why he does that.

He caresses my cheek and pushes hard and deep inside me. It's to help you, he says, hits me again, and then continues hard until he comes.

• • •

We talk about it in detail afterward—how we're to find the way back to the divine dimension of our relationship. It's lack of trust. I know that. I have to trust him. How else will I ever succeed?

We are the most important thing
there is
to each other.

Annika walked into the newspaper entrance hall just before 9 A.M.
Tore Brand was at reception and gave her a glum greeting.

"Bombs and shootings," he said. "That's all they're interested in at
this paper."

He nodded toward the *Kvällspressen* table of contents that was
posted over by the elevator. Annika looked at it. It took her a few seconds to process the information. She felt the floor swaying beneath her
feet. It can't be, she thought, grabbing the reception counter and reading
the bill again: "Terrorist Act Last Night—Ninja Barbies Taunt the Police."

There was a big photograph of a burning car.

"Who wrote the story?" she whispered.

"Riots and scandals, that's all we do here," Brand muttered.

She walked over to the display and picked up a copy of the paper.
Almost the whole front page was devoted to a photo of Minister for Foreign Trade Christer Lundgren. Next to him, arm around his shoulders,
was the prime minister. Both men were smiling cheerfully. The picture
had been taken eight months ago, when the minister was appointed and
was being introduced to the media. Annika thought the headline was
lame: "Under Fire." Above the newspaper masthead was the headline

from the bill, referring to pages six and seven. She opened the paper to the spread with trembling hands. Her eyes flew across the page, looking for the byline. Carl Wennergren.

She let the paper drop.

"Isn't it a damn shame?" Tore Brand said.

"You're damn right it is," Annika said, and walked over to the elevators.

She sat down in the cafeteria with a big mug of coffee and a sandwich. The coffee went cold while she read the two stories, first the one about the Ninja Barbies and then the one about the minister accused of murder.

They got what they were after, she thought, and looked for a long time at the photo of the burning car. The car was turned on its side, the underside facing the photographer, who was Carl Wennergren. The caption noted that the car belonged to a Stockholm police commissioner. Behind the flames you could make out a sixties brick house. The Ninja Barbies got to deliver their puerile and violent message. Not a single critical word appeared in the entire article. Shame on him, she thought. Shame on him, the rotten bastard.

The copy about the minister was better. It took the accusations made on *Studio 69* for what they were, unconfirmed allegations of vague suspicions. They hadn't been able to get hold of the minister himself for a comment, but his press secretary, Karina Björnlund, declared that all accusations were pure invention.

Annika didn't know what to think. The police had in fact interviewed Christer Lundgren; the press officer had confirmed that yesterday. But all other statements in the program were definitely wrong. And what about their suspicions about Joachim?

She threw the sandwich in the wastebasket without even removing the wrapping. She drank the cold coffee in three greedy gulps.

Spike was at his post, telephone glued to his ear. He didn't react to Annika' showing up on her day off; it was common for the covers to do that.

"You were way off the mark on the murder," he said as he put the phone down.

"You mean about the minister? The story doesn't make sense," Annika said.

"Oh, doesn't it? Why not?"

"I want to look into that today, if that's all right with you."

"We were lucky to have the scoop on the Ninja Barbies. Or we'd have been forced to make more of the murder and the minister. It would have looked a bit weird to have two different murderers in two days, don't you think?"

Annika turned red. She couldn't think of a response.

Spike's eyes were cold, watchful. "Thanks to Carl we landed on our feet." The news editor spun around in his chair, showing her the back of his balding head.

"Sure. Is Berit in yet?"

"She's gone to Fårö to look for the speaker. The IB scoop," Spike said without turning around.

Annika walked over to her desk and dropped her bag on the floor; her cheeks were burning. She wouldn't be getting a picture byline for a while.

She skimmed through the other papers to see what they had on the minister and the suspicions against him. No one had made a particularly big thing of it. The morning broadsheets only mentioned in brief that Minister Christer Lundgren had been interviewed regarding the murder of a woman in Stockholm. The Rival had given the items the same ranking as *Kvällspressen*.

How could *Studio 69* be so sure of their information? Annika wondered. They've got to have more than they're letting on.

The thought of it made her stomach turn. Why do I feel so guilty? she asked herself.

Despite the air-conditioning, the room was stuffy and hot. She went out to the ladies' room and splashed cold water on her face.

I've got to get this straight, she thought. I've got to get the whole picture. What did I miss?

She leaned her forehead against the mirror and closed her eyes. The glass was ice-cold and the chill spread via her sinuses into the bone.

The woman, she thought. The fat woman with the dog, Daniella's neighbor.

She wiped her face dry with a paper towel. She left a sweaty mark on the mirror.

• • •

The new deputy editor, Anders Schyman, was troubled. Naturally, he was aware of the ethical difficulties that came with his new post, but he would have liked to have had a few days before having to do any acrobatics on the moral trapeze. What was this hysterical story Carl Wennergren had found? A feminist combat group that set fire to cars and sent threatening messages to police officers. What the hell was that? And not a single critical comment, only the extremely predictable statement from the police press officer that they took the incident seriously and had deployed all necessary resources to finding the perpetrators.

The deputy editor sighed and sat down on a couch with an orange flowery pattern that had come with his office. The upholstery reeked so badly of stale smoke that the couch smelled like an ashtray. He stood up again and sat by his desk instead. It was not a nice office. There were no windows; he only got indirect light from the newsroom through the glass walls. Beyond the sports desk he could just make out the contours of a multistory garage. Despondent, he looked at the mountain of boxes that had arrived from Swedish Television the night before.

Jesus, what a lot of crap a man can accumulate, he thought.

He decided to skip the unpacking for the time being. He spread out the paper before him. He slowly read through all the contentious articles. True, he wasn't legally responsible for the publication of the newspaper, but as of today, he knew that he had to learn the mechanisms that shaped it.

Something was not quite right about the terrorist article. How could the reporter be in the right place at exactly the right time? And why would the women speak to him? "He was tipped off about it," Spike had explained to him. That didn't make sense. If the group had wanted maximum publicity, they would have told all the media. But they wouldn't have had any control over the material. They must have made some kind of deal or made some special demands.

He would bring it up with the reporter.

The story about the minister wasn't that strange. Ministers could be interviewed for information in connection with various crimes. Personally, he thought the radio program had gone too far in singling out

Christer Lundgren as a suspect. As far as he understood, nothing indicated this was the case. Still, a paper like *Kvällspressen* had to cover the story.

Schyman sighed.

He might as well get used to it.

Nobody came to the door. Annika pushed the doorbell over and over, but the woman pretended not to be at home. Through the mail drop she could hear the panting dog and the woman's heavy steps.

"I know you're in there!" she called through the mail drop. "I just want to ask a few questions. Please open the door!"

The footsteps disappeared but she could still hear the dog. She waited another five minutes.

Stupid woman, Annika thought. She rang Daniella Hermansson's doorbell instead. The young mother opened the door, the child on her arm and a bottle in her hand. "Oh, hi!" Daniella said cheerily. "Come in! The place is a mess, but you know what it's like when you have kids."

Annika mumbled something and stepped into the dark hallway. The apartment was long and narrow, meticulously decorated and tidy. Straight ahead were a mirror wall and a rustic-style chest of drawers, a vase of wooden tulips on top. Annika winced when she caught a glimpse of her own face. She looked pale and the skin was taut over her cheekbones. She quickly looked away and took off her shoes.

"Isn't it a marvelous summer we're having?" Daniella chirped from the kitchen. "Feel free to look around, see what our apartment looks like."

Annika dutifully had a quick look at the bedroom facing the yard and the living room facing the street. She said it was a lovely apartment. Do you own or rent, it must have been expensive. No—really? What a bargain!

"It's horrible, this thing with Christer Lundgren," Daniella said while the coffeemaker spluttered next to them on the kitchen table. The child clung to Annika's legs and dribbled on her skirt. She tried to ignore him.

"How do you mean?" She bit into a cracker.

"As if he'd be a murderer? It's so silly. Sure, I know he's tightfisted, but he's no killer."

"It sounds like you know him personally."

"Of course I do," the woman said, offended. "He's put off the repairs to the facade for a year now. Milk and sugar?"

Annika blinked. "I'm sorry. I'm not following you."

"It isn't really his apartment. It belongs to some Social Democratic local paper in Luleå. He's the chairman of the board and he's been using their overnight apartment. He's a real cheapskate." Daniella topped up Annika's cup.

"You mean he lives in this building!" Annika exclaimed.

"Left stairwell on the fifth floor. He's got a four hundred square foot studio apartment with a balcony. Nice little place. Our apartments are close to fifteen hundred kronor a square foot, you know."

Annika finished her second cup of coffee and leaned back.

"Jesus. Fifty yards from the murder scene."

"More coffee?"

"Tightfisted, you said. In what way?"

"I'm the secretary of the board of the condominium. Christer used to be a member of the board. Every time we'd discuss any form of improvements or repairs, he'd oppose them. He absolutely doesn't want the charges to go up. I think it's pathetic. He doesn't even pay for his apartment like the rest of us but is sponging off the party paper. All he pays is the monthly charge— Hello, Skruttis, so you want your momma now?"

Daniella took her son into her arms. He immediately tipped over his mother's cup so that the hot drink flowed over the table and down onto Annika's lap. It didn't burn her but made yet another stain on her skirt.

"It's okay," Annika said.

When Daniella came running with an evil-smelling dishcloth and tried to wipe her skirt, Annika quickly retreated to the hallway and put her shoes on.

"I have to go," she said, and left the apartment.

"I'm sorry, Skruttis didn't mean to do it . . ."

Annika took the stairs to the ground floor and pushed the button for the left elevator. It wasn't working. She groaned and started walking up the stairs. By the time she reached the fourth floor she was exhausted. She had to stop to catch her breath.

I should start taking vitamins, she thought.

She tiptoed up the last set of steps, breathing soundlessly with her mouth open while studying the eight apartment doors. Hessler. Carlsson. Lethander & Son Trading Co. Lundgren. Her eyes landed on the minister's mail slot. The nameplate was handwritten and taped to the mail slot. She approached the door slowly, listening for any noise. She placed her finger on the doorbell, hesitated. Instead she opened the mail slot. Warm air from inside the apartment washed over her face.

At that moment a telephone rang somewhere behind the door. Frightened, she dropped the slot, which closed without a sound. She put her ear against the door. The ringing signal wasn't repeated, so someone must have answered the phone. She caught the sound of a man's mumbling voice. Sweat trickled down her upper lip and she wiped it off with the back of her hand. She looked at the mail slot. She shouldn't be doing this.

But then the Social Democrats carried out burglaries and bugged people, she thought. So I can eavesdrop a little.

She stooped down and opened the mail slot again. The air hit her in the face. She turned her head and put her ear against the slot; the draft made a whistling sound.

"They want me to go back for another interview," she thought she heard the man's voice say.

Silence. She shifted her head to hear better.

"I don't know. It's not good."

New silence. The sweat trickled between her breasts. When the voice returned again, it was louder, more agitated.

"What the hell do you want me to do? The girl's dead!"

Annika shifted position to be more comfortable, going down on her knees. She thought she heard someone clearing his throat and steps, then the voice again, but softer now.

"Yes, yes, I know. I won't say anything. . . . No, I'll never confess. Who the hell do you take me for?"

The door opposite, Hessler, opened slowly. Annika's heart jumped and she quickly and clumsily got to her feet. She resolutely put her finger on the doorbell and glanced at Hessler. The man had to be close to eighty years old, with a small white dog on a lead. He eyed Annika suspiciously.

Annika gave him a big smile. "Isn't it hot?"

The man didn't answer but walked over to the elevator.

"It's not working, I'm afraid." Annika pushed the doorbell again.

She focused on the gleaming spot in the middle of the peephole. Suddenly it went dark. Someone had got in the way of the light. She looked straight ahead at the peephole, trying to look reassuring. No one opened the door. She rang the bell again. The peephole gleamed brightly again. Nothing happened. She rang the bell for the fourth time.

"Hello?" she called through the mail slot. "My name is Annika Bengtzon and I'm from *Kvällspressen*. Could I ask you a few questions?"

Huffing and puffing, old man Hessler began walking downstairs, the dog straining at its lead ahead of him.

She rang the bell again.

"Go away," a voice said from inside the apartment.

Annika started breathing faster and realized she desperately needed the bathroom.

"You'll only make it worse for yourself if you don't make any comments," she said, and swallowed.

"Bullshit."

She closed her eyes and breathed. "I'm sorry, could I borrow your bathroom?"

"What?"

She crossed her legs. Daniella's weak coffee threatened to burst her bladder.

"Please! I really need to go," she pleaded.

The door opened. "I've never heard that one before."

"Where is it? Please."

He pointed at a light green door to the left. She staggered inside and pulled the door closed behind her. She sat down on the toilet, breathing a big sigh of relief. She flushed and washed her hands.

The apartment was extremely bright and unbearably hot. You could walk all around it from one room into another—from the kitchen into the dining recess, out into the big room and back into the hallway.

"Now you have to go," the minister said, standing in the doorway.

She scrutinized the man. He looked tired and pale, dressed in a white, unbuttoned shirt and crumpled black pants. His hair was untidy and he hadn't shaved. Good-looking, Annika thought.

She smiled. "Thanks. Necessity knows no law."

The words hung in the air. He turned around and walked inside the room. "Close the door behind you."

She followed him into the room.

"I don't think you did it."

"How did you find me?" he asked, sounding dog-tired.

"Research."

He sat down on the bed.

Annika went up and stood in front of him. "You saw something, didn't you? That's why they're questioning you, isn't it?"

The minister looked up at her with weary eyes. "Hardly anyone knows where I live. How did you know where to find me?"

Annika watched the man closely. "You're hiding something, aren't you? What is it you can't talk about?"

The minister got to his feet suddenly and walked up close to her.

"You don't know shit. Now go, before I throw you out!"

Annika swallowed, held up both her hands, and started backing toward the door. "Okay. I'm on my way. Thanks for letting me use the bathroom."

She quickly left the apartment, quietly shutting the door behind her. She caught up with Hessler on the second floor.

"Fantastic summer, isn't it?" she said to him.

The minister unbuttoned his shirt. He might as well go down to Bergsgatan straightaway. He sighed, sat down on his bed, and tied his shoes.

The tricks they get up to, he thought, and looked at the door the reporter had disappeared through. The bathroom—my ass!

He stood up and was in two minds about whether to put on a jacket. He chose one made of light linen.

How the hell *did* she find him here? Not even Karina Björnlund knew where he lived when he was in Stockholm. She always called him on his cell phone.

The telephone rang, the regular one, not his mobile. He answered it immediately. Only a handful of people had this number.

"How are you?"

His wife was worried about him. He slumped down on the bed again and to his amazement started to cry.

"Darling, tell me what's wrong!" She was also crying.

"Are you with Stina?"

"We arrived yesterday."

He blew his nose. "I can't tell you."

"These terrible stories, I mean, there's nothing to them . . ."

He rubbed his forehead with his hand. "How can you even ask me that?"

"But what am I supposed to think?" Offended, frightened, suspicious.

"Do you think that I could . . . kill someone?"

She hesitated. "Not of your own accord," she said eventually.

"But if . . ."

"There's nothing you wouldn't do for the party." A note of resignation was in her voice.

Q answered the phone. Annika was beside herself with joy, short-lived though it turned out to be.

"I can't say a word."

"Is the minister really a suspect?" Annika leaned back in her chair and put her feet on her desk.

He gave a coarse laugh. "What an intelligent question! Did you come up with that all by yourself?"

"There's something about him. He's scared of something coming out. What's he hiding?"

Q's laughter died out and was followed by a brief silence. "Where do you get your information?"

"I listen, check things out, observe. He lives very close to the murder scene, for one thing."

"You've figured that out."

"Does that have anything to do with it?"

"All the tenants at sixty-four Sankt Göransgatan have been interviewed."

"It's a condo."

"What?"

"They're not tenants, they own their apartments."

"Oh, for Christ's sake!" the captain exclaimed.

"Do you really think he did it?"

Q sighed. "It's not unthinkable."

Annika was at a loss. "But . . . what about the boyfriend? Joachim?"

"He's got an alibi."

Annika leaned forward in her chair. "So it wasn't . . . It seemed like you—"

"It would be better for everybody concerned if there wasn't so much speculating going on in the media. You make life very difficult for people sometimes."

Annika flared up. "You're one to talk! Who called a press conference at 10 P.M. on a Saturday evening so you could maximize the media coverage? Don't bullshit me. What do you mean 'make life very difficult'? Journalists never beat people up. The police have a lot more to answer for than the media!"

"I don't need to sit here and listen to this." The police captain hung up.

"Hello? Hello! Damn!"

Annika threw the phone down, which earned her an annoyed look from Spike.

"You're sitting at my desk."

A woman in a tailored suit was haughtily eyeing her.

Annika looked at her. "What?"

"Aren't you off today?"

Annika put her feet on the floor, stood up, and held out her hand.

"You must be Mariana. Nice to meet you. I'm Annika Bengtzon."

The well-dressed dragon had a complicated, aristocratic-sounding surname. Annika knew she was held to be a great talent.

"I'd be grateful if you could tidy up after yourself. It's not very pleasant to be met by this kind of thing when you go on your shift."

"I agree. I had to clear both the bookshelf and the desk after you when I came in last Thursday."

Annika quickly grabbed the papers she'd put on the desk.

"I'm getting something to eat," she said to the news editor, and took her bag and left.

She bumped into Carl Wennergren by the elevators. He was with some of the other summer freelancers, and they all seemed to be laughing at something Carl had just said. Annika had been wondering how she would react when she next saw him. She'd been thinking about what she would say. Now she didn't need to puzzle about it any longer. She resolutely blocked the group's way.

"Could I have a word with you?" she said curtly.

Carl Wennergren pushed out his chest and flashed a smile that sparkled in his tanned face. His hair was still damp from his morning swim, his fringe tumbling onto his forehead.

"Sure, babe. What about?"

Annika started walking down the stairs. Carl, self-assured and relaxed, waved off his friends before he followed her. She waited for her colleague on a landing, her back against the wall, staring hard at him.

"I had an offer last Monday," she said in a low voice. "A group calling themselves the Ninja Barbies wanted to sell me a scoop. For fifty thousand in cash they'd let me be present when they carried out some kind of attack against a police official."

She watched Carl closely. The young man had stopped smiling. A blush spread over his face and out to his ears. He compressed his lips into a thin line.

"What do you mean?" he said, his voice a bit stifled.

"How did that story get into the paper?"

Carl tossed back his fringe. "What the hell's that got to do with you? Since when are you the editor in chief?"

She looked at him without saying anything. He turned around and started walking upstairs. Annika didn't move. After four steps he turned around and came back down, coming to a stop two inches from Annika's face.

"I didn't pay them a goddamn cent," he hissed. "Who the hell do you think I am?"

"I'm not thinking anything," she said, noticing that her voice was a bit shaky. "I just thought it was odd."

"They wanted to spread their message," Carl hissed, "but they couldn't sell the scoop. There isn't a paper in the world that's stupid enough to finance a terrorist attack on a police official. You know that."

"So they gave it to you for free?"

"Exactly."

"And then you thought it was cool to be in on it?"

Carl spun around and took the stairs two steps at a time.

"Did they wait for you to load the film before they started the fire?" she called after him.

The reporter disappeared into the newsroom without looking back.

Annika continued downstairs. Carl might be telling the truth. It would be pointless to start setting fire to cars if no one knew why they were doing it. The Ninja Barbies could have given him an ordinary tip-off.

But he hadn't known that the offer had been made to her first, she was sure of that. She had caught him off guard.

She walked out through the main entrance hall, pretending not to hear Tore Brand's complaints.

It was hotter than ever. The sun was beating down on the forecourt in front of the entrance and the asphalt was soft. She walked over to the kiosk on Rålambsvägen and bought a hot dog with mashed potatoes and shrimp cocktail, which she ate right there.

The early broadcast of *Aktuellt* didn't mention Josefin's murder, the minister, or the Ninja Barbies in the headlines. Maybe those stories would turn up later on in the program, but for the time being nobody at *Kvällspressen* was watching. But everything stopped dead when the electric guitar in the *Studio 69* signature tune reverberated around the newsroom. Annika sat at Berit's desk, staring at the radio loudspeakers.

"The police investigation into the murder of nineteen-year-old Josefin Liljeberg grows increasingly complex," the program presenter announced over the music. "The young woman was a stripper at an infamous strip club, and Minister for Foreign Trade Christer Lundgren has been brought in for further questioning. More on these matters in today's current affairs program with debate and analysis, live from Studio 69."

Annika could feel the eyes on her from the news desk without even looking up, the gazes burning through the back of her head.

"Wednesday, August first. Welcome to *Studio 69* from Radio House in Stockholm," boomed the voice of the program presenter.

"Josefin Liljeberg was a stripper at the notorious strip club that has taken the name of this radio program, Studio 69. In other media, principally in the tabloid *Kvällspressen*, she has been portrayed as a quiet family girl dreaming of a journalistic career and wanting to help children in need. The truth is quite different. We will now hear a recording of the woman's voice."

A tape began rolling in the control room. A young woman, trying hard to sound sensual, invited you to Studio 69, the most intimate club in Stockholm. She gave the opening hours: 1 P.M. to 5 A.M. You could meet gorgeous girls, buy them champagne, watch the floor show or a private show, watch movies or buy them.

Annika had difficulty breathing and hid her face in her hands. She hadn't known the voice was Josefin's.

The program carried on with information about the murder. The minister had been brought in for another interview at Stockholm police headquarters. They started up another tape, a door slamming shut and reporters shouting questions as Christer Lundgren entered the building.

Annika got up, hung her bag over her shoulder, and walked out the back door. The looks burning in her back ate away the oxygen from her. She had to have air before she died.

Patricia had set the clock radio for 17:58 on the P3 station. This would give her time to go to the bathroom and drink some water before *Studio 69* started. She had slept a deep and dreamless sleep and felt almost drugged when she stumbled back to the mattress. Clumsily, she propped up the pillows against the wall. She listened in the dark behind her black curtains, Josefin's curtains. The man on the radio tore Jossie to pieces, dragging her name through the mud, sullying everything about her. Patricia cried. It was so unfair.

She switched off the radio and went to the kitchen. With trembling hands she made a pot of tea. Just as she was about to pour the first cup, the doorbell rang. It was the journalist.

"The fucking bastards!" Annika exclaimed, and stormed into the apartment. "How the hell can they make her out to be some kind of prostitute? It's insane!"

Patricia wiped away her tears. "Would you like a cup of tea? I've just made a pot."

"Please." Annika sank down on a chair. "I wonder if you can do something—report them to the press ombudsman or make a complaint to the Broadcast Commission, or something. They can't do this!"

Patricia took out another cup and put it in front of the journalist. She didn't look well. She was even paler and thinner than last time she'd seen her.

"Do you want a sandwich? I've got some flat bread." It was Jossie's favorite, with Port Salut cheese.

"No thanks, I've been eating all day." Annika pushed the cup away and leaned over the table, staring straight into Patricia's eyes. "Did I get it all wrong, Patricia? Did I get it wrong in my articles?"

Patricia swallowed and looked down. "Not that I know,"

"Tell me honestly, Patricia. Have you ever seen that minister, Christer Lundgren?"

"I don't know," she whispered. "Maybe."

Annika leaned back on the chair, resigned. "Jesus. So it could be true. A cabinet minister. Jesus Christ!" She got to her feet and started pacing up and down. "But it's fucking indefensible to depict Josefin as a hooker. And to play that tape with her voice—it's so awful."

"That wasn't Jossie." Patricia blew her nose.

Annika stopped and gaped at her. "It wasn't? Then who the hell was it?"

"It was Sanna, the hostess. It's her job to keep a check on the answering machine. Drink your tea, it's getting cold."

The journalist sat down again. "Those jerks at the radio don't know as much as they think."

Patricia didn't reply. She put her hands over her face. Her own life had disappeared along with Josefin's, replaced by an uncontrollable reality. She was being pulled further into an abyss each day.

"It's all a bad dream," she said, her voice muffled behind her hands. She felt the journalist's gaze on her.

"Have you talked with anyone about all this?"

Patricia let her hands drop from her face, sighed, and lifted her cup. "How do you mean?"

"A therapist or a counselor?"

Patricia looked affronted. "Why would I want to do that?"

"Perhaps you need to talk to somebody?"

Patricia drank her tea—it was tepid. She swallowed. "What could anyone do? Josefin is dead."

Annika looked at her intently. "Patricia. Please, tell me what you know. It's important. Was it Joachim?"

Patricia placed her cup on the saucer and looked down on her lap. "I don't know," she said in a low voice. "It could have been someone else. Some VIP . . ." Her voice trailed off; suddenly the kitchen was heavy with silence.

"Why do you think that?"

Tears welled up in her eyes again.

"I can't tell you," she whispered.

"Why not?"

She looked up at the journalist, tears rolling down her cheeks; her voice was squawky and shrill. "Because he'd know that it was me who'd ratted on him! Don't you get it? I can't! I won't!"

Patricia jumped to her feet and ran out of the kitchen. She threw herself on her mattress, pulling the cover over her head. The reporter stayed in the kitchen. After a while Patricia heard her voice over by the door.

"I'm sorry. I really didn't mean to upset you. I'll check if it's possible to report *Studio 69* for the shit they've been circulating about Josefin. I'll call you tomorrow. Okay?"

Patricia didn't answer but stayed under the cover, breathing rapidly and shallowly, inhaling stuffy, clammy air that seemed to have lost its oxygen.

The journalist opened the front door and closed it quietly behind her. Patricia threw the cover to the side. She lay still, looking out through a gap in the black curtains.

Soon it would be night again.

Jansson was back, thank God! At least he had a brain, unlike Spike.

"You look tired," Jansson said.

"Thanks," Annika retorted. "Have you got a moment?"

He clicked away something on his screen. "Sure. Smoke room?"

They sat down in the glass cubicle next to the sports desk. The night editor lit up a cigarette and blew the smoke up toward the fan.

"The minister lives fifty yards from the murder scene. Everybody in the house has been interviewed."

Jansson whistled. "That puts it in a different light. Have you found out anything more?"

She looked down at the floor. "The boyfriend has an alibi. One of my sources tells me that it could have been someone important who killed her."

Jansson smoked and looked at the young journalist in silence. He couldn't figure her out. She was smart, inexperienced, and unbelievably ambitious. A not completely healthy combination.

"Tell me. What are your sources?"

She pressed her lips together. "You won't tell, will you?"

He shook his head.

"The murdered girl's roommate and the police captain in charge of the investigation at Krim. Neither of them will speak openly, but they do tell me things off the record."

Jansson's eyes widened a bit. "Not bad. How did you manage that?"

"I've been calling and hassling them. I went to the girl's house. Her name's Patricia. I'm a bit worried about her."

Jansson stubbed out the cigarette. "We'll go harder after the minister today. They've had him in for questioning three times now. There has to be something more than his apartment that's motivating them. That he lives so close is interesting, I haven't read that anywhere else. Let's do a story on that. How did you find out, by the way?"

"I had coffee with a neighbor. Then I rang on his door."

Jansson was taken aback. "And he opened the door?"

She blushed. "I needed to use the bathroom."

The night editor leaned back in his chair. "What did he say?"

She gave an embarrassed laugh. "He threw me out."

Jansson laughed heartily.

"Where's Carl?" Annika wondered.

"He got another tip-off about those Barbie dolls. They seem to have something new going on."

Annika stiffened. "What happened yesterday?"

"I don't know, actually. He just came in with the pictures around nine."

"Did you know he was bringing them in?"

Jansson shook his head and lit up again. "Nope. They came like a gift from the skies."

"Do you think it's ethically justifiable to stand around and watch people setting fire to police cars?"

Jansson sighed and stubbed the cigarette out after two drags. "That's too big a discussion for right now." He stood up. "Will you check with Carl to see if you should add anything to his story?"

Annika also got up. "Sure thing, babe."

Jansson hurried over to answer his phone.

"Hi, Berit! How the hell's it going? . . . No? The son of a bitch!"

Annika sat down at Berit's desk and wrote her pieces. The minister's association with the crime scene was tricky to string together. She didn't have much to make a show of. She just sat staring at the screen for a long while, then she lifted the phone and rang Christer Lundgren's press secretary.

"Karina Björnlund," the woman answered.

Annika introduced herself and asked if she was interrupting anything.

"Well, yes, I'm getting ready for a dinner party. Could you call back tomorrow?"

"Are you serious?"

"I told you I'm busy."

"Why are they questioning the minister?"

"I haven't the faintest idea."

"Is it because he lives right next to the murder scene?"

The press secretary's surprise sounded real. "He does?"

Annika groaned. "Thanks for letting me interrupt you," she said dryly. "It was very helpful."

"That was nothing," Karina Björnlund chirped. "Have a nice evening!"

Jesus Christ! Annika thought.

She called the switchboard and asked where Berit was staying in Gotland and got the number of a hotel. The reporter was in her room.

"No luck?" Annika said.

Berit heaved a sigh. "The Speaker refuses to admit any knowledge of the IB affair."

"What is it you're trying to dig out?"

"He was one of the principal players in the sixties. Among other things, his wartime posting was with IB."

"Really?"

"Formally, he was posted at the Defense Staff Headquarters intelligence outfit, but in reality he carried on with his normal political work. How are you doing?"

Annika paused. "So-so. *Studio 69* reported that she was a stripper."

"Did you know that?"

Annika closed her eyes. "Yep."

"So why didn't you write about it?" Berit sounded surprised.

Annika scratched her ear. "I just described her as a person. It didn't seem relevant."

"Of course it's relevant, come on."

Annika swallowed. "You get a one-dimensional picture if you bring up that stuff with the strip joint: she's just a simple hooker. There was a lot more to her. She was a daughter and a sister and a friend and a schoolgirl—"

"And a stripper. Of course it matters, Annika."

The phone was silent.

"I'm going to report *Studio 69* to the press ombudsman," Annika said in the end.

Berit's response was short but she sounded mad: "Why?"

"Patricia didn't know they were going to broadcast the information."

"Who's Patricia?"

"Josefin's best friend."

"Don't get pissed now, Annika, but I think you're taking the coverage of this murder a little too personally. Beware of mixing with the people involved. It never ends up well. You've got to keep a professional distance or you can't help anyone, least of all yourself."

Annika closed her eyes and felt she was turning pink. "I know what I'm doing," she said, a bit too shrilly.

"I'm not convinced you do."

They quickly finished the call. Annika sat with her face in her hands for a long while. She felt battered, on the verge of tears.

"Have you finished the apartment story?" Jansson shouted over from the news desk.

She quickly got ahold of herself. "Sure. I'm putting it on the server . . . now!"

She typed in the command and let the article zoom through the cables. Jansson gave her the thumbs-up when the copy landed on his screen. She collected her things and got up to leave. At that moment Carl Wennergren came galloping from the elevators.

"Get out my full picture byline, 'cause tonight I'm a star!" he shouted.

All the men around the news desk looked up at the reporter while he performed a war dance on the newsroom floor, pad in one hand, camera in the other.

"The Ninja Barbies have tried to set fire to the whorehouse where the stripper worked. Guess who's got exclusive rights to the pictures!"

The men around the desk all got up and went to slap Carl on the back. Annika saw the reporter's camera floating like a trophy above their heads. She quickly took her bag and left through the back door.

The temperature had dropped a few degrees but the air was thicker than ever. It felt like a real thunderstorm was on its way. Annika walked past the closed hot dog kiosk and ignored the bus stop. Instead she slowly walked toward Fridhemsplan and without noticing soon found herself in Kronoberg Park.

All the cordons were gone, but the mountain of flowers had

grown. They were in the wrong place, next to the entrance of the cemetery, but that didn't matter. The truth about Josefin wasn't important, only that the myth lived on. People could project whatever they wanted onto it.

She turned to the right and reached Hantverkargatan, where blue lights of emergency vehicles were flashing in the night.

The Ninja Barbies' arson, she thought, and in the next instant, oh my God, Patricia!

Annika ran past Kungsholmen High School and down the hill. The three crowns on top of City Hall glowed in the last rays of the sun. A group of bystanders had collected, and she saw Arne Påhlson from the Rival hanging about over by one of the fire engines. She edged closer. One of the narrow lanes of the street was closed off, so the cars had to crawl past in one lane. Three fire engines, two police cars, and one ambulance were parked outside the anonymous entrance to Studio 69. The sidewalk and the facade were blackened with soot. She stopped behind a group of young men with beer cans in their hands excitedly discussing what had happened.

Suddenly the door to the club swung open and a plainclothes officer stepped outside. Annika immediately recognized him, even though he wasn't wearing a Hawaiian shirt this time. He was talking to someone who was obscured by the door. Annika pushed her way nearer to the front and saw a thin woman's arm point at something on the street.

"Where?" Annika heard the police captain say.

Patricia stepped out onto the sidewalk. It took a couple of seconds before Annika registered that it was her. She wore heavy makeup and had her hair in a high ponytail. She was dressed in a red, glittering bra and panties with a G-string. The men surrounding Annika started howling and wolf-whistling. Patricia winced and looked over at the group. She instantly recognized Annika, and Patricia's face lit up as their eyes met. She lifted her hand to wave and Annika stiffened. Without thinking she ducked behind the men and drew back. The men pushed forward, and she heard a woman crying out. She rushed into the nearest side street, one she'd never been in before, and ran over to Bergsgatan, past the police headquarters and its parking lot, and then turned into Agnegatan. She took the shortcut across the yard and reached the street door of her house, trembling and out of breath. The key in her hand shook so badly that she could hardly get it into the lock.

I'm losing it, she thought, and bowed her head when she became conscious of her cowardice.

She was ashamed of Patricia.

EIGHTEEN YEARS, ONE MONTH, AND
TWENTY-FIVE DAYS

When deepest trust vanquishes dread, that's when true confidence is born. Everything else is a failure; I know that.

He wants me to relive horrible old memories.

He pushes me into the bathroom and tells me to masturbate.

He opens the door while I'm sitting with the showerhead between my thighs, his face white with anger.

"So you can fuck with that, but not with me?" he screams.

The hotel corridor, the door that locks. Panic, pulling and tugging, naked and wet.

Voices, the pool area, daren't call out. Dark and quiet, the tiled floor cold under my feet.

I creep into the bushes, step on a big insect, and nearly cry out. Hate spiders, hate small creeping things. Crying, freezing, shaking.

It's all about overcoming your fear, defeating your demons.

At regular intervals I try the door.

He unlocks it just before dawn, warm, dry, hot, loving.

We are the most important thing
there is
to each other.

THURSDAY 2 AUGUST

The prime minister saw the news photographers in the distance and heaved a sigh. The journalists had formed an impromptu wall by the entrance to the government offices at Rosenbad. He knew they'd be there, of course, yet he'd been hoping, somehow, that he could avoid them. So far he hadn't commented on the suspicions surrounding Christer Lundgren. He'd referred the media to the young woman who was minister for integration, who was acting head of government during the summer holidays. He couldn't go on doing this any longer. The few days that constituted this year's holiday had shrunk to almost nothing. He gave another sigh and yawned. He always did that when he was nervous. People around him thought it gave a casual impression, which could be a positive thing. Like now—the men in the car had no idea about the turmoil going on inside him or the tight knot in his stomach. His intestines were twirling with the anxiety; he'd have to go to the bathroom soon.

The media scrum caught sight of the car as it turned onto Fredsgatan. The entire group gave a start like one organism. The photographers struggled to hang the cameras with their long lenses around their necks. The prime minister watched them through the darkened windows. He could see radio, TV, and print reporters waving their little tape recorders in the air.

"They all look like toy figures," he said to the security man in the front seat. "He-Man with his detachable accessories. Don't you think?"

The security man agreed. All his people agreed with what he said. He gave a tired smile. If only the media and the opposition were so co-operative.

The car stopped with a soft rocking movement. The bodyguard was out of the car before the wheels had stopped, opening the back door and protecting the prime minister with his body.

The questions washed over the head of government.

"What do you think of the suspicions about the minister for foreign trade?"

"What are the effects on the party?"

"Will this change the focus of your election campaign?"

"Should Christer Lundgren resign?"

He wriggled out of the car and drew himself up full length. With all his extra weight, he could produce a highly theatrical sigh. Micro-phones, tape recorders, lenses, and film recorded this little exhalation. Everybody could see that the prime minister didn't look on the matter very seriously. He was dressed in a light-blue shirt that was open at the neck, crumpled trousers. His bare feet were in sandals.

"Now listen," the prime minister said, and stopped in the glare of a TV light. He spoke slowly and quietly, in a relaxed and somewhat long-suffering manner.

"Christer is not suspected of anything at all. And this business will have no effect whatsoever on our successful election campaign. I cer-tainly hope that Christer will stay in the cabinet, for the sake of the government and for the sake of Sweden and Europe. We need people with energy to carry our policies as the twenty-first century pro-gresses."

End of line one, he thought, and started walking toward the en-trance. The media people followed him like limpets, as he knew they would.

"Why have you interrupted your holiday?"

"Who will be at today's emergency meeting?"

"Do you still have confidence in Christer Lundgren?"

The prime minister took a few more steps before answering, just as he'd done when practicing with the media coach. Time for his cue.

As he turned around to the group, he gave a wry grin. "Do I look like it's an emergency?" He tried to get a sparkle in his eyes. It seemed to work. Several of the limpets were laughing.

He reached the door and the security people were prepared to open it. It was time for the grand finale. He adopted his slightly concerned face.

"Joking apart, though," he said, his hand on the big brass handle of the door. "Naturally, I feel for Christer at a time like this. This kind of unwarranted media attention is always a trial. But I assure you, for the government—and the party—this business is of no consequence whatever. I suppose you've all seen *Kvällspressen* today. They've realized why the police have been interviewing Christer. He happens to have an overnight apartment next to Kronoberg Park. Even cabinet ministers have to have somewhere to live."

He gave a pensive smile and nodded at his own words of wisdom before he entered the security doors of the government offices. As the doors shut, he could hear the questions seeping in through the crack.

" . . . a reason for several police interviews?"

" . . . seen anything in particular?"

" . . . comment on the latest statements from . . ."

He focused on walking up the stairs slowly and calmly for as long as the journalists could see him through the glass door. Goddamn hyenas!

"Shit, it's hot in here," he burst out, and opened a few more buttons on his shirt. "If I have to sit here all day, at least you could see to it that I can breathe!"

He stepped into an elevator and let the doors slide shut before the security people had time to get in. He really had to get to the bathroom.

The shoelace broke and Annika cursed. She didn't have any new ones at home. With a sigh she sat down on the hallway floor, pulled the sneaker off, and made yet another knot. Soon there wouldn't be any lace left to tie the shoes with. She had to remember to buy new ones.

She ran downstairs cautiously, not wanting to put too much strain on her knees. Her legs felt stiff and numb; she'd neglected her running all summer.

The air in the backyard was stagnant and heavy. All the windows of the building were open wide, baring black holes in the dilapidated facade. Curtains hung tiredly, not moving an inch. Annika threw in a towel in the shared basement bathroom and slowly jogged out through the gateway to Agnegatan.

The newsstand on the corner of Bergsgatan already had the *Kvälls-pressen* table of contents up. Carl Wennergren had the lead story again with his Ninja Barbies. She jogged in place for a couple of seconds while reading the headlines.

EXCLUSIVE PICTURES IN *KVÄLLSPRESSEN:*
STRIP CLUB ATTACK

Her pulse quickened and she began to sweat. In the picture, the door of the club was blown open, a fire blazing in the doorway.

I wonder where Patricia was when the explosion went off, she mused. Was she frightened?

She picked up a copy of the paper and skimmed the front-page story. There hadn't been any major damage to the club. She was relieved.

She put the paper back, turned around, and started jogging down Agnegatan toward Kungsholmsstrand. Down by the canal she turned left and increased the pace. Pretty soon her lungs started to ache. She was seriously out of condition. She let her feet slam down on the asphalt with increasing intensity, not minding the pain. When she saw Karlberg Palace ahead on her right, she moved into high gear. Her chest heaved like bellows, and the sweat ran into her eyes. She came back on Lindhagensgatan, through Rålambshov Park and up via Kungsholms Square. When she finally stepped into the shower, she was exhausted.

I have to take care of myself, she thought. I have to get regular exercise. As she returned up the stairs to her apartment, her legs were shaking.

• • •

She walked into the newsroom just before lunch. Berit still hadn't returned from Gotland, so Annika used her desk again.

Her own contribution for the day was the story on the minister's
overnight apartment. The headline was eye-catching, "*Kvällspressen* Re-
veals: Why Police Questioned Minister."

She was happy with the intro: "Christer Lundgren lives next to the
murder scene. He has a secret overnight apartment only 50 yards from
the cemetery.

"Not even Lundgren's press secretary knew the apartment existed.

" 'How did you find me?' the minister asked when *Kvällspressen*
yesterday visited him in the studio apartment."

Then followed a description of the apartment, the fact that everybody in the house had been interviewed, and then Daniella's words:
"As if he'd be a murderer? It's so silly. He's no killer."

Annika had left out the part about his being a cheapskate.

Then she'd added a few cryptic lines about the police still taking a
greater interest in the minister than the rest of the occupants in the
building. She'd kept that paragraph brief as she didn't quite know what
the police were after.

The bitch Mariana with the fancy surname had done a short piece
on Josefin's having worked in a club called Studio 69.

Berit had a short piece on the Speaker's denial of any knowledge of
the IB affair.

A stranger was sitting at the news desk with Spike's telephone receiver
glued to his ear. Annika turned on her computer and peeked at him
from behind her screen. Did he know who she was? It occurred to her
that she should go up and introduce herself. She hesitated for a moment, smoothing down her half-dry hair. When he put down the phone,
she hurried up to him. Just when she'd drawn breath to begin speaking
behind his back, the phone rang again and he answered it. Annika was
left standing behind his chair, looking around her. That's when she saw
a copy of the Rival. The picture of Josefin in her white graduation cap
dominated the front page. The headline was fat and black: "A Stripper."
Annika held on to the news editor's chair and leaned over the paper.
The caption added, "Murdered Josefin a sex worker."

"How the hell could we miss that angle? Maybe you can tell me that!"

Annika looked into the man's cold gaze. She wet her lips and held out her hand. "I'm Annika Bengtzon, nice to meet you," she said in a slightly hushed voice.

He released her eyes, quickly pressed her hand, and mumbled his own, Ingvar Johansson. He picked up the Rival and held it out in front of Annika.

"From what I hear, you've been covering this story. How the hell could we miss out on the fact that she was a hooker?"

Annika felt her pulse racing; her mouth was as dry as dust. She knew Johansson was the news editor. Her mind raced.

"She wasn't a hooker," she said with a trembling voice. "She danced in her boyfriend's club."

"Well, she wasn't dancing ballet. She was bare-assed."

"No, she wore panties. And the boyfriend was strictly legit."

Johansson stared at her. "So why didn't you write that if you knew all about it?"

She swallowed hard, her heartbeat thundering in her ears. "Well, I guess I was . . . wrong. I didn't think it mattered."

The telephone rang again and the news editor turned away. Annika swallowed and felt the tears welling up. Shit. Shit. Shit. She'd blown it. She'd fucked up.

She turned around and started walking toward Berit's desk, the floor rolling underneath her feet. She didn't seem to be able to do anything right.

Her telephone was ringing like mad. She hurried up to it, cleared her throat, and picked it up.

"Yes, hello, this is Lisbeth," she heard a mature woman's voice say.

Annika dropped down on the chair and closed her eyes. She was trying not to hyperventilate.

"Who?"

"You know, Lisbeth the counselor." The voice sounded reproachful.

Annika sighed soundlessly. "Oh, yes, of course, the youth club in Täby. What can I do for you?"

"The young people here are going ahead with their protest against violence today. They'll be leaving here at two P.M. in three coaches. They should be at the murder scene around two-thirty."

Annika swallowed and rubbed her forehead. "At two-thirty," she echoed.

"Yes, I thought you might want to know."

"Yeah, that's great. Thanks."

Annika hung up and went out to the ladies' room and ran cold water on her face and wrists. Slowly, the feelings of panic subsided.

It isn't that bad, she told herself. I've got to try to get things into perspective. Of course people might think I did the wrong thing—so what?

She smoothed down her hair and then went to the cafeteria and bought a sandwich. From a purely ethical point of view, it could be argued that she'd done the right thing. It was worth looking into.

She took the sandwich and a diet Fanta back to Berit's desk.

The press ombudsman was kind and patient: "You have to be a relation of the deceased to make a report, or have the consent of the family."

Annika thought about it. "This partly concerns a newspaper, partly a radio program. Would you deal with that?"

"We could look at the newspaper article but not the radio program. You'll have to go to the Broadcast Commission for that."

"I thought they only do impartiality and objectivity."

"It's true, but they also look at ethical and journalistic issues. The rules are roughly the same as for the print media. What form of publication is this about?"

"Thanks a lot for your help," Annika said quickly, and rang off.

She called the Broadcast Commission.

"Yes, we could look into that," said the chief administrative officer who answered the phone.

"Even if I'm the one bringing it up?" Annika asked.

"No, we only look into complaints from the public concerning impartiality and objectivity. When it comes to issues of intrusion into a deceased's family privacy, the complaint has to come from the people concerned."

Annika shut her eyes and leaned her head in her hand. "If that happened, what do you think would be your conclusion?"

The officer considered the question. "The outcome often isn't clear-cut. We've had a few cases, and in a couple of them the family's complaint has been upheld. Could you be a bit more specific?"

Annika drew a breath. "It's about a murdered woman. She's been depicted as a stripper in a radio program. Her family had not approved making this information public."

This wasn't strictly true; Annika hadn't talked to Josefin's parents. But as far as Patricia was concerned, she was like family.

"I see." The administrative officer hesitated. "It's not completely straightforward," she said in the end. "The commission would have to receive a complaint and then consider the case. There is the public interest to take into account."

Annika gave up. She felt she wouldn't be getting any further. She thanked her and hung up.

But I'm not completely talking through my hat, she thought. There might be a privacy case to be made.

The lunchtime *Eko* started. Annika put her feet on the desk and listened absentmindedly to Berit's transistor radio. They headlined five stories: the Middle East, the prime minister's comment on the Christer Lundgren affair, and three other things that Annika forgot about as soon as she'd heard them. She let her thoughts roam free while they droned on about the Middle East. When they announced the prime minister, she turned up the volume.

The familiar voice sounded mischievous: "Do I look like it's an emergency?"

The reporter described the prime minister as having been relaxed and in excellent spirits when arriving at Rosenbad this morning. He wasn't the least worried about the accusations against Foreign Trade Minister Christer Lundgren, but was looking forward to the forthcoming election campaign with confidence. He did feel sympathy for his colleague, however, and knew what he was going through.

The prime minister again: "Naturally, I feel for Christer at a time like this. This kind of unwarranted media attention is always a trial. But I assure you, for the government—and the party—this business is of no consequence whatever."

That was the end of the report. The next item was about some offi-cial report from the Association of Local Authorities. Annika turned the radio off. If one thing really bored the pants off her, it was Local Author-ities' reports.

"Is it you who's been talking all this rubbish?"

Patricia blinked sleepily at the strip of light between the curtains. She tried to sit up straight on the mattress and moved the receiver to the other ear.

"Hello."

"Don't try to get out of it. Just tell me the truth!" The shrill voice broke.

Patricia coughed and rubbed her eyes, wishing the pollen season would soon be over.

"Is that you, Barbro?" she said cautiously.

"Of course it's me! Who else would it be? One of your porn friends, perhaps!"

Josefin's mother was raging down the phone, a rant so inarticulate and incoherent Patricia hadn't even recognized her voice at first. Patri-cia took a deep breath and tried to collect her thoughts. The words en-twined, mixed up, and blurred. Spanish took over, as it sometimes did when she was under stress.

"No entiendo . . ."

"Do you understand what you have done?" Josefin's mother yelled. "You've blackened her memory forever. How could you?"

Patricia's mind cleared—something was wrong. "What's hap-pened? What are you talking about?"

The voice on the phone dropped to a whisper. "We know what you are. You're a greaseball whore. Do you hear that? And as if that weren't enough, you had to drag Josefin down with you!"

Patricia stood up and shouted back, "That's not true! Not at all! I didn't drag Josefin into anything!"

"Now listen to me," Barbro Liljeberg Hed hissed. "I want you out of my apartment today. Pack your dirty things and go back to Africa or wherever you came from."

"But—"

"I want you gone before six o'clock."

Click. The line went dead. Patricia listened to the empty noise for a while. Then she slowly put the phone down and sank down on the mattress. She sat down with her chin on her knees, her arms around her legs, and began rocking slowly back and forth, back and forth.

Where would she go?

The phone rang again. She flinched, as if from a slap. Without thinking she grabbed the phone, ripped the cord from the socket, and hurled it out in the hallway.

"Fucking bitch!" she screamed, and started to cry.

Annika let it ring for a long time. Patricia ought to be home by now. Maybe she was asleep, but she should still hear the telephone.

What if something had happened to her?

Worry mingled with the shame that lingered from the day before. First for being associated with the woman and then for her betrayal.

She walked restlessly around the newsroom, had a cup of coffee, and watched CNN for a while. When she came past the news desk, she realized that she had forgotten to tell them about the demonstration at the murder scene.

"You'll have to do it," Ingvar Johansson said curtly. "All the other reporters are busy."

She walked over to Picture Pelle and booked a photographer for 14:15.

"Pettersson will go with you," Pelle said. "He's on his way in."

Annika smiled nicely but groaned inwardly. The clapped-out VW again.

"I'll wait outside," she said, and went to pick up her bag.

She took the elevator down, walked outside, and sat down on one of the concrete foundations outside the multistory garage. The air was boiling and electrically charged; her lungs crackled as she breathed. She closed her eyes and listened to the sounds of the city; they might not be hers for much longer.

When she opened her eyes, she couldn't make sense of the image at first. The woman walking into the entrance looked familiar, but it took her a second to recognize her.

"Patricia!" Annika called out, and ran after her. "What on earth are you doing here?"

Confused, the woman looked around and saw Annika. She walked outside and nearly got caught between the automatic sliding doors. Tore Brand yelled something and Patricia stopped.

"What's happened?"

"They're throwing me out."

Annika breathed freely again. "But that's just as well. You'll soon find a new job."

Patricia looked at her, taken aback. "Not the club. The apartment."

"Josefin's parents?"

Patricia nodded and wiped away the tears. "Jossie's mother's a real bitch. A racist bitch."

"Where will you go?"

The young woman tossed her hair back defiantly and shrugged. "Don't know. Maybe I'll shack up with some guy. There's plenty of sugar daddies around."

Without really thinking about it, Annika rummaged around in her bag. "Here." She put her keys in Patricia's hand. "Thirty-two Hantverkargatan, across the yard, top floor. Have you got any money? Make some copies, my boyfriend has my extra set."

"What?"

"I've got an extra bedroom. It's an old maid's bedroom behind the kitchen. You can have it. Do you have a mattress?"

Patricia nodded.

"What about the other furniture in the apartment?"

"The bed belongs to Joachim, and the table Jossie bought second-hand."

"Are you working tonight?"

She nodded again.

"Do you work every night?"

"Almost," she said in a low voice.

"Okay, that's your business. Just don't mess the place up. That would make me unhappy."

Patricia looked at her with wide eyes. "How do you know you can trust me? You don't know me."

Annika smiled wryly. "There's nothing to steal."

At that moment Pettersson came driving along Gjörwellsgatan; Annika could hear that by the way he stalled at the entrance.

"Take the bus over there on Rålambsvägen. Number sixty-two will take you all the way down Hantverkargatan."

Patricia stood there looking at the keys.

Annika left her and walked toward the photographer.

"We'll have a thunderstorm tonight," Pettersson said through the window.

Patricia waved good-bye and walked off. Annika forced a smile in Pettersson's direction. He was some freaking weather prophet too.

"Let's park a little ways away," she said as she climbed into the passenger seat.

"Why?"

"I'm not a hundred percent sure they're going to like us being there."

They drove in silence over to the cemetery. The car only stalled twice. They parked in a garage that had its entrance down by Fleminggatan.

Annika slowly walked along Kronobergsgatan up to the park. They were out in good time; the coaches would only have just left Täby. She sat down on a doorstep where she had a good view of the cemetery. The photographer wandered around on the other side of the street.

In the winter I'll wish I was back in this heat, she mused. When the wind is blowing hard and the snow falling, when I'm scraping the ice off the windshield in the morning—then I'll be longing for these days. When I drive into Katrineholm to cover yet another council meeting and talk to some angry women about the closure of another post office, then I'll be remembering this. Here and now. Chaos and murder. The hot city.

She looked straight up at the sky—it was bluer than blue. Beyond the park it was a shade of steely gray, shiny and sharp.

So maybe Pettersson was right, she thought. Maybe we'll have a thunderstorm.

The first coach drove up along Kronobergsgatan at twenty past two. Annika stayed in the doorway while the photographer put on a telephoto lens and started snapping the youngsters as they stepped out of the coach. The other two coaches appeared a few minutes later. Annika got to her feet and brushed off her pants. She swallowed; her mouth was dry. Damn it, she always forgot to bring water with her on assignments. She approached the group slowly, looking out for Martin Larsson-Berg, Lisbeth, and Charlotta. She didn't see them.

The youngsters were loud and seemed aggressive. Several of them were crying. She came to a stop in Sankt Göransgatan. She didn't feel good about this. Despite the distance, she could see that many of the kids looked tired. Their faces were gray with lack of sleep. She crossed the street to Pettersson's side.

"Hey," she said. "Let's give this one a miss."

The photographer lowered his camera and looked at her, surprised. "Why, for Christ's sakes?"

Annika nodded toward the coaches. "Look at them. They're hysterical. I don't know if it's healthy to encourage mass psychosis like they do at that youth club. These kids probably haven't been home since last Sunday."

"But they called us."

Annika nodded. "Yeah, they did. This is probably very important to them. But it's our responsibility to use our brains, even if they can't."

The photographer was getting impatient. "Goddammit. I'm not going to ditch a job just because you've suddenly developed a conscience."

The group of youngsters was milling around, spreading out around the cemetery. Annika was still wavering.

At the same moment, Annika saw the car from the rival newspaper drive up and park in Sankt Göransgatan. Arne Påhlson stepped out.

That settled it. "Come on, then. Let's go closer," she said to Pettersson.

She approached the cemetery with the photographer in tow, aiming at the wrought-iron arches of the fence. Her mouth was dry as dust as she swallowed, her pulse quickening. When she was a few yards away from the kids, one pointed at her and started screaming.

"There they are. They're here! The vultures! The vultures!" Everybody's attention was directed at the two journalists.

"Is Lisbeth here?" Annika asked, but her voice didn't carry over the noise.

"Beat it, fucking assholes!" a boy of no more than thirteen or fourteen screamed at them. He took a few hostile steps toward Annika, who drew back instinctively. The boy's face was swollen from crying and lack of sleep, his whole body shaking with adrenaline and fury. She stared at him, speechless.

"Listen," she said, "we didn't mean to intrude—"

A big girl stepped forward and gave Annika's shoulder a hard shove. "Fucking hyenas!" she bawled, the spit flying.

Annika stumbled backward. She tried to catch the girl's furious gaze with calm. "Please. Let's try to talk about this—"

"Fucking hyena!" the girl screamed. "Asshole!"

The group of young people surrounding Annika grew denser. She was frightened. Someone pushed her in the back so she stumbled forward and collided with the big girl.

"What are you doing, bitch?" the girl screamed. "Are you starting something?"

Annika frantically looked around for Pettersson. Where was he?

"Pettersson!" she cried out. "Pettersson, where the hell are you?"

His voice reached her from somewhere over by the garage entrance.

"Bengtzon!" he yelled in panic. "They're trying to take my cameras!"

Suddenly one voice could be heard above all the others. Menacing and frenzied, it cut through the noise.

"Where? Where are they?"

A girl who had grabbed hold of Annika's bag let go of it and turned her attention toward the voice. Annika saw a copy of *Kvällspressen* bobbing above the heads of the youths. The group parted and she saw several kids opening up newspapers. Charlotta from Josefin's class was making her way forward through a passage in the crowd. Annika drew back another few steps at the sight.

The girl was on the verge of collapse. Her eyes were red and the pupils were dilated and dark, and her movements were jerky and uncoordinated. Her hair was dirty and messy and her breathing ragged.

"You . . . scavenger!" she screamed, and made a lunge at Annika. "You scumbag!"

With all her might, Charlotta whacked Annika over the head with the paper. Annika instinctively held up her hands as the blows rained down on her. The papers hit her on the arms and across her back while the screams around her rose to a collective roar.

Annika felt all thoughts disappear from her mind as she turned around, pushed kids out of the way, and started running. Away, God help her, away from here, and she heard her own steps thudding on the street. The green of the park flashed past on the right. She sensed Pettersson somewhere behind her, but so were the youths.

The slope down to the garage was pitch-dark after the strong sunlight in the park, and she stumbled.

"Pettersson!" she cried. "Are you there?"

She had reached the car, and once her eyes had grown used to the dark, she could see the photographer running down the ramp. He had his cameras in one hand, his photographer's vest hung loose from one shoulder, and his hair stood on end.

"They tried to tear my clothes off," he said, visibly disturbed. "That was fucking stupid, walking up to them."

"Just shut the fuck up," Annika shouted. "Get into the fucking car and let's get out of here!"

He opened the door, got in, and opened her door. Annika jumped in; it must have been a hundred degrees inside the car. She quickly wound down the window. Unbelievably, the car started on the first try, and Pettersson drove toward the exit on screeching tires. Outside, the light hit them and Annika was momentarily blinded.

"There they are!"

The howls reached her through the open side window and she saw the mob rushing toward them like a wall.

"Step on it, damn it!" she screamed, and wound up the window.

"It's a one-way street," the photographer wailed. "I've got to drive past the cemetery!"

"No way!" Annika yelled at him. "Just drive!"

Pettersson had just reached Kronobergsgatan when the car stalled. Annika wound up the window, locked her door, and put her hands over her ears. Pettersson turned the ignition key repeatedly. The starter went around and around without igniting. The mob reached them, surrounding them on all sides. Someone tried to climb up on the roof. They were thumping the car with their fists.

Annika saw a copy of *Kvällspressen* pushed against the windshield, open to her article about the mourning youth in Täby. The picture of the girls with their poems left marks of printing ink on the window.

Someone crumpled up the paper on the hood and set fire to it. Annika yelled, frantic.

"Just get the fucking car started, damn it! We've got to get out of here!"

At once, there were more burning papers, pictures of girls and poems went up in flames. The car was rocking, they were trying to turn the car over. The noise from the thumping fists grew louder. Pettersson roared and suddenly the car started. It jumped forward as the photographer pushed the clutch down and revved the engine. He leaned on the horn and slowly, slowly the car crept through the crowd. The kid on the roof jumped off the car. Annika leaned forward toward her knees, closed her eyes, and blocked her ears with her hands. She didn't look up until the car turned into Fleminggatan.

Pettersson was shaking so badly he could barely drive. They drove in the direction of the city center and stopped in front of a hot dog place half a mile away.

"We shouldn't have gone up to them," he sobbed.

"Stop your blubbering," Annika said. "It was your idea. What's done is done."

Her hands were trembling, she felt listless, numb. The photographer was no younger than herself, but she felt it was her responsibility to see things through.

"Relax," she said in a more sympathetic tone of voice. "We're all right."

She rummaged through her bag and found an unopened pack of tissues. "Here, blow your nose. I'll buy you a cup of coffee."

Pettersson did as he was told, grateful to Annika for taking command. They went into the hot dog place, which turned out to have coffee and cakes.

"Shit, that was scary," Pettersson mumbled, and bit into his marzipan bar. "That's the worst thing that ever happened to me."

Annika gave a wry grin that was mostly meant for herself. "You're lucky then."

They drank their coffee in silence.

"You should get that car fixed," she said eventually.

"No shit."

They had a refill of coffee.

"So what do we do with this?" he wondered.

"Nothing, and we hope that no one else will do anything on it."

"Who would?" Pettersson said in disbelief.

"Trust me, there are some people that would."

They drove back to the paper, taking a long detour past the Old Town and South Island. Going anywhere near Kronoberg Park was out of the question.

It was almost half past four when they returned to the newsroom.

"How did it go out there?" the news editor Ingvar Johansson asked.

"All hell broke loose," Annika said. "They attacked us. They pretty much tried to set fire to the car."

Johansson blinked in disbelief. "Come off it."

"It's the truth," Annika said. "It was bad."

All of a sudden she felt she had to sit down. She sank down on the news desk.

"No interviews? No pictures?" the news editor said disappointedly.

Annika looked at him, feeling as if a thick Plexiglas screen were between them.

"That's right. There was nothing to write about. The kids were just getting a kick out of it. They'd worked themselves up into some kind of mass psychosis. We were lucky—they could have turned over the car and set fire to it."

Johansson looked at her, then turned around and reached for his phone.

Annika got up and went over to Berit's desk. She suddenly noticed her legs were shaking.

Christ, I'm turning into a real wimp, she thought.

She sat down and read the TT wires and some obscure trade journals until she heard the signature tune to *Studio 69* start playing.

Afterward, she would remember this hour as if it were a surreal nightmare. For the next ten years it would recur in her dreams. She could invoke the feeling she had had when the electric guitar started playing, how exposed and unprepared she had been, how naively she had just stood there and let them take aim at her.

"The tabloids have today reached a new low-water mark in their sensationalism," the studio reporter intoned. "They parade mourning teenagers in the paper, spread false rumors about family members, and are the tools of politicians with the purpose of pulling the wool over the public's eyes. More about this in today's current affairs program with debate and analysis, live from Studio 69."

Annika heard the words without really registering them. She had a feeling but didn't quite want to comprehend.

The electric guitar faded out and the studio reporter returned.

"It's Thursday, August second. Welcome to Studio 69 in Stockholm Radio House," he droned on.

"Today we'll be looking into the tabloid newspaper *Kvällspressen*'s coverage of the murder of the stripper Josefin Liljeberg. With us in the studio are two people who knew Josefin well, her best friend, Charlotta, and the deputy principal of her school, Martin Larsson-Berg. We have also talked to her boyfriend, Joachim . . ."

A dizziness like a slow rolling movement established itself in her consciousness. The realization of what was coming was reaching her. She reached out to turn off the radio but stopped herself.

It's better to listen to what they say than to hear about it second-hand, she thought.

Afterward, she would regret that decision many times. The words were to become stuck like a mantra in her speech center.

"Let's start with you, Charlotta. Could you describe to us what the paper *Kvällspressen* has done to you?"

Charlotta started bawling in the studio. The studio reporter must have thought it made good radio because he let it go on for almost half a minute before he asked her if she was okay. She stopped immediately.

"Well, you know," Charlotta said, giving a sob, "this reporter, Annika Bengtzon, called me at home. She wanted to wallow in my grief."

"In what way?" the studio reporter asked, sounding concerned and empathetic.

"My best friend had died and she called me in the middle of the night, going, 'How do you feel?' "

"That must have been very difficult for you!" the studio reporter exclaimed.

Charlotta gave another sob. "Yes, it's the worst thing that's ever happened to me. How can you move on after something like that?"

"Was it the same for you, Martin Berg-Larsson?"

"Larsson-Berg," the deputy principal corrected him. "Well, on the whole. I wasn't a close friend of the girl, of course, but I am close to the family. Her brother is a very gifted student. He graduated last spring and will be going to the USA to study this fall. We are always very pleased at Tibble High School when our students go on to a higher education abroad."

"So how did you feel being confronted with these questions in the middle of the night?"

"Well, I was shocked, naturally. At first I thought something had happened to my wife, who was out sailing—"

"How did you react?"

"It's all a bit muddled . . ."

"Was this the same reporter who thrust herself on Charlotta, Annika Bengtzon?"

"Yes, that's right."

The studio reporter made a rustling noise with a newspaper. "Let's hear what Annika Bengtzon wrote. Listen to this . . ."

In a mocking tone, the man began reading from Annika's articles about Josefin, her dreams and hopes, the quotes from Charlotta and finally the grief-stricken youth of Täby.

"So what do you think of this?" he said in a lugubrious voice.

"It's terrible that people can't leave you alone in your grief," Charlotta whimpered. "The media never shows respect for people in times of crisis. And then today, at our demonstration against violence, she intruded *again!*"

Martin Larsson-Berg cleared his throat. "Yes, but from the point of view of the media, we do have a very good crisis management team in Täby. We like to see ourselves as an inspiring example—"

The studio reporter cut him off. "But *Kvällspressen* and Annika Bengtzon haven't stopped at that. The tabloid has actively tried to clear the cabinet minister Christer Lundgren of suspicion. Dancing unquestioningly to the Social Democratic tune, she has thrown the blame on the person who was closest of all to Josefin, her boyfriend. Our reporter met him for an interview."

"I loved Josefin. She was the most important person in my life," said a high-pitched male voice that sounded young and vulnerable.

"What did it feel like to be practically accused of being a murderer in the newspaper?" the reporter asked cautiously.

The man sighed. "It's impossible to describe the feeling. What can you say? To read that you've . . . No, it's beyond comprehension." There was a catch in his voice.

"Have you considered suing the paper?"

Another catch. "No, everybody knows it's pointless. Giants like that can put up any amount of money to crush a person. I'd never win a case against the press. Besides, it would bring back too many memories."

The studio reporter returned, now with another reporter in the studio who seemed to play the part of some kind of expert.

"This is a problem, isn't it?" the studio reporter said.

"It certainly is," the commentator said in a concerned voice. "A young man is branded a murderer by a summer temp who's put on her Sunday best to do a piece of investigative journalism, and a lie is established as truth. Justice will rarely be done in a case like this. It would cost an enormous sum of money to pursue a libel case against a newspaper. However, we'd like to point out to anybody who feels used or abused by the media that you can receive legal aid to get at journalists who tell lies."

"Could this be something for Joachim to think about?"

"Yes, it could. One just has to hope he has the energy to take the matter to court. It would be very interesting to see what would be the outcome of a case like this."

The studio reporter rustled his papers. "But why would a young journalist do a thing like this?"

"One explanation might be that she would stop at nothing to get a permanent job with a tabloid. *Kvällspressen* lives off its newsstand circulation. The juicier the front page, the more copies they sell and the more money they make. Unfortunately, the reporters that stoop to this kind of work can benefit financially from their sordid activities."

"So the more salacious the front page, the higher the salary for the reporter?"

"Yes, you could say that."

"But do you think it's that simple, that she's sold herself to the highest bidder?"

"No, regrettably, the underlying motives may be even more dubious."

"And what might they be, do you think?"

The commentator cleared his throat. "The fact is, that there are up to ten thousand lobbyists in Stockholm. And these lobbyists are only after one thing: to get the decision makers and the media to do their employers' bidding. They influence the media by 'planting' news. You dupe or buy a journalist with a planted piece of news and the reporter becomes your tool."

"Do you think that has happened in this case?"

"Yes, I'm absolutely convinced it has," the commentator said authoritatively. "It's obvious to someone with any kind of knowledge of this trade that Annika Bengtzon's pieces about Christer Lundgren constitute a case of planting."

"How do you know?" the studio reporter asked, sounding impressed.

"I'd like to play you a tape that proves my case. It's a clip from this morning outside Rosenbad," the commentator said triumphantly.

The voice of the prime minister filled the air: "Naturally, I feel for Christer at a time like this. This kind of unwarranted media attention is always a trial. But I assure you, for the government—and the party— this business is of no consequence whatever. I suppose you've all seen *Kvällspressen* today. They've realized why the police have been interviewing Christer. He happens to have an overnight apartment next to Kronoberg Park. Even cabinet ministers have to have somewhere to live."

Back in the studio. "There we heard it plainly," the commentator said. "The prime minister refers directly to the statements in a newspaper, clearly wanting other media to follow suit."

"What exactly is the responsibility of the government in a case like this?"

"Well, they should obviously be censured for taking advantage of such a young and inexperienced journalist. It is unfortunately a lot easier to manipulate the summer freelancers."

The studio reporter took over again. "We tried to get hold of the editor in chief to offer him the chance to comment on our report, but were told that he wasn't available . . ."

Annika got up and walked toward the ladies' room; the floor under her feet was rolling. It got worse when she entered the corridor behind the newsroom. She had to support herself against the wall. I'm going to break, she thought. I can't do it. I won't make it. I'll throw up right here on the floor.

She made it to the bathroom and threw up in the disabled toilet, causing a blockage in the drain when she tried to flush it. She looked at her face in the mirror and was surprised to find that she was still in one piece, that she looked the same. She was still breathing and her heart was still working.

I can never show my face again, she thought. I'm disgraced. I'll never get another job. They won't even want me back at *Katrineholms-Kuriren;* I'm going to get fired. She couldn't think if what they had said had any validity. She had been skewered on national radio.

She started to cry.

Christ, where am I going to live? If I can't pay the rent, then where do I go?

She sank down on the floor, sobbing into her skirt.

Lyckebo, she thought suddenly and stopped crying. I'll move to Grandma's. No one will find me there. Grandma will move into her apartment in Hälleforsnäs in October and I could just stay in the cottage.

She blew her nose on some toilet paper and wiped away the tears.

Yes—of course that's what she'd do! Grandma had promised to stand by her; she wouldn't let her down. And Annika was a union member, so she'd get unemployment benefits at least for a year and then she could see. She could go abroad, a lot of people before her had done that. Pick oranges in Israel or grapes in France—or New Zealand?

She got to her feet. There were lots of alternatives.

"You can do it," she said out loud.

She'd made up her mind. Never again was she going to set foot in a newspaper office, especially not this one. She would take her bag and box up her notes and leave journalism behind her forever. Determined, she opened the door.

The feeling of being out on a rough sea wouldn't quite go away. She stayed close to the wall so she wouldn't fall over.

Once she reached Berit's desk she quickly gathered her things and put them in her bag.

"There you are! Could you come into my office for a moment?"

She recognized the voice of the new deputy editor, Anders Schyman.

Surprised, she turned around. "Who, me?"

"Yes, I'm in the fish tank with the hideous curtains over there. Come on in when you've got a minute."

"I can come right now."

She felt the furtive glances of the newsroom as she walked over to the boss's office. One thing I know for sure, she thought—it can't get any worse.

It wasn't a nice office. The tired curtains really were hideous and the air was dank and stale.

"What's that god-awful smell? Haven't you emptied the ash-tray?"

"I don't smoke. It's the couch. Don't sit on it, the smell gets into your clothes."

She remained standing in the middle of the floor while he sat on his desk.

"I've called *Studio 69*," he said. "I never heard the likes of such a personal attack, and we didn't even get a chance to respond. I've already faxed a complaint to the Broadcast Commission. The editor in chief may be away, but I've been here all day. Did they call you?"

She didn't answer, just shook her head.

"I know that so-called commentator. He worked for a while on my current affairs program, but I had to get rid of him. His behavior really was beyond the pale. He was forever conspiring and dissing people until the office nearly fell apart. Fortunately, he wasn't on staff but was freelancing, so once I'd decided, I could ask him to leave."

Annika stared at the floor.

"And on the subject of planting," Schyman said, pulling out a fax from the mess that had already accumulated on his desk, "we've received an anonymous tip that the leader of one of the other parties in Parliament has been interviewed by the police in connection with the Josefin case."

He held out the fax to Annika, who looked at it, stunned. "Where was it sent from?"

"My question, exactly. Do you see the caller ID in the corner? That's the phone number of the Social Democrats' public relations office."

"That's so cheap."

"Isn't it? Brazen too. They don't even care we'd know right away who sent it."

They fell silent.

Then Annika steeled herself. "Nobody planted anything with me."

Anders Schyman looked at her attentively, waiting for her to continue.

"I haven't discussed my coverage with anyone, except a little with Berit and Anne Snapphane."

"With the news editors?"

Annika shook her head. "Not much," she said quietly.

"So you've handled this all on your own?"

He sounded a bit skeptical; Annika felt a bit edgy.

"Well, almost," she said, tears welling up in her eyes. "I can't blame anyone else."

"Oh, no," Schyman hastened to say, "that's not what I meant. I think your coverage has been okay, good, even. The only thing you missed out on was the strip joint. You knew about that, didn't you?"

She nodded.

"We should have run that sooner. But to do what the Rival and *Studio 69* have done, practically making the girl out to be a prostitute, that's a hell of a lot worse. How did you find out about the minister's overnight apartment?"

Annika heaved a sigh. "I had coffee with his neighbor."

"Great!" Schyman said enthusiastically. "And what really happened with those youngsters in Täby?"

There was a quick gleam in Annika's eyes. "That is just too much.

They called us themselves and invited us to the youth center. They also told us about the rally in the park, or whatever that was."

"Things got a bit out of hand there, I heard."

Annika dropped her bag on the floor and threw up her hands in a gesture of exasperation. It felt good to be talking about this at last.

"They're in mourning so you can't have a serious conversation with them. We're supposed to feel sorry for them but not to go near them in any way. You're not allowed to breathe a word about anything in this country that's the least bit unpleasant or controversial. We think that death and violence and suffering will go away if we just bury them and never discuss them. That's wrong! It's getting worse every day! Those kids were crazy, they would have set fire to us!"

"I don't think they would have gone that far." Annika was worked up and Schyman thought he should try to calm her down.

"Yes, they would. You weren't there," Annika shouted. "Those pathetic social workers took control of the grieving process. 'Crisis management team'—my ass! All they've done is to work the kids into a frenzy. I bet most of them hadn't so much as spoken to Josefin! What are they doing joining in an orgy of grief for a whole goddamn week? They were in some kind of a trance, Schyman, they didn't know what they were doing. They made us into Evil. As though we were to blame. They offered us up as scapegoats. Don't tell me I'm exaggerating!" Her face was blotchy from agitation and anger, her breathing sharp and hard.

The deputy editor eyed her with interest. "I think you may be right."

"Of course I'm right, for fuck's sake." Annika was holding nothing back because that's exactly how much she had to lose.

He smiled. "It's a good thing you don't swear like that in your copy."

"Of course I don't."

Anders Schyman started laughing.

Annika took a step forward. "It's no laughing matter. It's serious. Those youngsters at the cemetery were like a lynch mob. I can't say for sure they would have harmed us, but they gave us a fucking good scare. We should report them to the police, really. Pettersson's car got badly banged up, not that you can tell with that wreck, but still. We should make it clear that people can't behave like that, even if they are grieving."

"There are crisis management teams that do a fantastic job," the deputy editor said gravely.

Annika didn't respond and the man watched her for a while in silence.

"You've been working quite a lot lately, haven't you?"

She immediately was on the defensive. "I'm not overreacting because I'm overworked," she snapped.

The deputy editor got to his feet. "That's not what I meant. Are you on your regular shift now?"

She cast down her eyes. "No, I'm on next on Saturday."

"Take the weekend off. Go away and take a rest, you could do with some peace and quiet after what just happened."

She turned around and left the room without saying a word.

On her way out from the newsroom she heard Jansson cheering out loud, "Holy smokes, are we putting out a great newspaper or what! 'The Speaker admits, "I was in charge of IB." ' We've got a comment from the prime minister on the murder suspicions, and the Ninja Barbies have been arrested, of which we have the exclusive pictures!"

Annika quickly stepped into the elevator.

Not until she was standing outside her apartment block did she remember she didn't have any keys. She needed a key to open the door from the street as there was no code lock. She almost began to cry again.

"Fuck!" she said, and pulled at the door in exasperation. To her surprise, the door opened. A small piece of light-green cardboard fell to the ground. Annika bent down to pick it up. She recognized the pattern; it came from the box of a Clinique moisturizer she had.

Patricia, Annika thought. She knew I wouldn't be able to get in so she put the piece of paper in the lock.

She walked up the stairs, a short journey that felt interminable. Taped to the front door was an envelope; the keys jangled inside when she took it off.

Thank you so much for everything. Here are your keys, I've made copies. I'm at the club and will be back early tomorrow morning.

P.S. I've done some shopping, I hope you don't mind.

Annika opened the door. She was met by the fresh smell of floor cleaner. The voile curtains flew dramatically in the draft. She shut the door and the curtains sank back down. She wandered slowly through the rooms, looking around.

Patricia had cleaned the whole apartment, except for Annika's room, which was as messy as ever. The fridge was full of fresh cheeses, olives, hummus, and strawberries, and on the counter were plums, grapes, and avocados.

I'll never be able to eat all this before it goes bad, Annika thought. Then she remembered there were two of them now.

She opened the door to the maid's room a crack. Patricia's mattress lay in a corner, neatly made with flowery bedclothes. Next to it was a carryall with clothes and, on a hanger on the wall, Josefin's pink suit.

I want to stay here, Annika thought. I don't want to go back to my old apartment. Neither do I want to spend the rest of my life in Grandma's cottage at Lyckebo.

That night she dreamed for the first time about the three men from the radio program *Studio 69:* the studio reporter, the field reporter, and the commentator. Silent, faceless, and dressed in black, they were standing at her bedside. She could feel their malice like a cramp in her stomach.

"How can you say it was my fault?" she cried out.

The men drew nearer.

"I've thought it through! Maybe I did the wrong thing, but at least I tried!"

The men tried to shoot her. Their weapons thundered inside her head.

"I'm not Josefin! No!"

All together they leaned over her, and when she felt their icy cold breaths, she was woken up by her own scream.

The room was pitch-dark. The rain was pouring down outside. The rolls of thunder and flashes of lightning were almost simultaneous. The bedroom window was banging in the wind and the room was quite cold.

She struggled to her feet to close the window; it was hard to push it against the wind. In the silence after the rain outside, she felt the trickle down her leg. Her period had started. The bag with sanitary napkins was empty, but she had a few loose ones in her handbag.

While the storm went by, she lay crying in her bed for a long time, curled up in a little ball.

EIGHTEEN YEARS, SIX MONTHS, AND FOURTEEN DAYS

He feels deeply offended and my protests seem so feeble. I know he's right. No one could ever love me the way he does. There is nothing he would hesitate to do for me, and yet I care more about the outside world than I do about him.

My despair grows, my imperfection blossoms: poisonous, ice-cold, blue. It's so demoralizing, never to be up to standard. I want to watch TV when he wants to make love, and he twists my arm out of joint. The big void gets the upper hand, black and wet, shapeless, impenetrable. He says I let him down, and I can't find a way out.

We have to work together, find the way back to our heaven. Love is eternal, fundamental. I will never doubt it. But who says it should be easy? If perfection were universal, then why should anyone strive for it?

I can't give up now.

We are the most important thing
ever to happen
to each other.

FRIDAY 3 AUGUST

Anders Schyman got soaked running the short distance to his car. It was teeming down, avenging all the boiling-hot days in one single cloudburst. Squeezed in behind the steering wheel, the deputy editor swore as he tried to wrestle out of his jacket. His shirt was soaked through on his back and shoulders.

"It'll dry off," he said to himself.

His breath had already misted up the windows, so he put the defroster on full blast.

His wife was waving from the kitchen window. He wiped the side window, blew her a kiss, and started his journey into town. He could hardly see a thing, even though the windshield wipers were on full speed. He had to wipe the inside of the windshield constantly to see anything at all.

Traffic was flowing reasonably well on Saltsjöbads Way, but once he was past Nacka, it came to a standstill. An accident on Värmdö Way had caused a five-mile backup. Schyman groaned out loud. Exhaust fumes rose like a fog into the rain. In the end he turned the engine off and let the defroster recycle the air.

He couldn't quite work *Kvällspressen* out. He'd been reading it closely for four months now, ever since he was asked to step into the driver's seat. Certain things were a given. The paper was always teetering on the brink of what was morally and ethically defensible, for example. Any self-respecting tabloid should be like that. Sure, there were occasional transgressions, but they were surprisingly few. He had analyzed complaints to the press ombudsman and the Press Council, and obviously the tabloids had far more complaints against them than all the other papers, which was as it should be. It was their job to provoke a reaction in the reader. And still, only a few complaints per year were upheld. He had been surprised to learn that the articles singled out for censure often came from small-town papers around the country that hadn't been able to judge where to draw the line.

He concluded that *Kvällspressen* was an extremely smart publication with well-balanced articles, front pages, and headlines. It was committed to openness and a dialogue with its readers.

So it was in theory at least. The reality was distant from that.

The people at *Kvällspressen* often didn't have a damn clue what they were doing. For instance, they'd sent that country girl out among the dead bodies and lynch mobs, expecting her to make clear and rational assessments of the situation. He'd spoken to the news and night editors the night before, and none of them had really discussed the coverage of the murder of Josefin Liljeberg with her. In his eyes, that was both irresponsible and incompetent.

And then there was the peculiar affair with the female terrorist group. None of the editors seemed to know how the story had got into the paper. A summer freelancer waltzed into the newsroom with the sensational pictures in his hand, and everybody just cheered and published them without a moment's thought.

It couldn't go on like that. To be able to sail that close to the wind, you had to know exactly which way it was blowing. A disaster was just waiting to happen; he could smell it. The radio program the day before was a first sign that *Kvällspressen* was becoming fair game. If the newsroom started bleeding, the vultures would soon be circling. The competition would line up to tear the paper apart. It wouldn't matter what they wrote or how they wrote it, it would all be wrong. Unless the general level of awareness of all the staff was raised, and quickly and thoroughly, they were ruined, in terms of the circulation, journalism, and finances.

He sighed. The cars were beginning to move in the lane next to his. He started the engine and let it run, but he left the parking brake on.

There was a lot of professionalism in the newsroom, there was no doubt about it. But there was a lack of leadership and overall responsibility. All the journalists at the paper had to be made aware of their specific job and what they were expected to do. The overall direction of the paper had to be clearer.

This had made him realize yet another function he was expected to fill: he would be the searchlight sweeping over the barbed wire, looking for intruders. Part of that would take the form of discussions, seminars, focus meetings, and new practices.

The cars to his left swished by faster and faster while he wasn't moving forward an inch. He swore and tried to look behind him but couldn't see a thing. In the end, he indicated and turned left without looking. The driver he'd cut off leaned on his horn.

He muttered something in the direction of the rearview mirror.

At that very moment the traffic came to a halt again. The cars to his right, in the lane he'd just left, started moving and soon picked up speed.

He put his forehead on the steering wheel and groaned out loud.

Annika cautiously put her head around the door of Patricia's room. She was asleep. Annika closed the door and quietly set about making coffee. She tiptoed out into the hall and picked up the morning paper, which she threw on the kitchen table. It fell open on a page with the column header "Yesterday on the Radio." Annika's eyes were drawn to the headline, and she read the radio columnist's words with a mounting feeling of sickness.

"The most lively and informative newsmagazine program on the air at the moment is undoubtedly *Studio 69* on P3. Yesterday they focused on the continual dumbing down of the tabloids and the ruthless exploitation of bereaved individuals. Sadly, this is a debate that never ceases to be topical and . . ."

Annika crumpled up the paper into a ball and pushed it into the trash can. Then she went to the phone in the living room, called the newspaper, and canceled her subscription.

She tried to eat half an avocado, but she gagged on the rich green flesh. She tried a few strawberries but with the same result. She could manage some coffee and orange juice but threw away the avocado and a few strawberries so that Patricia would think she'd eaten them. Then she wrote a note telling her that she was going to Hälleforsnäs for the weekend. She wondered to herself whether she'd ever return. If not, then Patricia could have the apartment. She needed it.

The rain formed a wall outside the door when she went to leave. She just stood staring toward the house opposite, which was barely visible behind the curtain of rain.

Perfect, she thought. No one will be out and about. No one will see me. Mum won't have to feel ashamed.

She stepped out into the heavy rain and was soaked to the skin before she'd even reached the communal refuse room. She threw the half-full trash bag away with the paper, strawberries, and bits of avocado and slowly walked toward the subway station.

She'd heard in a movie that you reach a point when you can't get any wetter.

When she got to the railway station, she found out she'd have to wait nearly two hours for a train that went past Flen. She sat down on a bench in the roomy, brightly lit hall. The noises from the travelers, the trains, and the station loudspeakers all fused into a cacophony of city chaos.

Annika closed her eyes and let the sounds bombard her brain. After a while she felt cold, so she went to the ladies' room and stood with her hands under a hand dryer until people got pissed off with her taking too long over it.

At least they don't know who I am, she thought. They don't know that I'm the big loser. Thank God, I never got a picture byline.

She took a small regional train that quickly got packed with people. Opposite her was a fat man wet with perspiration and rain. Breathing hard, he unfolded a copy of *Kvällspressen* that Annika tried to avoid looking at.

She couldn't help noticing that Berit had got the Speaker to admit his involvement in the IB affair.

"I was posted with Elmér during the war," said the front-page story.

Oh, well, she thought. That's none of my business anymore.

At Flen she had another hour's wait for the bus to Hälleforsnäs. The rain was still pouring down, and a small lake had formed in the street behind the bus stop. She sat facing the waiting room wall in the railway station, not wanting any contact with anyone.

It was afternoon when the bus pulled up at the foot of Tattarbacken. The water-filled parking lot next to the co-op lay deserted, so no one saw her step off the bus. Tired and shaky, she made her way up to her house on legs that ached after the previous day's run.

Her apartment was dark and smelled of dust. Without lighting any lamps, she pulled off her wet clothes and crept into bed. Three minutes later she was asleep.

"It's only a matter of time," said the prime minister.

The chief press secretary protested, "We can't know that for sure. Nobody knows where the media pack chooses to stop."

The chief press secretary knew what he was talking about. He had been one of the toughest and most experienced political reporters in the country. Nowadays his job was to spin the media coverage in a favorable direction for the Social Democrats. He was, together with the election strategists from the United States, the most influential person outlining the election campaign for the governing party. The prime minister knew he voted Liberal.

"I have to admit I'm worried," the prime minister said. "I don't want to leave this to chance."

The big man got to his feet and walked restlessly over to the window. The rain was like a gray screen outside, hiding the view over the water.

The press secretary stopped him. "You shouldn't be standing there brooding in full view of everyone in the street. Pictures like that make a brilliant illustration of a government in crisis."

Vexed, the prime minister stopped himself. His bad temper grew even worse, and he abruptly turned to his foreign trade minister and barked, "How the hell could you be so damned stupid?"

Christer Lundgren didn't respond, just went on staring at the lead-gray sky from his place in the corner.

The prime minister moved closer to him. "Goddammit, you know we can't go interfering in the work of a government authority!"

The minister looked up at his superior. "Exactly. Neither the police or anybody else's."

The prime minister's eyes narrowed behind his glasses. "Don't you realize the predicament you've put us in? Do you recognize what the consequences of your actions will be?"

Christer Lundgren jumped to his feet and rushed up face-to-face with the prime minister and yelled, "I know exactly what I've done! I've fucking saved this goddamn party, that's what I've done!"

The press secretary stepped in. "We can't undo what's already been done," he said in a conciliatory tone. "We have to make the best of the situation. Going in and altering documents after the fact could end in disaster. We simply can't do that. I really don't think the journalists are capable of locating those receipts of yours." He circled the two ministers. "The most important thing is to cooperate with the police without giving them too much information."

In a gesture of conciliation, he put a hand on the shoulder of the minister for foreign trade. "Christer, it all depends on you now."

The minister shrugged off the hand. "I'm a murder suspect," he said in a strained voice.

"Yes, it's ironic," the press secretary said. "The death business is your responsibility in the cabinet. As far as arms sales are concerned. I suppose it wasn't meant literally."

It was evening by the time she woke up. Sven was sitting next to her on the bed, watching her.

"Welcome home," he said, and smiled.

She returned the smile. She was thirsty and had a headache.

"You sound as if I've been gone for ages."

"It feels like it," he said.

She pushed away the bedcover and got out of bed, feeling dizzy and queasy. "I don't feel well," she mumbled.

She staggered out to the bathroom and took a Tylenol. She opened the bathroom window to get some air. The rain had eased off but not stopped completely.

Sven came and stood in the doorway. "Shall we go and get a pizza?"

She swallowed. "I'm not really hungry."

"You've got to eat something. Look at you, you've gotten so thin."

"I've been busy." She walked past him and into the hallway.

He followed her out to the kitchen. "I heard they gave you a hard time on the radio."

She poured herself a glass of water. "Have you started listening to the current affairs program with debate and analysis?" she said tartly.

"No. Ingela told me."

She paused with the glass next to her mouth. "The sperm bucket?" she said with surprise. "Are you seeing her?"

He got angry. "That's such a mean old nickname. She hates it."

Annika smiled. "It was you who came up with it."

He grinned. "Yeah, right." He chuckled.

Annika drank the water in big gulps, and he came up to her and hugged her from behind.

"I'm cold. I've got to put some clothes on." She wriggled free.

Sven kissed her. "Sure. I'll call Maestro in the meantime."

Annika went into the bedroom and opened her closet. The clothes she'd left here were creased and smelled musty. She heard Sven call the local pizzeria and order two *quattro stagioni*. He knew she didn't eat mussels.

"You'll stay here now, won't you?" he called out to her after hanging up.

She searched through her clothes. "Why do you think that? My contract lasts until the fourteenth of August. I've got a week and a half left."

He leaned against the doorpost. "Do they still want you, though, the way you were disgraced like that?"

Her cheeks were burning. She rummaged deeper inside the closet. "The paper doesn't give a damn about what they say in a ridiculous radio program like that."

He came up to her and hugged her again. "I don't care what they say about you," he whispered. "To me you'll always be the best, even though all the others say you're worthless."

She pulled on a pair of old jeans that were too big for her now and an old sweater.

Sven shook his head disapprovingly. "Do you have to look like that? Haven't you got a dress?"

She closed the door of the closet. "How long will the pizzas be?"

"I mean it. Put something else on."

Annika stopped, breathed. "Come on," she begged him. "I'm hungry. The pizzas will get cold."

EIGHTEEN YEARS, TEN MONTHS, AND SIX DAYS

I long to return to the light and bright times. When days floated into shadowy nights like a spirit: clean, clear, fragrant, and soft. Time was a hole, weightless. The elation, the first touch, the wind, the light, and the feeling of absolute perfection. More than anything else in the world I want that moment to return.

His darkness blocks out the horizon. It isn't easy to navigate in the dark. The circle is round and evil. I bring out in him the darkness that cloaks our love in a fog. My steps grow unsteady and I stumble on our path. His patience gives out. I pay the price.

But we are the most important thing
there is
to each other.

The water boiled over and then, pouring it into the filter, she spilled some and scalded herself.

"Shit!" she cried out, jamming her burned finger into her mouth.

"Did you hurt yourself?"

A drowsy Patricia was standing in the doorway to the maid's room, dressed in T-shirt and panties, her hair tousled.

Annika was immediately gripped by a pang of guilt. "Oh, I'm so sorry! I didn't mean to wake you up. I'm really sorry."

"What's the matter? Did something happen?"

Annika turned around and poured the rest of the water on the coffee. "My job's hanging by a thread. Do you want some coffee, or are you going back to bed?"

Patricia rubbed her eyes. "I'm off tonight. I'd love a cup."

She put on a pair of shorts and disappeared into the stairwell to go to the bathroom. Annika quickly blew her nose and wiped her eyes. She took out a couple of slices of bread from the freezer, put them in the toaster, and put cheese and marmalade and margarine on the table. She heard Patricia come back in and close the front door.

"What happened?"

Patricia was staring at Annika's legs, and Annika herself looked down at them.

"I was chased by a lynch mob last Thursday. They almost set fire to the car as we were driving away."

Patricia gaped. "Jesus, sounds like a James Bond movie!"

Annika laughed. The toaster clicked and threw the slices up in an arc, and as they caught one each, Patricia laughed too.

They sat down at the kitchen table and made breakfast. Annika missed the morning paper. She looked out the window; the rain was pattering on the windowsill.

"So how was the countryside?"

Annika let out a sigh. "Just what you'd expect in this weather. I spent Friday night with Sven, my boyfriend, and then I went to my grandmother's. She's got a cottage that's part of Harpsund. She can rent it for as long as she likes, as she was the housekeeper there for thirty-seven years."

"What's Harpsund?"

Annika poured the coffee. "It's an estate between Flen and Hälle-forsnäs. A man called Hjalmar Wicander donated it to the government when he died in 1952. The condition was that the prime minister could use it as a recreational residence."

"What's a recrea . . . residence?"

"It's a summerhouse but it has reception rooms." Annika smiled. "Harpsund has been a big hit among prime ministers, especially the present one. He's from Sörmland and most of his family still lives there. I met him there on Midsummer Eve a couple of years ago."

Patricia was impressed. "You've been there?"

"I often went with Grandma when I was a kid."

They ate in silence.

"Are you working today?" Patricia asked.

Annika nodded.

"You've got a really hard job, don't you?" Patricia said. "And dangerous—if there are people trying to set fire to you."

Annika gave a lopsided smile. "Someone set fire to your workplace too."

"That wasn't personal."

Annika sighed. "Still, I wish I could stay."

"Why do you have to go in?"

"My contract ends next week. Only one or two of the summer free-lancers will get to go on working at the paper."

"Couldn't you be one of them? You've written a lot."

Annika shook her head. "They've got a recruitment meeting with the union tomorrow, and after that we'll find out who gets to stay. What are you doing today?"

Patricia's gaze turned inward and disappeared out in the rain. "I'm going to think about Josefin. I'm going to speak to the spirits and look for her on the other side. When I make contact with her, I'm going to ask her who did it."

Anne Snapphane was at her desk when Annika walked into the news-room.

"So you're alive," Annika established.

"Barely. It's been a goddamn awful weekend. The bosses have been completely nuts. Any assignments the news editor has handed out during the day, the night editor has trashed at night. I've had five stories spiked."

Annika dropped down at her desk. The dragon had left behind a battlefield of empty coffee mugs, wire copy, and used Kleenex tissues.

"I did think twice before I came in," Annika said. "Now I know why."

Anne began to laugh. Annika swept everything on the desk, including five notepads, two books, and three mugs marked Mariana, into the wastebasket. "Take that, you upper-class bitch."

Anne laughed so hard she fell off her chair.

"It wasn't that funny, was it?" Annika said.

Anne sat up again and tried to stop laughing. "No, it wasn't that funny," she said, chuckling. "It won't take much to make me laugh today. I know that I'm going to be getting out of here."

Annika stared at her. "You've got a job? Where?"

"With a TV production company in Hammarby Dock. I'll be researcher on a cable-station talk show aimed at women. It starts in about five weeks. It could be really trashy. I'm really looking forward to it."

"What if you get a job here?"

"Christ knows if I want to. Besides, the TV job is a permanent post."

"Congratulations." Annika walked around the desk to give her friend a hug. "I'm so happy for you!"

"Hey, could you dykes spare a minute to do some work?"

Spike was back in the news editor's chair.

"Shove it, you randy old goat!" Anne shouted at him.

"Are you crazy?" Annika said under her breath.

"Who cares? I'm leaving." Anne got up.

Anne got the assignment, a story about a kitten rescued by the Norr-köping police. It had been living at the station for two weeks and now it had to be put to sleep.

"We've got to get a photo of the stupid cat in a cell," Anne said. "Just imagine the headline: 'Puss on Death Row.' "

Spike looked at Annika. "I've got nothing for you right now. Stand by for the time being."

Annika swallowed. She got it. The fridge door had slammed shut.

"Okay," she said. "I'll read the papers."

She walked over to the archive shelves and picked up all the *Kvälls-pressen* issues since last Friday. She had neither read a paper nor watched TV all weekend. She would never listen to the radio again unless she was forced to.

She started with Berit's IB piece. Without beating about the bush, the Speaker now admitted he'd used his contacts with Birger Elmér at the IB domestic bureau to escape a military posting, a training assignment, in the autumn of 1966.

It was in the middle of an election campaign, and the Speaker was the deputy chairman of the Young Social Democrats at the time. The posting came at an inconvenient moment so Elmér set him up with a war job at IB.

This meant he could go on as usual with his political work, while doing his military service at the same time.

According to the records that Berit had dug up, the Speaker had been called up for service at the Defense Staff Intelligence Division, which could be another name for the IB. In 1966 he was thirty-three years old and he was never called up again.

Annika let the paper drop. How did Berit get the Speaker to admit all of this? He'd been denying all involvement for three decades, and now suddenly he'd come clean about everything. Weird.

The following spread showed some sensational pictures of the arrest of the Ninja Barbies, all of them taken by Carl Wennergren. In the article the readers were told that the group had decided to attack a judge's house in the leafy Stockholm suburb of Djursholm. The judge had recently acquitted a suspected pedophile for lack of evidence. The police had been tipped off and had sent in the terrorist squad. They had evacuated the surrounding houses and set up roadblocks. Parts of the squad had taken up position in the Stockhagen sports field right next to the judge's house; the rest had hidden in the garden.

The Ninja Barbies were taken completely by surprise and had surrendered after two of the women were shot in the leg.

The article gave Annika a bad taste in her mouth. Gone was the uncritical reiteration of the Ninja Barbies' grievances that had been the framework of the earlier articles; now the police were the heroes. If any articles in *Kvällspressen* ever merited analysis, it was these, she thought.

"We're going to drown in the tears of readers wanting to take care of little Puss," Anne Snapphane said.

Annika smiled. "What's the cat's actual name?"

"It said Harry on the collar. Have you had lunch yet?"

The minister drove into the little village called Mellösa. He slowed down and looked left through the rain. His turn should be somewhere here.

A large yellow house appeared in the grayness down by the water, and he slowed further; it didn't seem quite right. The car behind beeped.

"Calm down, for Christ's sake!" the minister cried out, and slammed on the brakes. The Volvo behind him braked, swerved, and missed him by an inch.

His rented car coughed and died; the fan hissed and the windshield wipers continued to squeak. He noticed that his hands on the wheel were shaking.

Jesus! What am I doing? he thought. I can't risk other people's lives just because . . .

The irony in his reasoning hit him full force. He started the car and slowly drove on. Two hundred meters farther on he saw the sign: Harpsund 5.

He turned left and crossed the railway. The road wound past a church, a school, and farms in a landscape that belonged to another time; manor houses with sunporches and fir hedges drifted past in the mist.

Here the landowners had sucked the working class dry for a thousand years, he mused.

After a few minutes he drove through the massive stone gateposts that marked the entrance to the prime minister's summer residence. A large, well-kept barn lay on the left, and behind it he glimpsed the main house.

He parked to the right of the entrance and sat in the car for a moment, looking at the building. It was two stories high with a mansard roof, built in the 1910s. A Caroline pastiche. He fished out his umbrella, opened the car door, and ran to the door.

"Welcome. The prime minister called. I've prepared some lunch for you." The housekeeper took his wet umbrella and jacket.

"Thanks, I'm fine. I had lunch on the way. I just want to go to my room."

The woman didn't express any disappointment. "Of course. This way, please."

She walked ahead of him up to the second floor and showed him to a room with a view over the lake. "Just call if you want anything."

The housekeeper closed the door without making a sound, and he took off his shirt and shoes. The prime minister was right—they'd never find him here.

He sat down on the bed with the telephone on his lap and took three deep breaths. Then he dialed the number for Karungi.

"It's over," he said when she answered.

He listened to her for a long time.

"No, darling," he said. "Don't cry. I'm not going to jail. No, I promise."

He stared out the window, hoping he wasn't lying.

The afternoon dragged. She didn't get any assignments. She took the hint, which wasn't even particularly subtle. She was taken off everything to do with the Josefin murder and the minister suspect. Carl Wen-nergren got all those jobs.

In an attack of boredom she called Krim and asked for Q. He actually answered the phone.

"They were hard on you on the radio last Thursday," he said.

"They were wrong. I was right. They got the wrong end of the stick."

"I don't know if I agree," he said genially. "You can be damned pushy."

"I'm smooth as a ballet dancer!"

He laughed out loud. "That's not exactly the metaphor that comes to mind when you call," he snorted. "But you can handle that, I expect. You're a tough nut, so you'll take it in your stride. You have to take a few on the chin."

Amazingly enough, she felt he was right.

"Now listen," she said, "I have a few questions about the Ninja Barbies."

He immediately turned serious. "What?"

"Did they have any cash on them when they were arrested?"

She heard the police captain draw a breath. "Why the hell do you ask that?"

She shrugged and smiled. "Just wondering, that's all . . ."

He thought about it for a long while. "Do you know anything about this?" he said in a low voice.

"Maybe."

"Well, give it to me, baby."

She laughed coarsely. "You'd like that, wouldn't you!"

"They didn't have anything *on* them."

Annika's heart started beating faster. "But in the car? At home? In the basement?"

"In the house of one of them."

"Like around fifty thousand?" Annika said innocently.

He sighed. "I wish you'd tell me straight."

"I could say the same to you."

"Forty-eight thousand five hundred. In an envelope."

He'd done it, the bastard!

"Maybe you could tell me where it came from," he said, trying to sound sweet.

She didn't reply.

When she heard the signature tune to *Studio 69,* Annika turned off the radio and went down to the canteen. She'd just finished filling a plate with rabbit food from the salad bar when a counter attendant with a prominent perm called out her name.

"You've got a call," the Perm said.

It was Anne Snapphane.

"You should listen to this," she said in a low voice.

Annika closed her eyes and felt her heart sink deep into her shoes. "Why would I want to listen to them rip me again?"

"No, no. It's not about you. It's about the minister."

Annika took a deep breath. *"Qué?"*

"It seems he did it after all."

Annika hung up and walked toward the exit with her salad plate.

"Hey, you!" the Perm shouted after her. "You're not allowed to take the plate with you!"

"So call the police," Annika retorted, pushed the door open, and walked out.

The newsroom was deathly quiet. The voice of the studio reporter resounded from the loudspeakers in the open-plan office, and all the journalists at the paper were leaning forward, taking in the message.

Annika gingerly sat down at her desk. "What's up?" she whispered to Anne Snapphane.

Anne leaned over toward her. "They've found the receipt," she said quietly. "The minister was at the strip club on the night of Josefin's murder. She rang up his check half an hour before she died."

Annika went completely pale. "Jesus Christ!"

"It all adds up. Christer Lundgren attended a conference with German Social Democrats and trade union representatives here in Stockholm on Friday, July twenty-seventh. He spoke about trade and cross-border cooperation. Afterward he took the Germans out on a spree."

"What a loser," Annika said.

"The *Studio 69* reporters have found the receipt. And he noted down the names of the Germans on the reverse."

"Has he resigned yet?"

"Do you think he will?" Anne Snapphane said.

"Well, it doesn't look very good. You can picture the headline. 'Social Democrat Spends Taxpayers' Money at Strip Joint.' "

A man from the proofreading desk hushed them. Annika switched on her radio and turned up the volume.

"Our reporter found the fateful receipt from the strip club in the archive of the Ministry for Foreign Affairs. But by then the police were already on the minister's track."

The man's voice was full of restrained triumph. He was milking it, speaking slowly in an ominous voice.

"There was, it appears . . . a witness."

A reporter began speaking, sounding as if he were standing in an empty hallway. The echo bounced around between the walls.

"I'm standing in the stairwell of the house where Minister for Foreign Trade Christer Lundgren has his overnight apartment," the reporter whispered excitedly. "Up to a few days ago, no one knew about it, not even his press secretary, Karina Björnlund. But there was one thing the minister failed to reckon with: the neighbors."

A sound effect faded in, shoes walking up marble steps.

"I'm on my way up to the woman who was to become a key witness in the investigation into the murder of the stripper Josefin Liljeberg," the reporter said, slightly out of breath.

The elevator must be out of order again, Annika thought.

"Her name is Elna Svensson, and it was her early-morning routine and razor-sharp observations that were to nail the minister."

A doorbell rang; Annika recognized it. He was at 64 Sankt Göransgatan, no doubt about it. The door opened.

"He was coming into the building when Jasper and I were on our way out," Elna Svensson said.

Annika immediately recognized the whining voice. The fat woman with the dog.

"Jasper likes to play in the park for a while before I have my morning coffee. Coffee and a plain bun, that's what I have for breakfast."

"And this particular morning you met Minister for Foreign Trade Christer Lundgren on your way out?"

"Yes, as I said."

"And he was on his way in?"

"He came in, looking agitated. He nearly stepped on Jasper, and he didn't apologize either."

Agitated? Annika noted the word down on her pad.

"What time was this?"

"I rise at five o'clock, every day of the week. It was just after that."

"Did you see anything strange in the park?"

The woman sounded more nervous. "Absolutely not. Nothing at all. Neither did Jasper. He did his business and we came back in."

The studio reporter returned, now with the commentator in the studio. They discussed when the minister would resign, the impact on the election campaign, the future of Social Democracy. They even touched on national security. No issues were too important for *Studio 69* on a day like this.

"It pisses me off," Anne Snapphane said.

"What does?" Annika said.

"That it had to be them of all people that found the receipt. Why didn't *I* go up to the Ministry for Foreign Affairs and ask to see it?"

"The question is how they knew it was there to be asked for."

"We have tried to get hold of Christer Lundgren for a comment," the studio reporter said, "but the minister has gone underground. Nobody knows where he is, not even his press secretary, Karina Björnlund, who claims not to have known about the strip club visit either."

Karina Björnlund's nasal voice streamed out of the radio: "I haven't got the slightest idea where he was that night. He told me he was having an informal meeting with some foreign representatives."

"Could that have been the German union leaders?" the reporter insinuated.

"I couldn't say," she said.

"And where is he now?"

"I've been trying to get hold of him all day."

Anne Snapphane rolled her eyes. "She doesn't sound like the sharpest knife in the drawer."

Annika shrugged.

"The prime minister has declined to comment on our latest disclosures," the studio reporter said. "Instead he referred us to a press conference at Rosenbad, tomorrow at eleven A.M."

"Do you think Lundgren will resign then?" Anne asked.

Annika frowned. "It depends," she said thoughtfully. "If the Social Democrats want an end to the discussion, they'll drop him like a hot potato. They'll appoint him county governor or vice president of some bank or something else equally boring up in the tundra."

Anne wagged her finger at Annika. "Watch it, you, you're talking about my backyard."

"Provincialist," Annika retorted. "That, however, would mean that the government would be admitting the minister was a murderer, even if he's never convicted. So if all Social Democrats have a clear conscience, the minister should stay."

"Despite the receipt from the strip club?"

"I bet my boots they'd come up with a great excuse. It was all probably his driver's fault." Annika grinned.

The radio hosts were now ready to sum up and did so with authority. Annika reluctantly admitted to herself that the new disclosures were both sensational and well presented. They'd done a good job.

"A minister in the Social Democrat cabinet takes seven German union leaders to a strip club," the reporter said. "A busty, blond stripper rings up the check at half past four in the morning. The minister signs it and carefully notes down the names of his German guests on the reverse. Half an hour later he returns to his house, agitated, and nearly steps on his neighbor's dog. The stripper is later found murdered fifty yards from the same house. She died between five and seven A.M. that same morning. The minister has been interviewed by the police on several occasions and has now disappeared . . ."

The last words hung in the air when the electric guitar music began. Annika switched off.

The senior editors had gathered over by the news desk. She saw Spike and Jansson; Ingvar Johansson; Picture Pelle and the sports editor; Anders Schyman and the editor in chief. Their backs were turned to the newsroom.

"Check that out for an image," Annika said. "They're in the process of sinking the paper with that damned wall of backs."

"Whatever they're talking about, we're not involved," Anne Snapphane said. "It'll be golden boy who gets this treat."

And true enough, the group moved as one in Carl Wennergren's direction.

"Does Jansson work all the time?" Annika wondered.

"Three ex-wives and five kids on the installment plan," Anne
replied.

Annika slowly ate her wilting salad. Maybe that's where you end
up in this job, she thought. Maybe it's just as well I'm out before I've become like those guys, a bunch of addled old hypocrites with brains that
can only think in 72-point Bodoni.

"You take care of Creepy Calls," Spike said to her when he walked
past.

One and a half weeks left, Annika thought, held her tongue, and
walked off to return her plate to the cafeteria.

"I could do with a quiet night," she said when she returned to her
desk.

"Ha!" Anne said. "That's what you think. Look at the weather. All
the loons will be calling."

Anne was right.

"Immigration's gone too far," a voice said. It resonated with testos-
terone and the southern suburbs.

"Do you think?" Annika said. "In what way?"

"They're taking over. Why the hell can't they solve their own problems wherever it is they come from instead of bringing all their shit over
here?"

Annika leaned back in her chair and sighed soundlessly. "Could
you be a bit more precise?"

"First they rape and kill each other at home, then they come over
here and strangle our girls. Take that dead girl in the park, for example."

At least there was someone who didn't listen to *Studio 69*.

"Well," Annika said, "I'm not so sure the police share your suspicions."

"See! That's what really pisses me off. The cops are protecting the
fuckers!"

"So what do you think should be done about it?" Annika asked in a
silky voice.

"Throw them out. Just send them all back to the jungle, god-dammit!"

Annika grinned. "I find it a bit hard to share your opinion as I'm black myself."

The man on the phone went quiet. Anne stopped writing and looked up at her, and Annika had problems keeping a straight face.

"I want to talk to someone else," the man said when he'd collected himself.

"Sorry, there's no one else here."

"Who is that idiot you're talking to?" Anne asked.

"There is," the man said. "I can hear another woman in the back-ground."

"Oh, yes, of course, there's Anne. She's Korean. Hang on and I'll put you through to her."

"Oh, fuck it!" the man exclaimed, and hung up.

"What an asshole!" Annika said.

The phone rang again.

"So, I don't have to tell you my name, right?" The voice belonged to a frightened young girl.

"Yeah, sure." Annika said. "What's it about?"

"Well, you know, this TV guy, this program presenter . . ." The girl gave the name of one of Sweden's most popular and highly esteemed TV journalists.

"What about him?"

"He dresses up in women's clothes and he gropes young girls."

Annika groaned. She'd heard this one before. "People can dress up however they want in this country."

"He goes to sex clubs too."

"And we have freedom of opinion and religion and freedom of as-sociation."

The girl on the phone lost the thread. "Oh, so it's nothing you'll write about?"

"Has he done anything illegal?"

"No . . ."

"Groped, you said. Has he forced himself on anyone?"

"No, not really, they wanted to—"

"Has he bought sexual favors with public money?"

The girl was confused. "What do you mean?"

"Does he buy prostitutes with taxpayers' money?"

"I don't know . . ."

Annika thanked her for the tip-off and terminated the call. "You're right," she said to Anne. "Loon night."

The tip-off phone rang a third time. Annika grabbed it.

"My name is Roger Sundström and I live in Piteå. Are you busy, or do you have a minute?"

Annika sat down. This crazy man was actually polite.

"I've got time. What's it about?"

"Well," the man said in broad Norrland dialect, "it's about this minister, Christer Lundgren. "They're saying in this radio program, *Studio 69*, that he was at a strip club in Stockholm, but that's not true."

Annika pricked up her ears; something in the man's voice made her take him seriously. She found a pen beside the keyboard. "Tell me, what makes you think that?"

"Well, we went to Majorca on holiday, the whole family. Silly, 'cause it's been warmer in Sweden than in Spain, but we couldn't have known that when we . . . Well, anyway, we were on our way back to Piteå. We'd booked flights with Transwede from Stockholm, as they're a bit cheaper . . ."

A child laughed in the background and Annika heard a woman singing.

"Go on."

"That's when we saw the minister. He was at the airport when we were there."

"When was this?"

"Friday the twenty-seventh, at twenty oh five in the evening."

"How can you be that exact?"

"I remembered it was the time our plane was supposed to leave. It says on my ticket."

Of course! "But what makes you think the minister wasn't at the strip club? The check that the reporters on *Studio 69* are talking about was rung up at half past four the following morning. *And* a neighbor saw him."

"But he wasn't in Stockholm then."

"How do you know?"

"Because he got on the plane. We saw him at the check-in counter. He had a briefcase and a small suitcase."

Annika felt the hair on her neck stand up; this could be important. Yet, she was doubtful. She had to be sure.

"How come you paid such close attention to the minister? How come you recognized him?"

The children in the background started singing a silly song. Roger Sundström gave an embarrassed laugh.

"I tried to talk to him, but he was too stressed-out. I don't think he even registered me."

"Stressed? In what way?"

"He was in a sweat and his hands were shaking."

"It was very hot that day, everyone was sweating."

Sundström patiently replied, "Yes, but he didn't look like he normally does. His eyes were sort of staring."

Annika felt the excitement drop. Sundström was probably imagining things. "How do you mean, staring?"

The man paused. "He was all tense, and he's always so self-assured and relaxed."

"What do you mean 'always'? Do you know him?" That's what she thought he was implying.

"Oh, yes. Christer's married to my cousin Anna-Lena. They live somewhere in Luleå, and their twins are the same age as our Kajsa. We don't meet up very often—the last time was at Granddad's funeral, I think. But Christer sure doesn't look like that normally, not even at funerals."

He fell silent, feeling that Annika didn't believe him.

Annika was at a loss but for the time being decided the man was telling the truth. At least he believed what he was telling her.

"Did you see him on the plane as well?"

Roger Sundström hesitated. "It was one of those big planes and it was packed. No, I don't think I saw him."

Annika closed her eyes and thought about the claim on *Studio 69* that there were ten thousand lobbyists in Stockholm; maybe they had a local office in Piteå.

"There's something I want to ask you, Roger, and I want you to be absolutely honest with me. It's extremely important."

"Right, what's that?" Annika sensed a note of suspicion and fear in his voice.

"Did anyone ask you to make this call?"

Again, there was a pause. "Well, I talked it over with Britt-Inger first. She thought I should call you."

"Britt-Inger?"

"My wife."

"And why did your wife think you should call?"

"Because they're wrong on *Studio 69*." Sundström was getting more assertive. "I called them first, but they wouldn't talk to me. But I know what I saw. Britt-Inger saw him too."

Annika frantically racked her brains. "And nobody else asked you to call?"

"Nobody."

"You're absolutely sure about that?"

"Now listen—"

"Okay," Annika said quickly. "What you're saying is very interesting. It puts the allegations on *Studio 69* in a completely different light. I'll see whether I can use it in one way or another in the future. Thank you very much for . . ."

Roger Sundström had already hung up.

The moment she put the Creepy Calls phone down, her own phone started ringing.

"You've got to help us." It was Daniella Hermansson.

"What's happened?"

"They keep calling Auntie Elna. She's here with me now. There are fifteen journalists with TV cameras and God knows what outside our door, and they won't stop ringing the bell. What can we do?"

Daniella was in a real state. Annika heard the child screaming in the background and assumed her calmest tone of voice.

"You have absolutely no obligation to let anyone in if you don't want to. Neither you, nor Elna, has to talk to any journalists. Are they phoning too?"

"Constantly."

"When we hang up, take the phone off the hook. They'll only get the busy signal. If you feel threatened by the journalists outside your door, call the police."

"The police? Oh, I daren't."

"Do you want me to do it?"

"Could you? Please . . ."

"You just hold the line and I'll call them on another phone."

Annika picked up the Creepy Calls phone and dialed the direct number to the police control room.

"Oh, hi, I'm calling from sixty-four Sankt Göransgatan," she said. "The press have invaded. They're scaring the pensioners to death. They're yelling and shouting, ringing on all doors. The people from the radio are the worst. I've got five terrified pensioners with me right now. It's the stairwell to the right, third floor."

She changed receivers. "They're on their way."

Daniella breathed freely again. "Oh, thank you so much. How can I ever thank you? That was really good of you, I'll—"

Annika wasn't listening. "Why did Elna talk to the reporter from *Studio 69*?"

"She says she hasn't talked to any reporters."

"She must have, I heard her on the radio. It would have been today or yesterday."

Daniella put the phone down and talked to someone in the room.

"Auntie Elna says absolutely not."

Annika pondered her words. "Listen, is Aunty Elna okay? Does she ever get a little confused?"

The answer came fast and assuredly. "Not a bit, she's completely with it. No reporter, she's positive."

"Well, she talked to someone, unless I and the entire pack of hacks outside your door have been hallucinating."

"A policeman. She spoke to a police officer this morning. He said he wanted to clarify a few points from a previous interview."

"Did he record their conversation?"

"Did he record your conversation?" Daniella asked.

A long mumbling conversation followed.

"Yes," Daniella said into the phone. "He wanted a transcript. The documentation of all interviews is very important, the policeman said."

They have absolutely no shame, Annika thought to herself.

"And she's sure about the day and the time? About when she bumped into the minister?"

"Yes, she's absolutely sure."

"How can she be?"

"Can I tell her?" Daniella asked her neighbor.

Mumbling and muttering. Then back into the phone: "No, I can't tell you why, but she is. Oh, something's happening outside! Hang on, let me check . . ."

Daniella dropped the phone; Annika could hear her footsteps. She was probably looking through the peephole. Then the steps returned.

"The police are here now. They're clearing out the stairwell. Thanks a million for all your help."

"Don't mention it."

Annika hung up, her head spinning. Creepy Calls rang again.

"You take it, please," Annika said to Anne Snapphane, and walked off to the cafeteria. She bought a bottle of mineral water and sat down by a window, looking out at the rain. It was a dark and heavy night. Not even the lights at the Russian embassy could penetrate the gloom.

I wonder when Josefin's funeral is, she mused. I guess it'll be some time. The medical examiners and the police will want the chance to look at her body now so they won't have to dig her back up.

She thought about the minister, wondering what window he was staring out of.

Talk about being up shit creek, she thought. How can you be so damn stupid to hand in the receipt from a strip joint to the Ministry for Foreign Affairs?

He's just tightfisted, that's how.

While she finished her water, her thoughts returned to Josefin. The dead girl had been completely forgotten in all this. From the moment she was exposed as a stripper, she became nothing but a piece of meat, a men's toy. Annika thought about her parents.

I wonder how my mom would have reacted if it had been me, she mused. Would she have cried to a journalist from the local paper?

Probably not. Her mother disliked journalists. People should mind their own business was what she thought. She'd never said it straight out, but she wasn't happy with Annika's choice of profession. She'd gone along with Sven, who thought Annika shouldn't accept her place at college.

"It's a really tough job," Sven had said. "Confronting people and challenging them isn't for you. You're such a soft touch."

She got to her feet, annoyed, and walked back to her desk in the newsroom.

"I've had enough of this for today," she said to Anne Snapphane, and took her bag and left.

Patricia jumped when the front door opened. Annika was a black silhouette against the sharp light in the stairwell.

"Were you asleep?" Annika turned on the light.

Patricia blinked at the light. "I was letting the energies flow."

"And I sent them packing," Annika said with a wan smile.

Patricia returned the smile. "They're always there."

Annika hung up her things in the hall. Her jacket was wet.

Patricia sat up on the couch. "Josefin had one of those jackets," she said, amazed. "Exactly the same."

Annika gave a surprised look. "It's several years old. From H and M, I think."

Patricia nodded. "So was Jossie's. It's still hanging in the hall in Dalagatan. 'I'll always wear this jacket,' she used to say. She often said stuff like that, big exaggerations. 'I'll always.' 'I'll never ever.' 'This is the biggest one of all.' 'You're the best friend I've ever had.' 'I'll hate him till I die.' Till I die . . ."

Patricia started crying and Annika sat down next to her on the couch.

"Did you listen to *Studio 69*?"

Patricia nodded.

"What do you think? Was it the minister?"

Patricia looked down at her hands through the tears. "It could be one of the bigwigs—they left shortly after Jossie. They paid with one of those fancy government cards. And then the Germans—you know what they're like. Dad often talked about them."

Annika stayed silent while Patricia cried. "Everyone important to me dies."

"Oh, come on," Annika tried.

"First Dad, then Jossie . . ."

"Surely that's not 'everyone'? What about your mom?"

Patricia fished out a tissue and blew her nose. "She doesn't want anything to do with me, calls me a whore. And she's got the whole family on her side."

Annika went to get two glasses of water from the kitchen. She gave one to Patricia.

"So why do you work there?"

"Joachim thinks I'm good in the bar," she said defiantly. "And I make good money—I put away ten thousand every month. When I've got enough, I'm going to open a shop. I already know what I'm going to call it, The Crystal. I checked it. The name's available. I'm going to sell tarot cards and tell people's fortunes, help people find the right path—"

"You've seen the minister in the photographs. Was he with those guys at the club?"Annika interrupted.

Patricia shrugged. "They all look the same, you know."

Annika recognized her words, she'd heard them somewhere else before. She looked at the woman on the couch. Doubtless, she avoided looking at the men altogether.

"Did the police ask you about this?"

"Of course. They've asked about everything a million times."

"What, for example?"

Patricia got to her feet, irritated. "Everything, a thousand different things. I'm tired now. Good night."

She quietly closed the door to her room behind her.

EIGHTEEN YEARS, ELEVEN MONTHS, AND FIVE DAYS

We don't know where we're headed. The truth that was behind the clouds has drifted off into space. I can't see it any longer, can't even sense its presence.

He cries over the emptiness. All I feel is flat and cold. I'm unmoved: indifferent, sterile.

Resignation is next door to failure. The will that is either too strong or too weak; the love that is either too demanding or too pale.

I can't back out now.

We are, despite everything,
the most important thing there is
to each other.

TUESDAY 7 AUGUST

S he's got to go," said the first one.

"How do we get rid of her?" said the second one.

"Shoot her?" said the third.

The men from *Studio 69* were sitting around her kitchen table. Annika wasn't going to stay on at the newspaper, that much was clear.

"But you haven't asked *me!*" Annika called out.

They continued mumbling among themselves at the table, and Annika couldn't catch their words.

"Hey, listen!" she called to them. "Maybe I don't want to go with you! I don't want to go to Harpsund!"

"Do you want some breakfast?"

When Annika opened her eyes, she was looking straight at Patricia. "What's that?"

Patricia's hands flew up to her mouth. "Oh, I'm sorry, you were still sleeping. I thought . . . You were talking. It must have been a dream."

Annika closed her eyes and smoothed back her hair. "Weird."

Annika got out of bed, put on her dressing gown, and padded down to the toilet. She returned just as Patricia was pouring out coffee.

"Didn't you sleep well?"

Annika sat down with a sigh. "They make their decision today."

"I think they'll let you stay on." Patricia smiled.

Annika pondered. "I have a chance. I'm a member of the Union of Journalists, so I've got them behind me. Even if the senior editors have been influenced by *Studio 69*, the union will back me up."

She had a bite of her roll, her expression lighting up. "Of course, that's what'll happen. It's possible the bosses will want to drop me, because they're really out of touch. But the union will stand up for me."

"There you go," Patricia said, and this time Annika returned the smile.

The rain had stopped. Nevertheless, his first breath filled his lungs with dampness. The fog was so dense he could barely make out his rental car.

He stepped out onto the crunching gravel, dropping the heavy door behind him. The sounds were muffled, as if wrapped in cotton wool. He passed his hand through the veils. They danced.

He walked around the house and emerged at the back. You couldn't guess that the lake was only a few hundred yards away. He knew the fog would lift during the morning, but if he was to get any fresh air today, it would have to be now.

A car drove past in the road, but he couldn't see it.

Talk about a perfect hiding place, he thought.

He sat down on a park bench and the damp immediately penetrated the seat of his pants. He didn't care.

The feeling of failure burned in his lungs as he drew deep, misty breaths. The view over the lake was as clear as his future. The prime minister was unwilling to discuss what he'd be doing after it was all over. All his energy was now aimed at salvaging the election campaign. Nothing must jeopardize that. The prime minister would get rid of him today in a public axing, on some invented pretext, and he'd grovel to the media. The amoebas, as he called them, controlled the election campaign, and it took precedence over everything else.

Except the truth, he reflected.

This realization had the same effect on his future as if the sun had suddenly broken through the thick clouds and made the fog lift in a moment.

It was that simple!

He suddenly laughed out loud.

He could choose to do damn well anything he wanted.

As long as no one found them out.

His laughter froze, the fog swallowed and drowned it.

"He resigned," Anne Snapphane hollered. "The news flash just came in from TT."

Annika dropped her bag on the floor. "And?"

" 'At a press conference the prime minister announced that the minister for foreign trade has resigned,' " Anne read on her screen. " 'The prime minister expressed regret at Christer Lundgren's decision but understands his motives.' "

"Which were?" Annika sat down at her own desk and switched on her computer.

"Family reasons."

"Of course he'd say that. They always say that. But it's not that straightforward."

"Oh, you," Anne said, "you're just imagining things."

"And what's the alternative? That he really is the murderer?"

"There's a lot that's pointing toward that now."

Annika didn't respond. She clicked onto the list of cable copy on the TT page on her computer. They had already reached "Minister resigns 5." No one had been able to get hold of Christer Lundgren himself for a comment. The prime minister had once again pointed out that the minister wasn't suspected of any form of criminal act and that the police interviews had been routine.

"So why did he resign?" Annika muttered.

She read that an internal committee was at present looking at the former minister's receipt from Studio 69.

She let go of the mouse, leaned back in her chair, and looked out over the newsroom. "So where are all the führers?"

"At the recruitment meeting," Anne said.

Annika's heart jumped. "I'm getting some coffee," she said abruptly, and got to her feet.

Jesus, I'm so nervous, she thought.

She went to get a copy of today's paper, opened it to page six and seven, and burst out laughing.

She was looking at a photograph of a small cat sitting on a dark green, plastic mattress in a jail cell. He was wide-eyed and dazed, maybe from the camera flash. The tip of his tail lay neatly on top of his front paws.

"Puss on Death Row" read the headline across all of page seven.

"It's a good thing that the media, at least once in a while, takes on the really important issues," Annika said when she'd pulled herself together.

"We're getting a storm of protests from the readers," Anne said. "My assignment for the day is to choose where Puss's new home will be." She waved a big bundle of telephone message notes in the air. "The switchboard will sift out all callers outside of Östergötland. How does Arkösund sound to you? Does Puss look like an archipelago cat to you?"

Anne leaned forward, studied the picture for a few seconds, and gave the answer herself. "Nah. I don't see him as a herring lover. I think he likes mice and birds. Haversby sounds like a real rat-hole, doesn't it? Is that where he should go?"

Annika got to her feet again, fidgety.

Why didn't Christer Lundgren attend his own press conference? And how come the prime minister announced his resignation and not him? Didn't he want to resign? Or did the election campaign managers think he'd shoot his mouth off?

Both, perhaps, Annika thought. In any case, it all pointed to some kind of cover-up.

She walked over to the bulletin board; the recruitment meeting had started at ten o'clock. They should be done soon. She needed to go to the bathroom, again.

When she came out, she saw Bertil Strand standing talking to Picture Pelle over by the picture desk. She knew that the photographer sat on the executive committee of the local branch of the union. They must have taken part in the meeting. Without being aware of it, she half ran over to him.

"What's the decision?" she said, out of breath.

Bertil Strand slowly turned round. "The union executive is united," he said coldly. "We think you should leave immediately. Your careless way of handling the public has compromised the credibility of the entire newspaper."

Annika wasn't taking it in. "But, do I get to stay on?"

He narrowed his eyes. His voice became icy cold. "Aren't you listening? You should leave right away."

The blood drained from Annika's face. She had to grab hold of the photo desk to keep from falling over. "Leave?"

Bertil Strand turned away and she let go of the table. Oh, dear God, get me away from here, Jesus Christ, how do I get out, I'm going to throw up. The whole newsroom was heaving up and down, the walls were swaying.

Rage surged up inside her, crimson and razor-sharp.

Shit, she thought. I've had it with these idiots. I'm not the one who's been behaving like an ass. It's not my fault the paper is going to hell. How can they say that to me, my own union representatives!

"How dare you?" she said to Bertil Strand.

The man's back stiffened.

"It's people like me who pay for your dinners with the executive committee," she said. "You're supposed to be there for me. How the hell can you stab me in the back like this?"

He turned around again. "You're not a regular member of this union branch," he said tersely.

"No, because I don't have a permanent job. But I pay exactly the same dues as everybody else. How come I don't have the same rights? How the hell can the union recommend firing one of its own members? Are you completely out of your minds?"

"Don't say anything you might regret," the photographer said, his gaze drifting away above her head.

She took a big step nearer to him, making him take a frightened step back.

"It's you who should watch what you say," she said in a low voice. "I've made some mistakes, but none as big as the one you're making right now."

Out of the corner of her eye, she saw Anders Schyman walking toward his fish tank with a mug of coffee in his hand. She fixed her gaze on the back of his head and set off toward him. Computers, people, bookshelves, and plants moved past like fragments until she was face-to-face with him.

"Are you kicking me out?" she said, her voice much too shrill.

The deputy editor steered her into his room and drew the curtains. She flopped onto the tobacco couch and stared at him.

"Of course we aren't."

"The union wants to," she said, her voice trembling. Don't start blubbering now, she thought.

Schyman nodded, then sat down next to her on the couch. "I just can't make them out. They don't give a damn about their members. All they want is power."

She eyed him suspiciously. "Why are you saying this to me?"

He looked at her calmly. "Because that's what it's about in this case."

She blinked.

"Unfortunately, the truth is there's no opening for you at the moment. We can't hire everybody who's good, and there's only one available contract this fall."

"Oh, let me guess, that went to Carl Wennergren?"

"Yes." The deputy editor looked at the floor.

Annika laughed. "Well, congratulations! This newspaper certainly backs the people it deserves." She stood up.

"Please sit down."

"Why should I? There's no reason for me to stay in this building for another second. I'll be leaving immediately, just like the union wants me to."

"You've got a week and a half left. Stick it out."

She gave a short laugh again. "So I can eat more shit?"

"In small quantities and at the right moments, it can be good for one's character," Anders Schyman said with a smile.

She pulled a wry face. "I've got compensatory leave to take."

"You do. But I'd rather you stayed and worked."

She walked toward the door but checked herself and stopped. "Just tell me one thing. Would this paper pay for a tip-off from a terrorist group?"

"What do you mean?" He got to his feet.

"Exactly what I say—pay money to be present during a terrorist act."

He crossed his arms and gave her a searching look. "Do you know something?"

"I never disclose my sources," she said mockingly.

"You're employed by this newspaper, and I'm your boss."

She fished out her pass from her pocket and put it on his desk. "Not any longer, you're not."

"I want to know what made you ask."

"Answer my question first," she retorted.

He looked at her in silence for a few seconds. "Of course not. It would be out of the question. Never."

"If the paper had done this since you started, you would know about it?"

"I take that for granted."

"And you can guarantee that this hasn't happened?"

He slowly nodded.

"Okay," she said in a light tone. "Then I'm satisfied. Well, then . . . It was short but sweet."

She held out her hand nonchalantly.

He didn't take it. "What are you going to do now?"

Annika looked at the deputy editor with slight contempt. "And what's that to you?"

He answered calmly, "I'm interested."

"I'm going to the Caucasus. Actually, I'm leaving tomorrow."

Schyman blinked. "I don't think that's a good idea. There's a civil war down there."

"Oh, don't worry about me. I'll be with the guerrillas, so I'm cool. See, the government has no weapons. The international community has seen to it that the slaughter is one-sided. Well, good luck getting this newspaper back on its feet. You've got a hell of a job ahead of you. The bosses here don't know what the fuck they're doing."

She put her hand on the door handle, paused. "You've got to get rid of that couch. It really stinks."

She left the door wide open behind her, Anders Schyman watching her weave her way through the newsroom. As she walked toward her desk, her movements jerky and angry, she didn't stop to speak to a single person.

Anne Snapphane wasn't at her desk.

Just as well, Annika thought. I have to get out of here without breaking down. I'm not going to give them that.

She threw her things together, a few boxes of pens, a pair of scissors, and a stapler thrown in. That was the least this shitty rag could give her.

She left the newsroom without looking round. In the elevator down, she suddenly felt a heavy pressure across her chest. She had difficulty breathing as she stared at her face, bluish pale as usual, in the wall mirror.

Damned lighting, she thought, and it's summer. I wonder what you look like in this elevator in the winter.

I'll never find out was her next thought. This is the last time I'll ever use it.

The cage stopped with the familiar jerk. She pushed the door open, heavy as lead, and walked toward the fog outside. Tore Brand must have gone on holiday; a woman she didn't recognize was behind the reception desk. The entrance doors slid closed behind her and that was the end of that.

She stood for a while on the forecourt of the newspaper building, drawing the damp air into her lungs. It was raw and unpleasant.

She recalled her words to Schyman.

Where the hell did the idea about the Caucasus come from? she wondered. But maybe going abroad wasn't such a bad idea, to just grab a last-minute trip anywhere.

A figure emerged from the veils of fog in the street. Carl Wennergren was carrying two heavy bags full of bottles. Of course he was going to celebrate!

"Congratulations," Annika said tartly when he walked past her.

He stopped and put the bags down. "Yeah, I feel great." He flashed a wide smile. "Six months, that's the longest contract they give you. Any longer and they would have to employ the person permanently."

"It must feel good, to get in here like that, by your own efforts—and with your own money."

The man smiled hesitantly. "What do you mean?"

"Daddy's little rich boy. Did you have the money to hand, or did you have to sell some stock?"

His smile immediately faded and he looked away with a sneer on his face. "So they chucked you out?" he said nonchalantly.

Her answer was shrill. "I'd rather eat cat food than buy my job from terrorists."

His contemptuous gaze swept across her body. "Well, *bon appétit.* You look a bit scrawny, actually. You could use something to eat."

He picked up his bags and turned around to go inside the newspaper offices. Annika saw that they were filled with Moët & Chandon bottles.

"And not only did you buy a scoop and a contract, you also gave up your own sources. That's quite a triple."

He stopped dead and looked around. "That's bullshit." She could see a hint of anxiety stirring around his eyes.

She moved closer to him. "How the hell could the police know the Ninja Barbies would hit that place at that time? How the hell did they know to evacuate that particular block? And how could they know exactly where to hide?"

"I don't know." Carl licked his lips.

She took another step toward him and hissed straight in his face, "You sold out your own sources. You cooperated with the police to get pictures of the arrest, didn't you?"

He raised his eyebrows, leaned his head back, and gave her a contemptuous look. "And . . . ?"

She lost her head and started yelling. "You are such a fucking asshole! Fuck you!"

He turned around and stumbled toward the entrance. "You crazy bitch!" he yelled over his shoulder.

He disappeared through the glass doors and Annika felt the tears welling up in her eyes. Screw them! He gets to go in with the champagne while they throw me out on the street.

"Hey, Bengtzon, do you want a lift?"

She spun around and saw Jansson sitting in a clapped-out old Volvo at the exit to the street.

"What are you doing here?" she called to him.

"The recruitment meeting." He switched off the engine. She walked over toward the car and the night editor stepped out.

"You look tired," she said.

"Yeah, I was on last night. But I really wanted to go to this meeting. To do my bit of lobbying for you."

She gave him a skeptical look. "Why?"

He lit up a cigarette. "I think you're the best cover we had this summer. I thought the six-month contract should go to you. So did Schyman."

Annika raised her eyebrows. "Really. So why didn't it?"

"The editor in chief said no. He's a real idiot. He's shit-scared of criticism. And you had the union against you."

"Yeah, I know."

They stood there for a while in silence, Jansson smoking his cigarette.

"Are you leaving right away?"

Annika nodded. "No point in prolonging the agony."

"Maybe you could come back."

She laughed quietly. "I wouldn't bet my last dollar on it."

The night editor shrugged. "So, can I drop you anywhere?"

She looked into the man's dog-tired face and shook her head. "Thanks, I'll walk. Enjoy the fantastic weather."

They both looked around into the fog and laughed.

Her clothes stank of stale tobacco. She pulled them off and left them in a heap on the floor in the hallway. She put on her dressing gown and sat down on the couch.

Patricia had gone out somewhere. Just as well. She reached for the telephone directories.

"You can't leave the Union of Journalists just like that," an administrator at the union central office told her reproachfully.

"I can't? So how do I do it?"

"First you have to write to your local branch and withdraw your name from the union, and then you have to write to us here at the central office. Then, after six months, you have to confirm your withdrawal, both locally and centrally."

"You must be kidding."

"The waiting period is counted from the first day of the following month. So you can't leave the union until the first of March next year at the earliest."

"And I have to pay my dues in full until then?"

"Yes, unless you stop practicing journalism."

"Well, that's exactly what I'm going to do. As of this moment."

"So you've left your present employment?"

Annika sighed. "No, I've got a permanent job on the *Katrineholms-Kuriren.*"

"Then you can't leave the union just like that."

I'm going to reach down the telephone wire and strangle the woman. "Now listen. I'm leaving the union now. Today. Forever. What I'm doing is none of your damned business. I won't pay another cent. Just strike me off the register right now."

The woman on the phone got angry. "Obviously I can't do that. And it's not *our* union, it's *your* union."

Annika laughed out loud.

"You're too much! Well, then, if I can't leave, I just won't pay the full dues, only the unemployment benefit fund contribution. Just send me a form."

"Well, that's not the correct procedure."

Annika closed her eyes and swallowed. Her brain was about to explode.

"Okay. Tell you what. Forget it. I'll leave the unemployment benefit fund as well. Just go to hell."

She hung up, searched the phone directory, then phoned the syndicalist union, the SAC, the Swedish Workers Confederation.

"I'd like to join the unemployment benefit fund. . . . Oh, great! Sure, I'll send you the papers straightaway."

Things could be so simple.

She went into the kitchen and made a sandwich, ate half of it, and threw the rest away. Then she went and got her notepad and settled down. She closed her eyes and drew a deep breath, then she wrote both the letters. She could buy envelopes and stamps at the corner shop.

It was evening when Patricia got home and stepped on the heap of clothes on the floor.

"Hello?"she called out. "Have you been to a bar or something?"

Annika popped her head around the kitchen door. "Why?"

"Your clothes smell like an ashtray."

"I've been fired."

Patricia hung up her jacket and walked into the kitchen. "Have you eaten?"

Annika shook her head. "I'm not hungry."

"You've got to eat."

"Or what, I get bad karma?"

Patricia smiled. "Karma is sins from previous lives that strike you in your present life. This is called hunger. People die from it."

She went up to the stove and started cracking eggs. Annika looked out the window; the rain pattered, emphasizing the dark gray of the evening.

"It'll be fall soon," Annika said after a couple of minutes.

"Here you are, a mushroom omelette." Patricia sat down opposite her.

To her surprise, Annika finished the omelette.

"So, tell me, what do you mean, you've been fired?"

Annika stared down at her empty plate. "I didn't get another contract. The union wanted me out right away."

"Idiots," Patricia said with such force that Annika started laughing.

"Yes, they are actually. I've left the union."

Patricia cleared the table and did the dishes.

"So what are you going to do?"

Annika swallowed. "I don't know," she said quietly. "I've just resigned from my job at *Katrineholms-Kuriren* and given my landlord in Hälleforsnäs notice. I posted the letters this afternoon."

Patricia opened her eyes wide. "How are you going to make any money?"

Annika shrugged. "It'll be a month before I get unemployment benefits. I've got some money in the bank."

"Where are you going to live?"

Annika threw her arms out. "Here, for the time being. It's only a short lease, but it could be for as long as a year. After that, I'll have to see."

"We always need people at the club."

Annika gave a shrill, cheerless laugh. "Well, I've got the main qualifications: tits and a pussy. Mind you, I have spun the roulette wheel a few times in my day."

"Really?"

"I worked as a croupier at the Katrineholm Hotel while I was at college. I can spin the wheel eleven times. I used to be able to make the ball land on thirty-four if I snapped the ball out from zero just right."

"Actually we need someone for the roulette table."

"I'm going to go away for a while."

"Where to?"

Annika shrugged. "I can't remember what it's called. It's in Turkey, by the Mediterranean."

"That sounds nice."

They sat in silence for a long while.

"You should find out where you're going," Patricia said.

"Sure."

"Hang on, let me get my cards."

Patricia got up from her chair and padded into her room. Annika heard her unzip her bag. A few moments later, Patricia appeared in the doorway, holding a small brown box.

Patricia put the box on the kitchen table and opened it. Inside was a bundle wrapped in black material that she slowly untangled.

"What's that?"

"Tarot is an ancient source of knowledge." Patricia placed the deck on the table. "It's a philosophy described in esoteric images on cards. A tool for moving toward greater awareness."

"I'm sorry, but I don't believe in this kind of stuff."

Patricia sat down. "It's not about believing. It's about listening. Opening up and gazing into one's inner realm."

Annika couldn't help smiling.

"Don't laugh, this is serious," Patricia said sternly. "Look, there are seventy-eight cards, the Major Arcana, the Minor Arcana, and the court cards. They represent different insights and perspectives."

Annika shook her head and got to her feet.

"No, sit down." Patricia caught Annika's wrist. "Let me tell you your fortune!"

Annika hesitated, sighed, and sat down. "Well, all right. What do I have to do?"

"Here." Patricia placed the deck of cards in Annika's hand. "Shuffle and cut."

Annika shuffled the cards, cut the deck, and held it out to Patricia.

"No. First you cut it three times and then you shuffle again and cut it twice."

Annika gave her a skeptical look. "Why?"

"For the energies. Go ahead."

Annika sighed inwardly and shuffled and cut, shuffled and cut.

"Good," Patricia said. "Now, don't put the two piles together but choose one of them with your left hand and shuffle it again."

Annika rolled her eyes and did as she was told.

"Great. Now you have to concentrate on the question you want an answer to. Are you facing a great change?"

"Jesus, you know I am," Annika said sharply.

"Okay, then I'll do a Celtic cross."

Patricia laid out the cards all over the table.

"Nice pictures," Annika said. "Weird-looking creatures."

"The deck was designed by Frieda Harris, after sketches by Aleister Crowley. It took five years to finish the whole deck. The symbols have their roots in the Hermetic Order of the Golden Dawn."

"Whatever that is," Annika said incredulously. "And now they're going to show me my future?"

Patricia nodded gravely and pointed at a card that lay underneath another. "Here, in the first position, is the card that represents your present situation. Tower Struck by Lightning, the sixteenth card in the Major Arcana. As you can see, it's falling down. That's your life, Annika. Everything that has stood for security in your world is crumbling—I don't need to tell you that."

Annika gave Patricia a searching look. "What else?"

Patricia moved her finger and pointed at the card that lay on top of the tower. "Five of Disks crosses your present situation, obstructing or promoting it. The card signifies Mercury in Taurus—depression and fear."

"And?"

"You're afraid of the change, but there's no need to be."

"Right, and then what?"

"Your view of the situation is what might be expected, Aeon, the twentieth card, which stands for self-criticism and thoughtfulness. You feel you've failed and are searching yourself. But your unconscious interpretation is much more interesting. Look here, Knight of Swords.

He's a master of creativity. He's trying to break away from all the narrow-minded idiots."

Annika leaned back in her chair, and Patricia continued, "You come from the Seven of Disks, limitation and failure, and you are moving toward the Eight of Swords, interference."

Annika sighed. "Sounds like hard work."

"This is you. The Moon. That's funny—last time I told my own fortune I also got the Moon. The female sex, the final test. I'm sorry but it's not a good card."

Annika didn't reply. Patricia looked at the remaining cards in silence, then said, "This is what you're most afraid of. The Hanged Man. Rigidity, that your own spirit should be broken."

"But how's it going to end?" Annika sounded a little less dismissive.

Hesitating, Patricia pointed at the tenth card. "This is the outcome. Don't be afraid. It's only a symbol. Don't take it literally."

Annika leaned forward. The card showed the figure of a black skeleton wielding a scythe. "Death."

"It doesn't necessarily signify physical death but rather a radical change. Old relationships need to be dissolved. Death has two faces. One that tears down and destroys, another that sets you free of old bonds."

Annika stood up abruptly. "I don't give a damn about your cards. It's bullshit," she said, and marched off to her room, shutting the door behind her.

PART THREE

SEPTEMBER

NINETEEN YEARS, TWO MONTHS, AND EIGHTEEN DAYS

I think I'm quite good at living. I imagine that in reality my life is quite bright. My breath is so light, my legs so smooth, my mind so open. I believe I have a gift for being happy. I think I love to be alive. I sense a shimmer somewhere just beyond, just nearby, but intangible.

How simple it can all be. How little is really needed.
Sun. Wind. Direction. Context. Commitment. Love. Freedom.
Freedom . . .

But he says
he will never
let me go.

The landscape didn't materialize until about a minute before the plane touched the ground. The clouds hung just above the trees, spreading a fine mist of rain.

I hope the weather's been this bad all the time, Annika thought. It would serve the bastards right.

The plane taxied to Arlanda Terminal 2, the same one they'd taken off from. Annika had been seriously disappointed that Terminal 2 was only an annex to the real international terminal, with hardly any duty-free shops. It was where the marginal airlines carried on their business, international and domestic, charter and scheduled. No glamour whatsoever.

At least no customs agents were around.

It's something, she thought as she walked through the green channel.

Of course, her bags came last of all. The airport bus was packed, and she had to stand for the forty-five-minute journey into central Stockholm and the City Terminal. When she stepped out on the Klaraberg Viaduct, it was raining properly. Her cloth bags absorbed the rain and her luggage got soaked. She swore under her breath and jumped on the 52 bus on Bolindersplan.

The apartment was quiet, the curtains resting peacefully in the morning light. She put her bags on the rug in the hall and sank down on the living room couch, groggy with fatigue. The plane had been scheduled to leave yesterday at four in the afternoon, but for reasons that were never disclosed, they had spent eight hours in the Turkish airport and another five in the plane itself before they finally took off. Oh, well, that's the kind of thing that happened on last-minute trips. It wasn't as if she was in a hurry to get anywhere.

She leaned back on the couch, shut her eyes, and allowed the unease to come to her. She had suppressed it during all those hot days in Turkey, focusing on absorbing the Asian sounds, the light, and the smells. She had eaten well, salads and kabobs, and she'd drunk wine with her lunch. Now she felt her stomach tighten and her throat constrict. When she tried to visualize her future, she saw nothing. Blank. White. Empty. No contours.

I have to forget, she thought. It begins now.

Annika fell asleep on the couch but woke up after ten minutes, freezing in her wet clothes.

She undressed and sprinted down to the communal bathroom in the basement.

When she returned upstairs, she tiptoed into the kitchen and popped her head around the door to Patricia's room. No one was in. It was both disconcerting and surprising. On her way back to Stockholm, she'd been annoyed at the thought of Patricia's being there. But she'd been wrong to think she wanted to be alone. The absence of her black mane on the pillow filled her with a sense of loss; it wasn't a good feeling.

She restlessly paced the apartment, from one room to another. She made coffee that she couldn't drink. She emptied out her wet clothes on the floor, then draped them over chairs and on door handles. The rooms filled with a sour, damp smell, so she opened a window.

Now what? she thought.

What am I going to do with my life?

How am I going to make a living?

She slumped back down on the couch. Her tiredness squeezed into a small lump of anxiety just beneath her breastbone. She had difficulty breathing. The curtain in front of the open window rose and billowed into the room, then sank back down again. Annika noticed that the floor next to the window was getting wet and got up to wipe it dry.

The building's going to be renovated, she suddenly thought to herself. It doesn't matter. It's pointless. Nobody cares if the floor is ruined. Why make the effort?

The realization that this was somehow emblematic of her own situation filled her with oceans of self-pity. She sank back down on the couch. She pulled her knees up to her chin and rocked back and forth crying. She was clutching her arms so tightly round her legs that they ached.

It's all over, she thought. Where can I go? Who'll help me now?

The realization, clear as crystal, hit her.

Grandma.

She dialed the number and with closed eyes prayed that her grandmother would be in her apartment and not out at Lyckebo.

"Sofia Hällström," the old woman answered.

"Oh, Grandma!" Annika was crying.

"Dearest little girl, what's wrong?"

The woman sounded so frightened that Annika forced herself to stop crying. "I feel so lonely and miserable."

Her grandmother sighed. "Life's like that. Sometimes it really is a struggle. The main thing is to not give up. Do you hear that?"

"But what's the point?" Annika said, on the verge of breaking out in tears again.

The old woman's voice sounded a bit tired. "Loneliness is difficult. People can't manage without their tribe. You've been expelled from the set you wanted to belong to, it's cut the ground from under your feet. No wonder, Annika. It would be stranger if you were all right. Allow yourself to feel bad and you can take care of yourself."

Annika wiped her face with the back of her hand. "I just want to die."

"I know, but you won't. You're going to live so that you can put me in the earth when that day comes."

"What are you saying?" Annika whispered down the phone. "Are you ill? You mustn't ever die!"

The woman chuckled. "No, I'm not ill, but we're all going to die.

And you're going to take care of yourself and not do anything rash, my dear. Take it easy and allow the pain to come to you. You can outrun it for a while, but it will always catch up to you. Let it wash over you, feel it, live it. You won't die. You'll survive, and when you come out on the other side, you'll be a stronger person. Older and wiser."

Annika smiled. "Like you, Grandma."

The woman laughed. "Have a cup of cocoa, Annika. Curl up on the couch and watch one of those TV shows, that's what I do when things feel difficult. Put a rug over your legs, you have to be warm and comfy. Everything will be all right, you'll see."

They fell silent and Annika realized how selfish she was being.

"How are things with you?" she asked quickly.

"Well, it's been raining every day since you left. I only came here to do some shopping and do the washing, so you were lucky to catch me."

There is a God, Annika thought.

"I've talked to Ingegerd and she tells me Harpsund has been very busy," her grandmother said in her gossipy tone of voice.

Annika smiled. "And how's the prime minister's slimming plan coming along?"

"Not at all, it's been postponed indefinitely. Others have been there who've been a lot less hungry."

Her grandmother's gossip with the new housekeeper at Harpsund didn't really interest Annika, but she wanted to be polite. "Oh, who's that then?"

"The minister that resigned, Christer Lundgren. He arrived the day before it was announced and stayed for a week. Every journalist in the country was looking for him, but no one found him."

Annika laughed. "The things you know! You've been at the center of things, haven't you!"

They both laughed and Annika could feel the lump in her chest slowly dissolving and trickling away.

"Thanks, Grandma," she said in a low voice.

"Just come here to me if things get too difficult. Whiskas misses you."

"He does not. Not the way you spoil him. Give him a big kiss from me."

The warmth that came when she thought of her grandmother lin-

gered after they hung up; still, the tears began trickling down again—
sad but not desperate, heavy yet lighter.

When the phone rang again, the shrill signal made her jump.

"So you're back? Jesus, you've been gone for a long time. How
was it?"

Annika wiped her face with the back of her hand. "It was great.
Turkey is amazing."

"Glad to hear it," Anne Snapphane said. "Maybe I should go.
What's the medical service like?"

Annika couldn't hold back her laughter, it just bubbled up and over
before she had time to think. "They've got special clinics for hypochon-
driacs. X-ray treatment for breakfast, Prozac with your lunch, and an-
tibiotics for dinner."

"Sounds good, but what's the radon emanation in the buildings
like? Where did you end up?"

Annika laughed again. "In a half-built resort ten miles outside of
Alanya, full of Germans. I went up to Istanbul and stayed with a woman
I met on the bus and worked for a week in her hotel. Then I moved on to
Ankara, which is a lot more modern." A peaceful feeling spread over her
body, making her legs feel soft and relaxed.

"Where did you stay?"

"I arrived late at night and the bus station was pretty chaotic. I just
jumped into the first taxi I saw and said, 'Hotel International.' And there
was one, with really nice staff."

"And you stayed in a suite even though you only paid for a single
room?"

"How did you know?"

Anne laughed. "You were born lucky. You know that."

They both laughed. They had a real affinity. The silence that followed was warm and light.

"Have you left yet?" Annika wondered.

"Yep, I quit yesterday. My TV job starts on the twelfth with some
kind of fall kickoff. What about you, what are you going to do?"

Annika heaved a sigh. The lump became tangible again. "I don't
know, I haven't got that far yet. I could always work in the hotel in Istanbul."

"Come with me to Piteå. I'm flying up this afternoon."

"No thanks, I've spent the last twenty-four hours in planes."

"So you're used to it then. Come with me! Have you ever been north of the Klar River?"

"I haven't even unpacked."

"Even better. My parents have a huge house in Pitholm, so there's plenty of room for you. And you could always go back home tomorrow if you want to."

Annika looked at the depressing heap of wet clothes and made her mind up. "So there are seats available?"

After hanging up, Annika rushed to her bedroom, found her old work carryall, and threw in two pairs of panties and a T-shirt. She picked up her toilet bag from the living-room floor.

Before she went to meet Anne on Kungsholms Square, she got a rag and wiped the floor under the window.

Disappointed, Annika looked around. "Where are the mountains?"

"Don't be such a Stockholmer," Anne told her. "We're on the coast. The Riviera of the North. Come on, the airport taxis are over there."

The crossed the tarmac surrounding Kallax Airport. Annika's eyes took in the surroundings—mostly fir trees, flat land. The sky was almost clear and the sun was shining. It was quite cold, at least for someone just back from Turkey. A fighter plane roared past above their heads.

"Air Force Base Twenty-one," Anne said, and threw her bags in the trunk of the taxi. "Kallax doubles as a military air base. I learned to parachute here."

Annika kept her bag on her lap. Two men in suits squeezed into the car before they set off for Piteå.

They drove past small villages and little patches of tilled land, but the E4 road they traveled along was mostly surrounded by forest. The leaves were blazing in radiant autumnal colors even though it was only the beginning of September.

"When does the winter start up here?" Annika wondered.

"I passed my driving test on the seventh of October. Two days later there was a blizzard. I drove straight into a ditch."

They stopped at the turning to Norrfjärden to drop off one of the suits.

Twenty minutes later, Annika and Anne got out at the bus station in Piteå.

They put Anne's bags in a left-luggage locker inside the waiting room.

"Dad will pick us up in an hour. Do you want to go for a cup of coffee?"

At Ekbergs Café, Annika had a prawn sandwich. She'd got her appetite back.

"This was a great idea," she said.

"Haven't you had any withdrawal symptoms?" Anne wondered.

Annika looked up in surprise. "From what?"

"Life. The news. The minister."

Annika cut a large piece from her prawn sandwich. "I don't give a damn about any of that," she said morosely.

"Don't you want to know what's been happening?"

Annika shook her head and chewed frenetically.

"Okay," Anne said. "Why do you spell Bengtzon with a z?"

Annika shrugged. "I don't know, actually. My great-great-grandfather Gottfried came to Hälleforsnäs at the end of the 1850s. Lasse Celsing, the ironworks proprietor, had installed a new stamping machine, and my ancestor was in charge of it. A cousin of mine tried to do some genealogical research, but he didn't get very far. He came to a stop on Gottfried. Nobody knows where he came from—he may have been German or Czech. He entered himself on the list as Bengtzon."

Anne took a big bite from her marzipan cake. "What about your mom?"

"She's from Hälleforsnäs's oldest family of foundry men. I've practically got the blast furnace stamped on my forehead. What about you? How can you be called Snapphane and come from Lapland?"

Anne groaned and licked her spoon. "Like I said, this is the coast. Everybody up here, apart from the Sami, come from somewhere else. They were loggers, railway laborers, Walloons, and other drifters. According to the family legend, Snapphane was first used as a term of abuse for a light-fingered Danish ancestor who was hanged for theft on the gallows hill outside Norrfjärden sometime in the eighteenth century. As a warning to others, his kids were also called Snapphane, and they didn't do very well either. A furnace on your forehead, well, I wish! My family crest has a gallows at the center."

Annika smiled and licked up the last dollop of mayonnaise. "Good story."

"There's probably not a word of truth in it. Shall we go?"

Anne's father was called Hans. He seemed genuinely pleased to meet one of Anne's colleagues from Stockholm.

"There's so much to see here," he said with great enthusiasm while his Volvo cruised slowly down Sundsgatan. "There's Storfors, the Elias Cave, the Böleby Tannery, Grans Farm Museum. There's Altersbruk, the old ironworks with a pond and a mill—"

"Come off it, Dad," Anne said, a bit embarrassed. "Annika is here to see me. You sound like a tour guide."

Hans wasn't put out. "Just let me know if you want to go anyplace, and I'll give you a ride," he said cheerfully, and looked at Annika in the rearview mirror.

Annika nodded and then turned her gaze out through the window. She glimpsed a narrow canal and they suddenly left the town center.

Piteå. That's where he lived—the man who had called Creepy Calls on the same day that *Studio 69* revealed that Christer Lundgren had visited a strip club. Wasn't he married to the minister's cousin?

She instinctively fished around in her bag. Her notepad was still there and she opened it toward the back.

"Roger Sundström," she read out, "from Piteå. Do you know anyone by that name?"

Anne's father turned left in a traffic circle and thought out loud. "Sundström . . . Roger Sundström—what does he do?"

"I don't know." Annika turned the pages over. "Here we are, his wife's called Britt-Inger."

"Everybody's wife is called Britt-Inger up here," Hans said. "Sorry, can't help you there."

"Why are you asking?" Anne wondered.

"I got a weird tip-off about the minister for foreign trade on the eve of his resignation from a Roger Sundström in Piteå."

"And I know someone who doesn't give a damn about journalism anymore," Anne said in a sugary voice.

Annika shoved the pad into her bag and put it on the floor. "So do I."

Anne's parents' house was on Oli-Jans Street in Pitholm. It was spacious and modern.

"You girls get settled upstairs," Anne's father said. "I'll fix some dinner. Britt-Inger is working tonight."

Annika gave a look of surprise. "Mom. He wasn't joking."

The upper floor was open and bright. On the left, by a window, was a desk with a computer, a printer, and a scanner. On the right were two guest rooms. They took one each.

While Hans cooked dinner, they went over Anne's old record collection that still stood in the hi-fi bench in the living room.

"Jesus, you've got this?" Annika said in amazement, pulling out Jim Steinman's solo album *Bad for Good.*

"It's a collector's item," Anne said.

"I've never met anyone who's ever heard this record. Apart from me."

"It's fantastic. Did you know he used material from this for both his Meat Loaf productions and *Streets of Fire*?"

"Yep," Annika said, scrutinizing the record cover. "The hook from the title song went into 'Nowhere Fast' in the movie."

"Yeah, and 'Love and Death and an American Guitar' is an intro on Meat Loaf's *Back into Hell,* except it's called 'Wasted Youth.' "

"Genuinely awesome," Annika said.

"Godlike."

They sat in silence for a moment, reflecting on Jim Steinman's greatness.

"Have you got his Bonnie Tyler productions?" Annika wondered.

"Sure. Which one do you want? *Secret Dreams and Forbidden Fire*?"

Anne placed the pickup on the vinyl and they both sang along.

Hans came in and turned the volume down. "This is a built-up area," he said. "Have you ever eaten *palt*?"

"Nope." Annika had never fancied the idea of bread baked with blood and rye flour.

It was fried and tasted quite good, a bit like potato dumplings.

"Do you want to go see a movie?" Anne said when the dishwasher started rumbling.

"Is there a movie theater here?" Annika wouldn't have thought there would be.

Anne gave her father an inquiring look. "Are there any theaters still open?"

"Sorry, I don't know."

"Do you have a phone directory?" Annika asked.

"Upstairs, by the computer," Hans replied.

After she looked for a movie theater, Annika thought she might as well look up Roger Sundström. Why not? There were two, one whose wife was called Britt-Inger. They lived on Solandergatan.

"Djupviken," Anne told her. "Other side of town."

"Do you want to go for a walk?" Annika said.

The sun was going down behind the pulp mill. They walked through Strömnäs and crossed over the Nolia area behind the People's Palace. The Sundström family lived in a sixties yellow-brick bungalow with a basement. Annika could hear children singing.

"Do whatever you want," Anne said. "I'm just coming along for the ride."

Annika rang the doorbell; Roger Sundström was in. The man was surprised when Annika introduced herself, and then he became suspicious.

"I couldn't stop thinking about what you told me," Annika said. "Now I'm here in Piteå, visiting my friend Anne, and I thought I'd just drop by."

The children, a boy and a girl, came rushing into the hallway and hid behind their father's legs, filled with curiosity.

"You go and put on your pajamas," the man said, and tried to shoo them into a room on the left.

"Are we going to sing later, Dad?"

"Yeah, yeah, and brush your teeth."

"Can we come in for a minute?"

The man hesitated but then showed them into the living room: corner couch, glass coffee table, china ornaments in the bookcase. "Britt-Inger is at her evening class."

"Nice house you've got here," Anne said in much broader Norr-land accent than she usually spoke in.

"So what do you want?" Roger sat down in a plush armchair.

Annika sat down on the edge of the couch. "I'm sorry to intrude like this. I'm just wondering if I remember correctly. Did you fly from Arlanda with Transwede?"

The man scratched his stubble. "Yes. That's right. Would you like a cup of coffee?"

The question was tentative—he knew he should offer.

"No thanks," Anne said. "We won't stay long."

"So then you departed from Terminal Two, didn't you?" Annika said. "The small one?"

"Which one?" the man asked.

"Not the big domestic departure terminal, but one that's a bit far-ther away."

Roger nodded circumspectly. "That's right. We had to take a trans-fer bus, and we had to carry our luggage all the way, because it had to go through customs in Stockholm."

Annika nodded. "Exactly! And it was there, at that small terminal, that you and Britt-Inger saw the minister?"

Roger thought about it. "Yes, it must have been there. Because we were checking in."

Annika swallowed. "I know this may be difficult, but do you re-member which gate you left from?"

He shook his head. "No idea."

Annika sighed inwardly. Oh, well, it was a long shot.

"Although," the man said, "we let the kids ride on top of the bag-gage trolley and that was a sight. I think Britt-Inger filmed it. Maybe you can see it on the videotape."

Annika opened her eyes wide. "For real?"

"Let's have a look." The man went over to the bookcase. He opened the doors to the cocktail cabinet and started looking through the tapes.

"Majorca, here we are." He pushed the tape into a VCR and started the video. The picture flickered—the kids playing by a pool. The sun must have been high as the shadows were short. Two hairy legs, probably Roger's, appeared on the left. The text in the corner read July 24, 2:27 P.M.

"Is that clock right?" Annika wondered.

"I think so. I'll fast-forward it a bit."

A blond, sleeping woman on an airplane, her chin slack. The date had jumped forward to July 27, 4:53 P.M. "My wife."

And then a tanned, smiling Roger was pushing a trolley fully loaded with both luggage and children, July 27, 7:43 P.M. The boy was standing up, holding on to the handle of the trolley; the girl sat on top of the suitcases. Both were waving at their mother behind the camera. The picture wobbled a bit as the camera swept across the hall.

"There!" Annika yelled. "Did you see? Sixty-four!"

"What?" Roger said.

"Rewind a bit," Annika said. "Have you got freeze-frame?"

Roger pressed on the remote control buttons.

"Too much," Anne said. "How did you manage to see that?"

"I was there today, and I was thinking about this," Annika said. "Go on, maybe there's more."

A bunch of people were suddenly jostling in front of the camera. Someone knocked the camera and then Roger was back in the picture.

"Christer!" he called out on-screen, lifting his hand and waving.

On-screen Roger stood on tiptoe, looked to his left, toward his wife, and talked into the living room. "Did you see him? It was Anna-Lena's Christer! He must be on our flight."

"Why don't you go over and say hello?" an invisible woman's voice said.

Roger turned around, and Annika saw people moving to the side, and in the distance, albeit out of focus, she saw Christer Lundgren running toward a gate. It was the former minister for foreign trade, without a doubt.

"Do you see?" Annika yelled out. "He's holding a ticket! He *is* boarding a plane."

On-screen Roger lost the minister in the crowd, looked in another direction, and called out, "Christer!" and then the screen went black. The picture jumped as the tape was beginning to rewind.

Annika felt a violent wave of adrenaline sweeping through her. "No wonder you didn't see him on the plane. Christer Lundgren took the flight from gate sixty-five, not sixty-four."

"Where was it going?" a confused Anne asked.

"That's what we're going to find out," Annika said. "Thank you so much for letting us disturb you, Roger."

She gave his hand a quick squeeze and hurried outside.

"What did I tell you?" she shouted with joy once they were outside. "I'll be damned! He *did* go somewhere that night. But he can't say where!" She performed a short war dance in the street.

"We know where he was," Anne said wryly. "He was at a sex club."

"No, he wasn't. He made a trip somewhere and the destination is top secret." Annika did a pirouette. "It's so damn secret that he'd rather be accused of murder and resign."

"Rather than what?"

Annika stopped. "Tell the truth."

NINETEEN YEARS, FOUR MONTHS, AND SEVEN DAYS

I have to decide what's important. I have to arrive at a conclusion about what I am. Do I exist, other than through him? Do I breathe, except through his mouth? Do I think, outside of his world?

I have tried talking to him about it. His logic is plain and lucid.

Do I exist, he asks, other than through you? Do I live—without you? he asks. Can I love without your love?

Then he gives me the answer.

No.

He needs me. He can't live without me. Never leave me, he says. We are the most important thing there is to each other.

He says
he will never
let me go.

I've been alone for a long time.

TUESDAY 4 SEPTEMBER

Patricia had slept for a few hours when she woke up with a vague sense of unease. She sat up on her mattress, brushed her hair from her face, saw the man, and screamed.

"Who are you?" the guy in the doorway asked. He was crouching and looked at her as if he'd been there for a while.

Patricia pulled up the cover to her chin and backed up against the wall. "Who are *you*?"

"I'm Sven. Where's Annika?"

Patricia swallowed and tried to get a grip on the situation. "I . . . she . . . I don't know."

"Didn't she get back from her holiday yesterday?"

Patricia cleared her throat. "Yes . . . Yes, I think so. Her clothes had been hung out to dry when I got home."

"Home?"

She looked down. "Annika said I could stay here for a while. I was sharing with a friend who . . . I didn't see her yesterday. I don't know where she is. She didn't come home last night."

The words hung in the air, pulsating. Patricia was hit by a monstrous feeling of déjà vu.

"Where do you think she is now?"

She had heard that question before; the whole room spun, and she gave the same answer now as then. "Don't know, maybe she's gone shopping, maybe she's with you . . ."

The guy gave her a searching look. "And you don't know when she'll be back?"

She shook her head, tears burning behind her eyelids.

Sven stood up. "Well, we've established who I am and what I want. Who the hell are you?"

She swallowed. "I'm Patricia. I got to know Annika when she worked at *Kvällspressen*. She said I could stay here awhile."

The man looked at her closely; she pressed the cover tighter against her chin.

"So you're a journalist too? What do you write about? Have you known her long?"

The unease sent shivers up and down her spine. She had answered so many questions, had been held responsible for so much that had nothing to do with her.

The man moved a few steps closer so that he stood right above her. "Annika hasn't been herself lately. She thought she'd make some kind of career here in the big city, but it was a nonstarter. Was it you who got her into all this?"

The words flashed through Patricia's mind and she yelled straight back at him, "I didn't get anyone into anything! No way." She glared up at the man, who started back.

"Annika will be moving to Hälleforsnäs soon. I hope you've got somewhere else to go then. I'll be staying here a few days. Tell her I'll be back tonight."

Patricia heard him walk out of the apartment, the front door shutting. A whimper rose in her mouth; she curled up in a small, hard ball, clutching her hands tightly, desperately.

Hans Snapphane was having coffee and reading the local newspaper when Annika padded into the kitchen.

"There are some boiled eggs on the stove," he said.

Annika fished one out and ran cold water over it.

"My daughter is still asleep, I imagine?"

Annika nodded and smiled. "She's worked hard for a long time."

"I'm glad she got away from there. That place did her no good. This new TV job seems to have decent hours. There are more women in management too."

Annika glanced at him furtively; he seemed to have a brain.

"Could I use your phone to make a few calls?" she asked as he got up and grabbed his briefcase.

"Sure, but go easy on Jim Steinman for a while, will you? Britt-Inger's working late again tonight."

He waved to her from the car as he drove off.

Annika gobbled down the egg and sprinted upstairs. She began by phoning the Civil Aviation Administration flight information at Arlanda.

"Hello, I was wondering if you could help me with something. I need to know when a particular flight departed."

"Sure," the customer service man said. "Which one?"

"It's a bit complicated. I only know which gate it left from."

"That's no problem—if it was today or yesterday, that is."

"Oh . . . No, it wasn't. Is it impossible to find out?"

"Have you got the time of departure? We can see the flights one day back and six days ahead."

Annika's heart sank. "This was five weeks ago."

"And all you have is the gate number? That makes it a bit tricky. I can't check that far back, I'm afraid."

"Don't you have timetables?"

"You'd have to get in touch with the airline. What's it about? Is it an insurance matter?"

"No, not at all."

They fell silent.

"Well," the man said, "you'd have to contact the airline."

She sighed. "I don't know which airline it was," she said glumly. "Which airlines fly out of Terminal Two?"

The man listed them. "Maersk Air, a Danish company that runs services to Jutland, among other places; Sabena to Brussels; Alitalia; Delta to the U.S.; Estonian Air; Austrian Airlines; and Finnair."

Annika jotted down the names of the airlines. "And do they all fly from all gates by turns?"

"Not really. The international flights usually use gates sixty-five to sixty-eight. Seventy to seventy-three are on the floor below for bus transfers."

"Gate sixty-five is international?"

"Yes. Customs and the security checkpoint are inside."

"And sixty-four, what kind of gate is that?"

"Mostly domestic. The gates are in pairs. But that can be altered by moving the doors about in a certain way—"

"Thanks a lot for your help," Annika said quickly, and rang off.

International indeed . . . Christer Lundgren traveled abroad on the night of the twenty-seventh of July and returned just after five in the morning on the twenty-eighth.

"So he didn't go to the U.S.," Annika said out loud, crossing out Delta Airlines.

He could have flown to Jutland, Finland, Brussels, Tallinn, and Vienna and back. The distances were short enough for it to be possible. Italy was more unlikely.

The question was, however, how did he get home in the middle of the night? It must have been a damned important meeting. It must have taken some time as well.

She counted on her fingers.

Say he left at 20:00; so wherever he was going, he wouldn't get there and clear customs before 21:30. Then he probably had to get somewhere in a taxi or a car, unless the meeting took place at the airport.

Suppose 22:00 was the time of the meeting. And suppose it finished at 23:00. Back to the airport, check in—he couldn't have been on a return flight before midnight.

There can't be that many scheduled flights at that time of the night, not with these airlines. And what was Maersk Air?

She sighed.

He could have got home some other way, she thought—by car or boat. That would exclude Vienna, Brussels, and anywhere in Italy.

She looked down at her pad; that left Jutland, Finland, and Tallinn. She looked up Finnair's ticket office in the phone book, dialed the toll-free number, and got the company's call center in Helsinki.

"No," said the friendly voice of a man who sounded like the Moomin Troll in Tove Jansson's children stories, "I can't check data like that on my computer. Did you say you don't have a flight number? If you did, I could check back."

Annika closed her eyes and rubbed her forehead with her hand. "Which cities do you fly to from Stockholm?"

The man tapped on his computer. "Helsinki, of course. And Oslo, Copenhagen, Vienna, Berlin, and London."

Dead end. It was impossible to check this way where the plane went.

"One last question. When does the last flight to Stockholm leave?"

"From Helsinki? It leaves at twenty-one forty-five and arrives at twenty-one forty in Stockholm. You're one hour behind us."

She thanked him and rang off.

He must have got home some other way than on a regular flight. Private plane, she thought. He could have chartered a plane to return on.

It costs a lot of money, she thought, remembering the uproar surrounding the prime minister's private flights. You have to pay for a chartered plane, and she didn't think Christer Lundgren would do that out of his own pocket. It would be against his religion.

She raised her eyes and looked out of the window in Hans Snapphane's study. To the right she saw the most common house type in Piteå, a red, seventies, prefab bungalow. Straight ahead, on the other side of the street, was a larger white-brick house with brown-stained paneling, and in the distance a stretch of woodland.

There has to be an invoice somewhere. Regardless of how he got home, the former minister for foreign trade must surely have invoiced his travel expenses to some department or government office.

It struck her that she didn't even know to which department foreign trade belonged.

She went into Anne and woke her up.

"I've got to go back to Stockholm," Annika told her. "I've got a lot to do."

Anne wasn't surprised at Annika's reawakened enthusiasm for her job. She helped Annika make the return arrangements. Back in Stockholm, Annika went straight from City Terminal to the Ministry for Foreign Affairs in Gustav Adolfs Square. But the pink-and-yellow building was surrounded by shiny, dark cars. Important men stood around watchfully, and pensioners with cameras were dotted here and there. The people made her uneasy as she approached the entrance. A large black vehicle with a ridiculous registration plate in the form of a crown blocked the entrance. When she'd walked around it, an obese security guard in olive drab uniform blocked her way.

"Where are you going?"

"Inside," Annika replied.

"We've got enough reporters as it is."

Shit, Annika thought. "But I'm going to the registrar."

"Then you'll have to wait," the guard said, and with a peremptory gesture crossed his hands over his crotch.

Annika didn't move. "Why's that?"

The guard's gaze shifted slightly. "State visit. The president of South Africa is here."

"No shit?" Annika said, and realized how far out of the news loop she was already.

"Come back after three o'clock."

Annika turned on her heel and walked away across Norrbro. She looked at her watch. She had over an hour to kill. The rain had stopped, so she decided to take a quick walk up to South Island. She had run regularly in Turkey, feeling the need and enjoying the calm that returned to her body. Now she walked fast and vigorously through Old Town and over to the steps around Mosebacke Square. With her bag across her chest, she ran up and down the steps until her pulse was beating fast and she was dripping with sweat. She paused at the top of Klevgränd and looked out over Stockholm: the narrow alleys cutting in between the Skeppsbro facades; the white hull of the *af Chapman* sparkling in the water; the light-blue roller coaster of Gröna Lund, resting against the green foliage like a tangled ball of yarn.

I really have got to find a way to stay here, she thought.

By five to three, all the cars in front of the Arvfurstens Palace were gone.

"I'd like to know something about how the cabinet ministers arrange their travels," Annika said politely to the Foreign Ministry lady behind the counter. Annika felt a bead of perspiration run along the root of her nose and quickly wiped it off.

The woman raised her eyebrows slightly. "Oh," she said in a disdainful tone of voice. "And may I ask who's asking?"

Annika smiled. "I'm not obliged to prove my identity. You don't even have the right to ask me. But you *are* obliged to answer my questions."

The woman stiffened.

"So what happens when a cabinet minister wants to travel?" Annika asked in her silkiest voice.

The woman's voice was frosty around the edges. "The minister's assistant books the tickets through the agency that has the government contract. At present Nyman and Schultz has that remit."

"Do the ministers have their own travel budgets?"

The woman sighed soundlessly. "Yes, naturally."

"Right. Then I'd like to make a request to look at an official document. An invoice with a credit card slip handed in by the former minister for foreign trade Christer Lundgren on the twenty-eighth of July this year."

The woman could barely conceal her delight. "No, that will not be possible."

"Oh, no? Why not?"

"Because the minister for foreign trade falls under the Ministry of Industry, Employment, and Communications, not the Ministry of Foreign Affairs, which he or she did until the current prime minister took over. The prime minister transferred questions concerning the promotion of export trade from the Ministry of Foreign Affairs to the Ministry of Industry, Employment, and Communications. The Ministry of Foreign Affairs got asylum and immigration matters instead."

Annika blinked. "So the minister for foreign trade doesn't hand in his invoices here at all?"

"No, not at all."

"Not for entertainment expenses or anything?"

"No."

Annika was at a loss. The studio reporter on *Studio 69* had claimed they'd found the receipt from the strip joint at the Ministry of Foreign Affairs, she was absolutely sure of that. The entire program resonated like a stubborn tune in her head, whether she wanted it to or not.

"Where is the Ministry of Industry, Employment, and Communications?"

Annika got the directions and walked past the Museum of Mediterranean and Near East Antiquities to 8 Fredsgatan. She found the equivalent civil servant and asked, "A traveling-expenses invoice and an entertainment invoice from July twenty-eighth this year. Will it take long?"

The registry clerk was a friendly and efficient woman. "No, it won't take long. Come back in an hour and we'll have it ready for you. But don't come any later, as we'll be closed."

Annika went up to Drottninggatan and had a look around. There was a light drizzle, and a mass of black clouds behind the Parliament building signaled heavier rain later in the evening. She strolled around, indifferently looking at the music, posters, and cheap clothes on offer. It was all beyond her, she was flat broke. The impulsive flight up to Piteå had cleaned her out.

She walked down the mall toward Klarabergsgatan. She went into a vile American coffee place and ordered ice water. They wanted five kronor for a glass of tap water. Annika swallowed her cutting remark and dug into her pocket. The rain had gotten heavier and it was worth spending the money to avoid getting soaked.

She sat down at the bar and had a look around. The café was full of trendy people with their cappuccinos and espressos. Annika took a sip of water and chewed on an ice cube.

So far she'd resisted the thought, but now it was inescapable. By resigning voluntarily from *Katrineholms-Kuriren,* she wasn't getting any unemployment benefits for a month and no more money was coming in from *Kvällspressen.*

But my expenses aren't that high, she thought. She began listing them.

Her rent was only 1,970 kronor a month, and now she had a roommate. Food didn't have to be that much, she could eat pasta. She didn't need a monthly travel ticket. She could buy reduced-rate tickets, walk or sneak in on the subway. She had to have a telephone, that was a priority. Forgoing clothes and makeup was no big sacrifice, at least not for a while.

I need a part-time job, she thought.

"Is this chair taken?"

A guy with two-tone hair and wearing mascara was standing in front of her.

"No, go ahead," Annika mumbled.

She took the opportunity to go to the bathroom. That didn't cost anything.

Fifty minutes later she was back at the office in Fredsgatan. The registry clerk went inside to collect the papers. She returned with a concerned look on her face.

"I couldn't find any travel-expenses invoices for that date, but here's the entertainment invoice."

She gave Annika a copy of the invoice. The receipt from Studio 69 was for 55,600 kronor and was specified as "entertainment and refreshments."

"Jesus," Annika said.

"I think they may have trouble getting that past the auditors," the clerk said without looking up.

"Have a lot of people asked to see this?"

The woman hesitated. "Not that many, actually." She looked up. "We thought a lot would, but so far only a handful have asked for it."

"But there's no travel-expenses invoice?"

The woman shook her head. "I checked both the preceding and the following weeks."

Annika thought a moment. She looked at the sprawling signature on the credit card slip. "Could he have handed in his travel-expenses invoice at another ministry?"

"The minister for foreign trade? I doubt it. It would still end up here."

"What about some other public authority? He travels a lot, lobbying for different organizations and companies, doesn't he?"

"Well, I suppose. Maybe the companies pay. I don't know."

Annika persisted. "But if he was traveling on behalf of the government and the invoices weren't handed in here, then where?"

The woman's phone rang. Annika noticed her tense up.

"I'm sorry, I honestly don't know," the woman said. "Keep the copy, it's on me."

Annika thanked her and left the woman to answer the call.

The apartment was quiet and still. She went straight to Patricia's room and peeped in.

"Annika!"

To her surprise, Patricia sounded frightened, and she entered the room.

"What is it?" Annika smiled.

Patricia jumped up, threw herself around Annika's neck, and cried.

"Jesus, what's wrong?" Annika said worriedly. "Has something happened?"

Patricia's hair got tangled up in her eyelashes, and she carefully tried to remove it so that she could see.

"You didn't come home. You didn't spend the night at home, and your boyfriend came here and asked where you were. I thought . . . something had happened."

Annika stroked Patricia's hair tenderly. "Silly. What would happen to me?"

Patricia let go of Annika and wiped her nose on her T-shirt. "I don't know," she whispered.

"I'm not Josefin," Annika said, smiling. "You don't need to worry yourself over me." She had to laugh. "Come on, Patricia, snap out of it! You're worse than my mom. Do you want some coffee?"

Patricia nodded and Annika went out into the kitchen.

"Toast?"

"Yes, please."

Annika set out evening coffee while Patricia put on a sweat suit. The mood at the table was a bit quiet.

"I'm sorry," Patricia said, spreading marmalade on a piece of toast.

"Don't worry. You're just a bit on edge, that's all."

They ate in silence.

"Are you moving out?" Patricia asked timidly after a while.

"Not right now. Why?"

Patricia shrugged. "Just wondering . . ."

Annika poured more coffee. "Has there been much in the papers about Josefin while I've been away?" She blew at the hot drink.

Patricia shook her head. "Hardly anything. The police say that suspicions point in one direction but that they won't be arresting anyone. Not at the moment, at least."

"And everybody's interpretation is that the minister is guilty?"

"Something like that."

"Have they written a lot about him?"

"Even less. It's as if he died rather than resigned."

Annika sighed. "Never kick a man when he's down."

"What?"

"That's how they reason—you stop digging when someone accepts the consequences of his actions and resigns. What else have they been writing about while I was gone?"

"They said on *Rapport* that the voters are abandoning the polls. A lot of people don't want to vote because they lack faith in the politicians. It's possible the Social Democrats will lose the election."

Annika nodded, it made sense. A minister suspected of murder in the middle of an election campaign was a nightmare.

Patricia wiped her fingers on a piece of paper towel and began clearing the table.

"Have you spoken to the police lately?"

Patricia stiffened. "No," she said.

"Do they know you're here?"

The woman got up and went over to the counter. "I don't think so."

Annika also got up. "Perhaps you should tell them. They might want to talk to you about something, and no one at the club knows you're staying here, right?"

"Please don't tell me what to do," Patricia replied curtly.

She turned her back and put a pan on the stove to heat water for the dishes.

Annika went back to the table and for a while sat watching the woman's back.

Well, go ahead and sulk, she thought, and went into her room.

The rain rattled hysterically on the windowsill. Will it never stop? Annika thought, and sank down on her bed. She lay on top of the bed without switching on the light. The room was dark and gray. She stared at the worn wallpaper, yellowed with a gray pattern.

It all has to come together somehow, she thought. Something happened just before the twenty-seventh of July that made the minister for foreign trade take a flight from Terminal 2 at Arlanda, so jittery and stressed-out that he didn't even notice his relatives calling out to him. Or he ignored them. The Social Democrats must have been in a real panic.

But it could have been something private, Annika suddenly realized. Maybe he wasn't on a government or party errand at all. Maybe he had a mistress somewhere.

Could it be that simple?

Then she remembered her grandmother.

Harpsund, she thought. If Christer Lundgren had committed a private indiscretion, the prime minister would never have let him use his summer residence as a hiding place. It had to be something political.

She stretched out on her back, put her hands behind her head, took a deep breath, and closed her eyes. She heard the clatter of the crockery; Patricia was puttering about in the kitchen.

Structure, she mused. Sort through what you've got. Start at the beginning. Toss out everything that's wishful thinking—be logical. What actually did happen?

A minister resigns following suspicions of murder, and not just any murder—a sex murder in a cemetery. Suppose the man is innocent. Say he was somewhere completely different on the morning when the woman was raped and killed. Suppose he's got a watertight alibi.

Then why the hell doesn't he clear his name? His life is ruined; politically he's washed-up, socially he's poison.

There can only be one explanation, Annika thought. My first idea holds up: his alibi is even worse than the crime.

Okay, even worse—but for whom? For himself? Not likely. That would be close to impossible.

Only one alternative remains: worse for the party.

Right, so she'd reached a conclusion.

What about the rest? What could be worse for the party than having a minister suspected of murder in the middle of an election campaign?

She squirmed restlessly on the bed, turned on her side, and stared out into the room. She heard Patricia open the front door and walk down the stairs, probably to have a shower.

The realization came like a puff of wind in her brain.

Only the loss of power was worse. Christer Lundgren did something that night that would lead to the Social Democrats losing power if it came to light. It had to be something fundamental, something crucial. What could pull the rug out from under the governing party's feet?

Annika sat bolt upright. She remembered the words, played them back in her brain. She went out to the telephone in the living room, sat down on the couch with the phone on her lap. She closed her eyes, took a few deep breaths.

Anne Snapphane still talked to her even though she'd been thrown out. Berit Hamrin might also look on her as a colleague even if she'd stopped working there. If she didn't try, she'd never know.

Resolutely she dialed the number to the *Kvällspressen* switchboard. She spoke in a squeaky voice when she asked for Berit, not wanting the operator to recognize her.

"Annika, how nice to hear from you!" Berit said cordially. "How are things?"

Annika's heart slowed down.

"Thanks, I'm fine. I've been to Turkey for a couple of weeks. It was really interesting."

"Writing about the Kurds?" Berit thought like a journalist.

"No, just a vacation. Listen, I've got a couple of questions concerning IB. Do you have time to meet up for a chat?"

If Berit was surprised, she wasn't letting it show. "Yes, sure. When?"

"What are you doing tonight?"

They agreed to meet at the pizzeria near the paper in half an hour's time.

Patricia came back in, dressed in her sweat suit and with her hair wrapped in a towel.

"I'm going out for a while." Annika got to her feet.

"I forgot to tell you something. Sven said he was staying here for a few days."

Annika went over to the coatrack. "Are you working tonight?" she said as she put her coat on.

"Yeah, why?"

It was pouring rain. Annika's umbrella was twisted by the wind, so when she stumbled through the door of the restaurant, she was soaked to the skin. Berit was already there.

"How nice to see you." Berit smiled. "You're looking well."

Annika laughed and wriggled out of her wet coat. "Leaving *Kvälls-pressen* does wonders for one's health. What's it like these days?"

Berit sighed. "Bit of a mess, actually. Schyman is trying to give the paper an overhaul, but he's meeting a lot of resistance from the rest of the senior editors."

Annika shook her wet hair and pushed it back. "In what way?"

"Schyman wants to set up new routines, have regular seminars about the direction of the paper."

"I get it. The others are in an uproar, whining that he's trying to turn *Kvällspressen* into Swedish Television, right?"

Berit nodded and smiled. "Exactly."

A waiter took their insignificant order, a coffee and a mineral water. He walked away unimpressed.

"So just how badly are the Social Democrats doing in the election campaign?" Annika wondered.

"Badly. They've fallen from forty-five percent in the opinion polls last spring to below thirty-five percent."

"Because of the IB affair or the strip-club business?"

"Probably a combination of both."

Both the glass and the cup were placed on the table with unnecessary force.

"Do you remember our talk about the IB archives?" Annika said when the waiter was gone.

"Of course. Why?"

"You thought the original foreign archive still exists. What exactly makes you think that?" Annika sipped at her mineral water.

Berit gave it some thought before answering. "Several reasons. People's political affiliations had been put on a register before, during the war. The practice was forbidden after the end of the war, and much later

Minister for Defense Sven Andersson said that the wartime archives had 'disappeared.' In reality, they had been at the Defense Staff Head-quarters' archive. This was made public a few years ago."

"So the Social Democrats have lied about vanished archives be-fore."

"That's right. And then, a year or two later, Andersson said that the IB archives were destroyed back in 1969. The latest version is that they were burned just before the exposure of IB in 1973. But the destruction was never entered in any official records, either domestic or foreign."

"And if the records had been destroyed, it would have been docu-mented?"

Berit drank some of her coffee and made a face. "Yuck, this isn't ex-actly freshly made. Yes, IB was a standard Swedish bureaucratic organi-zation. There are a lot of their documents in the Defense Staff Headquarters' intelligence archive. Everything was entered in a day-book, including reports of destroyed documents. There isn't one about these archives, which probably means that they're still there."

"Anything else?"

Berit thought about it for a moment. "They've always maintained that the foreign and domestic archives were destroyed at the same time and that there are no copies. We know that at least half of that is un-true."

Annika looked closely at Berit. "How did you get the Speaker to admit to his dealings with IB?"

Berit rubbed her forehead and sighed. "The force of reason," she said coyly.

"Can you tell me?"

Berit sat in silence for a while. She put two lumps of sugar in her coffee and stirred it.

"The Speaker has always refused to admit that he knew Birger Elmér," she said in a low voice. "He claimed he hadn't even met him. But I know that's not true."

She fell silent; Annika waited.

"In the spring of 1966," Berit said at length, "the Speaker, Ingvar Carlsson, and Birger Elmér met in the Speaker's home in Nacka. The Speaker's wife was also present. They had dinner, and the conversation turned to the fact the Speaker and his wife didn't have any children.

Elmér thought the two should adopt, which they later did. I told the Speaker I knew about this meeting, and that's when he began to talk."

Annika stared at Berit. "How the hell do you know that?"

"I can't tell you. You understand."

Annika leaned back in her chair. It was mind-boggling. Jesus H. Christ! Berit had to have a source within the party leadership.

Neither woman spoke for a long time. They could hear the rain thundering outside.

"Where were the archives held before they disappeared?" Annika asked eventually.

"The domestic archive was at twenty-four Grevgatan and the foreign one at fifty-six Valhallavägen. Why do you ask?"

Annika had taken out a pen and paper and was writing down the addresses. "Maybe it wasn't the Social Democrats themselves that made sure that the archives disappeared."

"How do you mean?"

Annika didn't reply and Berit crossed her arms. "Hardly anybody knew that the archives existed, let alone where they were kept."

Annika leaned forward. "The copy of the foreign archives was found in the incoming mail at the Defense Staff Headquarters, right?"

"Right. The parcel arrived at their printing and distribution office. It was registered, entered in the daybook, and classified. The documents were not considered secret."

"What day did they arrive?"

"Seventeenth of July."

"Where did they arrive from?"

"The official record didn't say. The sender was anonymous. It could have come from any dusty government department."

"But why would they want to be anonymous in this case?"

Berit shrugged. "Maybe they found the documents deep inside an old storeroom and didn't want to admit to having them all these years."

Annika groaned, yet another dead end.

They sat in silence for a while and looked at the other customers in the restaurant. A couple of men in overalls were having an evening pizza. Two women were noisily drinking beer.

"Where were the documents when you looked at them?" Annika wondered.

"They'd just arrived at the archives."

Annika smiled. "You've got friends everywhere."

Berit returned her smile. "Always be nice to telephone operators, secretaries, registry clerks, and archivists."

Annika emptied her glass. "And there was nothing that indicated where the documents came from?"

"No. They were delivered in two big sacks."

Annika raised her eyebrows. "What do you mean, 'sacks'? Like potato sacks?"

Berit sighed lightly. "I didn't really pay much attention to what they were. I was interested in their contents. It was one of my all-time best tip-offs."

Annika smiled. "I believe you. What did the sacks look like?"

Berit looked at her for a few seconds. "Now that you mention it, there was something printed on the sacks."

"You didn't see what it said?"

Berit closed her eyes, pinched the bridge of her nose with her thumb and forefinger, and sighed, then rubbed her forehead and licked her lips.

"What?"

"It could have been a courier's bag."

"What the heck is a courier's bag?"

"Under the Vienna Convention on Diplomatic Relations, there's an article that deals with inviolability of the communication between a state and its foreign missions. Article twenty-seven, I think. The diplomatic mail is sent in a special bag that is immune to inspection. Diplomatic couriers carry the bags through customs. It could have been one of those."

Annika felt the hair on her neck stand on end. "How could it have ended up at the Defense Staff Headquarters?"

Berit shook her head. "A Swedish courier bag would never be sent there. They always travel between the Ministry for Foreign Affairs and the various embassies around the world."

"But what if it were foreign?"

Berit shook her head. "No. I think I must be mistaken. Swedish courier bags are blue with yellow lettering and it says 'Diplomatic' on them. This was gray with red lettering. I really didn't pay attention to what it said, I was trying to get an idea of how comprehensive the archive material was, whether it contained any original documents. Unfortunately there weren't any."

They were silent for a while.

Annika looked at her former colleague. "How do you know about all these things? Sections and conventions . . ."

Berit smiled at her. "You get to write about most things over the years. Some of it sticks."

Annika's gaze traveled out through the window. "But it could have been a foreign courier's bag?"

"And it could have been a potato sack."

"Can you see where this is heading?"

"Where?" Berit didn't think it was going anywhere.

"I'll tell you when I know for sure. Thanks for talking to me!"

Annika gave Berit a quick hug, opened her umbrella, and braved the rain.

NINETEEN YEARS, FOUR MONTHS, AND THIRTY DAYS

*H*e can sense the chasm like a shooting sensation in the dark; he's walking on the edge without being aware of the abyss. It's manifested in desperate demands and hard lips. He licks me and sucks until my clitoris is big as a plum, maintaining that I cry from pleasure and not pain. The swelling remains for days, rubbing when I move.

I'm groping my way. The darkness is so vast. Depression hangs like a gray dampness inside me, impossible to exhale. My tears lie just below the surface, constantly present, unreliable, harder and harder to keep in check. Reality shrinks, contracted from the pressure and the cold.

My only source of warmth is spreading icy brutality at the same time.

And he says
he will never
let me go.

You can't fucking live here. No hot water, not even a damned toilet! When are you going to come home?"

Sven was sitting in the kitchen eating yogurt, dressed only in his briefs.

"Put some clothes on," Annika said, tightening the sash around her dressing gown. "Patricia's sleeping in there."

She walked over to the stove and poured herself some coffee.

"Yeah, and what the hell is she doing here?"

"She needed a place to stay. I had a room available."

"That stove, it's lethal. You'll set fire to the entire building."

Annika sighed inwardly. "It's a gas stove, it's no more dangerous than an electric one."

"Bullshit," Sven said truculently.

Annika didn't reply, just drank her coffee in silence.

"Hey, listen," Sven said in a conciliatory voice after a couple of minutes. "Stop what you're doing and come back home. You've had a go at it here and you can see it's not working. You're not a big-time reporter, you don't belong in this city."

He got to his feet, walked behind her chair, and started massaging her shoulders.

"But I love you anyway," he whispered, leaning forward and biting her earlobe. His hands slipped down along her neck and gently cradled her breasts.

Annika got up and poured out her coffee in the sink. "I'm not coming back yet," she said warily.

Sven gave her a penetrating look. "What about your job? You're going back to *Katrineholms-Kuriren* again after the election, right?"

She drew a sharp breath and swallowed. "I've got to get going. I've got things to do."

She quickly left the kitchen and got dressed.

Sven stood in the doorway watching her while she put on a pair of jeans and a sweater. "What do you do during the day?"

"Find out about things."

"You're not seeing someone else?"

Annika's arms fell down in a gesture of resignation. "Please. Even if you think I'm a terrible journalist, there are others who think I'm okay—"

He interrupted her by taking her in his arms. "I don't think you're terrible. On the contrary—I get mad when I hear them bad-mouthing you on the radio when I know how wonderful you are."

They kissed fiercely and Sven started opening her zipper.

"No," Annika said. "I've got to get going if I'm to—"

He shut her up with a kiss and moved her down onto the bed.

The archive of the highbrow broadsheet newspaper was located next door to the entrance of *Kvällspressen*. Annika walked quickly through the door, her eyes firmly on the ground. She didn't want to bump into anyone she knew. She walked past the reception and in among the shelves. Three men were standing over by the microfilm desk and the big table. She put her bag on the small table.

Issue nine of *Folket i Bild Kulturfront*, 1973, that Berit had mentioned had come out at the beginning of May. Annika pulled out the file containing the broadsheet from April the same year and began looking through it. She had to admit it was a long shot. She tore out the note from her pad and put it in front of her.

Domestic archive, 24 Grevgatan.

Foreign archive, 56 Valhallavägen.

The newspaper pages were yellowed and torn in places. The print was tiny, no more than seven points, and hard to read. The editing was untidy. The fashion ads made her want to laugh out loud, people looked so silly in the early seventies.

But the subject matter of the articles felt surprisingly familiar. Millions of people were threatened with starvation in Africa; young people had difficulties fitting into the labor market; Lasse Hallström had made a new TV film called *Are We Going to My Place, Your Place, or Each to Our Own?*

The world ice hockey championships were in progress, it seemed, and Olof Palme had made a speech in Kungälv. Wars were being fought in Vietnam and Cambodia, and the Watergate scandal was unfolding in Washington. She sighed. Not a single line about what she was looking for.

She moved to the next file, from the April 16–30 to April 1–15.

Monday, April 2, was the same as every other. Guerrillas in Cambodia had attacked government forces in Phnom Penh. A Danish lawyer by the name of Mogens Glistrup was successful with a new one-man party called the Progressive Party. The former American attorney general John Mitchell had agreed to testify before a Senate committee. And then at the bottom left of page 17, next to the short item "Bright Aurora Borealis over Stockholm," she found it:

"Mysterious Break-In at Office Building."

Annika's pulse quickened, racing until it thudded through her head and filled the entire room.

According to the short piece, an office at 24 Grevgatan had been searched sometime during the weekend, probably Sunday night. But strangely, nothing was missing. All office equipment had been left untouched, but all cabinets and drawers had been gone through.

I know what was stolen, she thought. Good God, I know what disappeared!

She found the second item in Section 2, at the top left of page 34. An office in 56 Valhallavägen had been vandalized over the weekend. It was a short piece, squeezed in between a picture of Crown Prince Carl Gustaf, who had caught two trout in the Mörrum River, and a piece about Gullfiber AB in Billesholm closing down.

None of the paper's editors had spotted a connection between the two break-ins; maybe the police hadn't either.

She copied the two pieces and put the file back on the shelf.

I'm on the right track, she thought.

She left the archive and took the 62 bus to Hantverkargatan.

Sven had left and Patricia was still asleep. Annika sat down with her pad and the phone in the living room.

What are the areas of responsibility of the minister for foreign trade? she wrote.

Trade and export, she thought. Promoting trade with other countries. What government department would pay for such travels? *The Swedish Trade Council,* she wrote.

What *does* Sweden export? Cars. Timber. Paper. Iron ore. Electricity. Nuclear power, perhaps?

The Nuclear Power Inspectorate, she wrote.

What else? Pharmaceuticals.

The National Board of Health and Welfare, she wrote.

Electronic products. Weapons.

Weapons? Yes, the arms export was the foreign trade minister's responsibility.

The War Matériel Inspectorate, she wrote, and then looked at her list. These were the ones she could think of; there had to be lots of other departments that she didn't know of.

What is there to think about? she said to herself, and looked up the Trade Council.

The information officer wasn't available; some other woman took the call.

"We're not a public authority. You can't get any documents from us," she said curtly.

"Are you sure? Do you think you could ask the information officer to call me later?" Annika gave her name and number.

"I'll give him the message, but he'll give you the same answer."

Jerk, Annika thought.

Instead she looked up the Nuclear Power Inspectorate and noted that they were located at 90 Klarabergsviadukten. They were closed until 12:30. She couldn't find the War Matériel Inspectorate, so she called directory assistance.

"They've changed names to the National Inspectorate of Strategic Products," the operator informed her.

The registrar there was out to lunch. Annika sighed, put the pen down, and leaned back on the couch.

She might as well have something to eat.

Number 90 Klarabergsviadukten was a relatively new glass complex on the Kungsholm side of the bridge. Annika stood outside the entrance and read the list of companies and organizations housed there: the AMU Group; the National Environmental Protection Agency; the Nuclear Power Inspectorate; the Inspectorate of Strategic Products—ISP.

I can kill two birds with one stone, Annika thought.

She rang the bell for the Nuclear Power Inspectorate but got no reply. Instead she pushed the bell for the inspectorate with a new name, ISP.

"Block A, fifth floor," a hesitant voice said in the loudspeaker.

She stepped out of the elevator on the fifth floor and saw herself in numerous versions in a hall of burnished steel mirrors. There was only the one door, for the ISP. She pushed the bell.

"Who are you here to see?" The blond woman who opened the door was friendly but reserved.

Annika looked around. It seemed to be a small and informal outfit with corridors leading in two directions. There was no reception desk, and the woman who had opened the door apparently occupied the room nearest to the door.

"My name is Annika Bengtzon," Annika said nervously. "I'd like to have a look at an official document."

The woman looked concerned. "Almost ninety percent of our documents are classified," she said apologetically. "But you can always make a request, and we'll investigate whether we can hand over the document."

Annika sighed quietly. Sure. She could have figured that out for herself.

"Do you have a registrar here?"

"Yes." The woman pointed down the corridor. "She's down that way, the second door from the end."

"I don't suppose you have an archive here, do you?" Annika prepared to leave.

"Oh, yes, we do."

Annika stopped. "So travel-expenses invoices that are five, six weeks old—do you keep them here?"

"Yes, though not in the archive. I deal with the invoices. I keep them in my office so we can balance the books. I'm the one who books all trips. There are quite a lot of them, actually, as the ISP takes part in a number of international meetings."

Annika looked at the woman closely. "Are the invoices secret?"

"No. They are part of the ten percent that we do hand out."

"How often do cabinet ministers take part in these meetings?"

"To the extent that any cabinet ministers take part on behalf of the inspectorate, it's usually the Ministry for Foreign Affairs who picks up the tab."

"And what if the minister for foreign trade goes?"

"Well, then it's the Ministry for Foreign Affairs that pays."

"But he falls under the Ministry of Industry, Employment, and Communications."

"Oh, right. Well, then the invoice should be sent there."

"Would it always?"

The woman suddenly became more reticent. "Not quite always."

Annika swallowed. "I was wondering if you received any invoices from Christer Lundgren from the twenty-seventh and twenty-eighth of July this year."

The woman gave Annika a searching look. "Yes, as a matter of fact we did get one."

Annika blinked. "Could I have a look at it?"

The woman licked her lips. "I think I'd have to talk to my boss first." She backed into her office.

"Why? You told me that travel-expenses invoices were official documents."

"Yes, but this one was special."

Annika could hear her pulse thunder in her ears. "In what way?"

The woman hesitated. "Listen. When the invoices from a cabinet minister turn up on your desk, especially without any warning, it's a surprise."

"What did you do?"

The woman sighed. "I took it to my boss. He called someone at the ministry and got it cleared. I paid it about a week ago."

Annika swallowed, her mouth was completely dry. "Could I get photocopies of the receipts and tickets?"

"I really have to ask my boss first." The woman vanished into her office. A few moments later she came out and hurried down the corridor. Thirty seconds later she came back and handed Annika a sheaf of photocopies.

"Here you go." She smiled.

Annika's fingers were trembling as she accepted the documents. "Where did he go?" She leafed through the papers.

"He flew Estonian Air to Tallinn on the night of the twenty-seventh and chartered a private plane back the same night. It landed at Barkarby. The plane was Estonian. Would you like the amount converted into Swedish kronor?"

"Thanks, I'm fine."

Annika stared down at the photocopied credit card slip in her hand. It had arrived at the inspectorate already on Monday the thirtieth of July. The minister had charged the cost of the plane to his government credit card. She had expected to see the same sprawling signature as on the slip from Studio 69, but this was round and childish.

"Thank you so much." Annika smiled at the woman. "You've no idea how much this means to me."

"Don't mention it."

Her feet were beating down on the asphalt but she couldn't feel them. They were bouncing on air. She laughed giddily as she skipped along.

What a cheapskate! He had to invoice someone for his expenses right away.

She floated homeward to Hantverkargatan—she'd been right! The minister had gone away and wouldn't for the life of him say why.

The so-and-so, she thought. He's done for now.

The telephone was ringing when she opened the front door. She sprinted for it and answered all out of breath.

"I'm the information officer at the Trade Council," said a man with a cut-glass accent. "You were interested in seeing some documents."

Annika sank down onto the couch with her coat on and the bag still across her shoulder. "I was told that the council isn't a public authority and that I couldn't."

"Well, we are. Just send us a written request, and we'll enter it in the daybook and decide whether the document in question can be handed out. Some papers are classified."

Oh, really, she thought. You've changed your tune now. "Thanks a lot for phoning back."

The woman she'd first spoken to had been talking through her hat, but Annika couldn't be bothered to get irritated by the autocratic stupidity of civil servants. So many of them still didn't know that the principle of public access to official records was part of the freedom of the press law as established in the Constitution. All documents at all public authorities had to be handed over at once to someone who asked to see them, unless they had been statutorily declared secret.

Everything in the world you should do yourself, Annika thought, so you could be sure it got done properly.

She got up and hung up her coat and bag, and then she called the Cherry Company to see if she could get a job.

"We're full at the moment," said the head of personnel. "Try again in the spring."

It hit her like a brick in the back of her head. She put the phone down and swallowed. Now what was she going to do?

She got to her feet, drank some water in the kitchen, and looked in on Patricia. The woman was fast asleep with her mouth open. Annika stood watching her for a while.

Patricia knows a lot more than she's telling me, she thought. The police should know where she's staying. And she had something to tell them now.

She closed the door cautiously and went back to the phone.

Q was in. "Course I remember you. You're the one fishing for information on Josefin Liljeberg."

"I was working as a journalist then. I don't anymore."

"So," the police captain said, clearly amused, "why are you calling me now?"

"I know where Patricia can be found."

"Who?"

Annika felt stupid. "Josefin's roommate."

"Right. Where is she then?"

"With me. Sharing my apartment."

"Sounds familiar. Better be careful. Anyway, we can find her at the club. What do you want?"

"Don't be an asshole," Annika snapped. "I'd like to know what's happened in your investigation."

He laughed. "You would, would you?"

"I know the minister was in Tallinn that night. Why doesn't he want that to be made public?"

The police officer's laughter died away. "You're a devil at digging things up. How did you find out about that?"

"You knew all along, didn't you?"

"Of course we did. We know a lot of things we don't let on to the media."

"Do you know what he was doing there?"

The police officer hesitated. "Actually, we don't. It wasn't part of the investigation."

"Didn't you wonder?"

"Not really. Some politicians' meeting, I imagine."

"On a Friday night?"

They fell silent.

"I don't care what the minister was up to. All I'm interested in is the perpetrator."

"And it's not Christer Lundgren?"

"No."

"So as far as the police are concerned, the case has been cleared up, is that right?"

Q sighed. "Thanks for telling me where Patricia's staying. Not that we've missed her, but you never know."

"Couldn't you tell me something more about the investigation?" Annika pleaded.

"Then you'll have to bring me something better. Now, I've got stuff to do."

He rang off. Annika dropped down on her back on the couch and closed her eyes. She had some thinking to do.

• • •

"Have you got a moment?"

Anders Schyman looked up; Berit Hamrin had popped her head around the door.

"Sure." The deputy editor closed the document on his screen. "Come on in."

Berit closed the door carefully behind her and sat down on the new leather couch. "How's it going?"

"So-so. This is an unwieldy ship we have here."

Berit smiled. "It's not going to alter course that easily. For what it's worth, I think you're doing the right thing. We should look at what we are doing more closely."

The man gave a light sigh. "I'm glad someone agrees with me. It doesn't always feel that way."

Berit rubbed her hands together. "Well, I was wondering about the crime desk. We've got a vacancy now, since Sjölander was moved to current affairs. Are you going to fill it?"

Schyman turned around to the bookcase, pulled out a ring binder, and leafed through it. "No. The senior editors decided to keep Sjölander at current affairs, and crime will have to make do with you and the other two. The editor in chief wants to keep a low profile on crime stories for the time being. He's still reeling from the criticism on *Studio 69.*"

Berit chewed on her lip. "I think he's wrong," she said cautiously. "I don't think we'll get out of this crisis by slamming on the brakes. I think we should go full speed ahead but carefully. But we can't do that with the present staff."

Schyman nodded. "I agree with you. But the way things are looking at the moment, there's no way I could do anything like you're suggesting. It would mean reorganizing and recruiting new reporters."

"Then I've got a suggestion."

The deputy editor smiled at her. "I'm sure you do."

"Annika Bengtzon is a very alert young woman. She turns things around fast, and she has a completely different approach in her thinking. She goes too far sometimes, but I think that could be remedied. I think we should try to hire her back."

The deputy editor made a gesture of resignation. "Sorry, but she's stone dead here right now. The editor in chief gets a rash at the mere mention of her name. I argued pretty strongly in favor of her when Carl Wennergren's contract was up for grabs, and that nearly cost me my job. Jansson was on my side, but the rest of the senior editors wanted to throw her out on her ear."

"And so you did," Berit said a bit tartly.

Schyman shrugged. "Sure, but it's not going to kill her. I talked to her just before she left. She was pissed off, all right, but she was in control."

Berit stood up. "I met Annika last night. She's got something going, something to do with the IB affair, I'm not quite sure what."

"I'm happy for her to write freelance."

Berit smiled. "I'll tell her that if I see her."

Patricia knocked on Annika's bedroom door.

"I'm sorry, but the kitchen's empty and it's your turn to do the shopping."

Annika put down her book and looked up. "Oh, I'm sorry. I'm broke."

Patricia crossed her arms. "Why don't you get a job then?"

Annika got up and they went out into the kitchen. The fridge was empty except for a tin of sardines.

"Shit. I phoned the Cherry Company but they had nothing until the spring."

"Have you checked at the unemployment office?" Patricia asked.

"That horror show? Nope."

"Maybe there's some journalist gigs out there."

"I'm not a journalist anymore," Annika replied curtly, pouring herself a glass of water. She sat down at the table.

"Well, why don't you come and work at the club?" Patricia sat down opposite her. "We need a croupier."

"I'm not working in a strip club!" Annika exclaimed, and emptied the glass.

Patricia raised her eyebrows and gave Annika a contemptuous look. "You're that superior to Josefin and me, are you? It's not good enough for you?"

Annika felt her cheeks blush. "I didn't mean it like that."

Patricia leaned forward. "We're not whores, you know. We're not even naked. I wear a red bikini—it's really nice. You've got big enough tits, you could have Josefin's. It's blue."

Annika's cheeks deepened a shade. "Are you serious?"

Patricia snorted. "It's not that big a deal. But I've got to talk to Joachim first. Do you want me to?"

Annika hesitated. I'll get a chance to see where she worked, she thought. I'll get to know her boyfriend and boss. I'll be wearing her bra and panties.

The last thought made her crotch tingle, a feeling that filled her with both excitement and shame.

She nodded.

"Okay," Patricia said. "I'll put a note on the table if you're asleep when I get back."

Then she left to go to work.

Annika sat at the kitchen table for a long time.

NINETEEN YEARS, FIVE MONTHS, AND TWO DAYS

*T*here are no cheap insights. Experience is never sold short. When you buy it, the price always seems too high, impossible to pay. Yet we stand there with our credit cards, running our peace of mind into debt for years to come.

Eventually, when the accounts have been settled and the payments are behind us, we always think it was worth it. That's my comfort now, because I made up my mind today. I've understood what I have to do. I've fished out my plastic and cashed in my soul.

It came close yesterday. I can barely remember the reason; something he couldn't find and claimed I'd thrown away. It wasn't true, of course, and he knew it.

I know what I have to do. My back against the wall.
I have to confront him and I know it's going to come at a high price.

Because he says
he will never
let me go.

THURSDAY 6 SEPTEMBER

The folded note lay on the kitchen table, the text consisted of two letters: *OK.*

Annika shuddered and swallowed, quickly throwing the note away. Sven entered the kitchen, naked and with tousled hair.

Annika had to smile. "You look like a little boy."

He kissed her softly. "Are there any good places to run around here?"

"No tracks that are illuminated, but there are footpaths all around Kungsholmen where you can run."

"Last man out is a monkey!" Sven rushed out into the hallway and into his jogging suit.

They raced each other the whole way. Sven won, of course, but Annika wasn't far behind. Then they made love in the basement shower, fervently but quietly so the whole backyard wouldn't hear.

Back up in the flat, Annika made coffee.

"My training starts next week," Sven said.

Annika poured coffee into mugs and sat down opposite him at the table. "I'll be staying here a while longer."

Sven fidgeted.

"I've been thinking about something. It's silly for us to have one apartment each in Hälleforsnäs. We could rent a bigger one together, or buy a house."

Annika got up and opened the fridge. It was as empty as it had been the night before. "Do you think you could do some shopping? There's a market down on the square."

"You're not listening to me."

She sat down with a sigh. "I am. But you're not listening to *me*. I'm going to stay here."

Sven stared into his coffee mug. "How long?"

Annika breathed for a few seconds. "I don't know. At least a few more weeks."

"What about your job?"

"I told you, I'm on leave."

Sven leaned across the table and put his hand across hers. "I miss you."

She gave his fingers a quick squeeze, then got up and picked out the recycling from the cupboard under the sink. "If you can't do the shopping, I'll do it."

He got to his feet. "You're not listening, damn it! I want us to move in together. I want to get married. I want us to have children."

Annika felt her hands drop. She stared down at the cans. "Sven, I'm not ready for any of that."

He threw his hands out. "What are you waiting for?"

She looked up at him, fighting to keep her cool. "All I'm saying is that I want to finish off a project first. And it may take a while."

He took a step closer to her. "And I'm saying that I want you to come home. Now. Today."

She put the last Coke can in the bag, the last drops splashing onto the floor. "You're the one who's not listening now." She left the kitchen. She got dressed and went down to the shop in Kungsholms Square. She didn't really like this place; it was cramped, confusing, and pretentious. The shelves were full of fancy little jars with umpteen different kinds of marinated garlic cloves. The staff frowned at her as she lugged the bags with cans and bottles to the deposit machines. She didn't care. She got enough deposit money to buy a loaf of bread and a carton of eggs.

The apartment was quiet and empty when she returned. Sven had taken off.

She found a bottle of cooking oil and a can of mushrooms in the kitchen cupboard, fried them up with three eggs, and made a big omelette. She sat staring out at the building opposite while she ate, then she lay down on her bed and stared up at the ceiling.

Patricia opened the door to Studio 69 with a key and by punching in a code on a code lock.

"You'll get your own key eventually," she said over her shoulder.

Annika swallowed and felt her heartbeat. She was regretting this so badly her whole body was screaming.

The darkness inside the door had a red shimmer to it. A spiral staircase led down toward the red light.

"Be careful on these stairs," Patricia said. "We've had customers nearly break their necks here."

Annika desperately hung on to the banister while she slowly glided into the underworld.

The underworld of porn, she thought. This is what it looks like. She felt shame and anticipation, curiosity and revulsion.

Straight ahead in the foyer was the roulette table, the sight of which filled her with some sense of calm and self-confidence. There were a couple of black leather armchairs and a round table; to the right, a small, high reception desk with a phone and a cash register.

"This is the entrance," Patricia said. "That's Sanna's responsibility."

Annika looked at the grubby white plaster walls. The parquet floor was covered with cheap IKEA copies of Oriental carpets. A low-wattage lamp was in the ceiling, the dim light barely penetrating the lampshade.

Behind the reception desk were two doors.

"These are the locker room and the office," Patricia said, nodding at the doors. "We'll start by getting changed. I've washed Jossie's bikini for you."

Annika took a deep breath and forced down the feeling of morbid excitement. Patricia stepped inside the locker room, turned a switch, and the cold, bluish light from strip lights in the ceiling filled the room.

"This is my locker. You can have number fourteen."

Annika put her bag in the metal locker she'd been allotted. "There's no lock." She thanked God she had emptied her bag of anything that could point to her identity.

"Joachim says we don't need them. Here, I think they'll fit you." Patricia held out a bra with sky-blue sequins and a minimal G-string. Annika took them, the material burning her hands, turned around, and undressed.

"We've got exotic dancing, a bar, and private shows." Patricia took out a plastic bag with makeup from her locker. "I do the bar and hardly ever do any shows. Jossie mostly danced, Joachim wouldn't let her work the booths. It made him too jealous."

Patricia did up her bra at the back. Annika saw that she rolled up her socks and put them in the cups.

"Joachim thinks they're too small," Patricia explained, and closed her locker. "Here, take these shoes."

Annika put on her bra. "Does everybody wear these?"

"No." Patricia started to put on makeup. "Most of the girls are completely naked, except when they dance. Then they have to wear a G-string. Dancing naked is illegal in Sweden."

Annika swallowed, then bent forward and did up the ridiculously high stilettos. "What kinds of men come here?"

Patricia brushed her eyelashes upward. "All kinds. But they all have money. I check out the credit cards, for fun mostly. They're lawyers, car dealers, company directors, politicians, police officers, guys that work in the laundry business, real estate, advertising, the media . . ."

Annika stiffened. Jesus, what if someone she knew turned up? She licked her lips. "A lot of celebrities?"

Patricia handed her the bag with makeup. "Here. Put lots on. Yes, some celebrities. We've got one TV guy who's a regular. He's always dressed in women's clothes and pays for two girls to come into a private room. Joachim checked last week—so far the guy had spent two hundred sixty thousand kronor over twenty or so visits this year."

Annika raised her eyebrows, recalling Creepy Calls. "How can he afford it?"

"Do you think he's paying for it himself?"

Patricia picked up a bunch of keys from the vanity table. "Joachim will come in later. Hurry up and I'll show you around and explain the prices before the other girls arrive. You'll have to talk to Joachim about the roulette."

Patricia waited for Annika in the doorway, a commanding air about her. Annika quickly put on a thick layer of dark green eye shadow, blush, and eyeliner. On her way out of the locker room, she caught sight of herself in a full-length mirror. She looked like a Las Vegas hooker.

"Admission is six hundred kronor." Patricia patted the reception desk. "The customer can pay for a private room straightaway; that costs twelve thousand kronor and then we waive the admission. He can choose any girl he wants in the bar."

"Do you mean this is a brothel?"

Patricia gave a laugh. "Course not! The girls can touch the customer, massage him and stuff, but they must never touch his dick. The guys can satisfy themselves while the girl has to stay at least six feet away."

"Why the hell would somebody shell out twelve thousand to jerk off?" Annika said in disbelief.

Patricia shrugged. "Don't ask me. I don't care. I've got my hands full at the bar. Here's the office."

Patricia unlocked the door with one of the keys on the bunch. The room was the same size as the locker room, furnished with plain office furniture, a photocopier, and a safe.

"I'll leave the door unlocked," Patricia said. "I've got to enter the bar takings for August. Joachim will only keep the books here until Saturday."

They came into the main room, and in spite of herself Annika held her breath. The walls and the ceiling were black, and the floor had dark red, wall-to-wall carpeting. The furniture was black and chrome and smacked of cheap eighties styling. All along the left wall was a long bar; on the right were black-painted doors leading to the private rooms. Straight ahead was a small stage with a chrome pole from floor to ceiling. The room had no windows, and the low ceiling was supported by black concrete pillars, which intensified the sensation that you were in a bunker.

"What was this place originally? A parking garage?"

"I think so." Patricia walked behind the bar. "Plus a car wash and repair shop. Joachim put a Jacuzzi in the inspection pit." She put some bottles on the bar. "Check this out. Nonalcoholic champagne at sixteen hundred a bottle. The girls get to keep twenty-five percent on the first two bottles they sell; the third one they get fifty."

Annika blinked with her stiff eyelashes. "Unbelievable."

Patricia looked at the stage. "Jossie was great at selling. She was the most beautiful of all the girls. She would drink with the johns all night but she never went into a private room. The guys would keep paying, she was so pretty." Patricia's eyes were moist with emotion. She quickly removed the bottles.

"Josefin must have made a lot of money."

"Not really. Joachim took her money to pay for the breast job. That's why she worked here. And she was only here on the weekends, she did her schoolwork during the week."

"Does Joachim take the other girls' money as well?"

"No. Everyone's here for the money. They make a packet, around ten thousand a night, tax free."

Annika's eyes narrowed. "What do the authorities think of that?"

Patricia let out a sigh. "No idea. Joachim and Sanna handle the accounts."

"But if you're entering the bar takings in the accounts, you'll have to pay tax on it."

Patricia got annoyed. "They keep two sets of books. Come on, let's go out to the roulette table."

Annika hesitated. "What about me? How much will I get?"

Patricia frowned and walked off into the foyer. "I don't know what Joachim has in mind."

Annika turned her back on the horrible, dark room. She wobbled on her high heels, which sank dangerously into the carpet.

The roulette table was worn, and the green baize was marked with cigarette burns and covered in ash. The table layout with its familiar figures and squares dispelled slightly her feelings of insecurity.

"It needs a good brush," Annika said.

While Patricia was finding the equipment, Annika let her hand slide along the edge of the table. She'd be all right, it wasn't so bad. She wouldn't be in a booth, and this foyer wasn't so different from the hotel lobby in Katrineholm.

Patricia showed Annika where the equipment was kept. Then Annika brushed the table and took out the chips.

"Why are there different colors?" Patricia asked.

"To separate the players." Annika put the chips in stacks around the wheel, twenty in each pile. "Where's the ball?"

"There are two, a small one and a big one." Patricia took out a box. "I don't know which one's the right one."

Annika smiled and weighed the balls in her hand. It was a familiar feeling as well. "They have different spinning times. I prefer the big ones."

She started the wheel spinning counterclockwise, took the big ball between her middle finger and thumb, held it against the inside rim of the wheel, and shot it off clockwise.

Patricia was impressed. "How did you do that?"

"It's in the wrist. The ball has to do at least seven turns around the wheel or the spin is invalid. I used to average eleven."

The ball slowed down and fell into number 19. Annika leaned over the wheel. "Next time I spin the ball, I have to start on the number I last picked it up from."

"Why?"

"So you can't cheat."

"How do you calculate the winnings?"

Annika gave a brief account of what *en plein, à cheval, transversale pleine, sixain, en carré, simple,* and all the other bets stood for. All the different bets gave different payoffs.

Patricia shook her head despairingly. "How on earth can you calculate all that?"

"It's quite simple once you've figured it out. It helps at first if you're good at mental arithmetic, but you soon learn the different combinations."

Annika demonstrated how she calculated the winnings—twenty chips in each stack, halve them and let your fingers slide along the edge so the rest of the chips followed.

Patricia watched Annika's nimble movements with fascination. "That's so neat. Maybe roulette is for me after all."

Annika laughed and spun the ball.

At that moment the other girls turned up.

• • •

Sanna, the hostess, was standing stark naked next to the reception desk when the men started arriving. She smiled and teased, flirted and coaxed, telling the guys what a good time they were going to have. Annika recognized Sanna's voice from the answering machine. When Sanna had got the men to part with their money, they would turn their gazes toward Annika. Their stares bore into her like steel arrows, making her feel as if the bra were shrinking, baring more of each of her breasts. She averted her eyes and stared at the burns on the table. She had to force herself not to cover herself with her hands. Nobody was interested in the roulette.

"You've got to flirt with them," Sanna said coldly when a group of Italian businessmen had disappeared inside the strip bar. "Be sexy, girl."

Annika swallowed self-consciously. "I'm not very good at it," she said in a far too high-pitched voice.

"You've got to learn. There's no point in your being there if you don't bring in any money."

Annika's eyes flashed. "The table's here," she said, raising her voice. "Does it hurt you if I'm standing here? Or do you want me to pay you for the air that I'm using?"

A man's big burst of laughter emanating from the spiral staircase shut them up. "Sounds like we've got two wildcats in a cage down here."

Annika knew immediately that this was the famous Joachim. He had long blond hair and expensive, fashionable clothes. A thick gold chain dangled on his chest. This was the guy Josefin had had her breasts done for.

She walked up to him and introduced herself. "I'm Annika. It's nice to be here."

Sanna pursed her lips.

Joachim looked Annika up and down, giving an approving nod when he reached her chest. "You'd look good onstage. If you want, you can go on tonight."

No one has asked for my surname, Annika thought, and tried hard to give him a natural smile. "Thanks, but I think I'll try the roulette first."

"You know, Sanna is right. You have to bring in your share of dough, or you're gone."

Annika's smile died. "I'll try." She looked down.

"Maybe you should start in the bar with the other girls for a few nights, have them show you the ropes."

The man stood a bit too close for comfort; Annika could feel his electricity. He was a looker, she had to admit that.

She closed her eyes for a moment before looking up and meeting his gaze. "Yeah, that's a good idea. But I'd like to try and see if I can make some of the customers stay here on their way out."

At that very moment, two half-drunk men in business suits staggered out of the strip bar. Their brows were damp and their clothes were rumpled.

Annika walked up to them, pushed her tits in their faces, and put her arms around them. "Hi, guys. You've just fallen in love, right? But if the night's going to be really good, you need to try your luck with me."

She smiled her most playful smile, her knees shaking. Joachim now had his thigh pressed against her behind, and she just wanted to scream out loud.

"Nah," one of them said.

Annika took a step forward to escape Joachim and gave the other guy a hug. "What about you? You look like a lucky guy, a real gentleman. Why don't you come and play with me?"

The man grinned. "What do I win? You?"

Annika managed a laugh. "Who knows? Maybe you'll win enough to buy any girl you want."

"Okay," the man said, and pulled out his wallet. His friend reluctantly followed suit.

The first man put a hundred on the table.

Annika smiled a troubled smile. The guy had just shelled out several thousand to drink sparkling apple juice and to look at naked girls, and now he was going to make her sweat for a hundred kronor.

"That won't even spin the ball," she said sweetly. "We play for high stakes here, handsome. High stakes, high winnings. It's a thousand for twenty chips."

The man was wavering, and Annika made a sweeping movement with her hand over the table. "A corner bet pays five thousand, a street, six thousand eight hundred. That's nearly seven thousand. Fifteen seconds, boys. You could win back all the money you've spent here tonight."

A light came on simultaneously in both men's eyes. She was right . . .

They bought chips for a thousand each on their credit cards and placed streets on numbers 11 and 16, their bets worth twelve hundred in all. Annika spun the wheel and launched the ball fast and hard. It rolled almost thirteen turns before it started slowing down.

"No more bets," she said, remembering how it went.

The ball dropped on slot number 3. With practiced movements she cleared the table and stacked the chips.

"Place your bets," she said, glancing at the men's disappointed faces. They were more careful this time, only doing corner bets and changing to numbers 9 and 18. New spin, no more bets, number 16. One of the guys won ten chips.

"Here you go." Annika pushed the small pile over to him. "Five hundred kronor. Didn't I say you were a lucky guy?"

The man lit up like a sun, and Annika knew she had them right where she wanted them. Both men spent another three thousand each before they paid Sanna with their credit card and slunk away. Annika saw that Sanna wrote "food and drink" on the receipt.

Joachim had been watching her from behind the reception desk.

"You know what you're doing," he said, and came closer. "Where did you learn to spin the wheel?"

"At the hotel in . . . Piteå." She smiled and swallowed hard.

"Then you must know Peter Holmberg?" He flashed a smile.

Annika felt her own smile quiver in the corners of her mouth. Shit, she thought, he'll catch me out before I even get started.

"No, but I know Roger Sundström on Solandergatan. Do you know him? Or Hans on Oli-Jansgatan out in Pitholm?"

Joachim dropped the subject. "You're charging too much for the chips, by the way. That's illegal. The stakes are too high."

"I can adjust the price according to the players. Nobody knows what anybody else pays for their chips, it doesn't say on them. I'm following the rules."

"You'll risk breaking the bank."

Annika stopped smiling. "There's only one way for a gambler to win at roulette, and that's to win straightaway, stop at once, and keep the winnings. And nobody who starts winning does that. It's a snap being a croupier. All you need to do is keep the people playing until they've lost all they've won."

Joachim smiled subtly. "I think we'll get along, you and me." He let his hand slide down her arm.

He went into his office. Annika turned around, feeling Sanna's eyes bore into her back. They're an item, she realized. Joachim and Sanna are a couple.

The sound of high heels coming down the spiral staircase made Annika look up. She couldn't believe her eyes. The TV presenter Patricia had told her about was teetering down the stairs of Studio 69 dressed in a miniskirt, stockings, and a see-through blouse showing the bra underneath.

"Hello, my friends," said the man in a squeaky voice.

"Welcome, madam," Sanna said, and flashed a flirtatious smile at him. "What little goodies can we tempt you with tonight?"

As the man named a few of the girls, Annika realized she was staring at him. She used to watch his show, irreverent panel debates with politicians and celebrities. She knew the man had a family.

He maneuvered himself into the strip bar with Sanna. Annika heaved a weary sigh. The shoes hurt her feet. For a moment, she contemplated taking them off; nobody would notice the difference behind the table, but at that moment some Italian guys showed up. Annika went up to them and talked to them in English. It didn't work. She tried French, no luck, but Spanish was okay.

They gambled away thirteen thousand, and Sanna's face got darker and darker the more the men lost.

She doesn't like me, Annika thought. She knows I'm Patricia's friend, and she sees me as a continuation of Josefin. Maybe it's not so strange.

She glanced down at her minimal sequined, sky-blue bikini, Josefin's work clothes.

The evening dragged and faded into intangible night. Down in the old garage it was always nighttime. Annika sat with her eyes closed in the bluish light of the locker room, feeling the tears burn inside her eyelids.

What am I doing here? she thought. Is there any chance I might slowly slip into this world and get comfortable? I could make more money modeling in the private rooms. Will I do that? What I'm doing with the price of the chips is illegal. I could go to jail if I get caught.

She put on more makeup. Her face looked pale without it.

Patricia came into the locker room and smiled encouragingly. "You're doing well, I hear."

Annika nodded. "Not bad."

Patricia looked proud. "I knew you were good."

Annika closed her eyes, I mustn't take it in, she thought, mustn't listen to it. I mustn't find my new affirmation here. I'm not going to make my career in a strip joint. I deserve better. Patricia deserves better.

She touched up her lipstick and went out.

In the small hours, Sanna disappeared into a private room with an older man.

"He's a regular," the hostess whispered as she left with the guy. "There are hardly any customers left. You get the money from them when they leave—the checks are on the desk."

Confused, Annika stood in front of the roulette table, not knowing the procedure. If she tried to get people to play roulette, then who would take the money if someone was leaving?

She made a quick decision to skip the roulette, and just then the TV guy appeared in the foyer.

"Where's Sanna?" Annika recognized the man's voice from the show.

"She's busy," Annika said, smiling. "Can I help you?"

The man put his card on the reception desk, and Annika anxiously licked her lips. She walked over to the desk and searched among the papers on it. There, she found the man's check.

She put the card in the machine and made out the credit card slip. She knew Sanna would get the cut on the sum; her code was logged in. The man signed the slip.

"Sweetie, are you leaving already?" a girl in the doorway squeaked. She was naked, with her pubes shaved off. She had pigtails and painted-on freckles.

"Oh, my little baby," TV man said, and gave her a bear hug.

"Just one moment, please," Annika said, and stole into the office. The room was empty. She put the credit card slip in the photocopier, shut her eyes, and prayed.

Dear God, please don't let it be noisy, don't let it be slow, let there be paper in the tray.

Rapidly and without a sound, the selenium-coated aluminum drum got to work underneath the glass; paper was released and fed into the machine; was sprayed with ink particles; then fixed and fed out again. She breathed out, but where the hell was she going to put the copy?

She quickly rolled it up into a hard tube, folded it in half, and pushed it in the crack behind the G-string—it was going to rub like hell.

"There we go," Annika said, and put the check and the slip on the desk.

The man was sucking at one of the baby doll's nipples. When the girl saw Annika, she pushed the man away. "I'm sorry," she said fearfully.

Annika blinked, puzzled. She suddenly realized the other girls saw her as a person of authority, maybe because Josefin had been one. She thought she'd try to make the most of it.

"Just don't let it happen again," she said sternly, and handed the man his receipt.

He left and the girl vanished into the bar. Annika waited for a couple of seconds, listening for noises from in there. The Muzak from the stage leaked out through the door, and she suddenly gave a shudder. It wasn't especially warm in here.

She slipped into the locker room, pulled out the photocopy, and pushed it down inside her shoe. She quickly returned to lean against the roulette table. She stood there until Sanna's hour in the private room was up.

"Everything okay?" the hostess wondered.

"Sure." Annika pointed to the credit card slip.

Sanna looked at the sum, smiled contentedly, and gave Annika a roguish look. "Do you pay your TV license?" Sanna wondered. She didn't expect a reply, just fanned herself with the slip, laughed to herself, and went into the office.

Annika smiled at the closed door.

• • •

Patricia was making tea. Annika sat on the couch in the living room, staring into the turquoise-gray dusk of the room. She had blisters from the horrible stilettos and was so tired she could cry.

"How can you stand it?" she said quietly.

"What?" Patricia said in the kitchen.

"Nothing," Annika said, just as quietly.

The feeling of disgust lay like an undefined sensation of nausea somewhere in her midriff, and as she closed her eyes, she saw the scrawny nakedness of the baby-doll girl.

"Here you go." Patricia placed the tray next to the phone on the small table.

Annika sighed heavily. "I don't know how I'm going to cope with another night. How do you do it?"

Patricia smiled faintly, poured out the tea, gave Annika a mug, and sat down next to her on the couch.

"Everybody uses you," Patricia said. "It's no worse than in any other place."

Annika drank some tea and burned her mouth. "You're wrong. It *is* worse. The girls in the club, including you, have crossed so many boundaries to end up where you are. You don't see it anymore."

Patricia swirled the lemon slice in her mug. "Maybe. Do you feel sorry for me?"

Annika gave it some thought. "No, not really. I guess you know what you're doing. You've stepped over the line of your own free will. It takes strength to do that, it shows a kind of flexibility. You're not the type to be scared and that's a quality."

Patricia gave Annika a searching look. "What about you? What boundaries have you crossed?"

Annika gave a lopsided smile and didn't reply.

Patricia put her mug on the floor, sighed quietly, and looked down at her hands. "That morning, that last night . . . Josefin and Joachim were fighting like mad. They were screaming at each other, at first in the office, then on the stairs. Josefin rushed out and he followed her."

Annika didn't say a word; she knew this was an important confidence. Patricia sat silent for a moment before continuing.

"Josefin wanted to quit the club. She wanted some time off before

starting her course. She'd been admitted to university, the media program, but Joachim didn't want her to leave. He was trying to trap her,
tie her to the club and make her give up her education. Jossie said she
would leave anyway and that she'd made enough money for him to pay
for ten breast operations. She split up with him, said they were over.
They were fighting."

Patricia fell silent again and the sounds of dawn crept in through
the open windows. The night bus stopping outside the street door in
Hantverkargatan, the never-ending sirens of the fire trucks, the fall
winds' whispers of chill and rain.

"They used to make love in that cemetery," Patricia whispered.
"Joachim got a kick out of it, but Jossie thought it was scary. They used
to climb the fence at the back where it's not so high. I thought it was horrible. Just imagine—among the graves . . ."

Annika said nothing and they sat in silence for a long time.

"I know what you're thinking."

"What?" Annika said in a hushed voice.

"You're wondering why she stayed with him. Why she didn't leave."

Annika sighed deeply. "I think I know. At first she was in love and
he was kind to her. Then he started making demands, affectionate little
demands that Josefin thought were cute. He had an opinion on who she
saw, what she should do, how she should talk. Everything was hunky-
dory until the bubble burst and Josefin wanted to enter the world again.
Study, go to the movies, talk on the phone to her friends. It pissed
Joachim off, he demanded that she stop and do what he wanted, and
when she didn't—he beat her up. Afterward he was full of remorse, crying and saying he loved her."

Patricia nodded. "How do you know all this?"

Annika smiled a mournful smile. "There are books on battered
women. The tabloids run series of articles on the violence. The abuse
usually follows a pattern; I'm sure Josefin's was no different. All the
time she thought things would improve if only she'd change and become like he wanted her. Some days were probably quite good, and
Josefin thought they were moving in the right direction. But the guy's
craving for control only grew and he probably got more and more jealous. He criticized her for everything, in front of other people, eroding
her self-esteem."

Patricia nodded. "It was like a slow brainwash. He made her doubt herself, told her she'd never cope with university. She was nothing but a lousy, fat whore, and the only one who could love her was him. Jossie cried more and more; toward the end she cried almost constantly. She didn't dare leave him, he'd swear he'd kill her if she tried."

"Did he rape her? Sexual violence is very common. Some men get excited when the woman is terrified . . . What's wrong?"

Patricia had put her hands over her ears, her eyes were tightly shut, and she was clenching her teeth.

"Patricia, what's wrong?"

Annika took the woman in her arms and rocked her slowly. Her tears poured down as hard as the rain outside. She shook uncontrollably.

"That was the worst," Patricia whispered when her tears were finally exhausted. "The worst of it all was when he raped her. Her screams were just too much."

NINETEEN YEARS, SIX MONTHS, AND THIRTEEN DAYS

I see him coming through the mists of memory, the pattern repeating, the chorus picking up. He starts by stomping around, working himself up into his usual rage, then cursing, pushing me, and shouting. The usual thing happens to me: my field of vision shrinks, my shoulders drop; with elbows pressed against my sides I hold my hands up to protect my head. I lose my focus, the sounds take over, paralysis sets in. A corner to sink into, a soundless plea for mercy.

His voice echoes in my head, I can't hear my own. The song of terror is wailing inside me, the nameless fear, the unarticulated horror. Maybe I try to scream, I don't know, his roar rising and falling. I'm transported, the warmth spreads, the redness appears. No, I don't feel any pain. The pressure is red and hot. The song fades under the hardest blows, jumps like the pickup on an old vinyl record, then returns a semitone higher. Horror, horror, fear and love. Don't hurt me! Oh, please, my darling, love me!

And he says
he will never
let me go.

Annika was dog-tired when the alarm went off. With a groan she switched it off. Her legs were aching, heavy as lead. The rain was still beating down on the windowsill, an abstract rhythm with an erratic beat.

She went and sat on the couch and made two phone calls. She was lucky: both men were in. She made a date with the first one for an hour later, the other for the following day. Then she crept back into bed and fought against sleep for half an hour. When she got out again, she was even more tired. She smelled of sweat, strong and pungent, but she didn't have the energy to go down to the shower. She rolled on some deodorant and put on a thick sweater.

He was already there, sitting at a window table staring at the rain streaming down the window. In front of him was a cup of coffee and a glass of water.

"Do you recognize me?" Annika held out her hand.

The man rose to his feet and smiled mockingly. "Sure. We've bumped into each other. Literally."

Annika blushed. They shook hands and sat down.

"What is it you want, exactly?" Q asked.

"Studio 69 is being creative with its bookkeeping. Joachim keeps two sets of books. The real ones, where the actual figures are entered, are only at the club occasionally."

Annika drank the police captain's water at one go.

Q raised his eyebrows. "Be my guest. I wasn't thirsty anyway."

"They're there at the moment and they'll be there until Saturday."

"How do you know?" the police captain said calmly.

"I've got a job there as a croupier. I'm not a journalist anymore. I've resigned from my job and left the union. The girls at the club are paid cash. They don't pay taxes or contributions."

"Who told you this?"

"Patricia. She enters the figures from the bar. And then I saw it myself this morning."

The police officer got up and walked over to the counter, bought another cup of coffee, and poured out two glasses of water. He put it all on the table. "You look like you could do with a shot of caffeine."

Annika drank some of the coffee. It was lukewarm.

"Why are you telling me this?" Q said in a low voice.

She didn't reply.

"Don't you see what you're doing?"

She drank some water. "What?"

"You're cooperating with the police. I thought that was beneath your dignity."

"I don't need to worry about protecting my sources anymore," Annika replied sharply. "I don't represent the media, so I can say what I like to the police."

He gave her an amused look. "Oh, no, a leopard never changes its spots. If I know you at all, you're writing the lead about our meeting in your head right now."

"Bullshit," she said, wincing. "You don't know me at all."

"Yes, I do. I know the journalist in you."

"She's dead."

"Bullshit to you. She's wounded and tired. But she's just taking a rest."

"I'm not going back."

"So you're going to be a croupier in strip joints for the rest of your life? Pity."

"I thought you thought I was a pain."

He grinned. "You are, a big pain in the ass. That's good, we need that so we know we're alive."

She looked at him suspiciously. "You're being sarcastic."

He sighed. "A little, maybe."

"You could get him for the bookkeeping. I don't know the law, but there should be enough to at least shut the club down. I'm breaking the law myself, actually—illegal gambling at the roulette table. Joachim said it was okay."

"You'll get busted. Sooner or later."

"I'm going back tonight, then I'm done with it. I made eight thousand kronor last night. One more night and I'll be all right until I start getting my unemployment checks."

"That's what they all say."

Annika fell silent, shame burning on her face. She knew he was right. She stared at her hands. "I've done enough talking now. Now I want to listen."

The police captain got up and returned with a cheese roll. "This is absolutely off the record. If you ever write a word about it, I'll roast you slowly over an open fire."

"Unlawful threat."

He flashed a quick smile, then turned serious again. "You're right. As far as the police are concerned, the murder of Josefin Liljeberg has been cleared up."

"Then why don't you bring him in?" Annika said, a bit too loud.

Q leaned forward across the table. "Don't you think we would if we could?" he said in a hushed voice. "Joachim has a watertight alibi. Six guys have vouched for him being at the Sturecompagniet club until five A.M. and then they all went in a limousine to another party. They all tell exactly the same story."

"But they're lying."

The police officer chewed on his dry roll. "Of course." He swallowed. "The problem is, how do we prove it? A waiter at the club has confirmed that Joachim was there, but he can't say exactly when. Neither can he say when Joachim left. The driver of the limousine confirms that he drove a bunch of drunken guys from Stureplan to Birkastan, and Joachim has the receipt. The driver can neither confirm nor deny that Joachim was there; he couldn't see the guys at the far back. At least

Joachim didn't ride in the front or pay. The girl who lives in the flat at Rörstrandsgatan says that Joachim fell asleep on her couch sometime after six. She's probably telling the truth."

"Joachim was at the club just before five," Annika said agitatedly. "He was fighting with Josefin. Patricia heard them."

Q sighed. "Yes, we know that. But it's Patricia's word against the seven guys'. And if, and that's a big if—*if* we ever get this case to court and manage to blow these guys' stories, we'd have to prosecute them all for perjury. That's unfeasible."

They sat in silence. Annika finished the by now cold coffee, he his cheese roll.

"One of them might talk," Annika said.

"Sure," Q said. "The only problem is that most of them were too drunk to remember anything. They've been served this story as the truth and they really believe what they're saying. My guess is that only one, possibly two of the guys are actually aware they're lying. They're Joachim's best pals, and both of them suddenly have come into a lot of money, I would imagine. They'll never squeal."

Annika was tired, to the point of feeling nauseated. "So what do you think really happened?" she said faintly.

"Exactly what you think. He strangled her behind that gravestone."

"And raped her?"

"No, not there, not then. We found semen inside her, and the DNA tests show that it was Joachim's. They had probably had sex a couple of hours earlier."

Annika closed her eyes and searched her memory. "But first you stated that it was a sex murder. You said there were signs of sexual violence."

The Krim captain rubbed his forehead. "They were mostly old injuries, especially in the anus. He must have raped her anally."

Annika felt like throwing up. "Oh, Christ . . ."

They were silent.

"That other woman who was murdered in the same park," Annika suddenly said. "Eva. That murder was never solved either, was it?"

Q sighed. "No, but it's the same thing there. We consider it cleared up. It was her ex-husband. We brought him in after a couple of years but had to release him. We never managed to nail him for it. He's dead now."

"And Joachim's going to get away scot-free?"

Q put on his jacket. "Not if your information is correct. We won't have time to organize a raid tonight, but we'll go in tomorrow. Stay well away."

He got up and stood next to her chair. "There's just the one thing we can't figure out."

"What's that?"

"How she got those injuries to her hand."

As Q left, Annika sat on her chair, her body like lead.

The hours at the club crept by. Patricia looked at Annika. "You look sick. Are you coming down with something?"

Annika wiped the cold sweat from her brow. Her hand was smeared with foundation. "I think so. I'm cold and I feel sick."

They were sitting on a wooden bench in the locker room; the blue light made the blisters on Annika's feet shine a glaring red.

"How much money have you made?" Patricia asked.

"Not enough." Annika looked down at her sky-blue bikini.

Now she really felt as if she was going to throw up. Today was Friday, and several more naked girls were prancing around the place. They would sit on the men's laps, rubbing themselves against their thighs, tempting them inside the private rooms where they would get to work with the body lotion. Generic, economy-size lotion that went a long way and was fragrance free.

"It has to be odorless, that's crucial," Patricia had explained. "They've got to go home to their wives afterward."

Annika was jittery and on edge. What if she'd misunderstood it all? She didn't dare ask Patricia any more questions about the double bookkeeping, and Patricia hadn't brought it up again. What if the police came tonight anyway? What if Joachim had already moved the books?

She brushed her hair away from her face with shaking hands.

"Would you like a sandwich, or some coffee?" Patricia asked with concern.

Annika forced a smile. "No thanks, I'll be all right."

Joachim was next door in the office. Mercifully, she'd been busy with some gamblers when he'd arrived.

How do you become like him? she wondered. What's wrong with

you when you kill the one you love? How can you kill another human being and go on living as if nothing has happened?

"I've got to go back out," Patricia said. "Are you coming?"

Annika leaned forward and put new Band-Aids on her blisters. "Sure."

The music was louder inside the strip bar. Two girls were onstage. One was wrapping herself around the pole, thrusting her hips toward the audience. The other had brought a man from the audience up onto the stage. He was smearing shaving foam all over her breasts while she arched backward, making as if she were groaning in ecstasy.

Annika followed Patricia behind the bar and poured herself a glass of Coke.

"Doesn't it get you down having to look at this all night?" Annika said into Patricia's ear.

"Put a bottle of champagne on the bald guy," one of the nudes said, and Patricia went over to the cash register.

Annika went back out to her foyer. She shuddered; it was cold out here. Sanna wasn't there. Annika sat down on a barstool she'd pulled in behind the roulette table.

"How's business?"

Joachim was standing in the office doorway, arms across his chest and a smile on his lips.

Annika immediately jumped down from the stool. "So-so. Yesterday was better."

He came up to the table, still smiling and holding her gaze with his. "I think you've got a real future here." He came up beside her behind the table.

Annika licked her lips and tried to smile. "Thanks." She batted her eyelashes.

"How did you decide to come work here?" His voice was a few degrees cooler.

Lie, she thought, but keep as close to the truth as you can.

"I need money." She looked up. "I got sacked from my old job, they thought I was a troublemaker. One of the . . . customers complained about me and my boss got cold feet."

Joachim laughed, then caressed her shoulder, his hand lingering just by her breast. "What was the job?"

She swallowed, fighting the instinct to recoil from his touch. "A grocery store. I worked in the deli section at Vivo on Fridhemsplan. Slicing salami all day long isn't exactly my idea of fun."

He laughed out loud and removed his hand. "I can understand why you quit. Who did you work with?"

Her heart stopped. Did he know someone there? "Why?" She smiled. "Do you have connections in the sausage business?"

He guffawed. "I think you should give the stage some thought." He moved closer to her. "You'd look fantastic in the spotlight. Have you ever wanted to be a star?"

He pushed both his hands into her hair and gave her neck a hug. To her dismay, she felt a pang of excitement in her genitals.

"A star? What, like Josefin?"

The words slipped out of her before she had time to think. He reacted as if she'd punched him, let go of her head, and took a step back.

"What the hell? What do you know about her?"

Jesus, how fucking stupid can I be? she thought, and cursed her big mouth.

"She worked here, didn't she? I heard about her," she said, unable to control her trembling voice.

Joachim backed off farther. "Why, did you know her or something?"

Annika smiled nervously. "No, not at all, I never met her. But Patricia told me she used to work here."

He went up and stood face-to-face with her. "Josefin came to a really fucking bad end," he said in a tense, deliberate voice. "We get some powerful people here, and she thought she could con some money out of them. Don't. Don't ever try to roll *anyone* here. Not the customers, not me."

Joachim spun round and went up the spiral staircase.

Annika was holding on to the roulette wheel, ready to faint.

NINETEEN YEARS, SEVEN MONTHS, AND FIFTEEN DAYS

I'm driven by my wish to understand. I realize that I'm looking for explanations and a framework where there aren't any. What do I really know about the terms of love?

He isn't really bad—only vulnerable and thin-skinned, scarred by his childhood. There is nothing to suggest his powerlessness will always find the same expression. When he becomes more mature, he'll stop hitting. My own mean doubts run stakes of shame through my abdomen; I've judged him far too rashly. I take my own development for granted, his I completely ignore.

Yet the chill has built a nest in my breast.

Because he says
he will never
let me go.

SATURDAY 8 SEPTEMBER

She felt strange using the elevator again. She remembered the last time she'd stood here, thinking she'd never be here again.

Nothing is forever, she thought. Everything goes around in circles.

The newsroom was bright, quiet, and weekend-empty, just as she preferred it. Ingvar Johansson had his back turned and was on the phone; he didn't see her.

Anders Schyman was sitting behind his desk in his fish tank.

"Come in." He indicated for her to sit down on his new burgundy leather couch. Annika pushed the door closed behind her and looked out at the newsroom behind the tired old curtains. It felt strange that everything should look exactly as it did when she'd left, as if she'd never existed.

"You're looking good."

I've heard that one before, Annika thought. "I wasn't *that* tired before," she said, and sat on the couch. The upholstery was hard, the leather cold.

"How was the Caucasus?"

She wasn't following and pressed her lips together.

"You were going," Schyman said.

"There were no last-minute trips left. I went to Turkey instead."

The deputy editor smiled. "Lucky for you. It looks like war down there. They seem to be mobilizing the army."

Annika nodded. "The government forces got hold of some weapons."

They sat in silence for a while.

"So what have you got cooking?" Schyman said after a while.

Annika took a deep breath. "I haven't written it. I don't have a computer. I was going to outline it to you and see what you think."

"Shoot."

Annika pulled up her photocopies from the bag. "It's about the murder of Josefin Liljeberg and the minister."

Anders Schyman waited in silence.

"The minister is innocent of the murder," she said. "As far as the police are concerned, the murder has been cleared up. The boyfriend did it, the strip-club owner Joachim. They can't nail him, though, as he has six witnesses that give him an alibi. They couldn't prosecute them all for perjury, but the police are convinced that they're lying."

Annika fell silent and leafed through her papers.

"So no one's going to be brought to trial for the murder?" Schyman said slowly.

"Nope. It'll remain unsolved unless the people giving the alibi start talking. And in twenty-five years the statute of limitations will expire."

She got up and put two photocopies on the deputy editor's desk. "Check this out. Here's the receipt from Studio 69 from the early hours on July twenty-eight. Seven people spent fifty-five thousand six hundred kronor on entertainment and refreshments. Josefin rang it up—you can see that on the code here, and it was paid for with a Diners Club card in Christer Lundgren's name. Look at the signature."

Anders Schyman picked up the photocopy and studied it. "It's illegible."

"Yep. Now look at this."

She held out the invoice for the Tallinn trip.

"Christer Lundgren," Schyman read, and looked up at Annika. "The two signatures were written by different people."

Annika nodded and licked her lips. Her mouth was completely dry.

She wished she had a glass of water. "The minister for foreign trade was never at the strip club. I think the Studio 69 receipt was signed by the undersecretary at the ministry."

Anders Schyman picked up the first slip and held it close to his glasses. "Yes. Could be."

"Christer Lundgren was in Tallinn that night. He flew out on Estonian Air at eight in the evening of the twenty-seventh of July, you can tell from the invoice. He met with someone there and flew back in a privately chartered plane the following morning."

The deputy editor changed papers. "What do you know . . . What was he doing there?"

Annika drew a light breath. "It was a highly secret meeting. It had to do with an arms deal. He didn't want to hand in his invoices to his own ministry where they could be found, so instead he sent them to the National Inspectorate of Strategic Products."

Schyman looked up at her. "The authority that controls Swedish arms exports?"

Annika nodded.

"Are you sure?"

She pointed at the verifications.

"Indeed," said the deputy editor. "Why, though?"

"I can only think of one reason. The export deal wasn't quite, shall we say, all in order."

A furrow appeared between Schyman's eyebrows. "It doesn't make sense. Why would this government do a shady arms deal? Who with?"

Annika straightened up and swallowed. "I don't think they had any choice," she said quietly.

Schyman leaned back in his swivel chair. "You'll have to be precise."

"I know, but the fact is that Christer Lundgren went to Tallinn that night on some business that's so controversial he'd rather get caught up in a murder investigation and resign than make it public. That's a fact. And what could be worse?"

She was standing up and gesticulating. Anders Schyman watched her with interest.

"I imagine you have a theory," he said, amused.

"IB. The lost archives, original documents that would sink the Social Democrats for a long time."

Schyman leaned forward. "But they've been destroyed."

"I don't believe so. A copy of the foreign archive turned up at the Defense Staff Headquarters on the seventeenth of July this year. It came from abroad, via diplomatic mail. I think it was a warning to the government: do as we say or we'll make the rest turn up. The originals."

"But how would this have happened?"

Annika sat on his desk and sighed. "The Social Democrats were spying on the Communists all through the postwar era, storing up as much information on them as they could lay their hands on. Meanwhile, do you think the guys over here were just sitting around doing nothing?" She pointed over her shoulder toward the Russian embassy. "Hardly. They knew exactly what the Swedes were up to." She got up, got her bag, and pulled out her pad. "In the spring of 1973, Elmér and the boys at IB knew that the journalists Guillou and Bratt were on their heels. The Social Democrats began to panic. Of course the Russians knew. And they knew that the Swedes would try to sweep away all traces of their spying. So what did they do?"

She held out her copies of the news items in the broadsheet from April 2, 1973.

"The Russians stole the archives. The Stockholm embassy's KGB man saw to it that they were taken out of the country, probably in large courier's bags."

Schyman took her pad and read.

"And who was the Stockholm head of KGB in the early seventies?" Annika said. "Yes, the man who today is the president of a troubled nation in the Caucasus region. He even speaks Swedish. This president has one gigantic problem: he's got no weapons to fight the guerrillas with and the international community has decided that he can't be sold any."

The deputy editor was fingering the papers.

Annika sat down on the couch to deliver her conclusion. "So what does the president do? He digs up the old documents from twenty-four

Grevgatan and fifty-six Valhallavägen. If the Swedish government doesn't supply him with weapons, he'll see to it that they lose power for a long time to come. At first the government refuses to listen. Maybe they don't believe he has any archives, so he sends his warning to the Defense Staff Headquarters. A selection of copies from the foreign archive—not enough to topple the government, but enough for the Social Democrats to be saddled with an IB debate in the middle of an election campaign. So the prime minister decides to send his minister for foreign trade to meet the president's representatives. They meet halfway, in Estonia. They make a deal and agree on the consignment of arms to be delivered immediately via some third country, probably Singapore. The army prepares for war."

Annika rubbed her forehead. "Everything goes according to plan. Except there's a hitch—a young woman is murdered outside the minister's front door on the same night that the meeting in Tallinn takes place. Through the most ill-fated coincidence it turns out that the minister's undersecretary has brought a bunch of German union reps to the strip club where the murder victim worked and paid the check with the minister's credit card. The minister's up the proverbial creek—his hands are tied. He can't say where he's been or what he's been doing."

The silence in the office was tangible. Annika could see that Schyman's brain was working at full speed. He fiddled with the pad and the photocopies, made a note, scratched his head.

"I'll be damned. I'll be damned. . . . What does he have to say for himself?"

Annika swallowed, desperately trying to moisten her throat. No success. "I've only spoken to his wife, Anna-Lena. Lundgren refuses to come to the phone. Then I tried reaching him through his former press secretary, Karina Björnlund. I gave her the whole scenario, how I think it all came about. She was going to try to get a comment, but she never phoned back."

They sat without talking for a while, then the deputy editor cleared his throat. "How many people have you told this to?"

"None," Annika instantly replied, "just you."

"And Karina Björnlund. Anyone else?"

Annika closed her eyes and thought. "No. Only you and Karina Björnlund." She felt herself tense up. The counterarguments would come now.

"This is incredibly interesting, but it's unpublishable."

"Why?" Annika quickly replied.

"Too many loose ends. Your line of argument is logical, even possible, but it can't be proved."

"I've got the copies of the invoices *and* the receipts!" Annika exclaimed.

"Sure, but it's not enough. You know that."

Annika didn't respond.

"That the minister was in Tallinn is news, but it doesn't give him an alibi for the time of the murder. He was home by five, the time when the girl was murdered. You remember the neighbor who bumped into him?"

Annika nodded.

Schyman continued, "Christer Lundgren has resigned, and you don't kick—"

"Someone who's down, I know. But you can publish facts, the burglaries at the addresses where the archives were kept, the invoices, the strip club receipt . . ."

The deputy editor sighed. "For what purpose? To show how the government smuggles arms? Imagine the court case involving the freedom of the press that would follow."

Annika stared down at the floor.

"This story is dead, Annika."

"What about the trip to Tallinn?" she said quietly.

Schyman sighed again. "Maybe, if circumstances had been different. Unfortunately, though, the editor in chief is allergic to this story. He won't hear the mere mention of either the murder or the minister. And for a minister to go to a meeting in a neighboring country isn't controversial enough for me to put my job on the line. We've got nothing to show who he met or for what purpose. The minister for foreign trade probably travels for three hundred days of the year."

"Why did he hand in his travel-expenses invoice to the Inspectorate of Strategic Products?"

"It's strange, but hardly worth writing about. The ministries hand

over hundreds of invoices for payment every day; this isn't even controversial. There's nothing fishy about a minister for foreign trade going
abroad."

Annika felt her chest tighten. At heart she knew that Anders Schyman was right. Now she just wanted to sink through the floor and disappear.

The deputy editor got to his feet, walked up to the window, and
looked out over the newsroom. "We need you here."

Annika was startled. "What?"

Schyman sighed. "We could do with someone of your character on
the crime desk. Right now there are only three people working there:
Berit Hamrin, Nils Langeby, and Eva-Britt Qvist. It would do Berit good
to have a competent person by her side."

"I've never met the other two," Annika said quietly.

"What are you doing now? Did you get another job?"

She shook her head.

The deputy editor came and sat down next to her on the couch.
"I'm sincerely sorry that we can't publish your stuff. You've done a fantastic piece of research, but the story is simply too incredible to be
told."

Annika didn't reply, just stared down at her hands.

Schyman watched her in silence. "The worst of it is that you're
probably right."

"I've got something else. I can't do it myself, but you can give it to
Berit."

She pulled out the copy of the TV guy's credit card slip. It was a
second-generation photocopy; she'd made a copy of her original copy at
the post office.

"He rented two girls and spent nearly an hour with them in a private room. On his way out he bought three videos. With animals. The
thing is, he paid for it all with a Swedish Television credit card."

Schyman whistled. "What do you know. This can go straight into
the paper—TV star visits brothel, pays with TV license-payers' money."

Annika smiled tiredly. "Glad to be of service," she said acer-
bically.

"Why don't you write it yourself?"

"You don't want to know."

"But you've got to have something for it. What do you want?"

Annika looked out over the deserted newsroom, which was bathed in the slanting rays of the fall sun.

"A job," she whispered.

Schyman walked over to his desk and flipped through the pages in a binder. "Subeditor on Jansson's night shift, starting in November, covering for parental leave. How does that sound?"

"Sounds fine. Offer accepted."

"It's a six-month contract so I have to take it up with the executive. The hours are awful; you start at ten P.M. and work until six A.M., four days on, four days off. You'll have to wait for a formal offer of a job, but this time I won't give in. This contract is yours. How about that?"

He got up and held out his hand to her. She got up and shook his hand, embarrassed at the cold clamminess of hers.

"Good to have you back." Schyman smiled.

"Just one more thing. Do you remember that they said on *Studio 69* that they'd found the strip-club receipt at the Ministry for Foreign Affairs?"

Schyman blinked, gave it some thought, then shook his head. "Don't remember."

"I'm sure they did. But the receipt wasn't there, it was at the Ministry of Industry, Employment, and Communication. What do you think that means?"

Schyman gave her a penetrating look. "Probably the same as you. They didn't find the slip themselves."

Annika gave a faint smile. "Exactly."

"Some lobbyist put it in their hands. It was planted."

"Now, isn't that ironic?" Annika said, and left the fish tank.

The rain was hanging in the air just above the treetops, and the wind was cold. She turned up her collar and walked toward Fridhemsplan. She felt a warm tranquillity inside. Perhaps she was going to make it. Subediting wasn't her favorite thing, but it still felt as if she'd hit the jackpot. She'd be sitting with the backbench subs at the night desk going through the other reporters' copy, correcting spelling and grammar, cutting where necessary, adding a sentence. She'd be writing captions and little fact boxes, making suggestions for headlines and rewriting bad intros.

She didn't have any illusions as to why Schyman had been able to offer her the job. Nobody else at the paper wanted it, they needed to get someone from outside. Even though the work was vital, it was seen as menial. No byline, no glamour, it was thoroughly uncool.

Well, they've never run an illegal gambling outfit in a brothel, Annika thought.

The wind was getting up as she came out onto the bridge. She walked slowly, pulling down the air into her lungs, holding it. She closed her eyes against the damp and let her hair fly free in the wind.

November, she thought. Nearly two months away. She had some time to think and refuel her energy supply. Clear out the apartment in Hälleforsnäs, draft-proof the windows in the apartment on Hantverkargatan. Go to the Museum of Modern Art, catch a musical at the Oscars Theater. See Grandma, hang out with Whiskas.

She suddenly missed her cat. But she couldn't have him with her in the city. He'd have to stay with Grandma.

She had to break up with Sven.

There it was—the thought that she'd been putting off all summer. She shuddered in the wind and pulled the jacket tighter around her. The summer was definitely over, time to get the winter clothes out.

She walked along Drottningholmsvägen, kicking at the wet leaves that were piling up on the sidewalk. Not until she was right next to the park did she look up at the foliage.

The vegetation sat brooding on the Kronoberg hill like a big, moldering mass.

She slowly walked up to the cemetery. The damp made the fence shine. The air stood still, the wind didn't reach here. The sounds of the city were muffled and drifted away.

Annika stopped by the entrance gate, put her hand on the padlock, and closed her eyes. All at once, the glow of the summer returned to her: the heat and the dizziness of the day Josefin lay in there among the graves; the sunlight dancing across the granite stones; the vibrations from the subway deep below.

How futile, she thought. Why did Josefin Liljeberg live? Why was she born? Why did she learn to read, count, write? Why did she worry about the changes in her beautiful body? For what purpose—only to die?

There has to be a meaning, Annika thought. There has to be a purpose to it all. How can we go on otherwise?

"Hi there! What are you doing here?"

Annika groaned inwardly. "Hi, Daniella. How are you?"

"I'm fine, just fine," Daniella Hermansson chirped. "We've been to the park, but it got a bit too cold. Skruttis is starting day care on Monday. We both feel a bit nervous about it. Don't we, Skruttis?"

The kid just looked up sadly at them.

"Do you want to come up for a cup of coffee? It's time for Skruttis's afternoon nap, so we could talk."

Annika remembered Daniella's weak coffee. "Some other day." Annika smiled. "I'm on my way home."

Daniella took a quick look around and stepped closer to Annika. "Listen, you're in the media," she said in a stage whisper, "did they ever catch the guy who did it?"

"Who killed Josefin? No, they didn't. Not for the murder."

Daniella sighed. "It's awful that he should be walking free."

"The police know who he is. They're going to bring him in anyway, for something else. He'll go to jail."

Daniella breathed a sigh of relief. "God, that's so good to know. Well, we never thought it was Christer."

"Not your neighbor either, the lady with the dog?"

Daniella giggled, a nervous and conspiratorial little laugh. "Now listen, you mustn't tell anybody about this, but Elna had already found the body at five in the morning."

Annika felt herself stiffen, forcing herself to look friendly. "Oh, how's that?"

"You know her dog, Jasper? Sweet little thing. Anyway, the dog went off inside the cemetery and chewed the girl a bit, and Auntie Elna was beside herself. She didn't dare call the police, for fear they'd put Jasper in jail. Did you ever hear of such a thing!" Daniella chuckled.

Annika swallowed. "No, actually, I haven't."

Skruttis started bawling. He wanted to get moving.

"There, there, darling. We'll go home and eat a banana now. You like that, don't you, little friend?"

The woman moved off down Kronobergsgatan toward her building. Annika looked at her for a long time.

There's an explanation for everything, she thought.

She slowly started walking in the opposite direction, toward the fire station. As she rounded the street corner, she saw the police cars blocking the whole street. She stopped.

They're early, she thought. I hope they find the books.

She took another way home.

NINETEEN YEARS, ELEVEN MONTHS, AND ONE DAY

Roughness against naked skin, the air full of dust, the oxygen used up: my living space shrunk to the size of a coffin. The ceiling presses against my brain, my knees and elbows get scratched.

Deep hole, dark grave, smell of dirt.

Panic.

He says that I've misunderstood it all, that I've got the wrong sense of proportion. It's not my life that's too small, I'm too big.

His love is infinite. He still loves me. No one else could give me what he gives me. There is only the one condition.

He says
he will never
let me go.

Her decision matured during the night. She was determined. She would break up with Sven. There was another life, she had found her way out.

The situation filled her with sadness and a sense of loss. She and Sven had been a couple for so long. She had never made love with another man. She cried a little in the shower.

The rain had stopped and the sun was pale and cold. She made coffee and called the railway station to check the departure times. The next train to Flen was in an hour and ten minutes.

She opened the window in the living room, sat down on the couch, and looked at the slow billowing of the curtains. She was going to stay here. She could live her own life.

Annika had put her jacket on and was getting ready to leave when she heard keys jangling in the front door. She stiffened, but relaxed when she saw it was Patricia. "Hi. Where have you been?"

Patricia closed the door quietly behind her, her hand staying on the door handle for a moment before she looked up at Annika.

"How could you?" she said in a stifled voice.

Her face was blotchy, her eyes red with weeping. Annika was dismayed at first, then realized what had happened.

"You sold me out. You blew the club sky-high. How could you?" Patricia came toward her, her mouth twisted, her hands like claws.

Annika tried to stay calm. "I didn't blow the club."

"It must have been you."

Patricia lunged forward and gave Annika a shove, throwing the keys on the floor. Annika stumbled backward.

"I did it to help you!" Patricia screamed. "You needed the money so I fixed you up with a job! How could you do this to me?"

Annika held up her hands and backed into the living room. "Patricia, please, I didn't want to hurt you, you know that. I wanted to help you, help you get away from that club and the degradation—"

"Don't you see what's going to happen?" Patricia screamed. "He'll finger me! He's been fucking all the other girls there, they've all been with him! I was Josefin's friend, he's got no loyalty toward me. He's going to drag me down with him! Oh, my God!"

She cried out loud, and Annika grabbed her by the shoulders and shook her. "No, that won't happen. The other girls will tell the truth. Go to the police and tell it like it is, they'll believe you."

Patricia threw her head back and gave a loud, shrill laugh. "You're so naive, Annika." Tears streamed down Patricia's cheeks. "You think that truth will always prevail. Grow up! It never does."

She broke away and rushed into her room, threw her things into her bag, and came out again, dragging the mattress behind her. It got jammed in the door. Patricia tore at it and cursed.

"Please, don't leave," Annika said.

The mattress came loose and Patricia nearly fell over. She was shaking with sobs, pulling at the foam-rubber mattress.

"I'm staying here. I got a job at *Kvällspressen*. You can stay for as long as you like."

Patricia had reached the front door and stopped dead. "What did you say? You got a job?"

Annika smiled nervously. "I got hold of a lot of information that I ran past the deputy editor, and he hired me again."

Patricia let go of the mattress, turned around, and walked up to Annika. Her black eyes were on fire. "Fuck you," she hissed. "Fuck anyone who stabs their friend in the back."

"But it had nothing to do with you, or the club . . ."

"And you ratted to the police, you fucking bitch! How the hell else could they know that the books were there just then? You sold me out, your friend, for a fucking job!" Patricia shrieked. "You are such a stinking piece of shit! Fuck you forever!"

Annika backed, hearing her own words inside her head. Jesus, Patricia was right. What have I done, what have I done?

The woman ran back to her mattress, pulled it along, and left the apartment without closing the door. Annika rushed up to the window and saw Patricia running across the yard dragging the mattress over the gravel. Annika pressed her forehead against the cold glass. Slowly she walked over to Patricia's room. A glass lay on its side on the floor, and hanging on the wall was Josefin's pink suit. Annika felt the tears welling up.

"I'm sorry," she whispered.

The numbness stayed with her all the way to Flen. Unable either to feel or eat, she saw the farmsteads of Sörmland fly past. The rhythmic beat of the wheels of the train became an incantation in her mind: *Your fault, Patricia, your fault, your fault, your fault, your fault . . .*

She covered her ears with her hands and shut her eyes.

At least the bus was waiting at the railway station. It left for Hälleforsnäs a few minutes later, passing Mellösa and stopping at the builders' merchant in Flenmo.

This may be the last time I go home when I come here, she mused.

Her mother wasn't particularly happy to see her: "Come on in. I've just made coffee."

Annika sat down at the kitchen table, still dazed and ashamed.

"I've found a house," her mother said, putting another cup on the table.

Annika pretended not to hear, just looked out at the roofs of the works.

"It's got a carport and a pool," her mother went on, a bit louder. "White brick. It's big, seven rooms in all. There's space for you and Sven."

"I don't want to live in Eskilstuna," Annika said without looking at her mother.

"It's in Svista, outside Eskilstuna—you know, Hugelstaborg. It's a nice area. Respectable people."

Annika blinked away the image before her eyes, closing her eyes tight in irritation. "What do you want with seven rooms?"

Her mother stopped puttering around. She sounded hurt. "I want to have space for you all, for you and Sven and Birgitta. And for my grandchildren, of course."

Annika hadn't thought about her sister in ages. Her mother must be really deluded if she thought they could all live together like a happy family. She got to her feet as her mother winked knowingly.

"Then you'll have to rely on Birgitta," Annika said. "I won't be having any kids for a while yet."

She walked over to the counter, took a glass out of the cupboard, and filled it from the tap. Her mother's gaze followed her, somewhat reproachful.

"Doesn't Sven have a say in that, then?"

Annika spun around. "What do you mean by that?"

Her mother bridled. "Some people think you push him around. Moving up to Stockholm just like that, without discussing it with him."

Annika turned white with rage. "What do you know about that?"

Her mother fumbled with a pack of cigarettes. She had to try the lighter a few times before she got it to work. She took a deep drag and started coughing immediately.

"You don't know a thing about me and Sven," Annika said while her mother coughed. "Are you saying I should have turned this opportunity down for his sake? Should my career and living be dependent on his whims? Is that really what you think? Huh?"

Her mother had tears in her eyes when she got her breath back. "My, my, I really should quit." She attempted a smile.

Annika didn't return it. "Of course I think you should concentrate on your job. You're very talented. Though it's a hard life up there, everybody knows that. No one's blaming you for failing to make it."

Annika turned around and filled her glass up.

Her mother came up to her and patted her arm awkwardly. "Annika, don't be mad at me."

"I'm not mad at you," Annika said in a low voice without turning around.

Her mother hesitated. "Seems like it sometimes."

Annika turned around and looked at her mother with tired eyes. "I just don't understand why you keep thinking that you're going to move into a fancy villa in Eskilstuna. You don't have the money. And what would you do if you did? Would you commute to work at the supermarket here?"

Now her mother turned her back. "There are plenty of jobs in Eskilstuna," she said sullenly. "Honest and scrupulous checkout assistants don't grow on trees."

"Why don't you start by finding a job then? You're starting at the wrong end by looking at luxury houses, surely you must see that?"

Her mother was sucking hard at her cigarette. "You don't respect me."

"Of course I do!" Annika exclaimed. "Jesus, you're my mother! I just want you to be realistic. If you want to live in a house so badly, then get one here in Hälleforsnäs. They cost next to nothing! I saw one for sale up on Flensvägen today. Do you know what they're asking for it?"

"Finns," said her mother contemptuously.

"Now you're being silly."

"What about you? You don't want to live here either. You just want to stay in Stockholm."

Annika flung her hands out. "Not because there's anything wrong with Hälleforsnäs! I love this place. But the job I want isn't here."

Her mother angrily stubbed her cigarette out in the sink. Her cheeks were burning with agitation, and her eyes were red around the edges. Her voice trembled as she said, "You must see that I don't want to live in any old rickety house in this godforsaken hole! I'd rather stay here in my apartment."

"Then do that," Annika said, and picked up her bag and left.

She got her bike and rode down to see Sven. No point in putting it off. He lived in the old works stables, a building that was once stately and

impressive but which was now part of the shabby end of Tattar-
backen.

He was at home, watching soccer on TV with a beer in his hand.

"Darling." He got to his feet and hugged her. "I'm so happy you're
home."

Gingerly, she pulled away from his arms, her heart thundering and
her legs shaking.

"I've come here to pack up, Sven," she said, her voice trembling.

He smiled. "So you think we can move in together?"

She swallowed and took a deep breath. "Sven, I've got a job in
Stockholm. At *Kvällspressen*. They want me back. I'm starting in November."

She was clutching her bag tightly with her hands.

Sven shook his head. "But you can't. You couldn't commute every
day, that'd be impossible."

She closed her eyes, feeling the tears welling up. "I'm moving, for
good. I've given the landlord here notice, and I've resigned from *Katrineholms-Kuriren*."

She instinctively backed toward the door.

"What the hell are you talking about?" Sven came closer.

"I'm sorry," she said through her tears. "I never wanted to hurt
you. I really have loved you."

"Are you leaving me?" he said in a stifled voice, grabbing her by
her upper arms.

She put her head back and closed her eyes, her tears rolling down
her face and neck.

"It has to be like this," she said breathlessly. "You deserve someone
who loves you more. I can't any longer."

He started shaking her, slowly at first, then more and more vio-
lently.

"What the hell do you mean?" he shouted. "Are you breaking up?
With *me*?"

Annika cried, her head hitting the door. She tried pushing him
back.

"Sven. Sven, listen to me—"

"Why the hell should I listen to you?" he screamed in her face.
"You've been lying to me the whole summer! You said you wanted to

give it a go in Stockholm, but you never intended to come back here, did you? You lying bitch!"

Annika suddenly stopped crying and looked him straight in the eye. "You're absolutely right. All I want is to be free of you."

He let go, staring at her in disbelief.

She turned around, kicked the door open, and ran away.

NINETEEN YEARS, ELEVEN MONTHS, AND TWENTY-FIVE DAYS

Yesterday the tears never came, nor the panicky fear after the attack. The heat got too much, it rose until the red became black. They say he saved my life. The kiss of life brought back the spirit that his hands tried to extinguish. I can't speak yet. The damage could be chronic. He says a piece of meat got stuck in my throat, but I can see in the doctors' eyes that they don't believe him. But no one asks any questions.

He cries with his face against my blanket. He's been holding my hand for many hours. He begs and pleads with me.

If I do what he wants, I'll dispose of the last barrier. I'll be erasing what's left of my personality and then there'll be nothing left. He'll have reached his goal. Nothing stops him from taking the final step. When he won't bring back my spirit.

He says
he will kill me
if I go.

Ho Lake sparkled like an icy sapphire in the morning sun. Annika walked slowly toward the water with Whiskas at her heels. The cat was bouncing and dancing around her feet, wild with happiness. She laughed and picked him up in her arms. The animal rubbed its nose against her chin, licked her neck, and purred like a machine.

"Aren't you the silliest little cat?" Annika said, and scratched him behind the ears.

She sat down on the jetty and looked out over the lake. The wind, gentle and mild, rippled the glittering surface. Annika screwed up her eyes and saw the flat, gray rocks across the lake rise out of the water and melt into the dark green wall of fir trees. Even farther away, where the lake ended and the real forest began, Old Gustav lived. She would look in on him someday. It had been a long time.

The future lay open before her like an unpainted watercolor. She could choose how she wanted to continue with the picture.

She'd make it warm and rich, she thought, light and bright.

The cat rolled itself up on her lap and fell asleep. She closed her eyes and let her fingers play with the animal's silky fur. She breathed deeply and was filled with an intense feeling of happiness. This is what living should be like, she mused.

Her grandmother called from the cottage. Annika straightened up, listened. Whiskas started and jumped down on the jetty. The old woman cupped her hands and called out, "Breakfast!"

Annika ran up to the house. Whiskas thought it was a race and rushed off like a maniac. He lay in wait on the steps and attacked her feet. Annika picked up the wriggling animal, burrowed her nose in his fur, and blew on his stomach. "What a silly kitty you are."

Her grandmother had put yogurt and wild raspberries, rye bread and cheese, on the table. The smell of coffee wafted in the air. Annika realized how ravenous she was.

"No, get down," she said to the cat, who was trying to jump up onto her lap.

"He's going to miss you," her grandmother said.

Annika sighed. "I'll come and visit often."

Her grandmother served coffee in fine china cups. "I want you to know that I think you're doing the right thing. You should concentrate on your work. I always thought that being able to support myself gave me a sense of self-esteem and satisfaction. You shouldn't be with a man who holds you back."

They ate in silence. The sun was shining in through the window, making the surface of the plastic tablecloth soft and warm to the touch.

"Are there a lot of mushrooms?"

Her grandmother chuckled. "I was just wondering how long it would be before you asked. The ground is covered!"

Annika jumped to her feet. "I'll go out and get some for lunch."

She dug out two plastic bags from a drawer and hurried out into the forest.

In the gloom of the forest, it took a few minutes before the pattern in the moss became visible to her blinking eyes. The ground really was covered with brown funnel chanterelles. They grew in clusters of hundreds, maybe thousands, on the edge of the forest clearing.

She filled both bags; it didn't even take her an hour. While she was picking the mushrooms, Whiskas caught two wood mice.

"Who's going to clean all these?" her grandmother said with mock alarm.

Annika laughed and emptied out the first bag on the table. "Let's do it!"

As usual, cleaning the mushrooms took longer than picking them.

They each had fried bread with a mountain of fried funnel chanterelles for lunch.

"I've run out of milk and bread," her grandmother said when they'd done the dishes.

"I'll cycle to the village and get some."

The old woman smiled. "That's nice of you."

Annika combed her hair and got her bag. "You stay with Grandma," she said to the cat.

Whiskas wasn't listening but merrily jumped ahead of her toward the barrier.

"No," Annika said, picking up the cat and carrying him back to the cottage. "I'm going to ride on the road, where you could get run over. Stay here."

The cat wriggled free and ran into the forest. Annika sighed.

"Put him inside when he comes back," she told her grandmother. "I don't want him running around on the road."

With swinging arms she walked to her bike. The sun shone over the landscape, clear and bright. She saw the chrome of the bike, resting against the barrier, from a long distance.

She didn't realize that something was wrong until she reached the bike. She grabbed the handlebars and looked. Both tires were slashed, the saddle as well. She stared at it in disbelief, not quite knowing what she was looking at.

"That's just the beginning, you fucking whore!"

She gasped and looked up. Sven was standing a few yards away. She knew what was coming.

"I've smashed up your whole goddamn place. I've cut all your fucking whore's clothes to pieces."

He sobbed and swayed. Annika saw that he was drunk. Watching him closely, she cautiously rounded the barrier.

"You're upset, Sven. And you're drunk. You're not yourself. Don't say anything you'll regret later."

He started to cry, waving his arms about. He came toward her.

"You're a *whore* and you're going to *die!*"

She dropped her bag on the ground and ran. She couldn't see. Everything went white. She ran, raced away; a branch hit her in the face, scratching her. She fell, got up. The sounds, where were all the sounds? Oh, God, run, run, legs hitting the ground, shit, shit, where is he, oh my God, help!

She ran blindly, in among the trees, across the road, down in the ditch, disappearing in the brush. She stumbled over a root and fell flat on her face, ants crawling over her cheek. She shut her eyes tight and waited for death, but it didn't come. Instead the sounds returned, the wind in the trees, her own panting breath, then silence.

He's not behind me, she thought. And then: I've got to get to where there are some people. I've got to get help.

Warily, soundlessly, she got to her feet and brushed away ants and bits of the forest floor. Listened. Where was he?

Not right here, not now. She looked around, she couldn't be far from Old Gustav's.

Cautiously, half crouching, she ran toward Lillsjötorp. The chanterelles squashed underneath her trainers. The tree trunks were brown and rough against her hands. She crossed a creek over by the deserted sawmill.

There, she glimpsed it between the trees, Old Gustav's red cottage. She straightened up and ran as fast as she could up to the house.

"Gustav!" she screamed. "Gustav, are you there?"

She dashed to the porch and tugged at the door. It was locked. She looked around, over to the woodshed where the old man spent most of his time, and someone was there—but it wasn't Gustav.

"I knew you'd come here, you little whore!"

Sven rushed toward her with something in his hand.

She jumped over the porch balustrade, landing in Gustav's bed of roses. Sweet fragrances filled her nose.

"Annika, I just want to talk to you. Stop!"

She stumbled into the forest, back down in the hollow, over the creek, rounding the fen—but the panting behind her didn't stop. Her feet crashed onto the moss, she flew over brush and stone, gasping, the surroundings dancing by.

I'm running, she thought, I'm not dead. I'm racing, I'm alive, it's not over, I've got a chance. Running isn't dangerous, running is the solution, I'm good at running.

She summoned up the idea of a tough workout, forcing the adrenaline back, focusing on breathing and the absorption of oxygen—breathe, breathe. Her vision returned, the roar inside her head lessened, thoughts began to take shape.

He can run faster than me, she thought, but he's drunk and I know the forest better. He's a better runner on flat ground so I'll have to stick to the rough terrain.

She immediately turned north, stopped following the road. Up there was Gorg Lake and Holm Lake; if she skirted them, she could go east, hit the big Sörmland Footpath and get to the village via the works.

Her legs were getting numb—she'd just eaten a pound of chanterelles. She forced them to speed up, gritting her teeth against the pain. The panting behind her was gone. She glanced over her shoulder: trees and bushes, sky and stones.

He could have taken one of the small roads to intercept me, she suddenly thought, and stopped dead.

Her pulse was beating hard and loud, she listened to the forest around her. Nothing, only the wind.

Where were the roads?

There was a rustle behind her, and she swung around, feeling the panic rising.

Oh, God, where is the road? There is a road here, but where?

She breathed and forced herself to think. What did the road look like?

It's a logging road, they drove timber on it, it's becoming overgrown, the brush is as tall as a man.

Run for the brush, she thought.

At the same moment her cat jumped out and rubbed against her legs so that she stumbled over him.

"Whiskas, you silly thing. Get out of here."

She kicked him lightly, tried to push him away.

"Run to Lyckebo. Run home to Grandma."

The cat meowed and jumped into the bushes.

She sprinted eastward and suddenly the terrain became more

scrubby. She was right, over there was the road. She waited for a few seconds in the bushes by the road before she emerged, holding her breath; all clear. She walked past Gorgnäs, nobody at home; Mastorp, nobody at home; then headed straight east, toward the footpath, straight ahead.

He was standing in the last bend before she hit the Sörmland Footpath. She saw him three seconds before he spotted her. She dashed north, up toward the cooling pond. She'd seen something gleaming in his hand and she knew what it was. She lost her wits. She ran, screamed, stumbled, scrambled, reached the water, and rushed out into it, gasping from the cold. She swam until she hit the beach snorting and spitting. She staggered toward the sheds, fences, ran to the left, climbed a tall ash tree, in among the buildings, into the works compound.

"You can't get away from me, you fucking whore!"

She looked around but she didn't see him. She dashed past a white building, pulled a faded light-blue door open, and rushed into the dark. Blinded, she stumbled over a slag heap and got ash in her mouth, moved farther in, farther away, crying. She began to see in the gloom: the shadows took shape—a blast furnace, empty ladles. Rows of grimy windows under the roof, soot and rust. The door she had come through was like a rectangle of light far away, with the silhouette of a man slowly approaching her. She saw the knife flashing in his hand. She recognized it, his hunting knife.

She turned around and ran, the metal flooring booming under her feet, past the shaft furnace. Stairs, up; darkness, new stairs; she stumbled and cut her knee; the light returned, a platform, windows, winches; she hit her head on a valve or something.

"End of the line."

He was breathing hard, his eyes gleaming with hatred and alcohol.

"Sven," she sobbed, backing up as far as she could. "Sven, don't . . . You don't want to . . ."

"You whore."

At the same instant she heard a faint meowing from the stairs. Annika peered into the shadows, searching among soot and slag. The cat; oh, the little cat, he'd followed her all the way.

"Whiskas!" she called out.

Sven took a step forward and she backed up. The cat came nearer, meowing and purring, making little turns and capering about, rubbing its nose against the rusty machine parts, playing with a piece of coal.

"Forget about the fucking cat," Sven said hoarsely. She knew that voice, he was on the verge of tears. "You can't leave me like this."

He cried out. Annika couldn't respond, her throat was constricted, couldn't produce a sound. She saw the contours of the knife glint in a beam of sunlight, waving aimlessly while the crying intensified.

"Annika, for Christ's sake, I love you!" he screamed.

She sensed rather than saw the cat go up to him, stand on its back legs to rub against his knee, followed the shiny steel of the knife as it sliced through the air and landed in the cat's belly.

"No!"

A nightmarish, unconscious cry. The cat's body soared through the air in a wide arc over the coke chute, leaving a bright red trail of blood, the intestines falling out of his body, coiling like a rope under his belly.

"You bastard!"

She felt the surge of power like fire and iron—like the mass her ancestors had melted and molded in this damned building—blazing, raging, and uncontrollable. Her field of vision turned red, everything came to her in slow motion. She bent down and reached for a pipe, black and rusty. She grabbed it with both hands, strong as iron. She wielded it with a power that she didn't really have. She walked down to where he stood, her eyes fixed on his.

The pipe hit him flat on the temple. She saw in her slow-motion vision how it smashed his skull bone, cracked it like an eggshell; his eyes rolled up and showed the whites; something squirted out from where she had hit him. His arms flailed out to the sides and the knife flew through space. His body was thrown to the left, tumbling; his feet scraped the ground, dancing, falling down.

The next blow hit his midriff, she could hear the ribs crack. His whole body moved with the power. He stood. Blindly he flailed around, swept along by fire and iron. He staggered to the rail and slowly tipped over the edge, down into the furnace throat.

"You bastard," Annika panted.

Using the pipe, she heaved him into the furnace. The last she saw of him was his feet following the rest of the body over the lip.

She dropped the pipe on the concrete floor, the metal ringing out in the sudden silence.

"Whiskas," she whispered.

He lay behind the stockhouse, his breastbone slit open, a bubbling, sticky mass inside. Still breathing faintly, his eyes looked into hers and he tried to meow. She hesitated before picking him up. She didn't want to hurt him even more. She carefully pushed some intestines back into the belly with her forefinger, sat down, and held him in her arms. She gently rocked him as his lungs slowly came to rest. His eyes let go of her, turned blank and still.

Annika cried, rocking the torn little body in her arms. The sounds coming from her were plaintive, drawn-out, monotonous howls. She sat there until the crying stopped and the sun was setting behind the factory.

The concrete floor was hard and cold. She was shivering. Her legs were numb, and she clumsily struggled to her feet with the cat still in her arms. She walked toward the stairs, the dust dancing in the air. It was a long climb down; she moved toward the light, toward the shining rectangle. Outside, the day was just as clear, a bit chillier, the shadows longer. She wavered for a moment and then walked off toward the factory gates.

The eight men still employed at the works had obviously just been leaving for the day. Two of them were already in their cars. The others stood talking while the foreman locked up.

The man who spotted her gave a shout and pointed in her direction. She was covered in blood from her head down to the waist, carrying the dead cat in her arms.

"What happened?" The foreman was the first to collect himself and run over to her.

"He's over there," Annika said in a flat voice. "In a furnace."

"Are you hurt? Do you need help?"

Annika didn't respond, just walked toward the exit.

"Come here, we'll help you," the foreman said.

The men gathered around her; the two who'd started their cars switched the engines off and walked back. The foreman unlocked the door and escorted her into his office.

"Has there been an accident?"

Annika didn't answer. She sat on a chair, clutching her cat tight.

"Check the forty-five-tonner in the old plant," the foreman said in a hushed voice.

Three of the men walked away.

The foreman sat down next to her, looking at the dazed woman. She was covered in blood but didn't seem to have any injuries herself.

"What's that you're holding?"

"Whiskas. My cat."

She leaned her head and gently rubbed her cheek against his soft fur, blew softly into his ear. He was so ticklish, always used to scratch his ear with his back leg when she did that.

"Do you want me to take care of him?"

She didn't reply, only turned away, clutching the dead cat tighter. The man sighed and walked out of the room.

"Keep an eye on her," he said to one of the men standing in the doorway.

She had no idea how long she'd been sitting there when a man put his hand on her shoulder. How clichéd, she thought.

"How are you, miss?"

She didn't reply.

"I'm Captain Johnsson from the Eskilstuna police department. There's a dead man in a furnace over there. Do you know anything about that?"

She didn't react.

The man sat down next to her. He watched her closely for a couple of minutes, then said, "You seem to have been involved in something really serious. Is that your cat?"

She nodded.

"What's her name?"

"His. Whiskas."

So she could talk. "What happened to Whiskas?"

She started to cry again. The police officer waited silently by her side until she stopped.

"He killed him, with his hunting knife," she said finally. "There was nothing I could do. He slashed his whole belly open."

"Who did?"

She didn't reply.

"The men out there think the dead man is Sven Matsson. Is that correct?"

She hesitated, then looked up at him and nodded. "He shouldn't have gone for my cat. He really shouldn't have gone for Whiskas. Do you understand?"

The man nodded. "Absolutely. And who are you?"

"Annika Sofia Bengtzon."

He took out a notepad from his pocket. "When were you born?"

She met his gaze. "I'm twenty-four years, five months, and twenty days old."

"Well! You're very precise."

"I keep a count in my diary," she said, and leaned over her dead cat.

Oh, hello! It's Karina Björnlund. Am I disturbing you?"

The prime minister sighed soundlessly into the phone. "No, not at all. What can I do for you?"

"Quite a lot, actually. As you must understand, I've been having quite a difficult time. In the middle of the election campaign and all . . ."

She fell silent; the prime minister waited for her to continue.

"Yes, well, I only got to work for eight months, so my severance pay wasn't very big."

Yes, he had to agree with that.

"So I was wondering if maybe I could go on working for the government. I've learned a lot and I think I could make quite a big contribution."

The prime minister smiled. "I'm sure, Karina. Working that close to the eye of the storm changes one forever. And I'm positive you'll find new work soon. Nobody can take your merits away from you."

"Or my knowledge."

"True. But you know the ministers like to have a say when it comes to choosing their press secretaries. I couldn't make any promises."

She gave a little laugh. "Of course you can. Everybody knows you're the one who decides. Nobody goes against your decisions."

That was true, he thought to his amusement. Maybe she wasn't so dim after all.

"Karina, I hear what you're saying. Okay? So you want to hang on, but I'm saying no. Are we agreed?"

The woman on the phone didn't say anything for a while.

"Well, if that was all . . ." The prime minister prepared to hang up.

"You don't get it, do you?" Karina Björnlund said quietly.

"I'm sorry?" A note of irritation was in his voice.

"Maybe I didn't make myself clear enough. This is not a negotiation. I'm telling you that in these eight months I've gained knowledge you couldn't put a price on. What I'm telling you is that I have a lot to contribute and that I want to go on working for the government."

The prime minister breathed down the phone; his brain had stopped working. How the hell . . . ? What the hell had the woman found out—

"Listen closely now," the woman said, "because I'm only going to tell you this once. I don't want to bring it up again, although the decision doesn't rest with me."

His mouth was completely dry. "You're not even a Social Democrat."

"What the hell does that matter?" she said.

Article in *Kvällspressen*
Date: 7 October
Page: 1 of 2
Written by: Sjölander

Two Surprises
in New Cabinet

Body text:
And so the prime minister has finally presented his new cabinet. The secrecy surrounding the new names has been profound. There were no
leaks before the complete cabinet was presented yesterday at Rosenbad.

"The pressure on the ministers is uncompromising," a source tells
Kvällspressen. "Anyone that talks to the media beforehand is out."

There are two big surprise names among the usual suspects. The
new minister for foreign trade after Christer Lundgren, who was recently appointed head of SSAB in Luleå, is Evert Andersson, former
chair of the local government social services committee in Katrineholm.
He has no experience of politics on a national level but is said to be a
close friend of the prime minister's.

The other surprise is even bigger. Karina Björnlund, the former
press secretary of Christer Lundgren, has been appointed new minister
for culture.

"Media commercialization has gone too far," the new minister said
in her first statement. "I will be appointing a committee that will take a
look at media concentration in order to maintain variety and confine
ownership. The media has far too much power."

But the question is to what extent Karina Björnlund and the rest of
the government will be able to implement any of their policies.

This year's election results were the worst in modern history for the
Social Democrats. They will have to rely on the support of at least two
other parliamentary parties to push through any of their policies and
(Page 2)

Wire from the Local Press Association (FLT)
Date: 10 November
Section: Current Affairs

Studio 69 Wins Media Award

STOCKHOLM (FLT) The current affairs radio program transmitted live from Studio 69 in the Radio House in Stockholm has been awarded this year's big media award in the radio category.

Studio 69 wins the prize for their investigation into the former minister for foreign trade Christer Lundgren's involvement in the murder of a stripper in July earlier this year.

"It's a victory for investigative journalism," the presenter says. "The award is proof that it's worth going for serious programming and competent journalists."

The award ceremony will take place on the 20th of November.

Copyright: FLT

Wire from the Swedish Central News Agency (TT)
Date: 24 February
Section: Home

Jail Sentence for Porn King

STOCKHOLM (TT) The 29-year-old man who ran the Stockholm strip club Studio 69 was yesterday sentenced to five and a half years imprisonment. The Stockholm City Court sentenced the man for fraud against creditors, fraudulent accounting, tax fraud, and obstruction of tax audit.

The 22-year-old woman, originating from South America, suspected of having run the business in conjunction with the man is still at large. A detention order has been issued in her absence.

Copyright: Swedish Central News Agency (TT)

Excerpt from *Lunchtime Eko*
Date: 15 March
Section: Political Affairs

Swedish Weapons Employed
in Bloody Caucasian Civil War

Report:

(Studio Reporter) Heavy fighting resumed last September in the small Caucasian mountain republic. In excess of ten thousand people have been killed in the war between the guerrillas and government forces during the past six months. The Swedish Peace and Arbitration Society now claims that the government forces are using arms from Swedish weapon manufacturers. This accusation is today made in an op-ed piece in the newspaper *Kvällspressen*.

The Swedish government are skeptical about the statement.

The prime minister's press officer says, "These claims are highly dubious. There is an embargo on arms exports to the republic in question, and we cannot see how any Swedish weapons could end up there. The Swedish government have not and will not sanction consignments to the area within the foreseeable future."

(end report)

payoff:
And the reporter was . . .

News item in *Eskilstuna-Kuriren*
Date: 23 June
Page: 17

Woman Convicted
of Death of Bandy Star

ESKILSTUNA The 25-year-old woman who last year in Hälleforsnäs killed the bandy player Sven Matsson was yesterday convicted of involuntary manslaughter by the Eskilstuna County Court. The woman was sentenced to a probational sentence.

The prosecution presented the case as manslaughter, but the judges went with the defense counsel. The decision reached by the court was influenced by the man's prolonged abuse of the woman. The act was to some extent seen as self-defense.

"The detailed description of physical and mental abuse as set down by the woman in her diary over the years has no doubt influenced the outcome of the case," the woman's lawyer stated.

The woman has declined to comment on the sentence.

"She has completely rebuilt her life following the tragic events," her lawyer says. "She lives in Stockholm and was yesterday, the day of the sentence, given a permanent position with her employer."

(EK)

ACKNOWLEDGMENTS

This is a work of fiction. The newspaper *Kvällspressen* doesn't exist, although it has traits of various existing media companies.

The account of the government departmental organization and the division of responsibility and premises is based on the situation prior to the formation of the new Ministry of Industry, Employment, and Communications.

Every character in the novel is a product of the author's imagination. All similarities between the characters in the novel and any real living persons are entirely accidental. Some existing political figures and civil servants do figure under their real names in the novel. They are to be found in the historical account of the twists and turns of the espionage carried out by the Swedish Social Democratic Party against the citizens of Sweden. All particulars in the case are based on previously known facts. However, the novel's assumption of the course of events and the repercussions of the IB affair are fictional.

My sources for the IB affair were:

Folket i Bild Kulturfront, no. 9, 1973, by Jan Guillou and Peter Bratt.

Kommunistjägarna (The Communist Hunters), by Jonas Gummesson and Thomas Kanger (Ordfront, 1990).

Aftonbladet, pullout section December 3, 1990, "Sanningen om den svenska neutraliteten" (The Truth about Swedish Neutrality), by Jonas Gummesson and Thomas Kanger.

Report on TV4 News during the 1998 election campaign.

The account and interpretation of the tarot cards were found in *Tarot: själens spegel* (Tarot—Mirror of the Soul), by Gerd Ziegler (Vattumannen Förlag).

The details surrounding the running of a strip club I found in *En strippas bekännelse* (Confessions of a Stripper), by Isabella Johansson.

I also want to thank all the people who have helped out with answers to my sometimes rather strange questions. They are:

Jonas Gummesson, current affairs editor at the TV4 News Desk, for supplying me with source material, checking of facts, and sharing his knowledge of Swedish domestic and foreign espionage.

Associate Professor Robert Grundin at the National Board of Forensic Medicine in Stockholm, for an introduction to the department's work.

Claes Cassel, the Stockholm police press officer, for guiding me through various police premises.

Kaj Hällström, filer at the Hälleforsnäs Works, for guiding and supplying trade terminology surrounding casting and deserted blast furnaces.

Eva Wintzell, district prosecutor in Stockholm, for legal advice and analysis.

Kersti Rosén, the press ombudsman, and Eva Tetzell, chief administrative officer at the Broadcasting Commission, for help with the analysis of media ethics issues.

Birgitta Wiklund, information officer at the Defense Staff information department, for an exposition of the principle of public access to official records and mail routines.

Nils-Gunnar Hellgren, senior administrative officer at the Ministry for Foreign Affairs' Courier Service, for background and rules governing diplomatic couriers and their bags.

Peter Rösth, winner of the Round Gotland Race, for yachting terminology.

Olov Karlsson, editor of TV Norrbotten, for special Piteå knowledge.

Maria Hällström and Catarina Nitz for Sörmland detail.

Nikolaj Alsterdal and Linus Feldt, my computer gurus.

Sigge Sigfridsson, my brilliant publisher, who has yet to fail me.

Lotta Snickare, management consultant at Föreningssparbanken, for continual fruitful discussions.

Johanne Hildebrandt, TV producer, war correspondent, and good friend, for daily shouts of encouragement.

And last and more than anyone, dramatist Tove Alsterdal, who read everything first; the perfect sounding board, reader, and critic.

In the end, any faults that may occur are entirely of my own making.